Everyman, I will go with thee,
and be thy guide

G. K. Chesterton

THE BEST OF
FATHER BROWN

Selected and introduced by
H. R. F. KEATING

EVERYMAN
J. M. DENT · LONDON
CHARLES E. TUTTLE
VERMONT

This selection first published in Great Britain
by J. M. Dent & Sons Ltd, 1987
Reissued 1991
Reprinted 1991

This edition first published in Everyman in 1993

The stories are taken from the
following collections:

J. M. Dent
Orion Publishing Group
Orion House, 5 Upper St Martin's Lane,
London WC2H 9EA
and
Charles E. Tuttle Co. Inc.
28 South Main Street,
Rutland, Vermont 05701, USA

Printed in Great Britain by
The Guernsey Press Co. Ltd,
Guernsey, Channel Islands.

British Library Cataloguing-in-Publication Data
is available upon request.

ISBN 0 460 87395 4

CONTENTS

NOTE ON THE AUTHOR AND EDITOR

GILBERT KEITH CHESTERTON was born at Campden Hill, London on 29th May 1874. He was educated at St Paul's school (where he started a magazine, *The Debater*) and the Slade School of Art. He married in 1901 and produced two volumes of verse. In 1904 he wrote *The Napoleon of Notting Hill* and followed this with studies of *Dickens* (1906) and *Robert Browning* (1909). He then wrote two works reflecting his religious and social beliefs and in 1911 the first in a series of detective stories, *The Innocence of Father Brown*, was published. In 1916 he took over the editorship of the *New Witness* from his brother and in 1922 was received into the Roman Catholic Church by his friend Father O'Connor, the original of 'Father Brown'. In the course of a busy life, he produced over 100 volumes, including various religious writings, poetry and essays as well as illustrating the novels of his friend, Hilaire Belloc. When he died in 1936, Chesterton was widely recognised as a stout, absent-minded and friendly character with a tremendous sense of fun, who was one of the most popular writers of the time.

H. R. F. KEATING is a crime novelist, creator of Inspector Ghote of Bombay, and a former reviewer of crime fiction for *The Times*. He is the author of *Murder Must Appetize*, a survey of the 1930s detective story, and *Sherlock Holmes: The Man and his World*. He is also the editor of *Agatha Christie: First Lady of Crime*, *Crime Writers* (from the BBC television series) and *Whodunit?*, a guide to crime fiction. In 1985 he was elected President of the Detection Club, a post first held by G. K. Chesterton.

CHRONOLOGY OF CHESTERTON'S LIFE

_____

Year	Age	Life
1874		Born Kensington, London, 29 May, first child of Edward Chesterton, estate agent, and the former Marie Louise Grosjean of French and Scottish parentage
		Baptised at St George's Church, opposite Notting Hill water tower ('I indignantly deny that the church was chosen because it needed the whole water-power of West London to turn me into a Christian')
1875		
1876		
1879	5	Birth of Cecil Chesterton, brother
1881	6	Enters preparatory school for St Paul's
1882		
1883	8	Meets E. C. Bentley, lifelong friend, at school
1885		
1886		
1887	12	Moves to St Paul's
1891		
1892	17	Leaves St Paul's (His comment on the school: 'I was being instructed by somebody I did not know, about something I did not want to know')
1893	18	Enters University College, London, studies Latin under A. E. Housman, the poet, and takes Fine Art classes at the Slade
1895	20	Leaves university without a degree; begins work at Redway, publishers, and then with Fisher Unwin
		Clarion prints his poem 'Easter Sunday'
		The Academy prints his review of a book on Ruskin

CHRONOLOGY OF HIS TIMES

Year	Literary Context	Historical Events
1874		Monarchy restored in Spain
1875	Wilkie Collins, *The Law and the Lady*	
1876		Telephone invented
1879		
1881		
1882		Britain occupies Egypt
1883		
1885		First petrol-driven car
1886	Arthur Conan Doyle, *A Study in Scarlet*	
1887		
1891	Arthur Conan Doyle, 'A Scandal in Bohemia' in the *Strand* (first Holmes short story)	
1892	G. B. Shaw (first play), *Widowers' Houses*	
1893		
1895		Marconi invents wireless First moving pictures

Year	Age	Life
1896	21	Meets Frances Blogg, his future wife, at a Boer War debate, speaking against
1898		
1899		
1900	25	Meets Hilaire Belloc, who was to form half of G. B. Shaw's imaginary creature, the Chesterbelloc Two volumes of verse published, *Greybeards at Play* and *The Wild Knight and Other Poems*
1901	26	Begins regular contributions to various journals
	27	Marries Frances, June 28
1902		
1903	29	Meets Fr John O'Connor (the basis for Father Brown)
1904	30	Publishes *The Napoleon of Notting Hill* (novel)
1905	31	*The Club of Queer Trades* (short stories) Canvasses on behalf of Liberals for Charles Masterman, future Cabinet Minister
1906	32	*Charles Dickens* (a biography) First fully recorded meeting with George Bernard Shaw, long-time friend and debating opponent, Rodin's studio, Paris
1907		
1908	34	Publishes *Orthodoxy* ('I did try to found a heresy of my own . . . I discovered that it was orthodoxy'); *The Man Who Was Thursday* (metaphysical thriller) Rents holiday house in Rye, next door to Henry James
1909	35	Moves to Beaconsfield, Buckinghamshire, where he is to live for the rest of his life
1910	36	First Father Brown story, 'The Blue Cross' in *The Storyteller* Canvasses for the Liberals in Beaconsfield during General Election
1911	37	First collection of Father Brown stories, *The Innocence of Father Brown* Poem 'Lepanto' in *The Eye-Witness* *The Ballad of the White Horse* ('I tell you naught for your comfort, Yea, naught for your desire')
1914	40	*The Wisdom of Father Brown*

Year	Literary Context	Historical Events
1896		
1898		American–Spanish War
		Sudan rebels defeated at
		Omdurman
1899	E. W. Hornung,	Boer War Begins
	The Amateur Cracksman	
	(Raffles)	
1900		
1901		Queen Victoria dies
1902		Boer War ends
1903		First aeroplane
1904		
1905		First Russian revolution
1906		
1907	Jacques Futrelle,	
	The Thinking Machine	
1908	Conrad, *The Secret Agent*	
1909		
1910		10,000 womens' suffrage march,
		London
1911		
1914		World War I begins
		Freud, *Psychopathology of*
		Everyday Life (Eng. trans.)

Year	Age	Life
1916	42	Takes on editorship of *The New Witness* when Cecil Chesterton is called up
1917		
1918	44	Cecil Chesterton dies as a result of illness contracted at the Front in France
1919		
1920		
1921	47	Tours America as lecturer; instant success
1922	48	Received into the Catholic Church, Beaconsfield, 30 July
1923	49	Founds *G. K. C.'s Weekly* ('When the title was first suggested my feeling was one of wild terror, which gradually softened into disgust'), later called *G. K.'s Weekly* and made the official organ of the Distributive League
1924		
1925		
1926	52	*The Incredulity of Father Brown* Elected President of the newly-formed Distributive League, founded to spread the principle of wider ownership by individuals
1927	53	*The Secret of Father Brown*
1928	54	Travels to Rome, meets Pope Pius XI and Mussolini
1929		
1931		
1932	58	Accepts presidency of the Detection Club
1933		

Year	Literary Context	Historical Events
1916		Easter Rising in Ireland
1917		October Revolution in Russia
1918	Melville Davisson Post, *Uncle Abner*	Armistice
1919	H. G. Wells, *An Outline of History* ('I do not believe the best way to produce an outline of history is to rub out the lines' G.K.C.)	Hitler and Mussolini found Fascist parties
1920	Agatha Christie, *The Mysterious Affair at Styles* (Poirot)	
1921		Warren Harding, U.S. President U.S. industrial depression
1922	James Joyce, *Ulysses* T. S. Eliot, *The Waste Land*	
1923	Virginia Woolf, *To the Lighthouse* Dorothy L. Sayers, *Whose Body?*	
1924	E. M. Forster, *A Passage to India* T. S. Eliot, *Poems 1919–25* ('The Hollow Men')	
1925	Edgar Wallace, *The Mind of Mr J. G. Reeder*	Television invented
1926		General Strike
1927		
1928		
1929	Dashiell Hammett, *Red Harvest*	Wall Street collapse
1931	Francies Iles, *Malice Aforethought*	
1932		
1933		Hitler becomes Chancellor

Year	Age	Life
1934		
1935	61	*The Scandal of Father Brown* Last broadcast, with poem 'Some sneer: some snigger; some simper; In the youth where we laughed, and sang. And they may end with a whimper But we will end with a bang.' Dies 14 June

Year	Literary Context	Historical Events
1934	Evelyn Waugh, *A Handful of Dust* James M. Cain, *The Postman Always Rings Twice*	
1935	John Dickson Carr, *The Hollow Men* (Locked-room classic)	

INTRODUCTION

It could be said of G.K. Chesterton as a writer of detective stories that, like the little girl who had a little curl right in the middle of her forehead, when he was good he was very, very good but when he was bad he was horrid. So selecting this triple handful of his best stories to put into one volume makes a lot of sense. It has enabled me, for one thing, to lead off with part of the fictional foreword Chesterton wrote for one of the later volumes of stories, *The Secret of Father Brown*, leaving out all his *aperçus* about the Spanish character and American mores, telling though they are, which somewhat cloud the whole. What remains is the central nugget, Chesterton's amusing and pointed explanation of the way in which his by then famous detective worked. All the other stories I have chosen can then be read in sequence by its light.

The curl in the middle of the Chestertonian forehead was his particular vision of the world, and it was not at all little but a great joyous swingeing affair. He possessed the gift of genuine and persistent paradox, a gift that particularly came into its own in his detective stories. Paradox, in fact, is something any detection writer might well beg as a blessing from the gods. Essentially, our curious sub-branch of the literary art depends simply on a sudden seeing of something the right way up, which is often upside-down. Edgar Allan Poe shows us that the place to hide a letter is in a letter-rack. Conan Doyle shows us that the really significant thing was that the dog did *not* bark in the night-time.

But this gift, all the better in Chesterton's case for being fuelled not just by a desire to tickle and puzzle but by the whole of the man and his beliefs, can also like a heavy swinging cavalry sabre sometimes topple its wielder over. So that a story may be interesting indeed to the amateur philosopher in us but may not be a success as a piece of detection.

Which brings me, paradoxically, to the first of the successful stories I have chosen, 'The Secret Garden', with the cavalry sabre that is the Weapon in it. I give a capital letter to the word because the sword's function in the story indicates how thoroughly the tale is a conventional, and brilliant, crime puzzle. It is the mystery of the locked garden. When you have read it, go back and look again at the second and third paragraphs. In them a couple of genuine clues are laid down with all the bland skill of Chesterton's world-renowned successor in this particular nook of literature, Agatha Christie. The solution, too, amply illustrates Poe's requirement that a Great Detective should be a person capable of seeing, in the words of his own Le Chevalier Dupin, 'that which has never occurred before', of providing an answer that is both startling and satisfying. As a further bonus in this tale, Father Brown's replies to Dr Simon's five impossible questions have all the delightful ambiguity of Sherlock Holmes teasing poor Watson to the top of his bent.

Just beating 'The Secret Garden' as my personal favourite among the tales is the next Chesterton wrote. (They appeared first in magazines such as *The Storyteller* and were collected together a year later, in 1911.) 'The Queer Feet' fascinated me when I read it as a boy, and I delight in it again at each re-reading when I am apt to find myself striding or scurrying up and down, attempting to imitate the two very different sets of footsteps that are the key to its mystery.

My high opinion of it was shared, though I never knew it then, by the first reviewers of the collection, *The Innocence of Father Brown*. A long, long piece in the *Manchester Guardian*, was perhaps a tribute more to the reputation Chesterton had already made for himself at this time than to the stories themselves. Born in 1874, Chesterton produced his first two books, essays and poems, in 1900, and by 1911 had written five well-praised biographies as well as *The Napoleon of Notting Hill*, that mad fantasy, and *The Man Who Was Thursday*, yet madder. But the *Guardian* reviewer, Dixon Scott, hailed the first stories in the book as 'simply goluptious' before going on to express some serious reservations about the place of evil in the detective story.

Still among the earlier goluptious tales, I think, comes 'The Invisible Man', another fine locked-room mystery which at the same time, and inextricably, tells us about life, and how it should be lived. The author's whole moral being is thrown behind the simple-sounding story. This is what accounts for its mysterious power to hold the reader three-quarters of a century after it was dashed down. It can be felt most clearly in the evocation of 'the speechless poetry of London'. Chesterton was capable of seizing on the whole concept of the mighty city and seeing it from an original, upside-down point-of-view, even if he has to use reverberant words like 'acephalous' (without a head) to do it.

This perception of London as a living whole was something Chesterton had vividly expressed long before he came to write of Father Brown. In one from a series of essays he produced for a periodical called *The Speaker* at the turn of the century, 'A Defence of Detective Stories', he hailed these then much despised tales as 'the earliest and only form of popular literature in which is expressed some sense of the poetry of modern life'. He goes on: 'Men lived among mighty mountains and eternal forests for ages before they realised they were poetical; it may reasonably be inferred that some of our descendants may see the chimney-pots as rich a purple as the mountain peaks, and find the lamp-posts as old and natural as the trees.' You have only to read the marvellously romantic and evocative London-set crime novels of the late Margery Allingham to see this supposition fully borne out.

The end of 'The Invisible Man' shows, in a truly Chestertonian paradoxical fashion, why he considered that murders, the play-things of this minor art (and which were no more than this in the hands of almost all his contemporaries), were truly important. Only murder is so heavy a crime that saving the murderer's soul comes before wringing his neck, and Father Brown walks off into the distance with the one who done it.

Of the next two stories I have chosen from that brilliant first collection, 'The Wrong Shape' and 'The Hammer of God', there is perhaps less to say. 'The Wrong Shape' shows early signs of that preoccupation with evil, nameless but very strongly sensed, which both helped and harmed the stories. Here the East, the whole of it from Cairo to Canton, is Chesterton's bogey, or at least the object on to which he fastens his genuine fears and feelings. Elsewhere he condemns the French or the Americans as sweepingly and with a still remaining substratum of truth.

Such blanket romantic or philosophical condemnations certainly make some of the stories 'horrid': but mostly they do not altogether spoil them as puzzles and pleasures. The critic of the American paper, *The Courant*, for instance, reviewing in 1926 a later collec-

tion, spoke of 'The Hammer of God' as 'one of the great short
stories of all literature'. It certainly holds its own in almost any
company.

From the next collection, *The Wisdom of Father Brown*, which
came out in 1914, I have chosen four tales, of which 'The Absence
of Mr Glass' and 'The Purple Wig' merit particular consideration.
'Mr Glass' stands out as being a funny story with, eventually, no
crime. As time went by, murder itself became less and less
important in the saga. Very funny the story is, too, to my mind,
besides containing one of Chesterton's best off-the-cuff descrip-
tions of his hero arriving 'with that beaming but breathless geniality which characterises a corpulent charwoman who has just
managed to stuff herself into an omnibus.'

How different is this muzzy figure from the real priest on whom
Chesterton based the inward Father Brown, Father John O'Connor of Keighley, Yorkshire, 'a small man with a smooth face and a
demure elvish complexion' as Chesterton described him before for
literary purposes he knocked him about, 'beating his hat and
umbrella shapeless, untidying his clothes, punching his intelligent
countenance into a condition of pudding-faced fatuity'. It was,
in fact, a glimpse of Father O'Connor's confessional-learnt knowledge of the criminal in man, as compared to the knowing innocence of a group of undergraduates they encountered when out
together one day, that gave Chesterton his essential idea for one of
the great characters of detective fiction, if not of wider pastures as
well.

In 'Mr Glass', in fact, Father Brown undergoes another small
transformation. In keeping perhaps with the light tone of the tale,
he is frequently referred to as Mr Brown or the Reverend Mr
Brown, becoming thus a quasi-Church of England clergyman, the
sort of figure who wanders mildly through many Agatha Christie
stories or even through many trousers-down stage farces.

In 'The Purple Wig' Father Brown becomes something of a
secondary figure to the foreground dance of journalists. Chesterton
here has some sharp and shrewd things to say about contemporary
newspaper practices (and, change for change, a lot of them still
apply). Chesterton had worked for the liberal *Daily News* as a
columnist for a dozen years and had made characteristically clear
assessments of what went on in Fleet Street. His contract with the
Daily News was, in fact, terminated when, as part of a campaign to

expose corruption in a paper edited by his brother Cecil, he produced a characteristically bouncy poem which included the lines, still to be found in dictionaries of quotations:

> Cocoa is a cad and coward,
>   Cocoa is a vulgar beast,
> Cocoa is a crawling, cringeing,
>   Lying, loathsome swine and clown . . .

Even today I feel a twinge of shame whenever I make myself a soothing cup.

From the next collection, *The Incredulity of Father Brown*, published in 1926, I have chosed just three stories. Chesterton was by now beginning to write them with more reluctance. Indeed, it was at this period that whenever his wife, Frances, told him they were short of money he would say, 'Oh, well, I suppose I shall have to write another Father Brown.' But it is a mistake, if for a moment I may be a little Chestertonian myself, to think that because a man writes for money he is bound to write cheaply. The later stories do, from the point of view of a crime connoisseur, deteriorate. But this is because the burden of thought they are made to carry often breaks the poor crime-donkey's back, not because the stories have any less of Chesterton's tumultuous genius behind them.

'The Oracle of the Dog' in this collection, for instance, has good claims to be the best of all Father Browns. In it puzzle and theological point mesh in together like the fingers of outstretched hands. You can almost see the moment when the puzzle core of the tale must have flashed into Chesterton's mind, his huge billowy figure striding somewhere beside the billows and seeing a dog deceived. It is hard to believe that this simple action did not give him a sure foundation on which to make a simple, paradoxical point about the human condition, even if his excellently shrewd observation about brutality and imperial police – one much harder to make in 1926 than today – must have come as an afterthought. To be confirmed, as it were, many years later when Paul Scott wrote with equal if lengthier insight in his *Raj Quartet* about Captain Merrick.

From the one but last collection, *The Secret of Father Brown* (1927), I take only two stories. But 'The Mirror of the Magistrate', with its insights into the making of poetry, fruit of the experience of a true, if minor (but diabolically memorable), poet, well earns its place. In it Chesterton takes, so to speak, a leaf in advance from the books of Agatha Christie, who might well be called the Mistress of the Mirrors, so often and so skilfully does she play on her readers' suppositions and unthinking assumptions about those deceptive objects. Here Father Brown is as tricksy about them as ever was Hercule Poirot or Miss Marple, and as triumphant in eventually showing how what seemed magic can be logically explained. That feat is perhaps what lies at the heart of detective fiction.

Admittedly, the story fails to achieve the highest success. There is one fearful piece of thin-ice skating in it (what about the second pistol shot?) and, frankly, the author should never have got away with it. But so ebullient is the writing that I noticed the error only long afterwards when I was reflecting on the tale's merits. But 'taking trouble was never a weakness of mine,' Chesterton is said to have said once. It was a weakness, in fact, that he did not often allow to spoil his detective stories, which he regarded as minor aspects of his life-work, unaware that they would become his most enduring monument.

From the final collection of stories, *The Scandal of Father Brown*, published in 1935, the year before Chesterton's death, I take the very last story in the book. It was not, alas and alas, the last Father Brown story he wrote. He sent one more to *The Storyteller* magazine, and they thought it so below standard that they declined it. Dorothy Collins, his secretary for many years, contrived to keep the fact from him for the short remainder of his life.

But for 'The Vampire of the Village' no apologies need to be made. It has all his old skills. For an adroitly placed clue you can hardly do better than the phrase, which comes somewhere about the middle of the story: 'the priest had again the weird feeling that . . .'; I give you no more hint than this. In its opening paragraph, too, we see another special characteristic, the vivid, splashed-in colours of Chesterton the artist, as we have seen him, perhaps even more strikingly in 'The Doom of the Darnaways' and in many places elsewhere. As E.C. Bentley, author of *Trent's Last Case* and Chesterton's friend from schooldays on, put it, Chesterton was possessed of a 'natural gift for decorative and grotesque drawing.' In words, that gift illuminates almost all the stories with a dazzling, even garish, overwhelming light.

Another long-time friend, Hilaire Belloc, described how, when he asked Chesterton to illustrate a novel he had written, as soon as the plot had been outlined Chesterton struck off drawing after drawing that 'with a soft pencil capable of giving every gradation of emphasis . . . set down, in gestures that were like caresses sometimes, sometimes like commands, sometimes like rapier-thrusts, the whole of what a man or woman was.' This gift of instant characterisation is also notable in his writing. Look at his swift sketch in this last tale of Dr Mulborough, 'called by his intimates Mulberry in apt allusion to something rich and fruity about his dark rotundity and rather empurpled visage.' The man jumps up in front of one.

And, here we have, too, Chesterton's last description of his great small hero, sitting in a train 'with the air of a patient baby absorbing instruction'. It gives us the essence of the ever-enduring character, echoing a phrase in the very first story I have selected, where we see the little priest at the moment the truth combines in his head, looking up 'with a face quite fresh and serious, like a child's'. Father Brown has the wisdom of the child, the directness to go to the heart of things and see them as they are, which is often, in fact, the reverse of the way we spoiled adults have taught ourselves to believe. And in his child-like vision the truth of many dark matters is made to shine out.

H. R. F. KEATING

THE BEST OF FATHER BROWN

THE SECRET OF FATHER BROWN

They were sitting in a sort of partly unroofed outer court of the house, such as often forms the entrance to Spanish houses. It was dusk turning to dark; and as all that mountain air sharpens suddenly after sunset, a small stove stood on the flagstones, glowing with red eyes like a goblin, and painting a red pattern on the pavement; but scarcely a ray of it reached the lower bricks of the great bare, brown brick wall that went soaring up above them into the deep blue night. Flambeau's big broad-shouldered figure and great moustaches, like sabres, could be traced dimly in the twilight, as he moved about, drawing dark wine from a great cask and handing it round. In his shadow, the priest looked very shrunken and small, as if huddled over the stove; but the American visitor leaned forward elegantly with his elbow on his knee and his fine pointed features in the full light; his eyes shone with inquisitive intelligence.

'I can assure you, sir,' he was saying, 'we consider your achievement in the matter of the Moonshine Murder the most remarkable triumph in the history of detective science.'

Father Brown murmured something; some might have imagined that the murmur was a little like a moan.

'We are well acquainted,' went on the stranger firmly, 'with the alleged achievements of Dupin and others; and with those of Lecocq, Sherlock Holmes, Nicholas Carter, and other imaginative incarnations of the craft. But we observe there is in many ways, a marked difference between your own method of approach and that of these other thinkers, whether fictitious or actual. Some have spec'lated, sir, as to whether the difference of method may perhaps involve rather the absence of method.'

Father Brown was silent; then he started a little, almost as if he had been nodding over the stove, and said: 'I beg your pardon. Yes. . . . Absence of method. . . . Absence of mind, too, I'm afraid.'

'I should say of strictly tabulated scientific method,' went on the inquirer. 'Edgar Poe throws off several little essays in a conversational form, explaining Dupin's method, with its fine links of logic.

Dr Watson had to listen to some pretty exact expositions of Holmes's method with its observation of material details. But nobody seems to have got on to any full account of your method, Father Brown, and I was informed you declined the offer to give a series of lectures in the States on the matter.'

'Yes,' said the priest, frowning at the stove; 'I declined.'

'Your refusal gave rise to a remarkable lot of interesting talk,' remarked Chace. 'I may say that some of our people are saying your science can't be expounded, because it's something more than just natural science. They say your secret's not to be divulged, as being occult in its character.'

'Being what?' asked Father Brown rather sharply.

'Why, kind of esoteric,' replied the other. 'I can tell you, people got considerably worked up about Gallup's murder, and Stein's murder, and then old man Merton's murder, and now Judge Gwynne's murder, and a double murder by Dalmon, who was well known in the States. And there were you, on the spot every time, slap in the middle of it; telling everybody how it was done and never telling anybody how you knew. So some people got to think you knew without looking, so to speak. And Carlotta Brownson gave a lecture on Thought-Forms with illustrations from these cases of yours. The Second Sight Sisterhood of Indianapolis——'

Father Brown, was still staring at the stove; then he said quite loud, yet as if hardly aware that anyone heard him:

'Oh, I say. This will never do.'

'I don't exactly know how it's to be helped,' said Mr Chace humorously. 'The Second Sight Sisterhood want a lot of holding down. The only way I can think of stopping it is for you to tell us the secret after all.'

Father Brown groaned. He put his head on his hands and remained a moment, as if full of a silent convulsion of thought. Then he lifted his head and said in a dull voice:

'Very well. I must tell the secret.'

His eyes rolled darkly over the whole darkling scene, from the red eyes of the little stove to the stark expanse of the ancient wall, over which were standing out, more and more brightly, the strong stars of the south.

'The secret is,' he said; and then stopped as if unable to go on. Then he began again and said:

'You see, it was I who killed all those people.'

'What?' repeated the other, in a small voice out of a vast silence.

'You see, I had murdered them all myself,' explained Father Brown patiently. 'So, of course, I knew how it was done.'

Grandison Chace had risen to his great height like a man lifted to the ceiling by a sort of slow explosion. Staring down at the other he repeated his incredulous question.

'I had planned out each of the crimes very carefully,' went on Father Brown, 'I had thought out exactly how a thing like that could be done, and in what style or state of mind a man could really do it. And when I was quite sure that I felt exactly like the murderer myself, of course I knew who he was.'

Chace gradually released a sort of broken sigh.

'You frightened me all right,' he said. 'For the minute I really did think you meant you were the murderer. Just for the minute I kind of saw it splashed over all the papers in the States: 'Saintly Sleuth Exposed as Killer: Hundred Crimes of Father Brown.' Why, of course, if it's just a figure of speech and means you tried to reconstruct the psychology——'

Father Brown rapped sharply on the stove with the short pipe he was about to fill; one of his very rare spasms of annoyance contracted his face.

'No, no, no,' He said, almost angrily; 'I don't mean just a figure of speech. This is what comes of trying to talk about deep things. . . . What's the good of words . . .? If you try to talk about a truth that's merely moral, people always think it's merely metaphorical. A real live man with two legs once said to me: "I only believe in the Holy Ghost in a spiritual sense." Naturally, I said: "In what other sense could you believe it?" and *then* he thought I meant he needn't believe in anything except evolution, or ethical fellowship, or some bilge. . . . I mean that I really did see myself, and my real self, committing the murders. I didn't actually kill the men by material means; but that's not the point. Any brick or bit of machinery might have killed them by material means. I mean that I thought and thought about how a man might come to be like that, until I realized that I really *was* like that, in everything except actual final consent to the action. It was once suggested to me by a friend of mine, as a sort of religious exercise. I believe he got it from Pope Leo XIII, who was always rather a hero of mine.'

'I'm afraid,' said the American, in tones that were still doubtful, and keeping his eye on the priest rather as if he were a wild animal, 'that you'd have to explain a lot to me before I knew what you were talking about. The science of detection——'

Father Brown snapped his fingers with the same animated annoyance. 'That's it,' he cried; 'that's just where we part company. Science is a grand thing when you can get it; in its real sense one of the grandest words in the world. But what do these men mean, nine times out of ten, when they use it nowadays? When they say detection is a science? When they say criminology is a science? They mean getting *outside* a man and studying him as if he were a gigantic insect: in what they would call a dry impartial light, in what I should call a dead and dehumanized light. They mean getting a long way off him, as if he were a distant prehistoric monster; staring at the shape of his 'criminal skull' as if it were a sort of eerie growth, like the horn on a rhinoceros's nose. When the scientist talks about a type, he never means himself, but always his neighbour; probably his poorer neighbour. I don't deny the dry light may sometimes do good; though in one sense it's the very reverse of science. So far from being knowledge, it's actually suppression of what we know. It's treating a friend as a stranger, and pretending that something familiar is really remote and mysterious. It's like saying that a man has a proboscis between the eyes, or that he falls down in a fit of insensibility once every twenty-four hours. Well, what you call 'the secret' is exactly the opposite. I don't try to get outside the man. I try to get inside the murderer. . . . Indeed it's much more than that, don't you see? I *am* inside a man. I am always inside a man, moving his arms and legs; but I wait till I know I am inside a murderer, thinking his thoughts, wrestling with his passions; till I have bent myself into the posture of his hunched and peering hatred; till I see the world with his bloodshot and squinting eyes, looking between the blinkers of his half-witted concentration; looking up the short and sharp perspective of a straight road to a pool of blood. Till I am really a murderer.'

'Oh,' said Mr Chace, regarding him with a long, grim face, and added: 'And that is what you call a religious exercise.'

'Yes,' said Father Brown; 'that is what I call a religious exercise.'

After an instant's silence he resumed: 'It's so real a religious exercise that I'd rather not have said anything about it. But I simply couldn't have you going off and telling all your countrymen that I had a secret magic connected with Thought-Forms, could I?

I've put it badly, but it's true. No man's really any good till he knows how bad he is, or might be; till he's realized exactly how much right he has to all this snobbery, and sneering, and talking about 'criminals,' as if they were apes in a forest ten thousand miles away; till he's got rid of all the dirty self-deception of talking about low types and deficient skulls; till he's squeezed out of his soul the last drop of the oil of the Pharisees; till his only hope is somehow or other to have captured one criminal, and kept him safe and sane under his own hat.'

Flambeau came forward and filled a great goblet with Spanish wine and set it before his friend, as he had already set one before his fellow guest. Then he himself spoke for the first time:

'I believe Father Brown has had a new batch of mysteries. We were talking about them the other day, I fancy. He has been dealing with some queer people since we last met.'

'Yes; I know the stories more or less – but not the application,' said Chace, lifting his glass thoughtfully. 'Can you give me any examples, I wonder. . . . I mean, did you deal with this last batch in that introspective style?'

Father Brown also lifted his glass, and the glow of the fire turned the red wine transparent, like the glorious blood-red glass of a martyr's window. The red flame seemed to hold his eyes and absorb his gaze that sank deeper and deeper into it, as if that single cup held a red sea of the blood of all men, and his soul were a diver, ever plunging in dark humility and inverted imagination, lower than its lowest monsters and its most ancient slime. In that cup, as in a red mirror, he saw many things; the doings of his last days moved in crimson shadows; the examples that his companions demanded danced in symbolic shapes; and there passed before him all the stories that are told here. Now, the luminous wine was like a vast red sunset upon dark red sands, where stood dark figures of men; one was fallen and another running towards him. Then the sunset seemed to break up into patches: red lanterns swinging from garden trees and a pond gleaming red with reflection; and then all the colour seemed to cluster again into a great rose of red crystal, a jewel that irradiated the world like a red sun, save for the shadow of a tall figure with a high head-dress as of some prehistoric priest; and then faded again till nothing was left but a flame of wild red beard blowing in the wind upon a wild grey moor. All these things, which may be seen later from other angles and in other moods than

THE SECRET GARDEN

Aristide Valentin, Chief of the Paris Police, was late for his dinner, and some of his guests began to arrive before him. These were, however, reassured by his confidential servant, Ivan, the old man with a scar and a face almost as grey as his moustaches, who always sat at a table in the entrance hall—a hall hung with weapons. Valentin's house was perhaps as peculiar and celebrated as its master. It was an old house, with high walls and tall poplars almost overhanging the Seine; but the oddity—and perhaps the police value—of its architecture was this: that there was no ultimate exit at all except through this front door, which was guarded by Ivan and the armoury. The garden was large and elaborate, and there were many exits from the house into the garden. But there was no exit from the garden into the world outside; all round it ran a tall, smooth unscalable wall with special spikes at the top; no bad garden, perhaps, for a man to reflect in whom some hundred criminals had sworn to kill.

As Ivan explained to the guests, their host had telephoned that he was detained for ten minutes. He was, in truth, making some last arrangements about executions and such ugly things; and though these duties were rootedly repulsive to him, he always performed them with precision. Ruthless in the pursuit of criminals, he was very mild about their punishment. Since he had been supreme over French—and largely over European—police methods, his great influence had been honourably used for the mitigation of sentences and the purification of prisons. He was one of the great humanitarian French freethinkers; and the only thing wrong with them is that they make mercy even colder than justice.

When Valentin arrived he was already dressed in black clothes and the red rosette—an elegant figure, his dark beard already streaked with grey. He went straight through his house to his study, which opened on the grounds behind. The garden door of it was open, and after he had carefully locked his box in its official place, he stood for a few seconds at the open door looking out upon the garden. A sharp moon was fighting with the flying rags and tatters of a storm, and Valentin regarded it with a wistfulness

9

unusual in such scientific natures as his. Perhaps such scientific natures have some psychic prevision of the most tremendous problem of their lives. From any such occult mood, at least, he quickly recovered, for he knew he was late and that his guests had already begun to arrive. A glance at his drawing-room when he entered it was enough to make certain that his principal guest was not there, at any rate. He saw all the other pillars of the little party: he saw Lord Galloway, the English Ambassador—a choleric old man with a russet face like an apple, wearing the blue ribbon of the Garter. He saw Lady Galloway, slim and thread-like, with silver hair and a face sensitive and superior. He saw her daughter, Lady Margaret Graham, a pale and pretty girl with an elfish face and copper-coloured hair. He saw the Duchess of Mont St Michel, black-eyed and opulent, and with her two daughters, black-eyed and opulent also. He saw Dr Simon, a typical French scientist, with glasses, a pointed brown beard, and a forehead barred with those parallel wrinkles which are the penalty of superciliousness, since they come through constantly elevating the eyebrows. He saw Father Brown of Cobhole, in Essex, whom he had recently met in England. He saw—perhaps with more interest than any of those—a tall man in uniform, who had bowed to the Galloways without receiving any very hearty acknowledgment, and who now advanced alone to pay his respects to his host. This was Commandant O'Brien, of the French Foreign Legion. He was a slim yet somewhat swaggering figure, clean-shaven, dark-haired, and blue-eyed, and as seemed natural in an officer of that famous regiment of victorious failures and successful suicides, he had an air at once dashing and melancholy. He was by birth an Irish gentleman, and in boyhood had known the Galloways—especially Margaret Graham. He had left his country after some crash of debts, and now expressed his complete freedom from British etiquette by swinging about in uniform, sabre and spurs. When he bowed to the Ambassador's family, Lord and Lady Galloway bent stiffly, and Lady Margaret looked away.

But for whatever old causes such people might be interested in each other, their distinguished host was not specially interested in them. No one of them at least was in his eyes the guest of the evening. Valentin was expecting, for special reasons, a man of world-wide fame, whose friendship he had secured during some of his great detective tours and triumphs in the United States. He was expecting Julius K. Brayne, that multi-millionaire whose colossal and even crushing endowments of small religions have occasioned so much easy sport and easier solemnity for the American and English papers. Nobody could quite make out whether Mr Brayne was an atheist or a Mormon, or a Christian Scientist; but he was ready to pour money into any intellectual vessel, so long as it was an untried vessel. One of his hobbies was to wait for the American Shakespeare—a hobby more patient than angling. He admired Walt Whitman, but thought that Luke P. Tanner, of Paris, Pa., was more 'progressive' than Whitman any day. He liked anything that he thought 'progressive.' He thought Valentin 'progressive,' thereby doing him a grave injustice.

The solid appearance of Julius K. Brayne in the room was as decisive as a dinner bell. He had this great quality, which very few of us can claim, that his presence was as big as his absence. He was a huge fellow, as fat as he was tall, clad in complete evening black, without so much relief as a watch-chain or a ring. His hair was white and well brushed back like a German's; his face was red, fierce and cherubic, with one dark tuft under the lower lip that threw up that otherwise infantile visage with an effect theatrical and even Mephistophelean. Not long, however, did that *salon* merely stare at the celebrated American; his lateness had already become a domestic problem, and he was sent with all speed into the dining-room with Lady Galloway upon his arm.

Except on one point the Galloways were genial and casual enough. So long as Lady Margaret did not take the arm of that adventurer O'Brien her father was quite satisfied; and she had not done so; she had decorously gone in with Dr Simon. Nevertheless, old Lord Galloway was restless and almost rude. He was diplomatic enough during dinner, but when, over the cigars, three of the younger men—Simon the doctor, Brown the priest, and the detrimental O'Brien, the exile in a foreign uniform—all melted away to mix with the ladies or smoke in the conservatory, then the English diplomatist grew very undiplomatic indeed. He was stung every sixty seconds with the thought that the scamp O'Brien might be signalling to Margaret somehow; he did not attempt to imagine how. He was left over the coffee with Brayne, the hoary Yankee who believed in all religions, and Valentin, the grizzled Frenchman who believed in none. They could argue with each other, but neither could appeal to him. After a time this 'progressive' logomachy had reached a crisis of tedium; Lord Galloway got up also and sought the drawing-room. He lost his way in long passages for some six or eight minutes: till he heard the high-pitched, didactic voice of the doctor, and then the dull voice of the priest, followed by general laughter. They also, he thought with a curse, were probably arguing about 'science and religion.' But the instant he opened the *salon* door he saw only one thing—he saw what was not there. He saw that Commandant O'Brien was absent, and that Lady Margaret was absent, too.

Rising impatiently from the drawing-room, as he had from the dining-room, he stamped along the passage once more. His notion of protecting his daughter from the Irish-Algerian ne'er-do-well had become something central and even mad in his mind. As he went towards the back of the house, where was Valentin's study, he was surprised to meet his daughter, who swept past with a white, scornful face, which was a second enigma. If she had been with O'Brien, where was O'Brien? If she had not been with O'Brien, where had she been? With a sort of senile and passionate suspicion he groped his way to the dark back parts of the mansion, and eventually found a servants' entrance that opened on to the garden. The moon with her scimitar had now ripped up and rolled away all the storm-wrack. The argent light lit up all four corners of the garden. A tall figure in blue was striding across the lawn towards the study door; a glint of moonlit silver on his facings picked him out as Commandant O'Brien.

He vanished through the french windows into the house, leaving Lord Galloway in an indescribable temper, at once virulent and vague. The blue-and-silver garden, like a scene in a theatre, seemed to taunt him with all that tyrannic tenderness against which his worldly authority was at war. The length and grace of the Irishman's stride enraged him as if he were a rival instead of a father; the moonlight maddened him. He was trapped as if by magic into a garden of troubadours, a Watteau fairyland; and, willing to shake off such amorous imbecilities by speech, he stepped briskly after his enemy. As he did so he tripped over some tree or stone in the grass; looked down at it first with irritation and then a second time with curiosity. The next instant the moon and the tall poplars looked at an unusual sight—an elderly English diplomatist running hard and crying or bellowing as he ran.

His hoarse shouts brought a pale face to the study door, the beaming glasses and worried brow of Dr Simon, who heard the nobleman's first clear words. Lord Galloway was crying: 'A corpse in the grass—a bloodstained corpse.' O'Brien at least had gone utterly from his mind.

'We must tell Valentin at once,' said the doctor, when the other had brokenly described all that he had dared to examine. 'It is fortunate that he is here'; and even as he spoke the great detective entered the study, attracted by the cry. It was almost amusing to note his typical transformation; he had come with the common concern of a host and a gentleman, fearing that some guest or servant was ill. When he was told the gory fact, he turned with all his gravity instantly bright and business-like; for this, however abrupt and awful, was his business.

'Strange, gentlemen,' he said, as they hurried out into the garden, 'that I should have hunted mysteries all over the earth, and now one comes and settles in my own backyard. But where is the place?' They crossed the lawn less easily, as a slight mist had begun to rise from the river; but under the guidance of the shaken Galloway they found the body sunken in deep grass—the body of a very tall and broad-shouldered man. He lay face downwards, so they could only see that his big shoulders were clad in black cloth, and that his big head was bald, except for a wisp or two of brown hair that clung to his skull like wet seaweed. A scarlet serpent of blood crawled from under his fallen face.

'At least,' said Simon, with a deep and singular intonation, 'he is none of our party.'

'Examine him, doctor,' cried Valentin rather sharply. 'He may not be dead.'

The doctor bent down. 'He is not quite cold, but I am afraid he is dead enough,' he answered. 'Just help me to lift him up.'

They lifted him carefully an inch from the ground, and all doubts as to his being really dead were settled at once and frightfully. The head fell away. It had been entirely sundered from the body; whoever had cut his throat had managed to sever the neck as well. Even Valentin was slightly shocked. 'He must have been as strong as a gorilla,' he muttered.

Not without a shiver, though he was used to anatomical abortions, Dr Simon lifted the head. It was slightly slashed about the neck and jaw, but the face was substantially unhurt. It was a ponderous, yellow face, at once sunken and swollen, with a hawk-like nose and heavy lids—the face of a wicked Roman emperor, with, perhaps, a distant touch of a Chinese emperor. All present seemed to look at it with the coldest eye of ignorance. Nothing else could be noted about the man except that, as they had lifted his body, they had seen underneath it the white gleam of a shirtfront defaced with a red gleam of blood. As Dr Simon said, the man had never been of their party. But he might very well have been trying to join it, for he had come dressed for such an occasion.

Valentin went down on his hands and knees and examined with his closest professional attention the grass and ground for some twenty yards round the body, in which he was assisted less skilfully by the doctor, and quite vaguely by the English lord. Nothing rewarded their grovellings except a few twigs, snapped or chopped into very small lengths, which Valentin lifted for an instant's examination, and then tossed away.

'Twigs,' he said gravely; 'twigs, and a total stranger with his head cut off; that is all there is on this lawn.'

There was an almost creepy stillness, and then the unnerved Galloway called out sharply:

'Who's that? Who's that over there by the garden wall?'

A small figure with a foolishly large head drew waveringly near them in the moonlit haze; looked for an instant like a goblin, but turned out to be the harmless little priest whom they had left in the drawing-room.

'I say,' he said meekly, 'there are no gates to this garden, do you know.'

Valentin's black brows had come together somewhat crossly, as they did on principle at the sight of the cassock. But he was far too just a man to deny the relevance of the remark. 'You are right,' he said. 'Before we find out how he came to be killed, we may have to find out how he came to be here. Now listen to me, gentlemen. If it can be done without prejudice to my position and duty, we shall all agree that certain distinguished names might well be kept out of this. There are ladies, gentlemen, and there is a foreign ambassador. If we must mark it down as a crime, then it must be followed up as a crime. But till then I can use my own discretion. I am the head of the police; I am so public that I can afford to be private. Please Heaven, I will clear every one of my own guests before I call in my men to look for anybody else. Gentlemen, upon your honour, you will none of you leave the house till tomorrow at noon;

there are bedrooms for all. Simon, I think you know where to find my man, Ivan, in the front hall; he is a confidential man. Tell him to leave another servant on guard and come to me at once. Lord Galloway, you are certainly the best person to tell the ladies what has happened, and prevent a panic. They also must stay. Father Brown and I will remain with the body.'

When this spirit of the captain spoke in Valentin he was obeyed like a bugle. Dr Simon went through to the armoury and routed out Ivan, the public detective's private detective. Galloway went to the drawing-room and told the terrible news tactfully enough, so that by the time the company assembled there the ladies were already startled and already soothed. Meanwhile the good priest and the good atheist stood at the head and foot of the dead man motionless in the moonlight, like symbolic statues of their two philosophies of death.

Ivan, the confidential man with the scar and the moustaches, came out of the house like a cannon ball, and came racing across the lawn to Valentin like a dog to his master. His livid face was quite lively with the glow of this domestic detective story, and it was with almost unpleasant eagerness that he asked his master's permission to examine the remains.

'Yes; look, if you like, Ivan,' said Valentin, 'but don't be long. We must go in and thrash this out in the house.'

Ivan lifted his head, and then almost let it drop.

'Why,' he gasped, 'it's—no, it isn't; it can't be. Do you know this man, sir?'

'No, said Valentin indifferently; 'we had better go inside.'

Between them they carried the corpse to a sofa in the study, and then all made their way to the drawing-room.

The detective sat down at a desk quietly, and even with hesitation; but his eye was the iron eye of a judge at assize. He made a few rapid notes upon paper in front of him and then said shortly: 'Is everybody here?'

'Not Mr Brayne,' said the Duchess of Mont St Michel, looking round.

'No,' said Lord Galloway, in a hoarse, harsh voice. 'And not Mr Neil O'Brien, I fancy. I saw that gentleman walking in the garden when the corpse was still warm.'

'Ivan,' said the detective, 'go and fetch Commandant O'Brien and Mr Brayne. Mr Brayne, I know, is finishing a cigar in the dining-room; Commandant O'Brien, I think, is walking up and down the conservatory. I am not sure.'

The faithful attendant flashed from the room, and before anyone could stir or speak Valentin went on with the same soldierly swiftness of exposition.

'Everyone here knows that a dead man has been found in the garden, his head cut clean from his body. Dr Simon, you have examined it. Do you think that to cut a man's throat like that would need great force? Or, perhaps, only a very sharp knife?'

'I should say that it could not be done with a knife at all,' said the pale doctor.

'Have you any thought,' resumed Valentin, 'of a tool with which it could be done?'

'Speaking within modern probabilities, I really haven't,' said the doctor, arching his painful brows. 'It's not easy to hack a neck through even clumsily, and this was a very clean cut. It could be done with a battle-axe or an old headsman's axe, or an old two-handed sword.'

'But, good heavens!' cried the Duchess, almost in hysterics; 'there aren't any two-handed swords and battle-axes round here.'

Valentin was still busy with the paper in front of him. 'Tell me,' he said, still writing rapidly, 'could it have been done with a long French cavalry sabre?'

A low knocking came at the door, which for some unreasonable reason, curdled everyone's blood like the knocking in *Macbeth*. Amid that frozen silence Dr Simon managed to say: 'A sabre—yes, I suppose it could.'

'Thank you,' said Valentin. 'Come in, Ivan.'

The confidential Ivan opened the door and ushered in Commandant Neil O'Brien, whom he had found at last pacing the garden again.

The Irish officer stood disordered and defiant on the threshold. 'What do you want with me?' he cried.

'Please sit down,' said Valentin in pleasant, level tones. 'Why, you aren't wearing your sword? Where is it?'

'I left it on the library table,' said O'Brien, his brogue deepening in his disturbed mood. 'It was a nuisance, it was getting——'

'Ivan,' said Valentin: 'please go and get the Commandant's sword from the library.' Then, as the servant vanished: 'Lord Galloway says he saw you leaving the garden just before he found the corpse. What were you doing in the garden?'

The Commandant flung himself recklessly into a chair. 'Oh,' he cried in pure Irish; 'admirin' the moon. Communing with Nature, me boy.'

A heavy silence sank and endured, and at the end of it came again that trivial and terrible knocking. Ivan reappeared, carrying an empty steel scabbard. 'This is all I can find,' he said.

'Put it on the table,' said Valentin, without looking up.

There was an inhuman silence in the room, like that sea of inhuman silence round the dock of the condemned murderer. The Duchess's weak exclamations had long ago died away. Lord Galloway's swollen hatred was satisfied and even sobered. The voice that came was quite unexpected.

'I think I can tell you,' cried Lady Margaret, in that clear, quivering voice with which a courageous woman speaks publicly. 'I can tell you what Mr O'Brien was doing in the garden, since he is bound to silence. He was asking me to marry him. I refused; I said in my family circumstances I could give him nothing but my respect. He was a little angry at that; he did not seem to think much of my respect. I wonder,' she added, with rather a wan smile, 'if he will care at all for it now. For I offer it him now, I will swear anywhere that he never did a thing like this.'

Lord Galloway had edged up to his daughter, and was intimidating her in what he imagined to be an undertone. 'Hold your tongue, Maggie,' he said in a thunderous whisper. 'Why should you shield the fellow? Where's his sword? Where's his confounded cavalry——'

He stopped because of the singular stare with which his daughter was regarding him, a look that was indeed a lurid magnet for the whole group.

'You old fool!' she said, in a low voice without pretence of piety; 'what do you suppose you are trying to prove? I tell you this man was innocent while with me. But if he wasn't innocent, he was still with me. If he murdered a man in the garden, who was it who must have seen—who must at least have known? Do you hate Neil so much as to put your own daughter——'

Lady Galloway screamed. Everyone else sat tingling at the touch of those satanic tragedies that have been between lovers before now. They saw the proud, white face of the Scotch aristocrat and her lover, the Irish adventurer, like old portraits in a dark house.

The long silence was full of formless historical memories of murdered husbands and poisonous paramours.

In the centre of this morbid silence an innocent voice said: 'Was it a very long cigar?'

The change of thought was so sharp that they had to look round to see who had spoken.

'I mean,' said little Father Brown, from the corner of the room. 'I mean that cigar Mr Brayne is finishing. It seems nearly as long as a walking-stick.'

Despite the irrelevance there was assent as well as irritation in Valentin's face as he lifted his head.

'Quite right,' he remarked sharply. 'Ivan, go and see about Mr Brayne again, and bring him here at once.'

The instant the factotum had closed the door, Valentin addressed the girl with an entirely new earnestness.

'Lady Margaret,' he said, 'we all feel, I am sure, both gratitude and admiration for your act in rising above your lower dignity and explaining the Commandant's conduct. But there is a hiatus still. Lord Galloway, I understand, met you passing from the study to the drawing-room, and it was only some minutes afterwards that he found the garden and the Commandant still walking there.'

'You have to remember,' replied Margaret, with a faint irony in her voice, 'that I had just refused him, so we should scarcely have come back arm in arm. He is a gentleman, anyhow; and he loitered behind—and so got charged with murder.'

'In those few moments,' said Valentin gravely, 'he might really——'

The knock came again, and Ivan put in his scarred face.

'Beg pardon, sir,' he said, 'but Mr Brayne has left the house.'

'Left!' cried Valentin, and rose for the first time to his feet.

'Gone. Scooted. Evaporated,' replied Ivan, in humorous French. 'His hat and coat are gone, too; and I'll tell you something to cap it all. I ran outside the house to find any traces of him, and I found one, and a big trace, too.'

'What do you mean?' asked Valentin.

'I'll show you,' said his servant, and reappeared with a flashing naked cavalry sabre, streaked with blood about the point and edge. Everyone in the room eyed it as if it were a thunderbolt; but the experienced Ivan went on quite quietly:

'I found this,' he said, 'flung among the bushes fifty yards up the road to Paris. In other words, I found it just where your respectable Mr Brayne threw it when he ran away.'

There was again a silence, but of a new sort. Valentin took the sabre, examined it, reflected with unaffected concentration of thought, and then turned a respectful face to O'Brien. 'Commandant,' he said, 'we trust you will always produce this weapon if it is wanted for police examination. Meanwhile,' he added, slapping the steel back in the ringing scabbard, 'let me return you your sword.'

At the military symbolism of the action the audience could hardly refrain from applause.

For Neil O'Brien, indeed, that gesture was the turning-point of existence. By the time he was wandering in the mysterious garden again in the colours of the morning the tragic futility of his ordinary mien had fallen from him; he was a man with many reasons for happiness. Lord Galloway was a gentleman, and had offered him an apology. Lady Margaret was something better than a lady, a woman at least, and had perhaps given him something better than an apology, as they drifted among the old flower-beds before breakfast. The whole company was more light-hearted and humane, for though the riddle of the death remained, the load of suspicion was lifted off them all, and sent flying off to Paris with the strange millionaire—a man they hardly knew. The devil was cast out of the house—he had cast himself out.

Still, the riddle remained; and when O'Brien threw himself on a garden seat beside Dr Simon, that keenly scientific person at once resumed it. He did not get much talk out of O'Brien, whose thoughts were on pleasanter things.

'I can't say it interests me much,' said the Irishman frankly, 'especially as it seems pretty plain now. Apparently Brayne hated this stranger for some reason; lured him into the garden, and killed him with my sword. Then he fled to the city, tossing the sword away as he went. By the way, Ivan tells me the dead man had a Yankee dollar in his pocket. So he was a countryman of Brayne's, and that seems to clinch it. I don't see any difficulties about the business.'

'There are five colossal difficulties,' said the doctor quietly; 'like high walls within walls. Don't mistake me. I don't doubt that Brayne did it; his flight, I fancy, proves that. But as to how he did it. First difficulty: Why should a man kill another man with a great hulking sabre, when he can almost kill him with a pocket knife and put it back in his pocket? Second difficulty: Why was there no noise or outcry? Does a man commonly see another come up waving a scimitar and offer no remarks? Third difficulty: A servant watched the front door all the evening; and a rat cannot get into Valentin's garden anywhere. How did the dead man get into the garden? Fourth difficulty: Given the same conditions, how did Brayne get out of the garden?'

'And the fifth,' said Neil, with eyes fixed on the English priest, who was coming slowly up the path.

'Is a trifle, I suppose,' said the doctor, 'but I think an odd one. When I first saw how the head had been slashed, I supposed the assassin had struck more than once. But on examination I found many cuts across the truncated section; in other words, they were struck *after* the head was off. Did Brayne hate his foe so fiendishly that he stood sabring his body in the moonlight?'

'Horrible!' said O'Brien, and shuddered.

The little priest, Brown, had arrived while they were talking, and had waited, with characteristic shyness, till they had finished. Then he said awkwardly:

'I say, I'm sorry to interrupt. But I was sent to tell you the news!'

'News?' repeated Simon, and stared at him rather painfully through his glasses.

'Yes, I'm sorry,' said Father Brown mildly. 'There's been another murder, you know.'

Both men on the seat sprang up, leaving it rocking.

'And, what's stranger still,' continued the priest, with his dull eyes on the rhododendrons, 'it's the same disgusting sort; it's another beheading. They found the second head actually bleeding in the river, a few yards along Brayne's road to Paris; so they suppose that he——'

'Great Heaven!' cried O'Brien. 'Is Brayne a monomaniac?'

'There are American vendettas,' said the priest impassively. Then he added: 'They want you to come to the library and see it.'

Commandant O'Brien followed the others towards the inquest, feeling decidedly sick. As a soldier, he loathed all this secretive carnage; where were these extravagant amputations going to stop? First one head was hacked off, and then another; in this case (he told himself bitterly) it was not true that two heads were better than one. As he crossed the study he almost staggered at a shocking

20

coincidence. Upon Valentin's table lay the coloured picture of yet a third bleeding head; and it was the head of Valentin himself. A second glance showed him it was only a Nationalist paper, called *The Guillotine*, which every week showed one of its political opponents with rolling eyes and writhing features just after execution; for Valentin was an anti-clerical of some note. But O'Brien was an Irishman, with a kind of chastity even in his sins; and his gorge rose against that great brutality of the intellect which belongs only to France. He felt Paris as a whole, from the grotesques on the Gothic churches to the gross caricatures in the newspapers. He remembered the gigantic jests of the Revolution. He saw the whole city as one ugly energy, from the sanguinary sketch lying on Valentin's table up to where, above a mountain and forest of gargoyles, the great devil grins on Notre Dame.

The library was long, low, and dark; what light entered it shot from under low blinds and had still some of the ruddy tinge of morning. Valentin and his servant Ivan were waiting for them at the upper end of a long, slightly-sloping desk, on which lay the mortal remains, looking enormous in the twilight. The big black figure and yellow face of the man found in the garden confronted them essentially unchanged. The second head, which had been fished from among the river reeds that morning, lay streaming and dripping beside it; Valentin's men were still seeking to recover the rest of this second corpse, which was supposed to be afloat. Father Brown, who did not seem to share O'Brien's sensibilities in the least, went up to the second head and examined it with his blinking care. It was little more than a mop of wet, white hair, fringed with silver fire in the red and level morning light; the face, which seemed of an ugly, empurpled and perhaps criminal type, had been much battered against trees or stones as it tossed in the water.

'Good morning, Commandant O'Brien,' said Valentin, with quiet cordiality. 'You have heard of Brayne's last experiment in butchery, I suppose?'

Father Brown was still bending over the head with white hair, and he said, without looking up:

'I suppose it is quite certain that Brayne cut off this head, too.'

'Well, it seems common sense,' said Valentin, with his hands in his pockets. 'Killed in the same way as the other. Found within a few yards of the other. And sliced by the same weapon which we know he carried away.'

'Yes, yes; I know,' replied Father Brown, submissively. 'Yet, you know, I doubt whether Brayne could have cut off this head.'

'Why not?' inquired Dr Simon, with a rational stare.

'Well, doctor,' said the priest, looking up blinking, 'can a man cut off his own head? I don't know.'

O'Brien felt an insane universe crashing about his ears; but the doctor sprang forward with impetuous practicality and pushed back the wet, white hair.

'Oh, there's no doubt it's Brayne,' said the priest quietly. 'He had exactly that chip in the left ear.'

The detective, who had been regarding the priest with steady and glittering eyes, opened his clenched mouth and said sharply: 'You seem to know a lot about him, Father Brown.'

'I do,' said the little man simply. 'I've been about with him for some weeks. He was thinking of joining our church.'

The star of the fanatic sprang into Valentin's eyes; he strode towards the priest with clenched hands. 'And, perhaps,' he cried, with a blasting sneer: 'perhaps he was also thinking of leaving all his money to your church.'

'Perhaps he was,' said Brown stolidly; 'it is possible.'

'In that case,' cried Valentin, with a dreadful smile: 'You may indeed know a great deal about him. About his life and about his——'

Commandant O'Brien laid a hand on Valentin's arm. 'Drop that slanderous rubbish, Valentin,' he said: 'or there may be more swords yet.'

But Valentin (under the steady, humble gaze of the priest) had already recovered himself. 'Well,' he said shortly: 'people's private opinions can wait. You gentlemen are still bound by your promise to stay; you must enforce it on yourselves—and on each other. Ivan here will tell you anything more you want to know; I must get to business and write to the authorities. We can't keep this quiet any longer. I shall be writing in my study if there is any more news.'

'Is there any more news, Ivan?' asked Dr Simon, as the chief of police strode out of the room.

'Only one more thing, I think, sir,' said Ivan, wrinkling up his grey old face; 'but that's important, too, in its way. There's that old buffer you found on the lawn,' and he pointed without pretence of reverence at the big black body with the yellow head. 'We've found out who he is, anyhow.'

'Indeed!' cried the astonished doctor; 'and who is he?'

'His name was Arnold Becker,' said the under-detective, 'though he went by many aliases. He was a wandering sort of scamp, and is known to have been in America; so that was where Brayne got his knife into him. We didn't have much to do with him ourselves, for he worked mostly in Germany. We've communicated, of course, with the German police. But, oddly enough, there was a twin brother of his, named Louis Becker, whom we had a great deal to do with. In fact, we found it necessary to guillotine him only yesterday. Well, it's a rum thing, gentlemen, but when I saw that fellow flat on the lawn I had the greatest jump of my life. If I hadn't seen Louis Becker guillotined with my own eyes, I'd have sworn it was Louis Becker lying there in the grass. Then, of course, I remembered his twin brother in Germany, and following up the clue——'

The explanatory Ivan stopped, for the excellent reason that nobody was listening to him. The Commandant and the doctor were both staring at Father Brown, who had sprung stiffly to his feet, and was holding his temples tight like a man in sudden and violent pain.

'Stop, stop, stop!' he cried; 'stop talking a minute, for I see half. Will God give me strength? Will my brain make the one jump and see all? Heaven help me! I used to be fairly good at thinking. I could paraphrase any page in Aquinas once. Will my head split—or will it see? I see half—I only see half.'

He buried his head in his hands, and stood in a sort of rigid torture of thought or prayer, while the other three could only go on staring at this last prodigy of their wild twelve hours.

When Father Brown's hands fell they showed a face quite fresh and serious, like a child's. He heaved a huge sigh, and said: 'Let us get this said and done with as quickly as possible. Look here, this will be the quickest way to convince you all of the truth.' He turned to the doctor. 'Dr Simon,' he said, 'you have a strong head-piece, and I heard you this morning asking the five hardest questions about this business. Well, if you will now ask them again, I will answer them.'

Simon's pince-nez dropped from his nose in his doubt and wonder, but he answered at once. 'Well, the first question, you know, is why a man should kill another with a clumsy sabre at all when a man can kill with a bodkin?'

'A man cannot behead with a bodkin,' said Brown, calmly, 'and for *this* murder beheading was absolutely necessary.'

'Why?' asked O'Brien, with interest.

'And the next question?' asked Father Brown.

'Well, why didn't the man cry out or anything?' asked the doctor; 'Sabres in gardens are certainly unusual.'

'Twigs,' said the priest gloomily, and turned to the window which looked on the scene of death. 'No one saw the point of the twigs. Why should they lie on that lawn (look at it) so far from any tree? They were not snapped off; they were chopped off. The murderer occupied his enemy with some tricks with the sabre, showing how he could cut a branch in mid-air, or what not. Then, while his enemy bent down to see the result, a silent slash, and the head fell.'

'Well,' said the doctor slowly, 'that seems plausible enough. But my next two questions will stump anyone.'

The priest still stood looking critically out of the window and waited.

'You know how all the garden was sealed up like an air-tight chamber,' went on the doctor. 'Well, how did the strange man get into the garden?'

Without turning round, the little priest answered: 'There never was any strange man in the garden.'

There was a silence, and then a sudden cackle of almost childish laughter relieved the strain. The absurdity of Brown's remark moved Ivan to open taunts.

'Oh!' he cried; 'then we didn't lug a great fat corpse on to a sofa last night? He hadn't got into the garden, I suppose?'

'Got into the garden?' repeated Brown reflectively. 'No, not entirely.'

'Hang it all,' cried Simon, 'a man gets into a garden, or he doesn't.'

'Not necessarily,' said the priest, with a faint smile. 'What is the next question, doctor?'

'I fancy you're ill,' exclaimed Dr Simon sharply; 'but I'll ask the next question if you like. How did Brayne get out of the garden?'

'He didn't get out of the garden,' said the priest, still looking out of the window.

'Didn't get out of the garden?' exploded Simon.

'Not completely,' said Father Brown.

24

Simon shook his fists in a frenzy of French logic. 'A man gets out of a garden, or he doesn't,' he cried.

'Not always,' said Father Brown.

Dr Simon sprang to his feet impatiently. 'I have no time to spare on such senseless talk,' he cried angrily. 'If you can't understand a man being on one side of the wall or the other, I won't trouble you further.'

'Doctor,' said the cleric very gently, 'we have always got on very pleasantly together. If only for the sake of old friendship, stop and tell me your fifth question.'

The impatient Simon sank into a chair by the door and said briefly: 'The head and shoulders were cut about in a queer way. It seemed to be done after death.'

'Yes,' said the motionless priest, 'it was done so as to make you assume exactly the one simple falsehood that you did assume. It was done to make you take for granted that the head belonged to the body.'

The borderland of the brain, where all the monsters are made, moved horribly in the Gaelic O'Brien. He felt the chaotic presence of all the horse-men and fish-women that man's unnatural fancy has begotten. A voice older than his first fathers seemed to be saying in his ear: 'Keep out of the monstrous garden where grows the tree with double fruit. Avoid the evil garden where died the man with two heads.' Yet, while these shameful symbolic shapes passed across the ancient mirror of his Irish soul, his Frenchified intellect was quite alert, and was watching the odd priest as closely and incredulously as all the rest.

Father Brown had turned round at last, and stood against the window with his face in dense shadow; but even in that shadow they could see it was pale as ashes. Nevertheless, he spoke quite sensibly, as if there were no Gaelic souls on earth.

'Gentlemen,' he said; 'you did not find the strange body of Becker in the garden. You did not find any strange body in the garden. In face of Dr Simon's rationalism, I still affirm that Becker was only partly present. Look here!' (pointing to the black bulk of the mysterious corpse); 'you never saw that man in your lives. Did you ever see this man?'

He rapidly rolled away the bald-yellow head of the unknown, and put in its place the white-maned head beside it. And there, complete, unified, unmistakable, lay Julius K. Brayne.

'The murderer,' went on Brown quietly, 'hacked off his enemy's head and flung the sword far over the wall. But he was too clever to fling the sword only. He flung the *head* over the wall also. Then he had only to clap on another head to the corpse, and (as he insisted on a private inquest) you all imagined a totally new man.'

'Clap on another head!' said O'Brien, staring. 'What other head? Heads don't grow on garden bushes, do they?'

'No,' said Father Brown huskily, and looking at his boots; 'there is only one place where they grow. They grow in the basket of the guillotine, beside which the Chief of Police, Aristide Valentin, was standing not an hour before the murder. Oh, my friends, hear me a minute more before you tear me in pieces. Valentin is an honest man, if being mad for an arguable cause is honesty. But did you ever see in that cold, grey eye of his that he is mad? He would do anything, *anything*, to break what he calls the superstition of the Cross. He has fought for it and starved for it, and now he has murdered for it. Brayne's crazy millions had hitherto been scattered among so many sects that they did little to alter the balance of things. But Valentin heard a whisper that Brayne, like so many scatter-brained sceptics, was drifting to us; and that was quite a different thing. Brayne would pour supplies into the impoverished and pugnacious Church of France; he would support six Nationalist newspapers like *The Guillotine*. The battle was already balanced on a point, and the fanatic took flame at the risk. He resolved to destroy the millionaire, and he did it as one would expect the greatest of detectives to commit his only crime. He abstracted the severed head of Becker on some criminological excuse, and took it home in his official box. He had that last argument with Brayne, that Lord Galloway did not hear the end of; that failing, he led him out into the sealed garden, talked about swordsmanship, used twigs and a sabre for illustration and——'

Ivan of the Scar sprang up. 'You lunatic,' he yelled; 'you'll go to my master now, if I take you by——'

'Why, I was going there,' said Brown heavily; 'I must ask him to confess, and all that.'

Driving the unhappy Brown before them like a hostage or sacrifice, they rushed together into the sudden stillness of Valentin's study.

The great detective sat at his desk too occupied to hear their turbulent entrance. They paused a moment, and then something in the look of that upright and elegant back made the doctor run forward suddenly. A touch and a glance showed him that there was a small box of pills at Valentin's elbow, and that Valentin was dead in his chair; and on the blind face of the suicide was more than the pride of Cato.

The Queer Feet

If you meet a member of that select club, 'The Twelve True Fishermen,' entering the Vernon Hotel for the annual club dinner, you will observe, as he takes off his overcoat, that his evening coat is green and not black. If (supposing that you have the star-defying audacity to address such a being) you ask him why, he will probably answer that he does it to avoid being mistaken for a waiter. You will then retire crushed. But you will leave behind you a mystery as yet unsolved and a tale worth telling.

If (to pursue the same vein of improbable conjecture) you were to meet a mild, hard-working little priest, named Father Brown, and were to ask him what he thought was the most singular luck of his life, he would probably reply that upon the whole his best stroke was at the Vernon Hotel, where he had averted a crime and, perhaps, saved a soul, merely by listening to a few footsteps in a passage. He is perhaps a little proud of this wild and wonderful guess of his, and it is possible that he might refer to it. But since it is immeasurably unlikely that you will ever rise high enough in the social world to find 'The Twelve True Fishermen,' or that you will ever sink low enough among slums and criminals to find Father Brown, I fear you will never hear the story at all unless you hear it from me.

The Vernon Hotel, at which The Twelve True Fishermen held their annual dinners, was an institution such as can only exist in an oligarchical society which has almost gone mad on good manners. It was that topsy-turvy product—an 'exclusive' commercial enterprise. That is, it was a thing which paid, not by attracting people, but actually by turning people away. In the heart of a plutocracy tradesmen become cunning enough to be more fastidious than their customers. They positively create difficulties in overcoming them. If there were a fashionable hotel in London which no man could enter who was under six foot, society would meekly make up parties of six-foot men to dine in it. If there were an expensive restaurant which by a mere caprice of its proprietor was only open on Thursday afternoon, it would be crowded on Thursday afternoon. The Vernon Hotel stood, as if by accident, in the corner of a

28

square in Belgravia. It was a small hotel; and a very inconvenient one. But its very inconveniences were considered as walls protecting a particular class. One inconvenience, in particular, was held to be of vital importance: the fact that practically only twenty-four people could dine in the place at once. The only big dinner table was the celebrated terrace table, which stood open to the air on a sort of veranda overlooking one of the most exquisite old gardens in London. Thus it happened that even the twenty-four seats at this table could only be enjoyed in warm weather; and this making the enjoyment yet more difficult made it yet more desired. The existing owner of the hotel was a Jew named Lever; and he made nearly a million out of it, by making it difficult to get into. Of course he combined with this limitation in the scope of his enterprise the most careful polish in its performance. The wines and cooking were really as good as any in Europe, and the demeanour of the attendants exactly mirrored the fixed mood of the English upper class. The proprietor knew all his waiters like the fingers on his hand; there were only fifteen of them all told. It was much easier to become a Member of Parliament than to become a waiter in that hotel. Each waiter was trained in terrible silence and smoothness, as if he were a gentleman's servant. And, indeed, there was generally at least one waiter to every gentleman who dined.

The club of The Twelve True Fishermen would not have consented to dine anywhere but in such a place, for it insisted on a luxurious privacy; and would have been quite upset by the mere thought that any other club was even dining in the same building. On the occasion of their annual dinner the Fishermen were in the habit of exposing all their treasures, as if they were in a private house, especially the celebrated set of fish knives and forks which were, as it were, the insignia of the society, each being exquisitely wrought in silver in the form of a fish, and each loaded at the hilt with one large pearl. These were always laid out for the fish course, and the fish course was always the most magnificent in that magnificent repast. The society had a vast number of ceremonies and observances, but it had no history and no object; that was where it was so very aristocratic. You did not have to be anything in order to be one of the Twelve Fishers; unless you were already a certain sort of person, you never even heard of them. It had been in existence twelve years. Its president was Mr Audley. Its vice-president was the Duke of Chester.

If I have in any degree conveyed the atmosphere of this appalling hotel, the reader may feel a natural wonder as to how I came to know anything about it, and may even speculate as to how so ordinary a person as my friend Father Brown came to find himself in that golden gallery. As far as that is concerned, my story is simple, or even vulgar. There is in the world a very aged rioter and demagogue who breaks into the most refined retreats with the dreadful information that all men are brothers, and wherever this leveller went on his pale horse it was Father Brown's trade to follow. One of the waiters, an Italian, had been struck down with a paralytic stroke that afternoon; and his Jewish employer, marvelling mildly at such superstitions, had consented to send for the nearest Popish priest. With what the waiter confessed to Father Brown we are not concerned, for the excellent reason that the cleric kept it to himself; but apparently it involved him in writing out a note or statement for the conveying of some message or the righting of some wrong. Father Brown, therefore, with a meek impudence which he would have shown equally in Buckingham Palace, asked to be provided with a room and writing materials. Mr Lever was torn in two. He was a kind man, and had also that bad imitation of kindness, the dislike of any difficulty or scene. At the same time the presence of one unusual stranger in his hotel that evening was like a speck of dirt on something just cleaned. There was never any borderland or ante-room in the Vernon Hotel, no people waiting in the hall, no customers coming in on chance. There were fifteen waiters. There were twelve guests. It would be as startling to find a new guest in the hotel that night as to find a new brother taking breakfast or tea in one's own family. Moreover, the priest's appearance was second-rate and his clothes muddy; a mere glimpse of him afar off might precipitate a crisis in the club. Mr Lever at last hit on a plan to cover, since he might not obliterate, the disgrace. When you enter (as you never will) the Vernon Hotel, you pass down a short passage decorated with a few dingy but important pictures, and come to the main vestibule and lounge which opens on your right into passages leading to the public rooms, and on your left to a similar passage pointing to the kitchens and offices of the hotel. Immediately on your left hand is the corner of a glass office, which abuts upon the lounge—a house within a house, so to speak, like the old hotel bar which probably once occupied its place.

In this office sat the representative of the proprietor (nobody in this place ever appeared in person if he could help it), and just beyond the office, on the way to the servants' quarters, was the gentlemen's cloakroom, the last boundary of the gentlemen's domain. But between the office and the cloak-room was a small private room without other outlet, sometimes used by the proprietor for delicate and important matters, such as lending a duke a thousand pounds or declining to lend him sixpence. It is a mark of the magnificent tolerance of Mr Lever that he permitted this holy place to be for about half an hour profaned by a mere priest, scribbling away on a piece of paper. The story which Father Brown was writing down was very likely a much better story than this one, only it will never be known. I can merely state that it was very nearly as long, and that the last two or three paragraphs of it were the least exciting and absorbing.

For it was by the time he had reached these that the priest began a little to allow his thoughts to wander and his animal senses, which were commonly keen, to awaken. The time of darkness and dinner was drawing on; his own forgotten little room was without a light, and perhaps the gathering gloom, as occasionally happens, sharpened the sense of sound. As Father Brown wrote the last and least essential part of his document, he caught himself writing to the rhythm of a recurrent noise outside, just as one sometimes thinks to the tune of a railway train. When he became conscious of the thing he found what it was: only the ordinary patter of feet passing the door, which in an hotel was no very unlikely matter. Nevertheless, he stared at the darkened ceiling, and listened to the sound. After he had listened for a few seconds dreamily, he got to his feet and listened intently, with his head a little on one side. Then he sat down again and buried his brow in his hands, not now merely listening, but listening and thinking also.

The footsteps outside at any given moment were such as one might hear in any hotel; and yet, taken as a whole, there was something very strange about them. There were no other footsteps. It was always a very silent house, for the few familiar guests went at once to their own apartments, and the well-trained waiters were told to be almost invisible until they were wanted. One could not conceive any place where there was less reason to apprehend anything irregular. But these footsteps were so odd that one could not decide to call them regular or irregular. Father Brown followed them with his finger on the edge of the table, like a man trying to learn a tune on the piano.

First, there came a long rush of rapid little steps, such as a light man might make in winning a walking race. At a certain point they stopped and changed to a sort of slow-swinging stamp, numbering not a quarter of the steps, but occupying about the same time. The moment the last echoing stamp had died away would come again the run or ripple of light, hurrying feet, and then again the thud of the heavier walking. It was certainly the same pair of boots, partly because (as has been said) there were no other boots about, and partly because they had a small but unmistakable creak in them. Father Brown had the kind of head that cannot help asking questions; and on this apparently trivial question his head almost split. He had seen men run in order to jump. He had seen men run in order to slide. But why on earth should a man run in order to walk? Or, again, why should he walk in order to run? Yet no other description would cover the antics of this invisible pair of legs. The man was either walking very fast down one half of the corridor in order to walk very slow down the other half; or he was walking very slow at one end to have the rapture of walking fast at the other. Neither suggestion seemed to make much sense. His brain was growing darker and darker, like his room.

Yet, as he began to think steadily, the very blackness of his cell seemed to make his thoughts more vivid; he began to see as in a kind of vision the fantastic feet capering along the corridor in unnatural or symbolic attitudes. Was it a heathen religious dance? Or some entirely new kind of scientific exercise? Father Brown began to ask himself with more exactness what the steps suggested. Taking the slow step first; it certainly was not the step of the proprietor. Men of his type walk with a rapid waddle, or they sit still. It could not be any servant or messenger waiting for directions. It did not sound like it. The poorer orders (in an oligarchy) sometimes lurch about when they were slightly drunk, but generally, and especially in such gorgeous scenes, they stand or sit in constrained attitudes. No; that heavy yet springy step, with a kind of careless emphasis, not specially noisy, yet not caring what noise it made, belonged to only one of the animals of this earth. It was a gentleman of western Europe, and probably one who had never worked for his living.

Just as he came to this solid certainty, the step changed to the quicker one, and ran past the door as feverishly as a rat. The listener remarked that though this step was much swifter it was also much more noiseless, almost as if the man were walking on tiptoe. Yet it was not associated in his mind with secrecy, but with something else—something that he could not remember. He was maddened by one of those half-memories that make a man feel half-witted. Surely he had heard that strange, swift walking somewhere. Suddenly he sprang to his feet with a new idea in his head, and walked to the door. His room had no direct outlet on the passage, but led on one side into the glass office, and on the other into the cloakroom beyond. He tried the door into the office, and found it locked. Then he looked at the window, now a square pane full of purple cloud cleft by livid sunset, and for an instant he smelt evil as a dog smells rats.

The rational part of him (whether the wiser or not) regained its supremacy. He remembered that the proprietor had told him that he should lock the door, and would come later to release him. He told himself that twenty things he had not thought of might explain the eccentric sounds outside; he reminded himself that there was just enough light left to finish his own proper work. Bringing his paper to the window so as to catch the last stormy evening light, he resolutely plunged once more into the almost completed record. He had written for about twenty minutes, bending closer and closer to his paper in the lessening light; then suddenly he sat upright. He had heard the strange feet once more.

This time they had a third oddity. Previously the unknown man had walked, with levity indeed and lightning quickness, but he had walked. This time he ran. One could hear the swift, soft, bounding steps coming along the corridor, like the pads of a fleeing and leaping panther. Whoever was coming was a very strong, active man, in still yet tearing excitement. Yet, when the sound had swept up to the office like a sort of whispering whirlwind, it suddenly changed again to the old slow, swaggering stamp.

Father Brown flung down his paper, and, knowing the office door to be locked, went at once into the cloakroom on the other side. The attendant of this place was temporarily absent, probably because the only guests were at dinner, and his office was a sinecure. After groping through a grey forest of overcoats, he found that the dim cloakroom opened on the lighted corridor in the form of a sort of counter or half-door, like most of the counters across which we have all handed umbrellas and received tickets. There was a light immediately above the semi-circular arch of this opening. It threw little illumination on Father Brown himself, who seemed a mere dark outline against the dim sunset window behind him. But it threw an almost theatrical light on the man who stood outside the cloakroom in the corridor.

He was an elegant man in very plain evening-dress; tall, but with an air of not taking up much room; one felt that he could have slid along like a shadow where many smaller men would have been obvious and obstructive. His face, now flung back in the lamplight, was swarthy and vivacious, the face of a foreigner. His figure was good, his manners good-humoured and confident; a critic could only say that his black coat was a shade below his figure and manners, and even bulged and bagged in an odd way. The moment he caught sight of Brown's black silhouette against the sunset, he tossed down a scrap of paper with a number and called out with amiable authority: 'I want my hat and coat, please; I find I have to go away at once.'

Father Brown took the paper without a word, and obediently went to look for the coat; it was not the first menial work he had done in his life. He brought it and laid it on the counter; meanwhile, the strange gentleman who had been feeling in his waistcoat pocket, said, laughing: 'I haven't got any silver; you can keep this.' And he threw down half a sovereign, and caught up his coat.

Father Brown's figure remained quite dark and still; but in that instant he had lost his head. His head was always most valuable when he had lost it. In such moments he put two and two together and made four million. Often the Catholic Church (which is wedded to common sense) did not approve of it. Often he did not approve of it himself. But it was a real inspiration—important at rare crises—when whosoever shall lose his head the same shall save it.

'I think, sir,' he said civilly, 'that you have some silver in your pocket.'

The tall gentleman stared. 'Hang it,' he cried. 'If I give you gold, why should you complain?'

'Because silver is sometimes more valuable than gold,' said the priest mildly; 'that is, in large quantities.'

The stranger looked at him curiously. Then he looked still more curiously up the passage towards the main entrance. Then he looked back at Brown again, and then he looked very carefully at the window beyond Brown's head, still coloured with the after-glow of the storm. Then he seemed to make up his mind. He put one hand on the counter, vaulted over as easily as an acrobat and towered above the priest, putting one tremendous hand upon his collar.

'Stand still,' he said, in a hacking whisper. 'I don't want to threaten you, but——'

'I do want to threaten you,' said Father Brown, in a voice like a rolling drum. 'I want to threaten you with the worm that dieth not, and the fire that is not quenched.'

'You're a rum sort of cloakroom clerk,' said the other.

'I am a priest, Monsieur Flambeau,' said Brown, 'and I am ready to hear your confession.'

The other stood gasping for a few moments, and then staggered back into a chair.

The first two courses of the dinner of The Twelve True Fishermen had proceeded with placid success. I do not possess a copy of the menu; and if I did it would not convey anything to anybody. It was written in a sort of super-French employed by cooks, but quite unintelligible to Frenchmen. There was a tradition in the club that the *hors d'œuvres* should be various and manifold to the point of madness. They were taken seriously because they were avowedly useless extras, like the whole dinner and the whole club. There was also a tradition that the soup course should be light and unpretending—a sort of simple and austere vigil for the feast of fish that was to come. The talk was that strange, slight talk which governs the British Empire, which governs it in secret, and yet would scarcely enlighten an ordinary Englishman even if he could overhear it. Cabinet Ministers on both sides were alluded to by their Christian names with a sort of bored benignity. The Radical Chancellor of the Exchequer, whom the whole Tory party was supposed to be cursing for his extortions, was praised for his minor poetry, or his saddle in the hunting-field. The Tory leader, whom all Liberals were supposed to hate as a tyrant, was discussed and, on the whole, praised—as a Liberal. It seemed somehow that politicians were very important. And yet, anything seemed impor-tant about them except their politics. Mr Audley, the chairman, was an amiable, elderly man who still wore Gladstone collars; he was a kind of symbol of all that phantasmal and yet fixed society. He had never done anything—not even anything wrong. He was not fast; he was not even particularly rich. He was simply in the thing; and there was an end of it. No party could ignore him, and if he had wished to be in the Cabinet he certainly would have been put there. The Duke of Chester, the vice-president, was a young and rising politician. That is to say, he was a pleasant youth, with flat, fair hair and a freckled face, with moderate intelligence and enormous estates. In public his appearances were always successful and his principle was simple enough. When he thought of a joke he made it, and was called brilliant. When he could not think of a joke he said that this was no time for trifling, and was called able. In private, in a club of his own class, he was simply quite pleasantly frank and silly, like a schoolboy. Mr Audley, never having been in politics, treated them a little more seriously. Sometimes he even embarrassed the company by phrases suggesting that there was some difference between a Liberal and a Conservative. He himself was Conservative even in his private life. He had a roll of grey hair over the back of his collar like certain old-fashioned statesmen, and seen from behind he looked like the man the empire wants. Seen from the front he looked like a mild, self-indulgent bachelor, with rooms in the Albany—which he was.

As has been remarked, there were twenty-four seats at the terrace table, and only twelve members of the club. Thus they could occupy the terrace in the most luxurious style of all, being ranged along the inner side of the table, with no one opposite, commanding an uninterrupted view of the garden, the colours of which were still vivid, though evening was closing in somewhat luridly for the time of year. The chairman sat in the centre of the line, and the vice-president at the right-hand end of it. When the twelve guests first trooped into their seats it was the custom (for some unknown reason) for all the fifteen waiters to stand lining the wall like troops presenting arms to the king, while the fat proprietor stood and bowed to the club with radiant surprise, as if he had never heard of them before. But before the first chink of knife and fork this army of retainers had vanished, only the one or two required to collect and distribute the plates darting about in deathly silence. Mr Lever, the proprietor, of course had disappeared in convulsions of courtesy long before. It would be exaggerative, indeed irreverent, to say that he ever positively appeared again. But when the important course, the fish course, was being brought on, there was—how shall I put it?—a vivid shadow, a projection of his personality, which told that he was hovering near. The sacred fish course consisted (to the eyes of the vulgar) in a sort of monstrous pudding, about the size and shape of a wedding cake, in which some considerable number of interesting fishes had finally lost the shapes which God had given to them. The Twelve True Fishermen took up their celebrated fish knives and fish forks, and approached it as gravely as if every inch of the pudding cost as much as the silver fork it was eaten with. So it did, for all I know. This course was dealt with in eager and devouring silence; and it was only when his plate was nearly empty that the young duke made the ritual remark: 'They can't do this anywhere but here.'

'Nowhere,' said Mr Audley, in a deep bass voice, turning to the speaker and nodding his venerable head a number of times. 'Nowhere, assuredly, except here. It was represented to me that at the Café Anglais——'

Here he was interrupted and even agitated for a moment by the removal of his plate, but he recaptured the valuable thread of his thoughts. 'It was represented to me that the same could be done at the Café Anglais. Nothing like it, sir,' he said, shaking his head ruthlessly, like a hanging judge. 'Nothing like it.'

'Overrated place,' said a certain Colonel Pound speaking (by the look of him) for the first time for some months.

'Oh, I don't know,' said the Duke of Chester, who was an optimist, 'it's jolly good for some things. You can't beat it at——'

A waiter came swiftly along the room, and then stopped dead. His stoppage was as silent as his tread; but all those vague and kindly gentlemen were so used to the utter smoothness of the unseen machinery which surrounded and supported their lives, that a waiter doing anything unexpected was a start and a jar. They felt as you and I would feel if the inanimate world disobeyed—if a chair ran away from us.

The waiter stood staring a few seconds, while there deepened on every face at table a strange shame which is wholly the product of our time. It is the combination of modern humanitarianism with the horrible modern abyss between the souls of the rich and poor. A genuine historic aristocrat would have thrown things at the waiter, beginning with empty bottles, and very probably ending with money. A genuine democrat would have asked him, with a comrade-like clearness of speech, what the devil he was doing. But these modern plutocrats could not bear a poor man near to them, either as a slave or as a friend. That something had gone wrong with the servants was merely a dull, hot embarrassment. They did not want to be brutal, and they dreaded the need to be benevolent. They wanted the thing, whatever it was, to be over. It was over. The waiter, after standing for some seconds rigid, like a cataleptic, turned round and ran madly out of the room.

When he reappeared in the room, or rather in the doorway, it was in company with another waiter, with whom he whispered and gesticulated with southern fierceness. Then the first waiter went away, leaving the second waiter, and reappeared with a third waiter. By the time a fourth waiter had joined this hurried synod, Mr Audley felt it necessary to break the silence in the interests of Tact. He used a very loud cough, instead of the presidential hammer, and said: 'Splendid work young Moocher's doing in Burma. Now, no other nation in the world could have——'

A fifth waiter had sped towards him like an arrow, and was whispering in his ear: 'So sorry. Important! Might the proprietor speak to you?'

The chairman turned in disorder, and with a dazed stare saw Mr Lever coming towards them with his lumbering quickness. The gait of the good proprietor was indeed his usual gait, but his face was by no means usual. Generally it was a genial copper-brown; now it was a sickly yellow.

'You will pardon me, Mr Audley,' he said, with asthmatic breathlessness. 'I have great apprehensions. Your fish-plates, they are cleared away with the knife and fork on them!'

'Well, I hope so,' said the chairman, with some warmth.

'You see him?' panted the excited hotel keeper; 'you see the waiter who took them away? You know him?'

'Knew the waiter?' answered Mr Audley indignantly. 'Certainly not!'

Mr Lever opened his hands with a gesture of agony. 'I never send him,' he said. 'I know not when or why he come. I send my waiter to take away the plates, and he find them already away.'

Mr Audley still looked rather too bewildered to be really the man the empire wants; none of the company could say anything except the man of wood—Colonel Pound—who seemed galvanized into an unnatural life. He rose rigidly from his chair, leaving all the rest sitting, screwed his eyeglass into his eye, and spoke in a raucous undertone as if he had half-forgotten how to speak. 'Do you mean,' he said, 'that somebody has stolen our silver fish service?'

The proprietor repeated the open-handed gesture with even greater helplessness; and in a flash all the men at the table were on their feet.

'Are all your waiters here?' demanded the colonel, in his low, harsh accent.

'Yes; they're all here. I noticed it myself,' cried the young duke, pushing his boyish face into the inmost ring. 'Always count 'em as I come in; they look so queer standing up against the wall.'

'But surely one cannot exactly remember,' began Mr Audley, with heavy hesitation.

'I remember exactly, I tell you,' cried the duke excitedly. 'There never have been more than fifteen waiters at this place, and there were no more than fifteen tonight, I'll swear; no more and no less.'

The proprietor turned upon him, quaking in a kind of palsy of surprise. 'You say—you say,' he stammered, 'that you see all my fifteen waiters?'

'As usual,' assented the duke. 'What is the matter with that?'

'Nothing,' said Lever, with a deepening accent, 'only you did not. For one of zem is dead upstairs.'

There was a shocking stillness for an instant in that room. It may be (so supernatural is the word death) that each of those idle men looked for a second at his soul, and saw it as a small dried pea. One of them—the duke, I think—even said with the idiotic kindness of wealth, 'Is there anything we can do?'

'He has had a priest,' said the Jew, not untouched.

Then, as to the clang of doom, they awoke to their own position. For a few weird seconds they had really felt as if the fifteenth waiter might be the ghost of the dead man upstairs. They had been dumb under that oppression, for ghosts were to them an embarrassment, like beggars. But the remembrance of the silver broke the spell of the miraculous; broke it abruptly and with a brutal reaction. The colonel flung over his chair and strode to the door. 'If there was a fifteenth man here, friends,' he said, 'that fifteenth fellow was a thief. Down at once to the front and back doors and secure everything; then we'll talk. The twenty-four pearls are worth recovering.'

Mr Audley seemed at first to hesitate about whether it was gentlemanly to be in such a hurry about anything; but, seeing the duke dash down the stairs with youthful energy, he followed with a more mature motion.

At the same instant a sixth waiter ran into the room, and declared that he had found the pile of fish plates on a sideboard, with no trace of the silver.

The crowd of diners and attendants that tumbled helter-skelter down the passages divided into two groups. Most of the Fishermen followed the proprietor to the front room to demand news of any exit. Colonel Pound, with the Chairman, the vice-president, and one or two others, darted down the corridor leading to the servants' quarters, as the more likely line of escape. As they did so they passed the dim alcove or cavern of the cloakroom, and saw a short, black-coated figure, presumably an attendant, standing a little way back in the shadow of it.

'Hallo there!' called out the duke. 'Have you see anyone pass?'

The short figure did not answer the question directly, but merely said: 'Perhaps I have got what you are looking for, gentlemen.'

They paused, wavering and wondering, while he quietly went to the back of the cloakroom, and came back with both hands full of shining silver, which he laid out on the counter as calmly as a salesman. It took the form of a dozen quaintly shaped forks and knives.

'You—you——' began the colonel, quite thrown off his balance at last. Then he peered into the dim little room and saw two things: first, that the short, black-clad man was dressed like a clergyman; and, second, that the window of the room behind him was burst, as if someone had passed violently through.

'Valuable things to deposit in a cloakroom, aren't they?' remarked the clergyman, with cheerful composure.

'Did—did you steal those things?' stammered Mr Audley, with staring eyes.

'If I did,' said the cleric pleasantly, 'at least I am bringing them back again.'

'But you didn't,' said Colonel Pound, still staring at the broken window.

'To make a clean breast of it, I didn't,' said the other, with some humour. And he seated himself quite gravely on a stool.

40

'But you know who did,' said the colonel.

'I don't know his real name,' said the priest placidly, 'but I know something of his fighting weight, and a great deal about his spiritual difficulties. I formed the physical estimate when he was trying to throttle me, and the moral estimate when he repented.'

'Oh, I say—repented!' cried young Chester, with a sort of crow of laughter.

Father Brown got to his feet, putting his hands behind him. 'Odd, isn't it,' he said, 'that a thief and a vagabond should repent, when so many who are rich and secure remain hard and frivolous, and without fruit for God or man? But there, if you will excuse me, you trespass a little upon my province. If you doubt the penitence as a practical fact, there are your knives and forks. You are The Twelve True Fishers, and there are all your silver fish. But He has made me a fisher of men.'

'Did you catch this man?' asked the colonel, frowning.

Father Brown looked him full in his frowning face. 'Yes,' he said, 'I caught him, with an unseen hook and an invisible line which is long enough to let him wander to the ends of the world, and still to bring him back with a twitch upon the thread.'

There was a long silence. All the other men present drifted away to carry the recovered silver to their comrades, or to consult the proprietor about the queer condition of affairs. Bu the grim-faced colonel still sat sideways on the counter, swinging his long, lank legs and biting his dark moustache.

At least he said quietly to the priest: 'He must have been a clever fellow, but I think I know a cleverer.'

'He was a clever fellow,' answered the other, 'but I am not quite sure of what other you mean.'

'I mean you,' said the colonel, with a short laugh. 'I don't want to get the fellow jailed; make yourself easy about that. But I'd give a good many silver forks to know exactly how you fell into this affair, and how you got the stuff out of him. I reckon you're the most up-to-date devil of the present company.'

Father Brown seemed rather to like the saturnine candour of the soldier. 'Well,' he said, smiling, 'I mustn't tell you anything of the man's identity, or his own story, of course; but there's no particular reason why I shouldn't tell you of the mere outside facts which I found out for myself.'

He hopped over the barrier with unexpected activity, and sat beside Colonel Pound, kicking his short legs like a little boy on a gate. He began to tell the story as easily as if he were telling it to an old friend by a Christmas fire.

'You see colonel,' he said. 'I was shut up in that small room there doing some writing, when I heard a pair of feet in this passage doing a dance that was as queer as the dance of death. First came quick, funny little steps, like a man walking on tiptoe for a wager; then came slowly, careless, creaking steps, as of a big man walking about with a cigar. But they were both made by the same feet, I swear, and they came in rotation; first the run and then the walk, and then the run again. I wondered at first idly, and then wildly why a man should act these two parts at once. One walk I knew; it was just like yours, colonel. It was the walk of a well-fed gentleman waiting for something, who strolls about rather because he is physically alert than because he is mentally impatient. I knew that I knew the other walk, too, but I could not remember what it was. What wild creature had I met on my travels that tore along on tiptoe in that extraordinary style? Then I heard a clink of plates somewhere; and the answer stood up as plain as St. Peter's. It was the walk of a waiter—that walk with the body slanted forward, the eyes looking down, the ball of the toe spurning away the ground, the coat tails and napkin flying. Then I thought for a minute and a half more. And I believe I saw the manner of the crime, as clearly as if I were going to commit it.'

Colonel Pound looked at him keenly, but the speaker's mild grey eyes were fixed upon the ceiling with almost empty wistfulness.

'A crime,' he said slowly, 'is like any other work of art. Don't look surprised; crimes are by no means the only works of art that come from an infernal workshop. But every work of art, divine or diabolic, has one indispensable mark—I mean, that the centre of it is simple, however much the fulfilment may be complicated. Thus, in *Hamlet*, let us say, the grotesqueness of the grave-digger, the flowers of the mad girl, the fantastic finery of Osric, the pallor of the ghost and the grin of the skull are all oddities in a sort of tangled wreath round one plain tragic figure of a man in black. Well, this also,' he said, getting slowly down from his seat with a smile, 'this also is the plain tragedy of a man in black. Yes,' he went on, seeing the colonel look up in some wonder, 'the whole of this tale turns on a black coat. In this, as in *Hamlet*, there are the rococo excrescences—yourselves, let us say. There is the dead waiter, who was there when he could not be there. There is the invisible hand that swept your table clear of silver and melted its air. But every clever crime is founded ultimately on some one quite simple fact—some fact that is not itself mysterious. The mystification comes in covering it up, in leading men's thoughts away from it. This large and subtle and (in the ordinary course) most profitable crime, was built on the plain fact that a gentleman's evening dress is the same as a waiter's. All the rest was acting, and thundering good acting, too.'

'Still,' said the colonel, getting up and frowning at his boots. 'I am not sure that I understand.'

'Colonel,' said Father Brown, 'I tell you that this archangel of impudence who stole your forks walked up and down this passage twenty times in the blaze of all the lamps, in the glare of all the eyes. He did not go and hide in dim corners where suspicion might have searched for him. He kept constantly on the move in the lighted corridors, and everywhere that he went he seemed to be there by right. Don't ask me what he was like; you have seen him yourself six or seven times tonight. You were waiting with all the other grand people in the reception room at the end of the passage there, with the terrace just beyond. Whenever he came among you gentlemen, he came in the lightning style of a waiter, with bent head, flapping napkin and flying feet. He shot out on to the terrace, did something to the table-cloth, and shot back again towards the office and the waiters' quarters. By the time he had come under the eye of the office clerk and the waiters he had become another man in every inch of his body, in every instinctive gesture. He strolled among the servants with the absent-minded insolence which they have all seen in their patrons. It was no new thing to them that a swell from the dinner party should pace all parts of the house like an animal at the Zoo; they know that nothing marks the Smart Set more than a habit of walking where one chooses. When he was magnificently weary of walking down that particular passage he would wheel round and pace back past the office; in the shadow of the arch just beyond he was altered as by a blast of magic, and went hurrying forward again among the Twelve Fishermen, an obsequious attendant. Why should the gentlemen look at a chance waiter? Why should the waiters suspect a first-rate walking gentleman? Once or twice he played the coolest tricks. In the proprietor's private quarters he called out breezily for a syphon of soda water, saying he was thirsty. He said genially that he would carry it himself, and he did; he carried it quickly and correctly through the thick of you, a waiter with an obvious errand. Of course, it could not have been kept up long, but it only had to be kept up till the end of the fish course.

'His worst moment was when the waiters stood in a row; but even then he contrived to lean against the wall just around the corner in such a way that for that important instant the waiters thought him a gentleman, while the gentlemen thought him a waiter. The rest went like winking. If any waiter caught him away from the table, that waiter caught a languid aristocrat. He had only to time himself two minutes before the fish was cleared, become a swift servant, and clear it himself. He put the plates down on a sideboard, stuffed the silver in his breast pocket, giving it a bulgy look, and ran like a hare (I heard him coming) till he came to the cloakroom. There he had only to be a plutocrat again—a plutocrat called away suddenly on business. He had only to give his ticket to the cloakroom attendant, and go out again elegantly as he had come in. Only—only I happened to be the cloakroom attendant.'

'What did you do to him?' cried the colonel, with unusual intensity. 'What did he tell you?'

'I beg your pardon,' said the priest immovably, 'that is where the story ends.'

'And the interesting story begins,' muttered Pound. 'I think I understand his professional trick. But I don't seem to have got hold of yours.'

'I must be going,' said Father Brown.

They walked together along the passage to the entrance hall, where they saw the fresh, freckled face of the Duke of Chester, who was bounding buoyantly along towards them.

'Come along, Pound,' he cried breathlessly. 'I've been looking for you everywhere. The dinner's going again in spanking style, and old Audley has got to make a speech in honour of the forks being saved. We want to start some new ceremony, don't you know, to commemorate the occasion. I say, you really got the goods back, what do you suggest?'

'Why,' said the colonel, eyeing him with a certain sardonic approval. 'I should suggest that henceforward we wear green coats instead of black. One never knows what mistakes may arise when one looks so like a waiter.'

'Oh, hang it all!' said the young man, 'a gentleman never looks like a waiter.'

'Nor a waiter like a gentleman, I suppose,' said Colonel Pound, with the same lowering laughter on his face. 'Reverend sir, your friend must have been very smart to act the gentleman.'

Father Brown buttoned up his commonplace overcoat to the neck, for the night was stormy, and took his commonplace umbrella from the stand.

'Yes,' he said; 'it must be very hard work to be a gentleman; but, do you know, I have sometimes thought that it may be almost as laborious to be a waiter.'

And saying 'Good evening,' he pushed open the heavy doors of that palace of pleasures. The golden gates closed behind him, and he went at a brisk walk through the damp, dark streets in search of a penny omnibus.

THE INVISIBLE MAN

In the cool blue twilight of two steep streets in Camden Town, the shop at the corner, a confectioner's, glowed like the butt of a cigar. One should rather say, perhaps, like the butt of a firework, for the light was of many colours and some complexity, broken up by many mirrors and dancing on many gilt and gaily-coloured cakes and sweetmeats. Against this one fiery glass were glued the noses of many guttersnipes, for the chocolates were all wrapped in those red and gold and green metallic colours which are almost better than chocolate itself; and the huge white wedding-cake in the window was somehow at once remote and satisfying, just as if the whole North Pole were good to eat. Such rainbow provocations could naturally collect the youth of the neighbourhood up to the ages of ten or twelve. But this corner was also attractive to youth at a later stage; and a young man, not less than twenty-four, was staring into the same shop window. To him, also, the shop was of fiery charm, but this attraction was not wholly to be explained by chocolates; which, however, he was far from despising.

He was a tall, burly, red-haired young man, with a resolute face but a listless manner. He carried under his arm a flat, grey portfolio of black-and-white sketches which he had sold with more or less success to publishers ever since his uncle (who was an admiral) had disinherited him for Socialism, because of a lecture which he had delivered against that economic theory. His name was John Turn-bull Angus.

Entering at last, he walked through the confectioner's shop into the back room, which was a sort of pastry-cook restaurant, merely raising his hat to the young lady who was serving there. She was a dark, elegant, alert girl in black, with a high colour and very quick, dark eyes; and after the ordinary interval she followed him into the inner room to take his order.

His order was evidently a usual one. 'I want, please,' he said with precision, 'one halfpenny bun and a small cup of black coffee.' An instant before the girl could turn away he added, 'Also, I want you to marry me.'

The young lady of the shop stiffened suddenly, and said: 'Those are jokes I don't allow.'

The red-haired young man lifted grey eyes of an unexpected gravity.

'Really and truly,' he said, 'it's as serious—as serious as the halfpenny bun. It is expensive, like the bun; one pays for it. It is indigestible, like the bun. It hurts.'

The dark young lady had never taken her dark eyes off him, but seemed to be studying him with almost tragic exactitude. At the end of her scrutiny she had something like the shadow of a smile, and she sat down in a chair.

'Don't you think,' observed Angus, absently, 'that it's rather cruel to eat these halfpenny buns? They might grow up into penny buns. I shall give up these brutal sports when we are married.'

The dark young lady rose from her chair and walked to the window, evidently in a state of strong but not unsympathetic cogitation. When at last she swung round again with an air of resolution, she was bewildered to observe that the young man was carefully laying out on the table various objects from the shop-window. They included a pyramid of highly coloured sweets, several plates of sandwiches, and the two decanters containing that mysterious port and sherry which are peculiar to pastry-cooks. In the middle of this neat arrangement he had carefully let down the enormous load of white sugared cake which had been the huge ornament of the window.

'What on earth are you doing?' she asked.

'Duty, my dear Laura,' he began.

'Oh, for the Lord's sake, stop a minute,' she cried, 'and don't talk to me in that way. I mean what is all that?'

'A ceremonial meal, Miss Hope.'

'And what is *that?*' she asked impatiently, pointing to the mountain of sugar.

'The wedding-cake, Mrs Angus,' he said.

The girl marched to that article, removed it with some clatter, and put it back in the shop-window; she then returned, and, putting her elegant elbows on the table, regarded the young man not unfavourably, but with considerable exasperation.

'You don't give me any time to think,' she said.

'I'm not such a fool,' he answered; 'that's my Christian humility.'

She was still looking at him; but she had grown considerably graver behind the smile.

'Mr Angus,' she said steadily, 'before there is a minute more of this nonsense I must tell you something about myself as shortly as I can.'

'Delighted,' replied Angus gravely. 'You might tell me something about myself, too, while you are about it.'

'Oh, do hold your tongue and listen,' she said. 'It's nothing that I'm ashamed of, and it isn't even anything that I'm specially sorry about. But what would you say if there were something that is no business of mine and yet is my nightmare?'

'In that case,' said the man seriously, 'I should suggest that you bring back the cake.'

'Well, you must listen to the story first,' said Laura, persistently. 'To begin with, I must tell you that my father owned the inn called the 'Red Fish' at Ludbury, and I used to serve people in the bar.'

'I have often wondered,' he said, 'why there was a kind of a Christian air about this one confectioner's shop.'

'Ludbury is a sleepy, grassy little hole in the Eastern Counties, and the only kind of people who ever came to the 'Red Fish' were occasional commercial travellers, and for the rest, the most awful people you can see, only you've never seen them. I mean little, loungy men, who had just enough to live on, and had nothing to do but lean about in bar-rooms and bet on horses, in bad clothes that were just too good for them. Even these wretched young rotters were not very common at our house; but there were two of them that were a lot too common—common in every sort of way. They both lived on money of their own, and were wearisomely idle and over-dressed. But yet I was a bit sorry for them, because I half believe they slunk into our little empty bar because each of them had a slight deformity; the sort of thing that some yokels laugh at. It wasn't exactly a deformity either; it was more an oddity. One of them was a surprisingly small man, something like a dwarf, or at least like a jockey. He was not at all jockeyish to look at, though, he had a round black head and a well-trimmed black beard, bright eyes like a bird's; he jingled money in his pockets; he jangled a great gold watch chain; and he never turned up except dressed just too much like a gentleman to be one. He was no fool, though, though a futile idler; he was curiously clever at all kinds of things that couldn't be the slightest use; a sort of impromptu conjuring;

making fifteen matches set fire to each other like a regular firework; or cutting a banana or some such thing into a dancing doll. His name was Isidore Smythe; and I can see him still, with his little dark face, just coming up to the counter, making a jumping kangaroo out of five cigars.

'The other fellow was more silent and more ordinary; but somehow he alarmed me much more than poor little Smythe. He was very tall and slight, and light-haired; his nose had a high bridge, and he might almost have been handsome in a spectral sort of way; but he had one of the most appalling squints I have ever seen or heard of. When he looked straight at you, you didn't know where you were yourself, let alone what he was looking at. I fancy this sort of disfigurement embittered the poor chap a little; for while Smythe was ready to show off his monkey tricks anywhere, James Welkin (that was the squinting man's name) never did anything except soak in our bar parlour, and go for great walks by himself in the flat, grey country all round. All the same, I think Smythe, too, was a little sensitive about being so small, though he carried it off more smartly. And so it was that I was really puzzled, as well as startled, and very sorry, when they both offered to marry me in the same week.

'Well, I did what I've since thought was perhaps a silly thing. But, after all, these freaks were my friends in a way; and I had a horror of their thinking I refused them for the real reason, which was that they were so impossibly ugly. So I made up some gas of another sort, about never meaning to marry anyone who hadn't carved his way in the world. I said it was a point of principle with me not to live on money that was just inherited like theirs. Two days after I had talked in this well-meaning sort of way, the whole trouble began. The first thing I heard was that both of them had gone off to seek their fortunes, as if they were in some silly fairy tale.

'Well, I've never seen either of them from that day to this. But I've had two letters from the little man called Smythe, and really they were rather exciting.'

'Ever heard of the other man?' asked Angus.

'No, he never wrote,' said the girl, after an instant's hesitation. 'Smythe's first letter was simply to say that he had started out walking with Welkin to London; but Welkin was such a good walker that the little man dropped out of it, and took a rest by the roadside. He happened to be picked up by some travelling show, and, partly because he was nearly a dwarf, and partly because he was really a clever little wretch, he got on quite well in the show business, and was soon sent up to the Aquarium, to do some tricks that I forgot. That was his first letter. His second was much more of a startler, and I only got it last week.'

The man called Angus emptied his coffee-cup and regarded her with mild and patient eyes. Her own mouth took a slight twist of laughter as she resumed: 'I suppose you've seen on the hoardings all about this 'Smythe's Silent Service'? Or you must be the only person that hasn't. Oh, I don't know much about it, it's some clockwork invention for doing all the housework by machinery. You know the sort of thing: "Press a button—A Butler who Never Drinks." "Turn a handle—Ten Housemaids who Never Flirt." You must have seen the advertisements. Well, whatever these machines are, they are making pots of money; and they are making it all for that little imp whom I knew down in Ludbury. I can't help feeling pleased the poor little chap has fallen on his feet; but the plain fact is, I'm in terror of his turning up any minute and telling me he's carved his way in the world—as he certainly has.'

'And the other man?' repeated Angus with a sort of obstinate quietude.

Laura Hope got to her feet suddenly. 'My friend,' she said: 'I think you are a witch. Yes, you are quite right. I have not seen a line of the other man's writing; and I have no more notion than the dead of what or where he is. But it is of him that I am frightened. It is he who is all about my path. It is he who has half driven me mad. Indeed, I think he has driven me mad; for I have felt him where he could not have been, and I have heard his voice when he could not have spoken.'

'Well, my dear,' said the young man, cheerfully, 'if he were Satan himself, he is done for now you have told somebody. One goes mad all alone, old girl. But when was it you fancied you felt and heard our squinting friend?'

'I heard James Welkin laugh as plainly as I hear you speak,' said the girl, steadily. 'There was nobody there, for I stood just outside the shop at the corner, and could see down both streets at once I had forgotten how he laughed, though his laugh was as odd as his squint. I had not thought of him for nearly a year. But it's a solemn truth that a few seconds later the first letter came from his rival.'

'Did you ever make the spectre speak or squeak, or anything?' asked Angus, with some interest.

Laura suddenly shuddered, and then said with an unshaken voice:

'Yes. Just when I had finished reading the second letter from Isidore Smythe announcing his success, just then, I heard Welkin say: "He shan't have you, though." It was quite plain, as if he were in the room. It is awful; I think I must be mad.'

'If you really were mad,' said the young man, 'you would think you must be sane. But certainly there seems to me to be something a little rum about this unseen gentleman. Two heads are better than one—I spare you allusions to any other organs—and really, if you would allow me, as a sturdy, practical man, to bring back the wedding-cake out of the window——'

Even as he spoken, there was a sort of steely shriek in the street outside, and a small motor, driven at devilish speed, shot up to the door of the shop and stuck there. In the same flash of time a small man in a shiny top hat stood stamping in the outer room.

Angus, who had hitherto maintained hilarious ease from motives of mental hygiene, revealed the strain of his soul by striding abruptly out of the inner room and confronting the newcomer. A glance at him was quite sufficient to confirm the savage guesswork of a man in love. This very dapper but dwarfish figure, with the spike of black beard carried insolently forward, the clever unrestful eyes, the neat but very nervous fingers, could be none other than the man just described to him: Isidore Smythe, who made dolls out of banana skins and matchboxes: Isidore Smythe, who made millions out of undrinking butlers and unflirting housemaids of metal. For a moment the two men, instinctively understanding each other's air of possession, looked at each other with that curious cold generosity which is the soul of rivalry.

Mr Smythe, however, made no allusion to the ultimate ground of their antagonism, but said simply and explosively: 'Has Miss Hope seen that thing on the window?'

'On the window?' repeated the staring Angus.

'There's no time to explain other things,' said the small millionaire shortly. 'There's some tomfoolery going on here that has to be investigated.'

He pointed his polished walking-stick at the window, recently depleted by the bridal preparations of Mr Angus; and that gentleman was astonished to see along the front of the glass a long strip of paper pasted, which had certainly not been on the window when he had looked through it some time before. Following the energetic Smythe outside into the street, he found that some yard and a half of stamp paper had been carefully gummed along the glass outside, and on this was written in straggly characters: 'If you marry Smythe, he will die.'

'Laura,' said Angus, putting his big red head into the shop, 'you're not mad.'

'It's the writing of that fellow Welkin,' said Smythe gruffly. 'I haven't seen him for years, but he's always bothering me. Five times in the last fortnight he's had threatening letters left at my flat, and I can't even find out who leaves them, let alone if it is Welkin himself. The porter of the flats swears that no suspicious characters have been seen, and here he has pasted up a sort of dado on a public shop window, while the people in the shop——'

'Quite so,' said Angus modestly, 'while the people in the shop were having tea. Well, sir, I can assure you I appreciate your common sense in dealing so directly with the matter. We can talk about other things afterwards. The fellow cannot be very far off yet, for I swear there was no paper there when I went last to the window, ten or fifteen minutes ago. On the other hand, he's too far off to be chased, as we don't even know the direction. If you'll take my advice, Mr Smythe, you'll put this at once in the hands of some energetic inquiry man, private rather than public. I know an extremely clever fellow, who has set up in business five minutes from here in your car. His name's Flambeau, and though his youth was a bit stormy, he's a strictly honest man now, and his brains are worth money. He lives in Lucknow Mansions, Hampstead.'

'That is odd,' said the little man, arching his black eyebrows. 'I live myself in Himalaya Mansions round the corner. Perhaps you might care to come with me; I can go to my rooms and sort out these queer Welkin documents, while you run round and get your friend the detective.'

'You are very good,' said Angus politely. 'Well, the sooner we act the better.'

Both men, with a queer kind of impromptu fairness, took the same sort of formal farewell of the lady, and both jumped into the brisk little car. As Smythe took the wheel and they turned the great corner of the street, Angus was amused to see a gigantesque poster of 'Smythe's Silent Service,' with a picture of a huge headless iron doll, carrying a saucepan with the legend, 'A Cook Who is Never Cross.'

'I use them in my own flat,' said the little black-bearded man, laughing, 'partly for advertisement, and partly for real convenience. Honestly, and all above board, those big clockwork dolls of mine do bring you coals or claret or a time-table quicker than any live servants I've ever known, if you know which knob to press. But I'll never deny, between ourselves, that such servants have their disadvantages, too.'

'Indeed?' said Angus; 'is there something they can't do?'

'Yes,' replied Smythe coolly; 'they can't tell me who left those threatening letters at my flat.'

The man's motor was small and swift like himself; in fact, like his domestic service, it was of his own invention. If he was an advertising quack, he was one who believed in his own wares. The sense of something tiny and flying was accentuated as they swept up long white curves of road in the dead but open daylight of evening. Soon the white curves came sharper and dizzier; they were upon ascending spirals, as they say in the modern religions. For, indeed, they were cresting a corner of London which is almost as precipitous as Edinburgh, if not quite so picturesque. Terrace rose above terrace, and the special tower of flats they sought, rose above them all to almost Egyptian height, gilt by the level sunset. The change, as they turned the corner and entered the crescent known as Himalaya Mansions, was as abrupt as the opening of a window; for they found that pile of flats sitting above London as above a green sea of slate. Opposite to the mansions, on the other side of the gravel crescent, was a bushy enclosure more like a steep hedge or dyke than a garden, and some way below that ran a strip of artificial water, a sort of canal, like the moat of that embowered fortress. As the car swept round the crescent it passed, at one corner, the stray stall of a man selling chestnuts; and right away at the other end of the curve, Angus could see a dim blue policeman walking slowly. These were the only human shapes in that high suburban solitude; but he had an irrational sense that they expressed the speechless poetry of London. He felt as if they were figures in a story.

The little car shot up to the right house like a bullet, and shot out its owner like a bomb shell. He was immediately inquiring of a tall commissionaire in shining braid, and a short porter in shirt sleeves, whether anybody or anything had been seeking his apartments. He was assured that nobody and nothing had passed these officials since his last inquiries; whereupon he and the slightly bewildered Angus were shot up in the lift like a rocket, till they reached the top floor.

'Just come in for a minute,' said the breathless Smythe. 'I want to show you those Welkin letters. Then you might run round the corner and fetch your friend.' He pressed a button concealed in the wall, and the door opened of itself.

It opened on a long, commodious ante-room, of which the only arresting features, ordinarily speaking, were the rows of tall half-human mechanical figures that stood up on both sides like tailors' dummies. Like tailors' dummies they were headless; and like tailors' dummies they had a handsome unnecessary humpiness in the shoulders, and a pigeon-breasted protuberance of chest; but barring this, they were not much more like a human figure than any automatic machine at a station that is about the human height. They had two great hooks like arms, for carrying trays; and they were painted pea-green, or vermilion, or black for convenience of distinction; in every other way they were only automatic machines and nobody would have looked twice at them. On this occasion, at least, nobody did. For between the two rows of these domestic dummies lay something more interesting than most of the mechanics of the world. It was a white, tattered scrap of paper scrawled with red ink; and the agile inventor had snatched it up almost as soon as the door flew open. He handed it to Angus without a word. The red ink on it actually was not dry, and the message ran: 'If you have been to see her today, I shall kill you.'

There was a short silence, and then Isidore Smythe said quietly: 'Would you like a little whisky? I rather feel as if I should.'

'Thank you; I should like a little Flambeau,' said Angus, gloomily. 'This business seems to me to be getting rather grave. I'm going round at once to fetch him.'

'Right you are,' said the other, with admirable cheerfulness. 'Bring him round here as quick as you can.'

But as Angus closed the front door behind him he saw Smythe push back a button, and one of the clockwork images glided from its place and slid along a groove in the floor carrying a tray with syphon and decanter. There did seem something a trifle weird about leaving the little man alone among those dead servants, who were coming to life as the door closed.

Six steps down from Smythe's landing the man in shirt sleeves was doing something with a pail. Angus stopped to extract a promise, fortified with a prospective bribe, that he would remain in that place until the return with the detective, and would keep count of any kind of stranger coming up those stairs. Dashing down to the front hall he then laid similar charges of vigilance on the commissionaire at the front door, from whom he learned the simplifying circumstance that there was no back door. Not content with this, he captured the floating policeman and induced him to stand opposite the entrance and watch it; and finally paused an instant for a pennyworth of chestnuts, and an inquiry as to the probable length of the merchant's stay in the neighbourhood.

The chestnut seller, turning up the collar of his coat, told him he should probably be moving shortly, as he thought it was going to snow. Indeed, the evening was growing grey and bitter, but Angus, with all his eloquence, proceeded to nail the chestnut man to his post.

'Keep yourself warm on your own chestnuts,' he said earnestly. 'Eat up your whole stock; I'll make it worth your while. I'll give you a sovereign if you'll wait here till I come back, and then tell me whether any man, woman, or child has gone into that house where the commissionaire is standing.'

He then walked away smartly, with a last look at the besieged tower.

'I've made a ring round that room, anyhow,' he said. 'They can't all four of them be Mr Welkin's accomplices.'

Lucknow Mansions were, so to speak, on a lower platform of that hill of houses, of which Himalaya Mansions might be called the peak. Mr Flambeau's semi-official flat was on the ground floor, and presented in every way a marked contrast to the American machinery and cold hotel-like luxury of the flat of the Silent Service. Flambeau, who was a friend of Angus, received him in a rococo artistic den behind his office, of which the ornaments were sabres, harquebuses, Eastern curiosities, flasks of Italian wine, savage cooking-pots, a plumy Persian cat, and a small dusty-looking Roman Catholic priest, who looked particularly out of place.

'This is my friend, Father Brown,' said Flambeau. 'I've often wanted you to meet him. Splendid weather, this; a little cold for Southerners like me.'

'Yes, I think it will keep clear,' said Angus, sitting down on a violet-striped Eastern ottoman.

'No,' said the priest quietly; 'It has begun to snow.'

And indeed, as he spoke, the first few flakes, foreseen by the man of chestnuts, began to drift across the darkening window-pane.

'Well,' said Angus heavily. 'I'm afraid I've come on business, and rather jumpy business at that. The fact is, Flambeau, within a stone's throw of your house is a fellow who badly wants your help; he's perpetually being haunted and threatened by an invisible enemy—a scoundrel whom nobody has ever seen.' As Angus proceeded to tell the whole tale of Smythe and Welkin beginning with Laura's story, and going on with his own, the supernatural laugh at the corner of two empty streets, the strange distinct words spoken in an empty room, Flambeau grew more and more vividly concerned, and the little priest seemed to be left out of it, like a piece of furniture. When it came to the scribbled stamp-paper pasted on the window, Flambeau rose, seeming to fill the room with his huge shoulders.

'If you don't mind,' he said, 'I think you had better tell me the rest on the nearest road to this man's house. It strikes me, somehow, that there is no time to be lost.'

'Delighted,' said Angus, rising also, 'though he's safe enough for the present, for I've set four men to watch the only hole to his burrow.'

They turned out into the street, the small priest trundling after them with the docility of a small dog. He merely said, in a cheerful way, like one making conversation: 'How quick the snow gets thick on the ground.'

As they threaded the steep side streets already powdered with silver, Angus finished his story; and by the time they reached the crescent with the towering flats, he had leisure to turn his attention to the four sentinels. The chestnut seller, both before and after receiving a sovereign, swore stubbornly that he had watched the door and seen no visitor enter. The policeman was even more emphatic. He said he had had experience of crooks of all kinds, in top hats and in rags; he wasn't so green as to expect suspicious characters to look suspicious; he looked out for anybody, and, so help him, there had been nobody. And when all three men gathered round the gilded commissionaire, who still stood smiling astride of the porch, the verdict was more final still.

'I've got a right to ask any man, duke or dustman, what he wants in these flats,' said the genial and gold-laced giant, 'and I'll swear there's been nobody to ask since this gentleman went away.'

The unimportant Father Brown, who stood back, looking modestly at the pavement, here ventured to say meekly: 'Has nobody been up and down stairs, then, since the snow began to fall? It began while we were all round at Flambeau's.'

'Nobody's been in here, sir, you can take it from me,' said the official, with beaming authority.

'Then I wonder what that is?' said the priest, and stared at the ground blankly like a fish.

The others all looked down also; and Flambeau used a fierce exclamation and a French gesture. For it was unquestionably true that down the middle of the entrance guarded by the man in gold lace, actually between the arrogant, stretched legs of that colossus, ran a stringy pattern of grey footprints stamped upon the white snow.

'God!' cried Angus involuntarily; 'the Invisible Man!'

Without another word he turned and dashed up the stairs, with Flambeau following; but Father Brown still stood looking about him in the snow-clad street as if he had lost interest in his query.

Flambeau was plainly in a mood to break down the door with his big shoulder; but the Scotsman, with more reason, if less intuition, fumbled about on the frame of the door till he found the invisible button; and the door swung slowly open.

It showed substantially the same serried interior; the hall had grown darker, though it was still struck here and there with the last crimson shafts of sunset, and one or two of the headless machines had been moved from their places for this or that purpose, and stood here and there about the twilit place. The green and red of their coats were all darkened in the dusk, and their likeness to human shapes slightly increased by their very shapelessness. But in the middle of them all, exactly where the paper with the red ink had lain, there lay something that looked very like red ink spilled out of its bottle. But it was not red ink.

With a French combination of reason and violence Flambeau simply said 'Murder!' and, plunging into the flat, had explored every corner and cupboard of it in five minutes. But if he expected to find a corpse he found none. Isidore Smythe simply was not in the place, either dead or alive. After the most tearing search the two men met each other in the outer hall with streaming faces and staring eyes. 'My friend,' said Flambeau, talking French in his excitement, 'not only is your murderer invisible, but he makes invisible also the murdered man.'

Angus looked round at the dim room full of dummies, and in some Celtic corner of his Scotch soul a shudder started. One of the life-size dolls stood immediately overshadowing the blood stain, summoned, perhaps, by the slain man an instant before he fell. One of the high-shouldered hooks that served the thing for arms, was a little lifted and Angus had suddenly the horrid fancy that poor Smythe's own iron child had struck him down. Matter had rebelled, and these machines had killed their master. But even so, what had they done with him?

'Eaten him?' said the nightmare at his ear; and he sickened for an instant at the idea of rent, human remains absorbed and crushed into all that acephalous clockwork.

He recovered his mental health by an emphatic effort, and said to Flambeau: 'Well, there it is. The poor fellow has evaporated like a cloud and left a red streak on the floor. The tale does not belong to this world.'

'There is only one thing to be done,' said Flambeau, 'whether it belongs to this world or the other, I must go down and talk to my friend.'

They descended, passing the man with the pail, who again asseverated that he had let no intruder pass, down to the commissionaire and the hovering chestnut man, who rightly reasserted their own watchfulness. But when Angus looked round for his fourth confirmation he could not see it, and called out with some nervousness: 'Where is the policeman?'

'I beg your pardon,' said Father Brown; 'that is my fault. I just sent him down the road to investigate something—that I just thought worth investigating.'

'Well, we want him back pretty soon,' said Angus abruptly, 'for the wretched man upstairs has not only been murdered, but wiped out.'

'How?' asked the priest.

'Father,' said Flambeau, after a pause, 'upon my soul I believe it is more in your department than mine. No friend or foe has entered the house, but Smythe is gone, as if stolen by the fairies. If that is not supernatural, I——'

As he spoke they were all checked by an unusual sight; the big blue policeman came round the corner of the crescent running. He came straight up to Brown.

'You're right, sir,' he panted, 'they've just found poor Mr Smythe's body in the canal down below.'

Angus put his hand wildly to his head. 'Did he run down and drown himself?' he asked.

'He never came down, I'll swear,' said the constable, 'and he wasn't drowned either, for he died of a great stab over the heart.'

'And yet you saw no one enter?' said Flambeau in a grave voice.

'Let us walk down the road a little,' said the priest.

As they reached the other end of the crescent he observed abruptly: 'Stupid of me! I forgot to ask the policeman something. I wonder if they found a light brown sack.'

'Why a light brown sack?' asked Angus, astonished.

'Because if it was any other coloured sack, the case must begin over again,' said Father Brown; 'but if it was a light brown sack, why, the case is finished.'

'I am pleased to hear it,' said Angus with hearty irony. 'It hasn't begun, so far as I am concerned.'

'You must tell us all about it,' said Flambeau, with a strange heavy simplicity, like a child.

Unconsciously they were walking with quickening steps down the long sweep of road on the other side of the high crescent, Father Brown leading briskly, though in silence. At last he said with an almost touching vagueness: 'Well, I'm afraid you'll think it so prosy. We always begin at the abstract end of things, and you can't begin this story anywhere else.

'Have you ever noticed this—that people never answer what you say? They answer what you mean—or what they think you mean. Suppose one lady says to another in a country house, "Is anybody staying with you?" the lady doesn't answer "Yes; the butler, the three footmen, the parlour-maid, and so on," though the parlour-maid may be in the room, or the butler behind her chair. She says: "There is *nobody* staying with us," meaning nobody of the sort you mean. But suppose a doctor inquiring into an epidemic asks, "Who is staying in the house?" then the lady will remember the butler, the parlour-maid, and the rest. All language is used like that; you never get a question answered literally, even when you get it answered truly. When those four quite honest men said that no man had gone into the Mansions, they did not really mean that *no man* had gone into them. They meant no man whom they could suspect of being your man. A man did go into the house, and did come out of it, but they never noticed him.'

'An invisible man?' inquired Angus, raising his red eyebrows.

'A mentally invisible man,' said Father Brown.

A minute or two after he resumed in the same unassuming voice, like a man thinking his way. 'Of course, you can't think of such a man, until you do think of him. That's where his cleverness comes in. But I came to think of him through two or three little things in the tale Mr Angus told us. First, there was the fact that this Welkin went for long walks. And then there was the vast lot of stamp paper on the window. And then, most of all, there were the two things the young lady said—things that couldn't be true. Don't get annoyed,' he added hastily, noting a sudden movement of the Scotsman's head; 'she thought they were true all right, but they couldn't be true. A person *can't* be quite alone in a street a second before she receives a letter. She can't be quite alone in a street when she starts reading a letter just received. There must be somebody pretty near her; he must be mentally invisible.'

'Why must there be somebody near her?' asked Angus.

'Because,' said Father Brown: 'barring carrier-pigeons, somebody must have brought her the letter.'

'Do you really mean to say,' asked Flambeau, with energy, 'that Welkin carried his rival's letters to his lady?'

'Yes,' said the priest. 'Welkin carried his rival's letters to his lady. You see, he had to.'

'Oh, I can't stand much more of this,' exploded Flambeau. 'Who is this fellow? What does he look like. What is the usual get-up of a mentally invisible man?'

'He is dressed rather handsomely in red, blue and gold,' replied the priest promptly with decision, 'and in this striking, and even showy costume he entered Himalaya Mansions under eight human eyes; he killed Smythe in cold blood, and came down into the street again carrying the dead body in his arms——'

'Reverend sir,' cried Angus, standing still, 'are you raving mad, or am I?'

'You are not mad,' said Brown, 'only a little unobservant. You have not noticed such a man as this, for example.'

He took three quick strides forward, and put his hand on the shoulder of an ordinary passing postman who had bustled by them unnoticed under the shade of the trees.

'Nobody ever notices postmen, somehow,' he said thoughtfully; 'yet they have passions like other men, and even carry large bags where a small corpse can be stowed quite easily.'

The postman, instead of turning naturally, had ducked and tumbled against the garden fence. He was a lean fair-bearded man of very ordinary appearance, but as he turned an alarmed face over his shoulder, all three men were fixed with an almost fiendish squint.

Flambeau went back to his sabres, purple rugs and Persian cat, having many things to attend to. John Turnbull Angus went back to the lady at the shop, with whom that imprudent young man contrives to be extremely comfortable. But Father Brown walked those snow-covered hills under the stars for many hours with a murderer, and what they said to each other will never be known.

THE WRONG SHAPE

Certain of the great roads going north out of London continue far into the country a sort of attenuated and interrupted spectre of a street, with great gaps in the building, but preserving the line. Here will be a group of shops, followed by a fenced field or paddock, and then a famous public-house, and then perhaps a market garden or a nursery garden, and then one large private house, and then another field and another inn, and so on. If anyone walks along one of these roads he will pass a house which will probably catch his eye, though he may not be able to explain its attraction. It is a long, low house, running parallel with the road, painted mostly white and pale green, with a veranda and sun-blinds, and porches capped with those quaint sort of cupolas like wooden umbrellas that one sees in some old-fashioned houses. In fact, it is an old-fashioned house, very English and very suburban in the good old wealthy Clapham sense. And yet the house has a look of having been built chiefly for the hot weather. Looking at its white paint and sun-blinds one thinks vaguely of puggarees and even of palm trees. I cannot trace the feeling to its root; perhaps the place was built by an Anglo-Indian.

Anyone passing this house, I say, would be namelessly fascinated by it; would feel that it was a place about which some story was to be told. And he would have been right, as you shall shortly hear. For this is the story—the story of the strange things that did really happen in it in the Whitsuntide of the year 18—:

Anyone passing the house on the Thursday before Whit Sunday at about half-past four p.m. would have seen the front door open, and Father Brown, of the small church of St Mungo, come out smoking a large pipe in company with a very tall French friend of his called Flambeau, who was smoking a very small cigarette. These persons may or may not be of interest to the reader, but the truth is that they were not the only interesting things that were displayed when the front door of the white-and-green house was opened. There are further peculiarities about this house, which must be described to start with, not only that the reader may understand this tragic tale, but also that he may

62

realize what it was that the opening of the door revealed.

The whole house was built upon the plan of a T, but a T with a very long cross piece and a very short tail piece. The long cross piece was the frontage that ran along in face of the street, with the front door in the middle; it was two stories high, and contained nearly all the important rooms. The short tail piece, which ran out at the back immediately opposite the front door, was one story high, and consisted only of two long rooms, the one leading into the other. The first of these two rooms was the study in which the celebrated Mr Quinton wrote his wild Oriental poems and romances. The farther room was a glass conservatory full of tropical blossoms of quite unique and almost monstrous beauty, and on such afternoons as these was glowing with gorgeous sunlight. Thus when the hall door was open, many a passer-by literally stopped to stare and gasp; for he looked down a perspective of rich apartments to something really like a transformation scene in a fairy play: purple clouds and golden suns and crimson stars that were at once scorchingly vivid and yet transparent and far away.

Leonard Quinton, the poet, had himself most carefully arranged this effect; and it is doubtful whether he so perfectly expressed his personality in any of his poems. For he was a man who drank and bathed in colours, who indulged his lust for colour somewhat to the neglect of form—even of good form. This it was that had turned his genius so wholly to eastern art and imagery; to those bewildering carpets or blinding embroideries in which all the colours seem fallen into a fortunate chaos, having nothing to typify or to teach. He had attempted, not perhaps with complete artistic success, but with acknowledged imagination and invention, to compose epics and love stories reflecting the riot of violent and even cruel colour; tales of tropical heavens of burning gold or blood-red copper; of eastern heroes who rode with twelve-turbaned mitres upon elephants painted purple or peacock green; of gigantic jewels that a hundred negroes could not carry, but which burned with ancient and strange-hued fires.

In short (to put the matter from the more common point of view), he dealt much in eastern heavens, rather worse than most western hells; in eastern monarchs, whom we might possibly call maniacs; and in eastern jewels which a Bond Street jeweller (if the hundred staggering negroes brought them into his shop) might possibly not regard as genuine. Quinton was a genius, if a morbid one; and even his morbidity appeared more in his life than in his work. In temperament he was weak and waspish, and his health had suffered heavily from oriental experiments with opium. His wife—a handsome, hard-working, and, indeed, over-worked woman—objected to the opium, but objected much more to a live Indian hermit in white and yellow robes, whom her husband had insisted on entertaining for months together, a Virgil to guide his spirit through the heavens and the hells of the east.

It was out of this artistic household that Father Brown and his friend stepped on to the door-step; and to judge from their faces, they stepped out of it with much relief. Flambeau had known Quinton in wild student days in Paris, and they had renewed the acquaintance for a weekend; but apart from Flambeau's more responsible developments of late, he did not get on well with the poet now. Choking oneself with opium and writing little erotic verses on vellum was not his notion of how a gentleman should go to the devil. As the two paused on the doorstep, before taking a turn in the garden, the front garden gate was thrown open with violence, and a young man with a billycock hat on the back of his head tumbled up the steps in his eagerness. He was a dissipated-looking youth with a gorgeous red necktie all awry, as if he had slept in it, and he kept fidgeting and lashing about with one of those little jointed canes.

'I say,' he said breathlessly, 'I want to see old Quinton. I must see him. Has he gone?'

'Mr Quinton is in, I believe,' said Father Brown, cleaning his pipe, 'but I do not know if you can see him. The doctor is with him at present.'

The young man, who seemed not to be perfectly sober, stumbled into the hall; and at the same moment the doctor came out of Quinton's study, shutting the door and beginning to put on his gloves.

'See Mr Quinton?' said the doctor coolly. 'No, I'm afraid you can't. In fact, you mustn't on any account. Nobody must see him; I've just given him his sleeping draught.'

'No, but look here, old chap,' said the youth in the red tie, trying affectionately to capture the doctor by the lapels of his coat. 'Look here. I'm simply sewn up, I tell you. I——'

'It's no good, Mr Atkinson,' said the doctor, forcing him to fall back; 'when you can alter the effects of a drug I'll alter my decision,' and, settling on his hat, he stepped out into the sunlight with the other two. He was a bull-necked, good-tempered little man with a small moustache, inexpressibly ordinary, yet giving an impression of capability.

The young man in the billycock, who did not seem to be gifted with any tact in dealing with people beyond the general idea of clutching hold of their coats, stood outside the door, as dazed as if he had been thrown out bodily, and silently watched the other three walk away together through the garden.

'That was a sound, spanking lie I told just now,' remarked the medical man, laughing. 'In point of fact, poor Quinton doesn't have his sleeping draught for nearly half an hour. But I'm not going to have him bothered with that little beast, who only wants to borrow money that he wouldn't pay back if he could. He's a dirty little scamp, though he is Mrs Quinton's brother, and she's as fine a woman as ever walked.'

'Yes,' said Father Brown. 'She's a good woman.'

'So I propose to hang about the garden till the creature has cleared off,' went on the doctor, 'and then I'll go in to Quinton with the medicine. Atkinson can't get in, because I locked the door.'

'In that case, Dr Harris,' said Flambeau, 'we might as well walk round at the back by the end of the conservatory. There's no entrance to it that way but it's worth seeing, even from the outside.'

'Yes, and I might get a squint at my patient,' laughed the doctor, 'for he prefers to lie on an ottoman right at the end of the conservatory amid all those blood-red poinsettias; it would give me the creeps. But what are you doing?'

Father Brown had stopped for a moment, and picked up out of the long grass, where it had almost been wholly hidden, a queer, crooked Oriental knife, inlaid exquisitely in coloured stones and metals.

'What is this?' asked Father Brown, regarding it with some disfavour.

'Oh, Quinton's, I suppose,' said Dr Harris carelessly; 'he has all sorts of Chinese knick-knacks about the place. Or perhaps it belongs to the mild Hindu of his whom he keeps on a string.'

'What Hindu?' asked Father Brown, still staring at the dagger in his hand.

'Oh, some Indian conjuror,' said the doctor lightly; 'a fraud, of course.'

'You don't believe in magic?' asked Father Brown without looking up.

'Oh crikey! Magic!' said the doctor.

'It's very beautiful,' said the priest in a low, dreaming voice; 'the colours are very beautiful. But it's the wrong shape.'

'What for?' asked Flambeau, staring.

'For anything. It's the wrong shape in the abstract. Don't you ever feel that about Eastern art? The colours are intoxicatingly lovely; but the shapes are mean and bad—deliberately mean and bad. I have seen wicked things in a Turkey carpet.'

'*Mon Dieu!*' cried Flambeau, laughing.

'They are letters and symbols in a language I don't know; but I know they stand for evil words,' went on the priest, his voice growing lower and lower. 'The lines go wrong on purpose—like serpents doubling to escape.'

'What the devil are you talking about?' said the doctor with a loud laugh.

Flambeau spoke quietly to him in answer. 'The Father sometimes gets this mystic's cloud on him,' he said; 'but I give you fair warning that I have never known him have it except when there was some evil quite near.'

'Oh, rats!' said the scientist.

'Why, look at it,' cried Father Brown, holding out the crooked knife at arm's length, as if it were some glittering snake. 'Don't you see it is the wrong shape? Don't you see that it has no hearty and plain purpose? It does not point like a spear. It does not sweep like a scythe. It does not *look* like a weapon. It looks like an instrument of torture.'

'Well, as you don't seem to like it,' said the jolly Harris, 'it had better be taken back to its owner. Haven't we come to the end of this confounded conservatory yet? This house is the wrong shape, if you like.'

'You don't understand,' said Father Brown, shaking his head. 'The shape of this house is quaint—it is even laughable. But there is nothing *wrong* about it.'

As they spoke they came round the curve of glass that ended the conservatory, an uninterrupted curve, for there was neither door nor window by which to enter at that end. The glass, however, was clear, and the sun still bright, though beginning to set; and they could see not only the flamboyant blossoms inside, but the frail figure of the poet in a brown velvet coat lying languidly on the sofa, having, apparently, fallen half asleep over a book. He was a pale, slight man, with loose, chestnut hair and a fringe of beard that was the paradox of his face, for the beard made him look less manly. These traits were well known to all three of them; but even had it not been so, it may be doubted whether they would have looked at Quinton just then. Their eyes were riveted on another object.

Exactly in their path, immediately outside the round end of the glass building, was standing a tall man, whose drapery fell to his feet in faultless white, and whose bare, brown skull, face, and neck gleamed in the setting sun like splendid bronze. He was looking through the glass at the sleeper, and he was more motionless than a mountain.

'Who is that?' cried Father Brown, stepping back with a hissing intake of his breath.

'Oh, it is only that Hindu humbug,' growled Harris; 'but I don't know what the deuce he's doing here.'

'It looks like hypnotism,' said Flambeau, biting his black moustache.

'Why are you unmedical fellows always talking bosh about hypnotism?' cried the doctor. 'It looks a deal more like burglary.'

'Well, we will speak to it, at any rate,' said Flambeau, who was always for action. One long stride took him to the place where the Indian stood. Bowing from his great height, which overtopped even the Oriental's, he said with placid impudence:

'Good evening, sir. Do you want anything?'

Quite slowly, like a great ship turning into a harbour, the great yellow face turned, and looked at last over its white shoulder. They were startled to see that its yellow eyelids were quite sealed, as in sleep. 'Thank you,' said the face in excellent English. 'I want nothing.' Then, half opening the lids, so as to show a slit of opalescent eyeball, he repeated, 'I want nothing.' Then he opened his eyes wide with a startling stare, said, 'I want nothing,' and sent rustling away into the rapidly darkening garden.

'The Christian is more modest,' muttered Father Brown; 'he wants something.'

'What on earth was he doing?' asked Flambeau, knitting his black brows and lowering his voice.

'I should like to talk to you later,' said Father Brown.

The sunlight was still a reality, but it was the red light of evening, and the bulk of the garden trees and bushes grew blacker and blacker against it. They turned round the end of the conservatory, and walked in silence down the other side to get round to the front door. As they went they seemed to wake something, as one startles a bird, in the deeper corner between the study and the main building; and again they saw the white-robed fakir slide out of the shadow, and slip round towards the front door. To their surprise, however, he had not been alone. They found themselves abruptly pulled up and forced to banish their bewilderment by the appearance of Mrs Quinton, with her heavy golden hair and square pale face, advancing on them out of the twilight. She looked a little stern, but was entirely courteous.

'Good evening, Dr Harris,' was all she said.

'Good evening, Mrs Quinton,' said the little doctor heartily. 'I am just going to give your husband his sleeping draught.'

'Yes,' she said in a clear voice. 'I think it is quite time.' And she smiled at them, and went sweeping into the house.

'That woman's over-driven,' said Father Brown; 'that's the kind of woman that does her duty for twenty years, and then does something dreadful.'

The little doctor looked at him for the first time with an eye of interest.

'Did you ever study medicine?' he asked.

'You have to know something of the mind as well as the body,' answered the priest; 'we have to know something of the body as well as the mind.'

'Well,' said the doctor. 'I think I'll go and give Quinton his stuff.'

They had turned the corner of the front façade, and were approaching the front doorway. As they turned into it they saw the man in the white robe for the third time. He came so straight towards the front door that it seemed quite incredible that he had not just come out of the study opposite to it. Yet they knew that the study door was locked.

Father Brown and Flambeau, however, kept this weird contradiction to themselves, and Dr Harris was not a man to waste his thoughts on the impossible. He permitted the omnipresent Asiatic to make his exit, and then stepped briskly into the hall. There he found a figure which he had already forgotten. The inane Atkinson was still hanging about, humming and poking things with his knobby cane. The doctor's face had a spasm of disgust and decision, and he whispered rapidly to his companion: 'I must lock the door again, or this rat will get in. But I shall be out again in two minutes.'

He rapidly unlocked the door and locked it again behind him, just balking a blundering charge from the young man in the billycock. The young man threw himself impatiently on a hall chair. Flambeau looked at a Persian illumination on the wall; Father Brown, who seemed in a sort of daze, dully eyed the door. In about four minutes the door was opened again. Atkinson was quicker this time. He sprang forward, held the door open for an instant, and called out: 'Oh, I say, Quinton, I want——'

From the other end of the study came the clear voice of Quinton, in something between a yawn and a yell of weary laughter.

'Oh, I know what you want. Take it, and leave me in peace. I'm writing a song about peacocks.'

Before the door closed half a sovereign came flying through the aperture; and Atkinson, stumbling forward, caught it with singular dexterity.

'So that's settled,' said the doctor, and, locking the door savagely, he led the way out into the garden.

'Poor Leonard can get a little peace now,' he added to Father Brown; 'he's locked in all by himself for an hour or two.'

'Yes,' answered the priest; 'and his voice sounded jolly enough when we left him.' Then he looked gravely round the garden, and saw the loose figure of Atkinson standing and jingling the half-sovereign in his pocket, and beyond, in the purple twilight, the figure of the Indian sitting bolt upright upon a bank of grass with his face turned towards the setting sun. Then he said abruptly:

'Where is Mrs Quinton?'

'She has gone up to her room,' said the doctor. 'That is her shadow on the blind.'

Father Brown looked up, and frowningly scrutinized a dark outline at the gas-lit window.

'Yes,' he said, 'that is her shadow,' and he walked a yard or two and threw himself upon a garden seat.

Flambeau sat down beside him; but the doctor was one of those energetic people who live naturally on their legs. He walked away, smoking, into the twilight, and the two friends were left together.

'My father,' said Flambeau in French, 'what is the matter with you?'

Father Brown was silent and motionless for half a minute then he said: 'Superstition is irreligious, but there is something in the air of this place. I think it's that Indian—at least, partly.'

He sank into silence, and watched the distant outline of the Indian, who still sat rigid as if in prayer. At first sight he seemed motionless, but as Father Brown watched him he saw that the man swayed ever so slightly with a rhythmic movement, just as the dark tree-tops swayed ever so slightly in the little wind that was creeping up the dim garden paths and shuffling the fallen leaves a little.

The landscape was growing rapidly dark, as if for a storm, but they could still see all the figures in their various places. Atkinson was leaning against a tree, with a listless face; Quinton's wife was still at her window; the doctor had gone strolling round the end of the conservatory; they could see his cigar like a will-o'-the-wisp; and the fakir still sat rigid and yet rocking, while the trees above him began to rock and almost to roar. Storm was certainly coming.

'When that Indian spoke to us,' went on Brown in a conversational undertone, 'I had a sort of vision, a vision of him and all his universe. Yet he only said the same thing three times. When first he said, "I want nothing," it meant only that he was impenetrable, that Asia does not give itself away. Then he said again, "I want nothing," and I knew that he meant that he was sufficient to himself, like a cosmos, that he needed no God, neither admitted any sins. And when he said the third time, "I want nothing," he said it with blazing eyes. And I knew that he meant literally what he said; that nothing was his desire and his home; that he was weary for nothing as for wine; that annihilation, the mere destruction of everything or anything——'

Two drops of rain fell; and for some reason Flambeau started and looked up, as if they had stung him. And the same instant the doctor down the end of the conservatory began running towards them, calling out something as he ran.

As he came among them like a bombshell the restless Atkinson happened to be taking a turn nearer to the house front; and the doctor clutched him by the collar in a convulsive grip. 'Foul play!' he cried; 'what have you been doing to him, you dog?'

The priest had sprung erect, and had the voice of steel of a soldier in command.

'No fighting,' he cried coolly; 'we are enough to hold anyone we want to. What is the matter, doctor?'

'Things are not right with Quinton,' said the doctor, quite white. 'I could just see him through the glass, and I don't like the way he's lying. It's not as I left him, anyhow.'

'Let us go in to him,' said Father Brown shortly. 'You can leave Mr Atkinson alone. I have had him in sight since we heard Quinton's voice.'

'I will stop here and watch him,' said Flambeau hurriedly. 'You go in and see.'

The doctor and the priest flew to the study door, unlocked it, and fell into the room. In doing so they nearly fell over the large mahogany table in the centre at which the poet usually wrote; for the place was lit only by a small fire kept for the invalid. In the middle of this table lay a single sheet of paper, evidently left there on purpose. The doctor snatched it up, glanced at it, handed it to Father Brown, and crying, 'Good God, look at that!' plunged towards the glass room beyond, where the terrible tropic flowers still seemed to keep a crimson memory of the sunset.

Father Brown read the words three times before he put down the paper. The words were: 'I die by my own hand; yet I die murdered!' They were in the quite inimitable, not to say illegible, handwriting of Leonard Quinton.

Then Father Brown, still keeping the paper in his hand, strode towards the conservatory, only to meet his medical friend coming back with a face of assurance and collapse. 'He's done it,' said Harris.

They went together through the gorgeous unnatural beauty of cactus and azalea and found Leonard Quinton, poet and romancer, with his head hanging downward off his ottoman and his red curls sweeping the ground. Inside his left side was thrust the queer dagger that they had picked up in the garden, and his limp hand still rested on the hilt.

Outside, the storm had come at one stride, like the night in Coleridge, and garden and glass roof were darkening with driving rain. Father Brown seemed to be studying the paper more than the corpse; he held it close to his eyes; and seemed trying to read it in the twilight. Then he held it up against the faint light, and, as he did so, lightning stared at them for an instant so white that the paper looked black against it.

Darkness full of thunder followed, and after the thunder Father Brown's voice said out of the dark: 'Doctor, this paper is the wrong shape.'

'What do you mean?' asked Doctor Harris, with a frowning stare.

'It isn't square,' answered Brown. 'It has a sort of edge snipped off at the corner. What does it mean?'

'How the deuce should I know?' growled the doctor. 'Shall we move this poor chap, do you think? He's quite dead.'

'No,' answered the priest; 'we must leave him as he lies and send for the police.' But he was still scrutinizing the paper.

As they went back through the study he stopped by the table and picked up a small pair of nail scissors. 'Ah,' he said with a sort of relief; 'this is what he did it with. But yet——' And he knitted his brows.

'Oh, stop fooling with that scrap of paper,' said the doctor emphatically. 'It was a fad of his. He had hundreds of them. He cut all his paper like that,' as he pointed to a stack of sermon paper still unused on another and smaller table. Father Brown went up to it and held up a sheet. It was the same irregular shape.

'Quite so,' he said. 'And here I see the corners that were snipped off.' And to the indignation of his colleague he began to count them.

'That's all right,' he said, with an apologetic smile. 'Twenty-three sheets cut and twenty-two corners cut off them. And as I see you are impatient we will rejoin the others.'

'Who is to tell his wife?' asked Dr Harris. 'Will you go and tell her now, while I sent a servant for the police?'

'As you will,' said Father Brown indifferently. And he went out to the hall door.

Here also he found a drama, though of a more grotesque sort. It showed nothing less than his big friend Flambeau in an attitude to which he had long been unaccustomed, while upon the pathway at the bottom of the steps was sprawling with his boots in the air the amiable Atkinson, his billycock hat and walking-cane sent flying in opposite directions along the path. Atkinson had at length wearied of Flambeau's almost paternal custody, and had endeavoured to knock him down, which was by no means a smooth game to play with the Roi des Apaches, even after that monarch's abdication.

Flambeau was about to leap upon his enemy and secure him once more, when the priest patted him easily on the shoulder.

'Make it up with Mr Atkinson, my friend,' he said. 'Beg a mutual pardon and say "Good night." We need not detain him any longer.' Then, as Atkinson rose somewhat doubtfully and gathered his hat and stick and went towards the garden gate, Father Brown said in a more serious voice: 'Where is that Indian?'

They all three (for the doctor had joined them) turned involuntarily towards the dim grassy bank amid the tossing trees, purple with twilight, where they had last seen the brown man swaying in his strange prayers. The Indian was gone.

'Confound him,' said the doctor, stamping furiously. 'Now I know that it was that nigger that did it.'

'I thought you didn't believe in magic,' said Father Brown quietly.

'No more I did,' said the doctor, rolling his eyes. 'I only know that I loathed that yellow devil when I thought he was a sham wizard. And I shall loathe him more if I come to think he was a real one.'

'Well, his having escaped is nothing,' said Flambeau. 'For we could have proved nothing and done nothing against him. One hardly goes to the parish constable with a story of suicide imposed by witchcraft or auto-suggestion.'

Meanwhile Father Brown had made his way into the house, and now went to break the news to the wife of the dead man.

When he came out again he looked a little pale and tragic; but what passed between them in that interview was never known, even when all was known.

Flambeau, who was talking quietly with the doctor, was surprised to see his friend reappear so soon at his elbow; but Brown took no notice, and merely drew the doctor apart. 'You have sent for the police, haven't you?' he asked.

'Yes,' answered Harris. 'They ought to be here in ten minutes.'

'Will you do me a favour?' said the priest quietly. 'The truth is, I make a collection of these curious stories, which often contain, as in the case of our Hindu friend, elements which can hardly be put into a police report. Now, I want you to write out a report of this case for my private use. Yours is a clever trade,' he said, looking at the doctor gravely and steadily in the face. 'I sometimes think that you know some details of this matter which you have not thought fit to mention. Mine is a confidential trade like yours, and I will treat anything you write for me in strict confidence. But write the whole.'

The doctor, who had been listening thoughtfully with his head a little on one side, looked the priest in the face for an instant, and said: 'All right,' and went into the study, closing the door behind him.

'Flambeau,' said Father Brown, 'there is a long seat there under the veranda, where we can smoke, out of the rain. You are my only friend in the world, and I want to talk to you. Or, perhaps, be silent with you.'

They established themselves comfortably in the veranda seat; Father Brown, against his common habit, accepted a good cigar and smoked it steadily in silence, while the rain shrieked and rattled on the roof of the veranda.

'My friend,' he said at length, 'this is a very queer case. A very queer case.'

'I should think it was,' said Flambeau, with something like a shudder.

'You call it queer, and I call it queer,' said the other, 'and yet we mean quite opposite things. The modern mind always mixes up two different ideas: mystery in the sense of what is marvellous, and mystery in the sense of what is complicated. That is half its difficulty about miracles. A miracle is startling; but it is simple. It is simple because it *is* a miracle. It is power coming directly from God (or the devil) instead of indirectly through nature or human wills. Now you mean that this business is marvellous because it is miraculous, because it is witchcraft worked by a wicked Indian. Understand, I do not say that it was not spiritual or diabolic. Heaven and hell only know by what surrounding influences strange sins come into the lives of men. But for the present my point is this: If it was pure magic, as you think, then it is marvellous; but it is not mysterious—that is, it is not complicated. The quality of a miracle is mysterious, but its manner is simple. Now, the manner of this business has been the reverse of simple.'

The storm that had slackened for a little seemed to be swelling again, and there came heavy movements as of faint thunder. Father Brown let fall the ash of his cigar and went on:

'There has been in this incident,' he said, 'a twisted, ugly, complex quality that does not belong to the straight bolts either of heaven or hell. As one knows the crooked track of a snail, I know the crooked track of a man.'

The white lightning opened its enormous eye in one wink, the sky shut up again, and the priest went on:

'Of all these crooked things, the crookedest was the shape of that piece of paper. It was crookeder than the dagger that killed him.'

'You mean the paper on which Quinton confessed his suicide,' said Flambeau.

'I mean the paper on which Quinton wrote, "I die by my own hand," ' answered Father Brown. 'The shape of that paper, my friend, was the wrong shape; the wrong shape if ever I have seen it in this wicked world.'

'It only had a corner snipped off,' said Flambeau, 'and I understand that all Quinton's paper was cut that way.'

'It was a very odd way,' said the other, 'and a very bad way, to my taste and fancy. Look here, Flambeau, this Quinton—God receive his soul!—was perhaps a bit of a cur in some ways, but he really was an artist, with the pencil as well as the pen. His handwriting, though hard to read, was bold and beautiful. I can't prove what I say; I can't prove anything. But I tell you with the full force of conviction that he could never have cut that mean little piece off a sheet of paper. If he had wanted to cut down paper for some purpose of fitting in, or binding up, or what not, he would have made quite a different slash with the scissors. Do you remember the shape? It was a mean shape. It was a wrong shape. Like this. Don't you remember?'

And he waved his burning cigar before him in the darkness, making irregular squares so rapidly that Flambeau really seemed to see them as fiery hieroglyphics upon the darkness—hieroglyphics such as his friend had spoken of, which are undecipherable, yet can have no good meaning.

'But,' said Flambeau, as the priest put his cigar in his mouth again and leaned back, staring at the roof. 'Suppose somebody else did use the scissors. Why should somebody else, cutting pieces off his sermon paper, make Quinton commit suicide?'

Father Brown was still leaning back and staring at the room, but he took his cigar out of his mouth and said: 'Quinton never did commit suicide.'

Flambeau stared at him. 'Why, confound it all,' he cried; 'then why did he confess to suicide?'

The priest leaned forward again, settled his elbows on his knees, looked at the ground, and said in a low distinct voice: 'He never did confess to suicide.'

Flambeau laid his cigar down. 'You mean,' he said, 'that the writing was forged?'

'No,' said Father Brown; 'Quinton wrote it all right.'

'Well, there you are,' said the aggravated Flambeau; 'Quinton wrote: "I die by my own hand," with his own hand on a plain piece of paper.'

'Of the wrong shape,' said the priest calmly.

'Oh, the shape be damned!' cried Flambeau. 'What has the shape to do with it?'

'There were twenty-three snipped papers,' resumed Brown unmoved, 'and only twenty-two pieces snipped off. Therefore one of the pieces had been destroyed, probably that from the written paper. Does that suggest anything to you?'

A light dawned on Flambeau's face, and he said: 'There was something else written by Quinton, some other words. "They will tell you I die by my own hand," or "Do not believe that——" '

'Hotter, as the children say,' said his friend. 'But the piece was hardly half an inch across; there was no room for one word, let alone five. Can you think of anything hardly bigger than a comma which the man with hell in his heart had to tear away as a testimony against him?'

'I can think of nothing,' said Flambeau at last.

'What about quotation marks?' said the priest, and flung his cigar far into the darkness like a shooting star.

All words had left the other man's mouth, and Father Brown, said, like one going back to fundamentals:

'Leonard Quinton was a romancer, and was writing an Oriental romance about wizardry and hypnotism. He——'

At this moment the door opened briskly behind them and the doctor came out with his hat on. He put a long envelope into the priest's hands.

'That's the document you wanted,' he said, 'and I must be getting home. Good night.'

'Good night,' said Father Brown, as the doctor walked briskly to the gate. He had left the front door open, so that a shaft of gaslight fell upon them. In the light of this Brown opened the envelope and read the following words:

'DEAR FATHER BROWN,—*Vicisti, Galilaee! Otherwise, damn your eyes, which are very penetrating ones. Can it be possible that there is something in all that stuff of yours after all?*

'I am a man who has ever since boyhood believed in Nature and in all natural functions and instincts, whether men called them moral or immoral. Long before I became a doctor, when I was a schoolboy keeping mice and spiders, I believed that to be a good animal is the best thing in the world. But just now I am shaken; I have believed in Nature; but it seems as if Nature could betray a man. Can there be anything in your bosh? I am really getting morbid.

'I loved Quinton's wife. What was there wrong in that? Nature told me to, and it's love that makes the world go round. I also thought, quite sincerely, that she would be happier with a clean animal like me than with that tormenting little lunatic. What was there wrong in that? I was only facing facts, like a man of science. She would have been happier.

'According to my own creed I was quite free to kill Quinton, which was the best thing for everybody, even himself. But as a healthy animal I had no notion of killing myself. I resolved, therefore, that I would never do it until I saw a chance that would leave me scot free. I saw that chance this morning.

'I have been three times, all told, into Quinton's study today. The first time I went in he would talk about nothing but the weird tale, called "The Curse of a Saint," which he was writing, which was all about how some Indian hermit made an English colonel kill himself by thinking about him. He showed me the last sheets, and even read me the last paragraph, which was something like this: "The conqueror of the Punjab, a mere yellow skeleton, but still gigantic, managed to lift himself on his elbow and gasp in his nephew's ear: 'I die by my own hand, yet I die murdered!'" It so happened, by one chance out of a hundred, that those last words were written at the top of a new sheet of paper. I left the room, and went out into the garden intoxicated with a frightful opportunity.

'We walked round the house, and two more things happened in my favour. You suspected an Indian, and you found a dagger which the Indian might most probably use. Taking the opportunity to stuff it in my pocket I went back to Quinton's study, locked the door, and gave him his sleeping draught. He was against answering Atkinson at all, but I urged him to call out and quiet the fellow, because I wanted a clear proof that Quinton was alive when I left the room for the second time. Quinton lay down in the conservatory, and I came through the study. I am a quick man with my hands, and in a minute and a half I had done what I wanted to do. I had emptied all the first part of Quinton's romance into* *the fireplace, where it burnt to ashes. Then I saw that the quotation marks wouldn't do, so I snipped them off, and to make it seem likelier, snipped the whole quire to match. Then I came out with the knowledge that Quinton's confession of suicide lay on the front table, while Quinton lay alive, but asleep, in the conservatory beyond.*

'*The last act was a desperate one; you can guess it; I pretended to have seen Quinton dead and rushed to his room. I delayed you with the paper; and, being a quick man with my hands, killed Quinton while you were looking at his confession of suicide. He was half-asleep, being drugged, and I put his own hand on the knife and drove it into his body. The knife was of so queer a shape that no one but an operator could have calculated the angle that would reach his heart. I wonder if you noticed this.*

'*When I had done it the extraordinary thing happened. Nature deserted me. I felt ill. I felt just as if I had done something wrong. I think my brain is breaking up; I feel some sort of desperate pleasure in thinking I have told the thing to somebody; that I shall not have to be alone with it if I marry and have children. What is the matter with me? . . . Madness . . . or can one have remorse, just as if one were in Byron's poems! I cannot write any more.*—JAMES ERSKINE HARRIS.'

Father Brown carefully folded up the letter and put it in his breast pocket just as there came a loud peal at the gate bell, and the wet waterproofs of several policeman gleamed in the road outside.

The Hammer of God

The little village of Bohun Beacon was perched on a hill so steep that the tall spire of its church seemed only like the peak of a small mountain. At the foot of the church stood a smithy, generally red with fires and always littered with hammers and scraps of iron; opposite to this, over a rude cross of cobbled paths, was 'The Blue Boar,' the only inn of the place. It was upon this crossway, in the lifting of a leaden and silver daybreak, that two brothers met in the street and spoke; though one was beginning the day and the other finishing it. The Rev. and Hon. Wilfred Bohun was very devout, and was making his way to some austere exercises of prayer or contemplation at dawn. Colonel the Hon. Norman Bohun, his elder brother, was by no means devout, and was sitting in evening-dress on the bench outside 'The Blue Boar,' drinking what the philosophic observer was free to regard either as his last glass on Tuesday or his first on Wednesday. The colonel was not particular.

The Bohuns were one of the very few aristocratic families really dating from the Middle Ages, and their pennon had actually seen Palestine. But it is a great mistake to suppose that such houses stand high in chivalric traditions. Few except the poor preserve traditions. Aristocrats live not in traditions but in fashions. The Bohuns had been Mohocks under Queen Anne and Mashers under Queen Victoria. But, like more than one of the really ancient houses, they had rotted in the last two centuries into mere drunkards and dandy degenerates, till there had even come a whisper of insanity. Certainly there was something hardly human about the colonel's wolfish pursuit of pleasure, and his chronic resolution not to go home till morning had a touch of the hideous clarity of insomnia. He was a tall, fine animal, elderly, but with hair startlingly yellow. He would have looked merely blond and leonine, but his blue eyes were sunk so deep in his face that they looked black. They were a little too close together. He had very long yellow moustaches: on each side of them a fold or furrow from nostril to jaw, so that a sneer seemed to cut into his face. Over his evening clothes he wore a curiously pale yellow coat that looked more like a very light dressing gown than an overcoat, and on the back of his head was stuck an extraordinary broad-brimmed hat of a bright green colour, evidently some oriental curiosity caught up at random. He was proud of appearing in such incongruous attires—proud of the fact that he always made them look congruous.

His brother the curate had also the yellow hair and the elegance, but he was buttoned up to the chin in black, and his face was clean-shaven, cultivated and a little nervous. He seemed to live for nothing but his religion; but there were some who said (notably the blacksmith, who was a Presbyterian) that it was a love of Gothic architecture rather than of God, and that his haunting of the church like a ghost was only another and purer turn of the almost morbid thirst for beauty which sent his brother raging after women and wine. This charge was doubtful, while the man's practical piety was indubitable. Indeed, the charge was mostly an ignorant misunderstanding of the love of solitude and secret prayer, and was founded on his being often found kneeling, not before the altar, but in peculiar places, in the crypts or gallery, or even in the belfry. He was at the moment about to enter the church through the yard of the smithy, but stopped and frowned a little as he saw his brother's cavernous eyes staring in the same direction. On the hypothesis that the colonel was interested in the church he did not waste any speculations. There only remained the blacksmith's shop, and though the blacksmith was a Puritan and none of his people, Wilfred Bohun had heard some scandals about a beautiful and rather celebrated wife. He flung a suspicious look across the shed, and the colonel stood up laughing to speak to him.

'Good morning, Wilfred,' he said. 'Like a good landlord I am watching sleeplessly over my people. I am going to call on the blacksmith.'

Wilfred looked at the ground and said: 'The blacksmith is out. He is over at Greenford.'

'I know,' answered the other with silent laughter; 'that is why I am calling on him.'

'Norman,' said the cleric, with his eye on a pebble in the road, 'are you ever afraid of thunderbolts?'

'What do you mean?' asked the colonel. 'Is your hobby meteorology?'

'I mean,' said Wilfred, without looking up, 'do you ever think that God might strike you in the street?'

'I beg your pardon,' said the colonel; 'I see your hobby is folklore.'

'I know your hobby is blasphemy,' retorted the religious man, stung in the one live place of his nature. 'But if you do not fear God, you have good reason to fear man.'

The elder raised his eyebrows politely. 'Fear man?' he said.

'Barnes the blacksmith is the biggest and strongest man for forty miles round,' said the clergyman sternly. 'I know you are no coward or weakling, but he could throw you over the wall.'

This struck home, being true, and the lowering line by mouth and nostril darkened and deepened. For a moment he stood with the heavy sneer on his face. But in an instant Colonel Bohun had recovered his own cruel good humour and laughed, showing two dog-like front teeth under his yellow moustache. 'In that case, my dear Wilfred,' he said quite carelessly, 'it was wise for the last of the Bohuns to come out partially in armour.'

And he took off the queer round hat covered with green, showing that it was lined within with steel. Wilfred recognized it indeed as a light Japanese or Chinese helmet torn down from a trophy that hung in the old family hall.

'It was the first to hand,' explained his brother airily; 'always the nearest hat—and the nearest woman.'

'The blacksmith is away at Greenford,' said Wilfred quietly; 'the time of his return is unsettled.'

And with that he turned and went into the church with bowed head, crossing himself like one who wishes to be quit of an unclean spirit. He was anxious to forget such grossness in the cool twilight of his tall Gothic cloisters; but on that morning it was fated that his still round of religious exercises should be everywhere arrested by small shocks. As he entered the church, hitherto always empty at that hour, a kneeling figure rose hastily to its feet and came towards the full daylight of the doorway. When the curate saw it he stood still with surprise. For the early worshipper was none other than the village idiot, a nephew of the blacksmith, one who neither would nor could care for the church or for anything else. He was always called 'Mad Joe,' and seemed to have no other name; he was a dark, strong, slouching lad, with a heavy white face, dark straight hair, and a mouth always open. As he passed the priest, his moon-calf countenance gave no hint of what he had been doing or thinking of. He had never been known to pray before. What sort of prayers was he saying now? Extraordinary prayers surely.

Wilfred Bohun stood rooted to the spot long enough to see the idiot go out into the sunshine, and even to see his dissolute brother hail him with a sort of avuncular jocularity. The last thing he saw was the colonel throwing pennies at the open mouth of Joe, with the serious appearance of trying to hit it.

This ugly sunlight picture of the stupidity and cruelty of the earth sent the ascetic finally to his prayers for purification and new thoughts. He went up to a pew in the gallery, which brought him under a coloured window which he loved and which always quieted his spirit; a blue window with an angel carrying lilies. There he began to think less about the half-wit, with his livid face and mouth like a fish. He began to think less of his evil brother, pacing like a lean lion in his horrible hunger. He sank deeper and deeper into those cold and sweet colours of silver blossoms and sapphire sky.

In this place half an hour afterwards he was found by Gibbs, the village cobbler, who had been sent for him in some haste. He got to his feet with promptitude, for he knew that no small matter would have brought Gibbs into such a place at all. The cobbler was, as in many villages, an atheist, and his appearance in church was a shade more extraordinary than Mad Joe's. It was a morning of theological enigmas.

'What is it?' asked Wilfred Bohun rather stiffly, but putting out a trembling hand for his hat.

The atheist spoke in a tone that, coming from him, was quite startlingly respectful, and even, as it were, huskily sympathetic.

'You must excuse me, sir,' he said in a hoarse whisper, 'but we didn't think it right not to let you know at once. I'm afraid a rather dreadful thing has happened, sir. I'm afraid your brother——'

Wilfred clenched his frail hands. 'What devilry has he done now?' he cried in involuntary passion.

'Why, sir,' said the cobbler, coughing, 'I'm afraid he's done nothing, and won't do anything. I'm afraid he's done for. You had really better come down, sir.'

The curate followed the cobbler down a short winding stair which brought them out at an entrance rather higher than the street. Bohun saw the tragedy in one glance, flat underneath him like a plan. In the yard of the smithy were standing five or six men, mostly in black, one in an inspector's uniform. They included the doctor, the Presbyterian minister, and the priest from the Roman

Catholic chapel to which the blacksmith's wife belonged. The latter was speaking to her, indeed, very rapidly, in an undertone, as she, a magnificent woman with red-gold hair, was sobbing blindly on a bench. Between these two groups, and just clear of the main heap of hammers, lay a man in evening dress, spread-eagled and flat on his face. From the height above Wilfred could have sworn to every item of his costume and appearance, down to the Bohun rings upon his fingers; but the skull was only a hideous splash, like a star of blackness and blood.

Wilfred Bohun gave but one glance, and ran down the steps into the yard. The doctor, who was the family physician, saluted him, but he scarcely took any notice. He could only stammer out: 'My brother is dead. What does it mean? What is this horrible mystery?' There was an unhappy silence; and then the cobbler, the most outspoken man present, answered: 'Plenty of horror, sir,' he said, 'but not much mystery.'

'What do you mean?' asked Wilfred, with a white face.

'It's plain enough,' answered Gibbs. 'There is only one man for the forty miles round that could have struck such a blow as that, and he's the man that had most reason to.'

'We must not prejudge anything,' put in the doctor, a tall, black-bearded man, rather nervously; 'but it is competent for me to corroborate what Mr Gibbs says about the nature of the blow, sir; it is an incredible blow. Mr Gibbs says that only one man in this district could have done it. I should have said myself that nobody could have done it.'

A shudder of superstition went through the slight figure of the curate. 'I can hardly understand,' he said.

'Mr Bohun,' said the doctor in a low voice, 'metaphors literally fail me. It is inadequate to say that the skull was smashed to bits like an egg-shell. Fragments of bone were driven into the body and the ground like bullets into a mud wall. It was the hand of a giant.'

He was silent a moment, looking grimly through his glasses; then he added: 'The thing has one advantage—that it clears most people of suspicion at one stroke. If you or I or any normally made man in the country were accused of this crime, we should be acquitted as an infant would be acquitted of stealing the Nelson Column.'

'That's what I say,' repeated the cobbler obstinately, 'there's only one man that could have done it, and he's the man that would have done it. Where's Simeon Barnes, the blacksmith?'

'He's over at Greenford,' faltered the curate.

'More likely over in France,' muttered the cobbler.

'No; he is in neither of those places,' said a small and colourless voice, which came from the little Roman priest who had joined the group. 'As a matter of fact, he is coming up the road at this moment.'

The little priest was not an interesting man to look at, having stubbly brown hair and a round and stolid face. But if he had been as splendid as Apollo no one would have looked at him at that moment. Everyone turned round and peered at the pathway which wound across the plain below, along which was indeed walking, at his own huge stride and with a hammer on his shoulder, Simeon the smith. He was a bony and gigantic man, with deep, dark, sinister eyes and a dark chin beard. He was walking and talking quietly with two other men; and though he was never specially cheerful, he seemed quite at his ease.

'My God!' cried the atheistic cobbler; 'and there's the hammer he did it with.'

'No,' said the inspector, a sensible-looking man with a sandy moustache, speaking for the first time. 'There's the hammer he did it with, over there by the church wall. We have left it and the body exactly as they are.'

All glanced round, and the short priest went across and looked down in silence at the tool where it lay. It was one of the smallest and the lightest of the hammers, and would have caught the eye among the rest; but on the iron edge of it were blood and yellow hair.

After a silence the short priest spoke without looking up, and there was a new note in his dull voice. 'Mr Gibbs was hardly right,' he said, 'in saying that there is no mystery. There is at least the mystery of why so big a man should attempt so big a blow with so little a hammer.'

'Oh, never mind that,' cried Gibbs, in a fever. 'What are we to do with Simeon Barnes?'

'Leave him alone,' said the priest quietly. 'He is coming here of himself. I know these two men with him. They are very good fellows from Greenford, and they have come over about the Presbyterian chapel.'

Even as he spoke the tall smith swung round the corner of the church and strode into his own yard. Then he stood there quite still, and the hammer fell from his hand. The inspector, who had preserved impenetrable propriety, immediately went up to him.

'I won't ask you, Mr Barnes,' he said, 'whether you know anything about what has happened here. You are not bound to say. I hope you don't know, and that you will be able to prove it. But I must go through the form of arresting you in the King's name for the murder of Colonel Norman Bohun.'

'You are not bound to say anything,' said the cobbler in officious excitement. 'They've got to prove everything. They haven't proved yet that it is Colonel Bohun, with the head all smashed up like that.'

'That won't wash,' said the doctor aside to the priest. 'That's out of detective stories. I was the colonel's medical man, and I knew his body better than he did. He had very fine hands, but quite peculiar ones. The second and third fingers were the same in length. Oh, that's the colonel right enough.'

As he glanced at the brained corpse upon the ground the iron eyes of the motionless blacksmith followed them and rested there also.

'Is Colonel Bohun dead?' said the smith quite calmly. 'Then he's damned.'

'Don't say anything! Oh, don't say anything,' cried the atheist cobbler, dancing about in an ecstasy of admiration of the English legal system. For no man is such a legalist as the good Secularist.

The blacksmith turned on him over his shoulder the august face of a fanatic.

'It is well for you infidels to dodge like foxes because the world's law favours you,' he said; 'but God guards His own in His pocket, as you shall see this day.'

Then he pointed to the colonel and said: 'When did this dog die in his sins?'

'Moderate your language,' said the doctor.

'Moderate the Bible's language, and I'll moderate mine. When did he die?'

'I saw him alive at six o'clock this morning,' stammered Wilfred Bohun.

'God is good,' said the smith. 'Mr Inspector, I have not the slightest objection to being arrested. It is you who may object to arresting me. I don't mind leaving the court without a stain on my character. You do mind, perhaps, leaving the court with a bad set-back in your career.'

The solid inspector for the first time looked at the blacksmith with a lively eye—as did everybody else, except the short, strange priest, who was still looking down at the little hammer that had dealt the dreadful blow.

'There are two men standing outside this shop,' went on the blacksmith with ponderous lucidity, 'good tradesmen in Greenford whom you all know, who will swear that they saw me from before midnight till daybreak and long after in the committee-room of our Revival Mission, which sits all night, we save souls so fast. In Greenford itself twenty people could swear to me for all that time. If I were a heathen, Mr Inspector, I would let you walk on your downfall; but, as a Christian man, I feel bound to give you your chance and ask you whether you will hear my alibi now or in court.'

The inspector seemed for the first time disturbed and said: 'Of course I should be glad to clear you altogether now.'

The smith walked out of his yard with the same long and easy stride, and returned to his two friends from Greenford, who were indeed friends of nearly everyone present. Each of them said a few words which no one ever thought of disbelieving. When they had spoken the innocence of Simeon stood up as solid as the great church above them.

One of those silences struck the group which are more strange and insufferable than any speech. Madly, in order to make conversation, the curate said to the Catholic priest:

'You seem very much interested in that hammer, Father Brown.'

'Yes, I am,' said Father Brown; 'why is it such a small hammer?'

The doctor swung round on him.

'By George, that's true,' he cried; 'who would use a little hammer with ten larger hammers lying about?'

Then he lowered his voice in the curate's ear and said: 'Only the kind of person that can't lift a large hammer. It is not a question of force or courage between the sexes. It's a question of lifting power in the shoulders. A bold woman could commit ten murders with a light hammer and never turn a hair. She could not kill a beetle with a heavy one.'

Wilfred Bohun was staring at him with a sort of hypnotized

horror, while Father Brown listened with his head a little on one side, really interested and attentive. The doctor went on with more hissing emphasis:

'Why do those idiots always assume that the only person who hates the wife's lover is the wife's husband? Nine times out of ten the person who most hates the wife's lover is the wife. Who knows what insolence or treachery he had shown her—look there?'

He made a momentary gesture towards the red-haired woman on the bench. She had lifted her head at last and the tears were drying on her splendid face. But the eyes were fixed on the corpse with an electric glare that had in it something of idiocy.

The Rev. William Bohun made a limp gesture as if waving away all desire to know; but Father Brown, dusting off his sleeve some ashes blown from the furnace, spoke in his indifferent way.

'You are like so many doctors,' he said; 'your mental science is really suggestive. It is your physical science that is utterly impossible. I agree that the woman wants to kill the co-respondent much more than the petitioner does. And I agree that a woman will always pick up a small hammer instead of a big one. But the difficulty is one of physical impossibility. No woman ever born could have smashed a man's skull out flat like that.' Then he added reflectively, after a pause: 'These people haven't grasped the whole of it. The man was actually wearing an iron helmet, and the blow scattered it like broken glass. Look at that woman. Look at her arms.'

Silence held them all up again, and then the doctor said rather sulkily: 'Well, I may be wrong; there are objections to everything. But I stick to the main point. No man but an idiot would pick up that little hammer if he could use a big hammer.'

With the lean and quivering hands of Wilfred Bohun went up to his head and seemed to clutch his scanty yellow hair. After an instant they dropped, and he cried: 'That was the word I wanted; you have said the word.'

Then he continued, mastering his discomposure: 'The words you said were, "No man but an idiot would pick up the small hammer" '

'Yes,' said the doctor. 'Well?'

'Well,' said the curate, 'no man but an idiot did.' The rest stared at him with eyes arrested and riveted, and he went on in a febrile and feminine agitation.

'I am a priest,' he cried unsteadily, 'and a priest should be no shedder of blood. I—I mean that he should bring no one to the gallows. And I thank God that I see the criminal clearly now—because he is a criminal who cannot be brought to the gallows.'

'You will not denounce him?' inquired the doctor.

'He would not be hanged if I did denounce him,' answered Wilfred, with a wild but curiously happy smile. 'When I went into the church this morning I found a madman praying there—that poor Joe, who has been wrong all his life. God knows what he prayed; but with such strange folk it is not incredible to suppose that their prayers are all upside down. Very likely a lunatic would pray before killing a man. When I last saw poor Joe he was with my brother. My brother was mocking him.'

'By Jove!' cried the doctor, 'this is talking at last. But how do you explain——'

The Rev. Wilfred was almost trembling with the excitement of his own glimpse of the truth. 'Don't you see; don't you see,' he cried feverishly, 'that is only theory that covers both the queer things, that answers both the riddles. The two riddles are the little hammer and the big blow. The smith might have struck the big blow, but he would not have chosen the little hammer. His wife would have chosen the little hammer, but she could not have struck the big blow. But the madman might have done both. As for the little hammer—why, he was mad and might have picked up anything. And for the big blow, have you never heard, doctor, that a maniac in his paroxysm may have the strength of ten men?'

The doctor drew a deep breath and then said: 'By golly, I believe you've got it.'

Father Brown had fixed his eyes on the speaker so long and steadily as to prove that his large grey, ox-like eyes were not quite so insignificant as the rest of his face. When silence had fallen he said with marked respect: 'Mr Bohun, yours is the only theory yet propounded which holds water every way and is essentially unassailable. I think, therefore, that you deserve to be told, on my positive knowledge, that it is not the true one.' And with that the odd little man walked away and stared again at the hammer.

'That fellow seems to know more than he ought to,' whispered the doctor peevishly to Wilfred. 'Those popish priests are deucedly sly.'

'No, no,' said Bohun, with a sort of wild fatigue. 'It was the lunatic. It was the lunatic.'

The group of the two clerics and the doctor had fallen away from the more official group containing the inspector and the man he had arrested. Now, however, that their own party had broken up, they heard voices from the others. The priest looked up quietly and then looked down again as he heard the blacksmith say in a loud voice:

'I hope I've convinced you, Mr Inspector. I'm a strong man, as you say, but I couldn't have flung my hammer back here from Greenford. My hammer hasn't any wings that it should come flying half a mile over hedges and fields.'

The inspector laughed amicably and said: 'No; I think you can be considered out of it, though it's one of the rummiest coincidences I ever saw. I can only ask you to give us all the assistance you can in finding a man as big and strong as yourself. By George! you might be useful, if only to hold him! I suppose you yourself have no guess at the man?'

'I may have a guess,' said the pale smith, 'but it is not at a man.' Then, seeing the scared eyes turn towards his wife on the bench, he put his huge hand on her shoulder and said: 'Nor a woman either.'

'What do you mean?' asked the inspector jocularly. 'You don't think cows use hammers, do you?'

'I think no thing of flesh held that hammer,' said the blacksmith in a stifled voice; 'mortally speaking, I think the man died alone.'

Wilfred made a sudden forward movement and peered at him with burning eyes.

'Do you mean to say, Barnes,' came the sharp voice of the cobbler, 'that the hammer jumped up of itself and knocked the man down?'

'Oh, you gentlemen may stare and snigger,' cried Simeon; 'you clergymen who tell us on Sunday in what a stillness the Lord smote Sennacherib. I believe that One who walks invisible in every house defended the honour of mine, and laid the defiler dead before the door of it. I believe the force in that blow was just the force there is in earthquakes, and no force less.'

Wilfred said, with a voice utterly undescribable: 'I told Norman myself to beware of the thunderbolt.'

'That agent is outside my jurisdiction,' said the inspector with a slight smile.

'You are not outside His,' answered the smith; 'see you to it.' And, turning his broad back, he went into the house.

The shaken Wilfred was led away by Father Brown, who had an easy and friendly way with him. 'Let us get out of this horrid place, Mr Bohun,' he said. 'May I look inside your church? I hear it's one of the oldest in England. We take some interest, you know,' he added with a comical grimace, 'in old English churches.'

Wilfred Bohun did not smile, for humour was never his strong point. But he nodded rather eagerly, being only too ready to explain the Gothic splendours to someone more likely to be sympathetic than the Presbyterian blacksmith or the atheist cobbler.

'By all means,' he said; 'let us go in at this side.' And he led the way into the high side entrance at the top of the flight of steps. Father Brown was mounting the first step to follow him when he felt a hand on his shoulder, and turned to behold the dark, thin figure of the doctor, his face darker yet with suspicion.

'Sir,' said the physician harshly, 'you appear to know some secrets in this black business. May I ask if you are going to keep them to yourself?'

'Why, doctor,' answered the priest, smiling quite pleasantly, 'there is one very good reason why a man of my trade would keep things to himself when he is not sure of them, and that is that it is so constantly his duty to keep them to himself when he is sure of them. But if you think I have been discourteously reticent with you or anyone, I will go to the extreme limit of my custom. I will give you two very large hints.'

'Well, sir?' said the doctor gloomily.

'First,' said Father Brown quietly, 'the thing is quite in your own province. It is a matter of physical science. The blacksmith is mistaken, not perhaps in saying that the blow was divine, but certainly in saying that it came by a miracle. It was no miracle, doctor, except in so far as man is himself a miracle, with his strange and wicked and yet half-heroic heart. The force that smashed that skull was a force well known to scientists—one of the most frequently debated of the laws of nature.'

The doctor, who was looking at him with frowning intentness, only said: 'And the other hint?'

'The other hint is this,' said the priest: 'Do you remember the blacksmith, though he believes in miracles, talking scornfully of the impossible fairy tale that his hammer had wings and flew half a mile across country?'

'Yes,' said the doctor, 'I remember that.'

'Well,' added Father Brown, with a broad smile, 'that fairy tale was the nearest thing to the real truth that has been said today.' And with that he turned his back and stumped up the steps after the curate.

The Reverend Wilfred, who had been waiting for him, pale and impatient, as if this little delay were the last straw for his nerves, led him immediately to his favourite corner of the church, that part of the gallery closest to the carved roof and lit by the wonderful window with the angel. The little Latin priest explored and admired everything exhaustively, talking cheerfully but in a low voice all the time. When in the course of his investigation he found the side exit and the winding stair down which Wilfred had rushed to find his brother dead, Father Brown ran not down but up, with the agility of a monkey, and his clear voice came from an outer platform above.

'Come up here, Mr Bohun,' he called. 'The air will do you good.'

Bohun followed him, and came out on a kind of stone gallery or balcony outside the building, from which one could see the illimitable plain in which their small hill stood, wooded away to the purple horizon and dotted with villages and farms. Clear and square, but quite small beneath them, was the blacksmith's yard, where the inspector still stood taking notes and the corpse still lay like a smashed fly.

'Might be the map of the world, mightn't it?' said Father Brown.

'Yes,' said Bohun very gravely, and nodded his head.

Immediately beneath and about them the lines of the Gothic building plunged outwards into the void with a sickening swiftness akin to suicide. There is that element of Titan energy in the architecture of the Middle Ages that, from whatever aspect it be seen, it always seems to be rushing away, like the strong back of some maddened horse. This church was hewn out of ancient and silent stone, bearded with old fungoids and stained with the nests of birds. And yet, when they saw it from below, it sprang like a fountain at the stars; and when they saw it, as now, from above, it poured like a cataract into a voiceless pit. For these two men on the tower were left alone with the most terrible aspect of the Gothic: the monstrous foreshortening and disproportion, the dizzy perspectives, the glimpses of great things small and small things great; a topsy-turvydom of stone in the mid-air. Details of stone, enormous by their proximity, were relieved against a pattern of fields and farms, pygmy in their distance. A carved bird or beast at a corner seemed like some vast walking or flying dragon wasting the pastures and villages below. The whole atmosphere was dizzy and dangerous, as if men were upheld in air amid the gyrating wings of colossal genii; and the whole of that old church, as tall and rich as a cathedral, seemed to sit upon the sunlit country like a cloudburst.

'I think there is something rather dangerous about standing on these high places even to pray,' said Father Brown. 'Heights were made to be looked at, not to be looked from.'

'Do you mean that one may fall over?' asked Wilfred.

'I mean that one's soul may fall if one's body doesn't,' said the other priest.

'I scarcely understand you,' remarked Bohun indistinctly.

'Look at that blacksmith, for instance,' went on Father Brown calmly; 'a good man, but not a Christian—hard, imperious, unforgiving. Well, his Scotch religion was made up by men who prayed on hills and high crags, and learnt to look down on the world more than to look up at heaven. Humanity is the mother of giants. One sees great things from the valley; only small things from the peak.'

'But he—he didn't do it,' said Bohun tremulously.

'No,' said the other in an odd voice; 'we know he didn't do it.'

After a moment he resumed, looking tranquilly out over the plain with his pale grey eyes. 'I knew a man,' he said, 'who began by worshipping with others before the altar, but who grew fond of high and lonely places to pray from, corners or niches in the belfry or the spire. And once in one of those dizzy places, where the whole world seemed to turn under him like a wheel, his brain turned also, and he fancied he was God. So that though he was a good man, he committed a great crime.'

Wilfred's face was turned away, but his bony hands turned blue and white as they tightened on the parapet of stone.

'He thought it was given to *him* to judge the world and strike down the sinner. He would never have had such a thought if he had been kneeling with other men upon a floor. But he saw all men walking about like insects. He saw one especially strutting just below him, insolent and evident by a bright green hat—a poisonous insect.'

Rooks cawed round the corners of the belfry; but there was no other sound till Father Brown went on.

'This also tempted him, that he had in his hand one of the most awful engines of nature; I mean gravitation, that mad and quickening rush by which all earth's creatures fly back to her heart when released. See, the inspector is strutting just below us in the smithy. If I were to toss a pebble over this parapet it would be something like a bullet by the time it struck him. If I were to drop a hammer—even a small hammer——'

Wilfred Bohun threw one leg over the parapet, and Father Brown had him in a minute by the collar.

'Not by that door,' he said quite gently; 'that door leads to hell.'

Bohun staggered back against the wall, and stared at him with frightful eyes.

'How do you know all this?' he cried. 'Are you a devil?'

'I am a man,' answered Father Brown gravely; 'and therefore have all devils in my heart. Listen to me,' he said after a short pause. 'I know what you did—at least, I can guess the great part of it. When you left your brother you were racked with no unrighteous rage to the extent even that you snatched up the small hammer, half inclined to kill him with his foulness on his mouth. Recoiling, you thrust it under your buttoned coat instead, and rushed into the church. You pray wildly in many places, under the angel window, upon the platform above, and on a higher platform still, from which you could see the colonel's Eastern hat like the back of a green beetle crawling about. Then something snapped in your soul, and you let God's thunderbolt fall.'

Wilfred put a weak hand to his head, and asked in a low voice: 'How did you know that his hat looked like a green beetle?'

'Oh, that,' said the other with the shadow of a smile, 'that was common sense. But hear me further. I say I know all this; but no one else shall know it. The next step is for you; I shall take no more steps; I will seal this with the seal of confession. If you ask me why, there are many reasons, and only one that concerns you. I leave things to you because you have not yet gone very far wrong, as assassins go. You did not help to fix the crime on the smith when it was easy; or on his wife, when that was easy. You tried to fix it on the imbecile, because you knew that he could not suffer. That was one of the gleams that it is my business to find in assassins. And now come down into the village, and go your own way as free as the wind; for I have said my last word.'

They went down the winding stairs in utter silence, and came out into the sunlight by the smithy. Wilfred Bohun carefully unlatched the wooden gate of the yard, and going up to the inspector, said: 'I wish to give myself up; I have killed my brother.'

The Absence of Mr Glass

The consulting-rooms of Dr Orion Hood, the eminent criminologist and specialist in certain moral disorders, lay along the sea-front at Scarborough, in a series of very large and well-lighted french windows, which showed the North Sea like one endless outer wall of blue-green marble. In such a place the sea had something of the monotony of a blue-green dado: for the chambers themselves were ruled throughout by a terrible tidiness not unlike the terrible tidiness of the sea. It must not be supposed that Dr Hood's apartments excluded luxury, or even poetry. These things were there, in their place; but one felt that they were never allowed out of their place. Luxury was there: there stood upon a special table eight or ten boxes of the best cigars; but they were built upon a plan so that the strongest were always nearest the wall and the mildest nearest the window. A tantalus containing three kinds of spirit, all of a liqueur excellence, stood always on this table of luxury; but the fanciful have asserted that the whisky, brandy, and rum seemed always to stand at the same level. Poetry was there: the left-hand corner of the room was lined with as complete a set of English classics as the right hand could show of English and foreign physiologists. But if one took a volume of Chaucer or Shelley from that rank, its absence irritated the mind like a gap in a man's front teeth. One could not say the books were never read; probably they were, but there was a sense of their being chained to their places, like the Bibles in the old churches. Dr Hood treated his private bookshelf as if it were a public library. And if this strict scientific intangibility steeped even the shelves laden with lyrics and ballads and the tables laden with drink and tobacco, it goes without saying that yet more of such heathen holiness protected the other shelves that held the specialist's library, and the other tables that sustained the frail and even fairylike instruments of chemistry or mechanics.

Dr Orion Hood paced the length of his string of apartments, bounded—as the boys' geographies say—on the east by the North Sea and on the west by the serried ranks of his sociological and criminologist library. He was clad in an artist's velvet, but with none of an artist's negligence; his hair was heavily shot with grey, but growing thick and healthy; his face was lean, but sanguine and expectant. Everything about him and his room indicated something at once rigid and restless, like that great northern sea by which (on pure principles of hygiene) he had built his home.

Fate, being in a funny mood, pushed the door open and introduced into those long, strict, sea-flanked apartments one who was perhaps the most startling opposite of them and their master. In answer to a curt but civil summons, the door opened inwards and there shambled into the room a shapeless little figure, which seemed to find its own hat and umbrella as unmanageable as a mass of luggage. The umbrella was a black and prosaic bundle long past repair; the hat was a broad-curved black hat, clerical but not common in England; the man was the very embodiment of all that is homely and helpless.

The doctor regarded the newcomer with a restrained astonishment, not unlike that he would have shown if some huge but obviously harmless sea-beast had crawled into his room. The newcomer regarded the doctor with that beaming but breathless geniality which characterizes a corpulent charwoman who has just managed to stuff herself into an omnibus. It is a rich confusion of social self-congratulation and bodily disarray. His hat tumbled to the carpet, his heavy umbrella slipped between his knees with a thud; he reached after the one and ducked after the other, but with an unimpaired smile on his round face spoke simultaneously as follows:

'My name is Brown. Pray excuse me. I've come about that business of the MacNabs. I have heard you often help people out of such troubles. Pray excuse me if I am wrong.'

By this time he had sprawlingly recovered the hat, and made an odd little bobbing bow over it, as if setting everything quite right.

'I hardly understand you,' replied the scientist, with a cold intensity of manner. 'I fear you have mistaken the chambers. I am Dr Hood, and my work is almost entirely literary and educational. It is true that I have sometimes been consulted by the police in cases of peculiar difficulty and importance, but——'

'Oh, this is of the greatest importance,' broke in the little man called Brown. 'Why, her mother won't let them get engaged.' And he leaned back in his chair in radiant rationality.

The brows of Dr Hood were drawn down darkly, but the eyes under them were bright with something that might be anger or

might be amusement. 'And still,' he said, 'I do not quite understand.'

'You see, they want to get married,' said the man with the
clerical hat. 'Maggie MacNab and young Todhunter went to get
married. Now, what can be more important than that?'

The great Orion Hood's scientific triumphs had deprived him of
many things—some said of his health, others of his God; but they
had not wholly despoiled him of his sense of the absurd. At the last
plea of the ingenuous priest a chuckle broke out of him from inside,
and he threw himself into an armchair in an ironical attitude of the
consulting physician.

'Mr Brown,' he said gravely, 'it is quite fourteen and a half years
since I was personally asked to test a personal problem: then it was
the case of an attempt to poison the French President at a Lord
Mayor's Banquet. It is now, I understand, a question of whether
some friend of yours called Maggie is a suitable fiancée for some
friend of hers called Todhunter. Well, Mr Brown, I am a sports-
man. I will take it on. I will give the MacNab family my best
advice, as good as I gave the French Republic and the King of
England—no, better: fourteen years better. I have nothing else to
do this afternoon. Tell me your story.'

The little clergyman called Brown thanked him with unques-
tionable warmth, but still with a queer kind of simplicity. It was
rather as if he were thanking a stranger in a smoking-room for some
trouble in passing the matches, than as if he were (as he was)
practically thanking the Curator of Kew Gardens for coming with
him into a field to find a four-leaved clover. With scarcely a
semi-colon after his hearty thanks, the little man began his
recital:

'I told you my name was Brown; well, that's the fact, and I'm the
priest of the little Catholic Church I dare say you've seen beyond
those straggly streets, where the town ends towards the north. In
the last and straggliest of the streets which runs along the sea like a
sea-wall there is a very honest but rather sharp-tempered member
of my flock, a widow called MacNab. She has one daughter, and
she lets lodgings, and between her and the daughter, and between
her and the lodgers—well, I dare say there is a great deal to be said
on both sides. At present she has only one lodger, the young man
called Todhunter; but he has given more trouble than all the rest,
for he wants to marry the young woman of the house.'

'And the young woman of the house,' asked Dr Hood, with huge and silent amusement, 'what does she want?'

'Why, she wants to marry him,' cried Father Brown, sitting up eagerly. 'That is just the awful complication.'

'It is indeed a hideous enigma,' said Dr Hood.

'This young James Todhunter,' continued the cleric, 'is a very decent man so far as I know; but then nobody knows very much. He is a bright, brownish little fellow, agile like a monkey, clean-shaven like an actor, and obliging like a born courtier. He seems to have quite a pocketful of money, but nobody knows what his trade is. Mrs MacNab, therefore (being of a pessimistic turn), is quite sure it is something dreadful, and probably connected with dynamite. The dynamite must be of a shy and noiseless sort, for the poor fellow only shuts himself up for several hours of the day and studies something behind a locked door. He declares his privacy is temporary and justified, and promises to explain before the wedding. That is all that anyone knows for certain, but Mrs MacNab will tell you a great deal more than even she is certain of. You know how the tales grow like grass on such a patch of ignorance as that. There are tales of two voices heard talking in the room; though, when the door is opened, Todhunter is always found alone. There are tales of a mysterious tall man in a silk hat, who once came out of the sea-mists and apparently out of the sea, stepping softly across the sandy fields and through the small back garden at twilight, till he was heard talking to the lodger at his open window. The colloquy seemed to end in a quarrel. Todhunter dashed down his window with violence, and the man in the high hat melted into the sea-fog again. This story is told by the family with the fiercest mystification; but I really think Mrs MacNab prefers her own original tale: that the Other Man (or whatever it is) crawls out every night from the big box in the corner, which is kept locked all day. You see, therefore, how this sealed door of Todhunter's is treated as the gate of all the fancies and monstrosities of the 'Thousand and One Nights.' And yet there is the little fellow in his respectable black jacket, as punctual and innocent as a parlour clock. He pays his rent to the tick; he is practically a teetotaller; he is tirelessly kind with the younger children, and can keep them amused for a day on end; and, last and most urgent of all, he has made himself equally popular with the eldest daughter, who is ready to go to church with him tomorrow.'

A man warmly concerned with any large theories has always a relish for applying them to any triviality. The great specialist having condescended to the priest's simplicity, condescended expansively. He settled himself with comfort in his armchair and began to talk in the tone of a somewhat absent-minded lecturer:

'Even in a minute instance, it is best to look first to the main tendencies of Nature. A particular flower may not be dead in early winter, but the flowers are dying; a particular pebble may never be wetted with the tide, but the tide is coming in. To the scientific eye all human history is a series of collective movements, destructions or migrations, like the massacre of flies in winter or the return of birds in spring. Now the root fact in all history is Race. Race produces religion; Race produces legal and ethical wars. There is no stronger case than that of the wild, unworldly and perishing stock which we commonly call the Celts, of whom your friends the MacNabs are specimens. Small, swarthy, and of this dreamy and drifting blood, they accept easily the superstitious explanation of any incidents, just as they still accept (you will excuse me for saying) that superstitious explanation of all incidents which you and your Church represent. It is not remarkable that such people, with the sea moaning behind them and the Church (excuse me again) droning in front of them, should put fantastic features into what are probably plain events. You, with your small parochial responsibilities, see only this particular Mrs MacNab, terrified with this particular tale of two voices and a tall man out of the sea. But the man with the scientific imagination sees, as it were, the whole clans of MacNab scattered over the whole world, in its ultimate average as uniform as a tribe of birds. He sees thousands of Mrs MacNabs, in thousands of houses, dropping their little drop of morbidity in the tea cups of their friends; he sees——'

Before the scientist could conclude his sentence, another and more impatient summons sounded from without; someone with swishing skirts was marshalled hurriedly down the corridor, and the door opened on a young girl, decently dressed but disordered and red-hot with haste. She had sea-blown blonde hair, and would have been entirely beautiful if her cheek-bones had not been, in the Scotch manner, a little high in relief as well as in colour. Her apology was almost as abrupt as a command.

'I'm sorry to interrupt you, sir,' she said, 'but I had to follow Father Brown at once; it's nothing less than life or death.'

Father Brown began to get to his feet in some disorder. 'Why, what has happened, Maggie?' he said.

'James has been murdered, for all I can make out,' answered the girl, still breathing hard from her rush. 'That man Glass has been with him again; I heard them talking through the door quite plain. Two separate voices: for James speaks low, with a burr, and the other voice was high and quavery.'

'That man Glass?' repeated the priest in some perplexity.

'I know his name is Glass,' answered the girl, in great impatience. 'I heard it through the door. They were quarrelling—about money, I think—for I heard James say again and again, "That's right, Mr Glass," or "No, Mr Glass," and then, "Two or three, Mr Glass." But we're talking too much; you must come at once, and there may be time yet.'

'But time for what?' asked Dr Hood, who had been studying the young lady with marked interest. 'What is there about Mr Glass and his money troubles that should impel such urgency?'

'I tried to break down the door and couldn't,' answered the girl shortly. 'Then I ran round to the backyard, and managed to climb on to the window-sill that looks into the room. It was all dim, and seemed to be empty, but I swear I saw James lying huddled up in a corner, as if he were drugged or strangled.'

'This is very serious,' said Father Brown, gathering his errant hat and umbrella and standing up; 'in point of fact I was just putting your case before this gentleman, and his view——'

'Has been largely altered,' said the scientist gravely. 'I do not think this young lady is so Celtic as I had supposed. As I have nothing else to do, I will put on my hat and stroll down the town with you.'

In a few minutes all three were approaching the dreary tail of the MacNabs' street: the girl with the stern and breathless stride of the mountaineer, the criminologist with a lounging grace (which was not without a certain leopard-like swiftness), and the priest at an energetic trot entirely devoid of distinction. The aspect of this edge of the town was not entirely without justification for the doctor's hints about desolate moods and environments. The scattered houses stood farther and farther apart in a broken string along the seashore; the afternoon was closing with a premature and partly lurid twilight; the sea was of an inky purple and murmuring ominously. In the scrappy back garden of the MacNabs which ran down towards the sand, two black, barren-looking trees stood up like demon hands held up in astonishment, and as Mrs MacNab ran down the street to meet them with lean hands similarly spread, and her fierce face in shadow, she was a little like a demon herself. The doctor and the priest made scant reply to her shrill reiterations of her daughter's story, with more disturbing details of her own, to the divided vows of vengeance against Mr Glass for murdering, and against Mr Todhunter for being murdered, or against the latter for having dared to want to marry her daughter, and for not having lived to do it. They passed through the narrow passage in the front of the house until they came to the lodger's door at the back, and there Dr Hood, with the trick of an old detective, put his shoulder sharply to the panel and burst in the door.

It opened on a scene of silent catastrophe. No one seeing it, even for a flash, could doubt that the room had been the theatre of some thrilling collision between two, or perhaps more, persons. Playing-cards lay littered across the table or fluttered about the floor as if a game had been interrupted. Two wine glasses stood ready for wine on a side-table, but a third lay smashed in a star of crystal upon the carpet. A few feet from it lay what looked like a long knife or short sword, straight, but with an ornamental and pictured handle; its dull blade just caught a grey glint from the dreary window behind, which showed the black trees against the leaden level of the sea. Towards the opposite corner of the room was rolled a gentleman's silk top hat, as if it had just been knocked off his head; so much so, indeed, that one almost looked to see it still rolling. And in the corner behind it, thrown like a sack of potatoes, but corded like a railway trunk, lay Mr James Todhunter, with a scarf across his mouth, and six or seven ropes knotted round his elbows and ankles. His brown eyes were alive and shifted alertly.

Dr Orion Hood paused for one instant on the doormat and drank in the whole scene of voiceless violence. Then he stepped swiftly across the carpet, picked up the tall silk hat, and gravely put it upon the head of the yet pinioned Todhunter. It was so much too large for him that it almost slipped down on his shoulders.

'Mr Glass's hat,' said the doctor, returning with it and peering into the inside with a pocket lens. 'How to explain the absence of Mr Glass and the presence of Mr Glass's hat? For Mr Glass is not a careless man with his clothes. This hat is of a stylish shape and systematically brushed and burnished, though not very new. An old dandy, I should think.'

'But, good heavens!' called out Miss MacNab, 'aren't you going to untie the man first?'

'I say "old" with intention, though not with certainty,' continued the expositor; 'my reason for it might seem a little far-fetched. The hair of human beings falls out in very varying degrees, but almost always falls out slightly, and with the lens I should see the tiny hairs in a hat recently worn. It has none, which leads me to guess that Mr Glass is bald. Now when this is taken with the high-pitched and querulous voice which Miss MacNab described so vividly (patience, my dear lady, patience), when we take the hairless head together with the tone common in senile anger, I should think we may deduce some advance in years. Nevertheless, he was probably vigorous, and he was almost certainly tall. I might rely in some degree on the story of his previous appearance at the window, as a tall man in a silk hat, but I think I have more exact indication. This wine glass has been smashed all over the place, but one of its splinters lies on the high bracket beside the mantelpiece. No such fragment could have fallen there if the vessel had been smashed in the hand of a comparatively short man like Mr Todhunter.'

'By the way,' said Father Brown, 'might it not be as well to untie Mr Todhunter?'

'Our lesson from the drinking-vessels does not end here,' proceeded the specialist. 'I may say at once that it is possible that the man Glass was bald or nervous through dissipation rather than age. Mr Todhunter, as has been remarked, is a quiet thrifty gentleman, essentially an abstainer. These cards and wine cups are no part of his normal habit; they have been produced for a particular companion. But, as it happens, we may go farther. Mr Todhunter may or may not possess this wine-service, but there is no appearance of his possessing any wine. What, then, were these vessels to contain? I would at once suggest some brandy or whisky, perhaps of a luxurious sort, from a flask in the pocket of Mr Glass. We have thus something like a picture of the man, or at least of the type: tall, elderly, fashionable, but somewhat frayed, certainly fond of play and strong waters, and perhaps rather too fond of them. Mr Glass is a gentleman not unknown on the fringes of society.'

'Look here,' cried the young woman, 'if you don't let me pass to untie him I'll run outside and scream for the police.'

'I should not advise *you*, Miss MacNab,' said Dr Hood gravely, 'to be in any hurry to fetch the police. Father Brown, I seriously ask you to compose your flock, for their sakes not for mine. Well, we have seen something of the figure and quality of Mr Glass; what are the chief facts known of Mr Todhunter? They are substantially three: that he is economical, that he is more or less wealthy, and that he has a secret. Now, surely it is obvious that there are the three chief marks of the kind of man who is blackmailed. And surely it is equally obvious that the faded finery, the profligate habits, and the shrill irritation of Mr Glass are the unmistakable marks of the kind of man who blackmails him. We have the two typical figures of a tragedy of hush money: on the one hand, the respectable man with a mystery; on the other, the West End vulture with a scent for a mystery. These two men have met here today and have quarrelled, using blows and a bare weapon.'

'Are you going to take those ropes off?' asked the girl stubbornly.

Dr Hood replaced the silk hat carefully on the side table, and went across to the captive. He studied him intently, even moving him a little and half-turning him round by the shoulders, but he only answered:

'No; I think these ropes will do very well till your friends the police bring the handcuffs.'

Father Brown, who had been looking dully at the carpet, lifted his round face and said: 'What do you mean?'

The man of science had picked up the peculiar dagger-sword from the carpet and was examining it intently as he answered:

'Because you find Mr Todhunter tied up,' he said, 'you all jump to the conclusion that Mr Glass had tied him up; and then, I suppose, escaped. There are four objections to this: First, why should a gentleman so dressy as our friend Glass leave his hat behind him, if he left of his own free will? Second,' he continued, moving towards the window, 'this is the only exit, and it is locked on the inside. Third, this blade here has a tiny touch of blood at the point, but there is no wound on Mr Todhunter. Mr Glass took that wound away with him, dead or alive. Add to all this primary probability. It is much more likely that the blackmailed person would try to kill his incubus, rather than that the blackmailer would try to kill the goose that lays his golden eggs. There, I think, we have a pretty complete story.'

'But the ropes?' inquired the priest, whose eyes had remained open with a rather vacant admiration.

'Ah, the ropes,' said the expert with a singular intonation. 'Miss MacNab very much wanted to know why I did not set Mr Todhunter free from his ropes. Well, I will tell her. I did not do it because Mr Todhunter can set himself free from them at any minute he chooses.'

'What?' cried the audience on quite different notes of astonishment.

'I have looked at all the knots on Mr Todhunter,' reiterated Hood quietly. 'I happen to know something about knots; they are quite a branch of criminal science. Every one of those knots he has made himself and could loosen himself; not one of them would have been made by an enemy really trying to pinion him. The whole of this affair of the ropes is a clever fake, to make us think him the victim of the struggle instead of the wretched Glass, whose corpse may be hidden in the garden or stuffed up the chimney.'

There was a rather depressed silence; the room was darkening, the sea-blighted boughs of the garden trees looked leaner and blacker than ever, yet they seemed to have come nearer to the window. One could almost fancy they were sea-monsters like crakens or cuttlefish, writhing polypi who had crawled up from the sea to see the end of this tragedy, even as *he*, the villain and victim of it, the terrible man in the tall hat, had once crawled up from the sea. For the whole air was dense with the morbidity of blackmail, which is the most morbid of human things, because it is a crime concealing a crime; a black plaster on a blacker wound.

The face of the little Catholic priest, which was commonly complacent and even comic, had suddenly become knotted with a curious frown. It was not the blank curiosity of his first innocence. It was rather that creative curiosity which comes when a man has the beginnings of an idea. 'Say it again, please,' he said in a simple, bothered manner; 'do you mean that Todhunter can tie himself up all alone and untie himself all alone?'

'That is what I mean,' said the doctor.

'Jerusalem!' ejaculated Brown suddenly; 'I wonder if it could possibly be that!'

He scuttled across the room rather like a rabbit, and peered with quite a new impulsiveness into the partially-covered face of the captive. Then he turned his own rather fatuous face to the company. 'Yes, that's it!' he cried in a certain excitement. 'Can't you see it in the man's face? Why, look at his eyes!'

Both the Professor and the girl followed the direction of his glance. And though the broad black scarf completely masked the lower half of Todhunter's visage, they did grow conscious of something struggling and intense about the upper part of it.

'His eyes do look queer,' cried the young woman, strongly moved. 'You brutes; I believe it's hurting him!'

'Not that, I think,' said Dr Hood; 'the eyes have certainly a singular expression. But I should interpret those transverse wrinkles as expressing rather such slight psychological abnormality——'

'Oh, bosh!' cried Father Brown: 'can't you see he's laughing?'

'Laughing!' repeated the doctor, with a start; 'but what on earth can he be laughing at?'

'Well,' replied the Reverend Brown apologetically, 'not to put too fine a point on it, I think he is laughing at you. And indeed, I'm a little inclined to laugh at myself, now I know about it.'

'Now you know about what?' asked Hood, in some exasperation.

'Now I know,' replied the priest, 'the profession of Mr Todhunter.'

He shuffled about the room, looking at one object after another with what seemed to be a vacant stare, and then invariably bursting into an equally vacant laugh, a highly irritating process for those who had to watch it. He laughed very much over the hat, still more uproariously over the broken glass, but the blood on the sword point sent him into mortal convulsions of amusement. Then he turned to the fuming specialist.

'Dr Hood,' he cried enthusiastically, 'you are a great poet! You have called an uncreated being out of the void. How much more godlike that is than if you had only ferreted out the mere facts! Indeed, the mere facts are rather commonplace and comic by comparison.'

'I have no notion what you are talking about,' said Dr Hood rather haughtily; 'my facts are all inevitable, though necessarily incomplete. A place may be permitted to intuition, perhaps (or poetry if you prefer the term), but only because the corresponding details cannot as yet be ascertained. In the absence of Mr Glass——'

'That's it, that's it,' said the little priest, nodding quite eagerly; 'that's the first idea to get fixed; the absence of Mr Glass. He is so extremely absent. I suppose,' he added reflectively, 'that there was never anybody so absent as Mr Glass.'

'Do you mean he is absent from the town?' demanded the doctor.

'I mean he is absent from everywhere,' answered Father Brown; 'he is absent from the Nature of Things, so to speak.'

'Do you seriously mean,' said the specialist with a smile, 'that there is no such person?'

The priest made a sign of assent. 'It does seem a pity,' he said.

Orion Hood broke into a contemptuous laugh. 'Well,' he said, 'before we go on to the hundred and one other evidences, let us take the first proof we found; the first fact we fell over when we fell into this room. If there is no Mr Glass, whose hat is this?'

'It is Mr Todhunter's,' replied Father Brown.

'But it doesn't fit him,' cried Hood impatiently. 'He couldn't possibly wear it!'

Father Brown shook his head with ineffable mildness. 'I never said he could wear it,' he answered. 'I said it was his hat. Or, if you insist on a shade of difference, a hat that is his.'

'And what is the shade of difference?' asked the criminologist with a slight sneer.

'My good sir,' cried the mild little man, with his first movement akin to impatience, 'if you will walk down the street to the nearest hatter's shop, you will see that there is, in common speech, a difference between a man's hat and the hats that are his.'

'But a hatter,' protested Hood, 'can get money out of his stock of new hats. What could Todhunter get out of this one old hat?'

'Rabbits,' replied Father Brown promptly.

'*What?*' cried Dr Hood.

'Rabbits, ribbons, sweetmeats, goldfish, rolls of coloured paper,' said the reverend gentleman with rapidity. 'Didn't you see it all when you found out the faked ropes? It's just the same with the sword. Mr Todhunter hasn't got a scratch on him, as you say; but he's got a scratch in him, if you follow me.'

'Do you mean inside Mr Todhunter's clothes?' inquired Mrs MacNab sternly.

'I do not mean inside Mr Todhunter's clothes,' said Father Brown. 'I mean inside Mr Todhunter.'

'Well, what in the name of Bedlam *do* you mean?'

'Mr Todhunter,' explained Father Brown placidly, 'is learning to be a professional conjuror, as well as juggler, ventriloquist, and expert in the rope trick. The conjuring explains the hat. It is without traces of hair, not because it is worn by the prematurely bald Mr Glass, but because it has never been worn by anybody. The juggling explains the three glasses, which Todhunter was teaching himself to throw up and catch in rotation. But, being only at the stage of practice, he smashed one glass against the ceiling. And the juggling also explains the sword, which it was Mr Todhunter's professional pride and duty to swallow. But, again, being at the stage of practice, he very slightly grazed the inside of his throat with the weapon. Hence he has a wound inside him, which I am sure (from the expression of his face) is not a serious one. He was also practising the trick of a release from ropes, like the Davenport Brothers, and he was just about to free himself when we all burst into the room. The cards, of course, are for card tricks, and they are scattered on the floor because he had just been practising one of those dodges of sending them flying through the air. He merely kept his trade secret, because he had to keep his tricks secret, like any other conjurer. But the mere fact of an idler in a top hat having once looked in at his back window, and been driven away by him with great indignation, was enough to set us all on a wrong track of romance, and make us imagine his whole life overshadowed by the silk-hatted spectre of Mr Glass.'

'But what about the two voices?' asked Maggie, staring.

'Have you never heard a ventriloquist?' asked Father Brown. 'Don't you know they speak first in their natural voice, and then answer themselves in just that shrill, squeaky, unnatural voice that you heard?'

There was a long silence, and Dr Hood regarded the little man who had spoken with a dark and attentive smile. 'You are certainly a very ingenious person,' he said; 'it could not have been done better in a book. But there is just one part of Mr Glass you have not succeeded in explaining away, and that is his name. Miss MacNab distinctly heard him so addressed by Mr Todhunter.'

The Rev. Mr Brown broke into a rather childish giggle. 'Well, that,' he said, 'that's the silliest part of the whole silly story. When our juggling friend here threw up the three glasses in turn, he counted them aloud as he caught them, and also commented aloud when he failed to catch them. What he really said was: "One, two and three—missed a glass; one, two—missed a glass." And so on.'

There was a second of stillness in the room, and then everyone with one accord burst out laughing. As they did so the figure in the corner complacently uncoiled all the ropes and let them fall with a flourish. Then, advancing into the middle of the room with a bow, he produced from his pocket a big bill printed in blue and red, which announced that ZALADIN, the World's Greatest Conjuror, Contortionist, Ventriloquist and Human Kangaroo would be ready with an entirely new series of Tricks at the Empire Pavilion, Scarborough, on Monday next at eight o'clock precisely.

The Man in the Passage

Two men appeared simultaneously at the two ends of a sort of passage running along the side of the Apollo Theatre in the Adelphi. The evening daylight in the streets was large and luminous, opalescent and empty. The passage was comparatively long and dark, so each man could see the other as a mere black silhouette at the other end. Nevertheless, each man knew the other, even in that inky outline; for they were both men of striking appearance and they hated each other.

The covered passage opened at one end on one of the steep streets of the Adelphi, and at the other on a terrace overlooking the sunset-coloured river. One side of the passage was a blank wall, for the building it supported was an old unsuccessful theatre restaurant, now shut up. The other side of the passage contained two doors, one at each end. Neither was what was commonly called the stage door; they were a sort of special and private stage doors used by very special performers, and in this case by the star actor and actress in the Shakespearean performance of the day. Persons of that eminence often like to have such private exits and entrances, for meeting friends or avoiding them.

The two men in question were certainly two such friends, men who evidently knew the doors and counted on their opening, for each approached the door at the upper end with equal coolness and confidence. Not, however, with equal speed; but the man who walked fast was the man from the other end of the tunnel, so they both arrived before the secret stage door almost at the same instant. They saluted each other with civility, and waited a moment before one of them, the sharper walker who seemed to have the shorter patience, knocked at the door.

In this and everything else each man was opposite and neither could be called inferior. As private persons both were handsome, capable and popular. As public persons, both were in the first public rank. But everything about them, from their glory to their good looks, was of a diverse and incomparable kind. Sir Wilson Seymour was the kind of man whose importance is known to everybody who knows. The more you mixed with the innermost

109

ring in every polity or profession, the more often you met Sir Wilson Seymour. He was the one intelligent man on twenty unintelligent committees—on every sort of subject, from the reform of the Royal Academy to the project of bimetallism for Greater Britain. In the Arts especially he was omnipotent. He was so unique that nobody could quite decide whether he was a great aristocrat who had taken up Art, or a great artist whom the aristocrats had taken up. But you could not meet him for five minutes without realizing that you had really been ruled by him all your life.

His appearance was 'distinguished' in exactly the same sense; it was at once conventional and unique. Fashion could have found no fault with his high silk hat; yet it was unlike anyone else's hat—a little higher, perhaps, and adding something to his natural height. His tall, slender figure had a slight stoop yet it looked the reverse of feeble. His hair was silver-grey, but he did not look old; it was worn longer than the common yet he did not look effeminate; it was curly but it did not looked curled. His carefully pointed beard made him look more manly and militant than otherwise, as it does in those old admirals of Velázquez with whose dark portraits his house was hung. His grey gloves were a shade bluer, his silver-knobbed cane a shade longer than scores of such gloves and canes flapped and flourished about the theatres and the restaurants.

The other man was not so tall, yet would have struck nobody as short, but merely as strong and handsome. His hair also was curly, but fair and cropped close to a strong, massive head—the sort of head you break a door with, as Chaucer said of the Miller's. His military moustache and the carriage of his shoulders showed him a soldier, but he had a pair of those peculiar frank and piercing blue eyes which are more common in sailors. His face was somewhat square, his jaw was square, his shoulders were square, even his jacket was square. Indeed, in the wild school of caricature then current, Mr Max Beerbohm had represented him as a proposition in the fourth book of Euclid.

For he also was a public man, though with quite another sort of success. You did not have to be in the best society to have heard of Captain Cutler, of the siege of Hong Kong, and the great march across China. You could not get away from hearing of him wherever you were; his portrait was on every other postcard; his maps and battles in every other illustrated paper; songs in his honour in every other music-hall turn or on every other barrel-organ. His fame, though probably more temporary, was ten times more wide, popular and spontaneous than the other man's. In thousands of English homes he appeared enormous above England, like Nelson. Yet he had infinitely less power in England than Sir Wilson Seymour.

The door was opened to them by an aged servant or 'dresser,' whose broken-down face and figure and black shabby coat and trousers contrasted queerly with the glittering interior of the great actress's dressing-room. It was fitted and filled with looking-glasses at every angle of refraction, so that they looked like the hundred facets of one huge diamond—if one could get inside a diamond. The other features of luxury, a few flowers, a few coloured cushions, a few scraps of stage costume, were multiplied by all the mirrors into the madness of the Arabian Nights, and danced and changed places perpetually as the shuffling attendant shifted a mirror outwards or shot one back against the wall.

They both spoke to the dingy dresser by name, calling him Parkinson, and asking for the lady as Miss Aurora Rome. Parkinson said she was in the other room, but he would go and tell her. A shade crossed the brow of both visitors; for the other room was the private room of the great actor with whom Miss Aurora was performing, and she was of the kind that does not inflame admiration without inflaming jealousy. In about half a minute, however, the inner door opened, and she entered as she always did, even in private life, so that the very silence seemed to be a roar of applause, and one well-deserved. She was clad in a somewhat strange garb of peacock green and peacock blue satins, that gleamed like blue and green metals, such as delight children and aesthetes, and her heavy, hot brown hair framed one of those magic faces which are dangerous to all men, but especially to boys and to men growing grey. In company with her male colleague, the great American actor, Isidore Bruno, she was producing a particularly poetical and fantastic interpretation of *Midsummer Night's Dream:* in which the artistic prominence was given to Oberon and Titania, or in other words to Bruno and herself. Set in dreamy and exquisite scenery, and moving in mystical dances, the green costume, like burnished beetle-wings, expressed all the elusive individuality of an elfin queen. But when personally confronted in what was still broad daylight, a man looked only at the woman's face.

She greeted both men with the beaming and baffling smile which kept so many males at the same just dangerous distance from her. She accepted some flowers from Cutler, which were as tropical and expensive as his victories; and another sort of present from Sir Wilson Seymour, offered later on and more nonchalantly by that gentleman. For it was against his breeding to show eagerness, and against his conventional unconventionality to give anything so obvious as flowers. He had picked up a trifle, he said, which was rather a curiosity; it was an ancient Greek dagger of the Mycenæan Epoch, and might well have been worn in the time of Theseus and Hippolyta. It was made of brass like all the Heroic weapons, but, oddly enough, sharp enough to prick anyone still. He had really been attracted to it by the leaf-like shape; it was as perfect as a Greek vase. If it was of any interest to Miss Rome or could come in anywhere in the play, he hoped she would——

The inner door burst open and a big figure appeared, who was more of a contrast to the explanatory Seymour than even Captain Cutler. Nearly six-foot-six, and of more than theatrical thews and muscles, Isidore Bruno, in the gorgeous leopard skin and golden-brown garments of Oberon, looked like a barbaric god. He leaned on a sort of hunting-spear, which across a theatre looked a slight, silvery wand, but which in the small and comparatively crowded room looked as plain as a pike-staff—and as menacing. His vivid black eyes rolled volcanically, his bronzed face, handsome as it was, showed at that moment a combination of high cheekbones with set white teeth, which recalled certain American conjectures about his origin in the Southern plantations.

'Aurora,' he began, in that deep voice like a drum of passion that had moved so many audiences, 'will you——'

He stopped indecisively because a sixth figure had suddenly presented itself just inside the doorway—a figure so incongruous in the scene as to be almost comic. It was a very short man in the black uniform of the Roman secular clergy, and looking (especially in such a presence as Bruno's and Aurora's) rather like the wooden Noah out of an ark. He did not, however, seem conscious of any contrast, but said with dull civility: 'I believe Miss Rome sent for me.'

A shrewd observer might have remarked that the emotional temperature rather rose at so unemotional an interruption. The detachment of a professional celibate seemed to reveal to the others

112

that they stood round the woman as a ring of amorous rivals; just as a stranger coming in with frost on his coat will reveal that a room is like a furnace. The presence of the one man who did not care about her increased Miss Rome's sense that everybody else was in love with her, and each in a somewhat dangerous way: the actor with all the appetite of a savage and a spoilt child; the soldier with all the simple selfishness of a man of will rather than mind; Sir Wilson with that daily hardening concentration with which old Hedonists take to a hobby; nay, even the abject Parkinson, who had known her before her triumphs, and who followed her about the room with eyes or feet, with the dumb fascination of a dog.

A shrewd person might also have noted a yet odder thing. The man like a black wooden Noah (who was not wholly without shrewdness) noted it with a considerable but contained amusement. It was evident that the great Aurora, though by no means indifferent to the admiration of the other sex, wanted at this moment to get rid of all the men who admired her and be left alone with the man who did not—did not admire her in that sense at least; for the little priest did admire and even enjoy the firm feminine diplomacy with which she set about her task. There was, perhaps, only one thing that Aurora Rome was clever about, and that was one half of humanity—the other half. The little priest watched, like a Napoleonic campaign, the swift precision of her policy for expelling all while banishing none. Bruno, the big actor, was so babyish that it was easy to send him off in brute sulks, banging the door. Cutler, the British officer, was pachydermatous to ideas, but punctilious about behaviour. He would ignore all hints, but he would die rather than ignore a definite commission from a lady. As to old Seymour, he had to be treated differently; he had to be left to the last. The only way to move him was to appeal to him in confidence as an old friend, to let him into the secret of the clearance. The priest did really admire Miss Rome as she achieved all these three objects in one selected action.

She went across to Captain Cutler and said in her sweetest manner: 'I shall value all these flowers, because they must be your favourite flowers. But they won't be complete, you know, without *my* favourite flower. *Do* go over to that shop round the corner and get me some lilies-of-the-valley, and then it will be *quite lovely*.'

The first object of her diplomacy, the exit of the enraged Bruno, was at once achieved. He had already handed his spear in a lordly style, like a sceptre, to the piteous Parkinson, and was about to assume one of the cushioned seats like a throne. But at this open appeal to his rival there glowed in his opal eyeballs all the sensitive insolence of the slave; he knotted his enormous brown fists for an instant, and then, dashing open the door, disappeared into his own apartments beyond. But meanwhile Miss Rome's experiment in mobilizing the British Army had not succeeded so simply as seemed probable. Cutler had indeed risen stiffly and suddenly, and walked towards the door, hatless, as if at a word of command. But perhaps there was something ostentatiously elegant about the languid figure of Seymour leaning against one of the looking-glasses that brought him up short at the entrance, turning his head this way and that like a bewildered bulldog.

'I must show this stupid man where to go,' said Aurora in a whisper to Seymour, and ran out to the threshold to speed the parting guest.

Seymour seemed to be listening, elegant and unconscious as was his posture, and he seemed relieved when he heard the lady call out some last instructions to the Captain, and then turn sharply and run laughing down the passage towards the other end, the end on the terrace above the Thames. Yet a second or two after Seymour's brow darkened again. A man in his position has so many rivals, and he remembered that at the other end of the passage was the corresponding entrance to Bruno's private room. He did not lose his dignity; he said some civil words to Father Brown about the revival of Byzantine architecture in the Westminster Cathedral, and then, quite naturally, strolled out himself into the upper end of the passage. Father Brown and Parkinson were left alone, and they were neither of them men with a taste for superfluous conversation. The dresser went round the room, pulling out looking-glasses and pushing them in again, his dingy dark coat and trousers looking all the more dismal since he was still holding the festive fairy spear of King Oberon. Every time he pulled out the frame of a new glass, a new black figure of Father Brown appeared; the absurd glass chamber was full of Father Browns, upside down in the air like angels, turning somersaults like acrobats, turning their backs to everybody like very rude persons.

Father Brown seemed quite unconscious of this cloud of witnesses, but followed Parkinson with an idly attentive eye till he took himself and his absurd spear into the farther room of Bruno.

Then he abandoned himself to such abstract meditations as always amused him—calculating the angles of the mirrors, the angles of each refraction, the angle at which each must fit into the wall . . . when he heard a strong but strangled cry.

He sprang to his feet and stood rigidly listening. At the same instant Sir Wilson Seymour burst back into the room, white as ivory. 'Who's that man in the passage?' he cried. 'Where's that dagger of mine?'

Before Father Brown could turn in his heavy boots Seymour was plunging about the room looking for the weapon. And before he could possibly find that weapon or any other, a brisk running of feet broke upon the pavement outside, and the square face of Cutler was thrust into the same doorway. He was still grotesquely grasping a bunch of lilies-of-the-valley. 'What's this?' he cried. 'What's that creature down the passage? Is this some of your tricks?'

'My tricks!' hissed his pale rival, and made a stride towards him.

In the instant of time in which all this happened Father Brown stepped out into the top of the passage, looked down it, and at once walked briskly towards what he saw.

At this the other two men dropped their quarrel and darted after him, Cutler calling out: 'What are you doing? Who are you?'

'My name is Brown,' said the priest sadly, as he bent over something and straightened himself again. 'Miss Rome sent for me, and I came as quickly as I could. I have come too late.'

The three men looked down, and in one of them at least the life died in that late light of afternoon. It ran along the passage like a path of gold, and in the midst of it Aurora Rome lay lustrous in her robes of green and gold, with her dead face turned upwards. Her dress was torn away as in a struggle, leaving the right shoulder bare, but the wound from which the blood was welling was on the other side. The brass dagger lay flat and gleaming a yard or so away.

There was a blank stillness for a measurable time, so that they could hear far off a flower-girl's laugh outside Charing Cross, and someone whistling furiously for a taxicab in one of the streets off the Strand. Then the Captain, with a movement so sudden that it might have been passion or play-acting, took Sir Wilson Seymour by the throat.

Seymour looked at him steadily without either fight or fear. 'You need not kill me,' he said in a voice quite cold; 'I shall do that on my own account.'

The Captain's hand hesitated and dropped; and the other added with the same icy candour: 'If I find I haven't the nerve to do it with that dagger I can do it in a month with drink.'

'Drink isn't good enough for me,' replied Cutler, 'but I'll have blood for this before I die. Not yours—but I think I know whose.'

And before the others could appreciate his intention he snatched up the dagger, sprang at the other door at the lower end of the passage, burst it open, bolt and all, and confronted Bruno in his dressing-room. As he did so, old Parkinson tottered in his wavering way out of the door and caught sight of the corpse lying in the passage. He moved shakily towards it; looked at it weakly with a working face; then moved shakily back into the dressing-room again, and sat down suddenly on one of the richly cushioned chairs. Father Brown instantly ran across to him, taking no notice of Cutler and the colossal actor, though the room already rang with their blows and they began to struggle for the dagger. Seymour, who retained some practical sense, was whistling for the police at the end of the passage.

When the police arrived it was to tear the two men from an almost ape-like grapple; and, after a few formal inquiries, to arrest Isidore Bruno upon a charge of murder, brought against him by his furious opponent. The idea that the great national hero of the hour had arrested a wrongdoer with his own hand doubtless had its weight with the police, who are not without elements of the journalist. They treated Cutler with a certain solemn attention, and pointed out that he had got a slight slash on the hand. Even as Cutler bore him back across tilted chair and table, Bruno had twisted the dagger out of his grasp and disabled him just below the wrist. The injury was really slight, but till he was removed from the room the half-savage prisoner stared at the running blood with a steady smile.

'Looks a cannibal sort of chap, don't he?' said the constable confidentially to Cutler.

Cutler made no answer, but said sharply a moment after: 'We must attend to the . . . the death . . .' and his voice escaped from articulation.

'The two deaths,' came in the voice of the priest from the farther side of the room. 'This poor fellow was gone when I got across to him.' And he stood looking down at old Parkinson, who sat in a black huddle on the gorgeous chair. He also had paid his tribute, not without eloquence, to the woman who had died.

The silence was first broken by Cutler, who seemed not untouched by a rough tenderness. 'I wish I was him,' he said huskily. 'I remember he used to watch her wherever she walked more than—anybody. She was his air, and he's dried up. He's just dead.'

'We are all dead,' said Seymour in a strange voice, looking down the road.

They took leave of Father Brown at the corner of the road, with some random apologies for any rudeness they might have shown. Both their faces were tragic, but also cryptic.

The mind of the little priest was always a rabbit-warren of wild thoughts that jumped too quickly for him to catch them. Like the white tail of a rabbit he had the vanishing thought that he was certain of their grief, but not so certain of their innocence.

'We had better all be going,' said Seymour heavily; 'we have done all we can to help.'

'Will you understand my motives,' asked Father Brown quietly, 'If I say you have done all you can to hurt?'

They both started as if guiltily, and Cutler said sharply: 'To hurt whom?'

'To hurt yourselves,' answered the priest. 'I would not add to your troubles if it weren't common justice to warn you. You've done nearly everything you could do to hang yourselves, if this actor should be acquitted. They'll be sure to subpœna me; I shall be bound to say that after the cry was heard each of you rushed into the room in a wild state and began quarrelling about a dagger. As far as my words on oath can go, you might either of you have done it. You hurt yourselves with that; and then Captain Cutler must have hurt himself with the dagger.'

'Hurt myself!' exclaimed the Captain, with contempt. 'A silly little scratch.'

'Which drew blood,' replied the priest, nodding. 'We know there's blood on the brass now. And so we shall never know whether there was blood on it before.'

There was a silence; and then Seymour said, with an emphasis quite alien to his daily accent: 'But I saw a man in the passage.'

'I know you did,' answered the cleric Brown with a face of wood, 'so did Captain Cutler. That's what seems so improbable.'

117

Before either could make sufficient sense of it even to answer, Father Brown had politely excused himself and gone stumping up the road with his stumpy old umbrella.

As modern newspapers are conducted, the most honest and most important news is the police news. If it be true that in the twentieth century more space is given to murder than to politics, it is for the excellent reason that murder is a more serious subject. But even this would hardly explain the enormous omnipresence and widely distributed detail of 'The Bruno Case,' or 'The Passage Mystery,' in the Press of London and the provinces. So vast was the excitement that for some weeks the Press really told the truth; and the reports of examination and cross-examination, if interminable, even if intolerable are at least reliable. The true reason, of course, was the coincidence of persons. The victim was a popular actress; the accused was a popular actor; and the accused had been caught red-handed, as it were, by the most popular soldier of the patriotic season. In those extraordinary circumstances the Press was para-lysed into probity and accuracy; and the rest of this somewhat singular business can practically be recorded from the reports of Bruno's trial.

The trial was presided over by Mr Justice Monkhouse, one of those who are jeered at as humorous judges, but who are generally much more serious than the serious judges, for their levity comes from a living impatience of professional solemnity; while the serious judge is really filled with frivolity, because he is filled with vanity. All the chief actors being of a worldly importance, the barristers were well balanced; the prosecutor for the Crown was Sir Walter Cowdray, a heavy but weighty advocate of the sort that knows how to seem English and trustworthy, and how to be rhetorical with reluctance. The prisoner was defended by Mr Patrick Butler, K.C., who was mistaken for a mere *flâneur* by those who misunderstood the Irish character—and those who had not been examined by him. The medical evidence involved no contra-dictions, the doctor whom Seymour had summoned on the spot, agreeing with the eminent surgeon who had later examined the body. Aurora Rome had been stabbed with some sharp instrument such as a knife or dagger; some instrument, at least, of which the blade was short. The wound was just over the heart, and she had died instantly. When the doctor first saw her she could hardly have been dead for twenty minutes. Therefore when Father Brown found her she could hardly have been dead for three.

Some official detective evidence followed, chiefly concerned with the presence or absence of any proof of a struggle; the only suggestion of this was the tearing of the dress at the shoulder, and this did not seem to fit in particularly well with the direction and finality of the blow. When these details had been supplied, though not explained, the first of the important witnesses was called.

Sir Wilson Seymour gave evidence as he did everything else that he did at all—not only well, but perfectly. Though himself much more of a public man than the judge, he conveyed exactly the fine shade of self-effacement before the King's Justice; and though everyone looked at him as they would at the Prime Minister or the Archbishop of Canterbury, they could have said nothing of his part in it but that it was that of a private gentleman, with an accent on the noun. He was also refreshingly lucid, as he was on the committees. He had been calling on Miss Rome at the theatre; he had met Captain Cutler there; they had been joined for a short time by the accused, who had then returned to his own dressing-room; they had then been joined by a Roman Catholic priest, who asked for the deceased lady and said his name was Brown. Miss Rome had then gone just outside the theatre to the entrance of the passage, in order to point out to Captain Cutler a flower-shop at which he was to buy her some more flowers; and the witness had remained in the room, exchanging a few words with the priest. He had then distinctly heard the deceased, having sent the Captain on his errand, turn round laughing and run down the passage towards its other end, where was the prisoner's dressing-room. In idle curiosity as to the rapid movements of his friends, he had strolled out to the head of the passage himself and looked down it towards the prisoner's door. Did he see anything in the passage? Yes; he saw something in the passage.

Sir Walter Cowdray allowed an impressive interval, during which the witness looked down, and for all his usual composure seemed to have more than his usual pallor. Then the barrister said in a lower voice, which seemed at once sympathetic and creepy: 'Did you see it distinctly?'

Sir Wilson Seymour, however moved, had his excellent brains in full working-order. 'Very distinctly as regards its outline, but quite indistinctly, indeed not at all, as regards the details inside the outline. The passage is of such length that anyone in the middle of it appears quite black against the light at the other end.' The witness lowered his steady eyes once more and added: 'I had noticed the fact before, when Captain Cutler first entered it.' There was another silence, and the judge leaned forward and made a note.

'Well,' said Sir Walter patiently, 'what was the outline like? Was it, for instance, like the figure of the murdered woman?'

'Not in the least,' answered Seymour quietly.

'What did it look like to you?'

'It looked to me,' replied the witness, 'like a tall man.'

Everyone in court kept his eyes riveted on his pen, or his umbrella handle, or his book, or his boots or whatever he happened to be looking at. They seemed to be holding their eyes away from the prisoner by main force; but they felt his figure in the dock, and they felt it as gigantic. Tall as Bruno was to the eye, he seemed to swell taller and taller when all eyes had been torn away from him.

Cowdray was resuming his seat with his solemn face, smoothing his black silk robes, and white silk whiskers. Sir Wilson was leaving the witness-box, after a few final particulars to which there were many other witnesses, when the counsel for the defence sprang up and stopped him.

'I shall only detain you a moment,' said Mr Butler, who was a rustic-looking person with red eyebrows and an expression of partial slumber. 'Will you tell his lordship how you knew it was a man?'

A faint, refined smile seemed to pass over Seymour's features. 'I'm afraid it is the vulgar test of trousers,' he said. 'When I saw daylight between the long legs I was sure it was a man, after all.'

Butler's sleepy eyes opened as suddenly as some silent explosion. 'After all!' he repeated slowly. 'So you did think at first it was a woman?'

Seymour looked troubled for the first time. 'It is hardly point of fact,' he said, 'but if his lordship would like me to answer for my impression, of course I shall do so. There was something about the thing was not exactly a woman and yet was not quite a man; somehow the curves were different. And it had something that looked like long hair.'

'Thank you,' said Mr Butler, K.C., and sat down suddenly, as if he had got what he wanted.

Captain Cutler was a far less plausible and composed witness than Sir Wilson, but his account of the opening incidents was solidly the same. He described the return of Bruno to his dressing-room, the dispatching of himself to buy a bunch of lilies-of-the-valley, his return to the upper end of the passage, the thing he saw in the passage, his suspicion of Seymour, and his struggle with Bruno. But he could give little artistic assistance about the black figure that he and Seymour had seen. Asked about its outline, he said he was no art critic—with a somewhat too obvious sneer at Seymour. Asked if it was a man or a woman, he said it looked more like a beast—with a too obvious snarl at the prisoner. But the man was plainly shaken with sorrow and sincere anger, and Cowdray quickly excused him from confirming facts that were already fairly clear.

The defending counsel also was again brief in his cross-examination; although (as was his custom) even in being brief, he seemed to take a long time about it. 'You used a rather remarkable expression,' he said, looking at Cutler sleepily. 'What do you mean by saying that it looked more like a beast than a man or a woman?'

Cutler seemed seriously agitated. 'Perhaps I oughtn't to have said that,' he said; 'but when the brute has huge humped shoulders like a chimpanzee, and bristles sticking out of its head like a pig——'

Mr Butler cut short his curious impatience in the middle. 'Never mind whether its hair was like a pig's,' he said, 'was it like a woman's?'

'A woman's!' cried the soldier. 'Great Scott, no!'

'The last witness said it was,' commented the counsel, with unscrupulous swiftness. 'And did the figure have any of those serpentine and semi-feminine curves to which eloquent allusion has been made? No? No feminine curves? The figure, I understand you, was rather heavy and square than otherwise?'

'He may have been bending forward,' said Cutler, in a hoarse and rather faint voice.

'Or again, he may not,' said Mr Butler, and sat down suddenly for the second time.

The third witness called by Sir Walter Cowdray was the little Catholic clergyman, so little, compared with the others, that his head seemed hardly to come above the box, so that it was like cross-examining a child. But unfortunately Sir Walter had some-how got it into his head (mostly by some ramifications of his family's religion) that Father Brown was on the side of the prisoner, because the prisoner was wicked and foreign and even partly black. Therefore he took Father Brown up sharply whenever that proud pontiff tried to explain anything; and told him to answer yes or no, and tell the plain facts without any jesuitry. When Father Brown began, in his simplicity, to say who he thought the man in the passage was, the barrister told him that he did not want his theories.

'A black shape was seen in the passage. And you say you saw the black shape. Well, what shape was it?'

Father Brown blinked as under rebuke; but he had long known the literal nature of obedience. 'The shape,' he said, 'was short and thick, but had two sharp, black projections curved upwards on each side of the head or top, rather like horns, and——'

'Oh! the devil with horns, no doubt,' ejaculated Cowdray, sitting down in triumphant jocularity. 'It was the devil come to eat Protestants.'

'No,' said the priest dispassionately; 'I know who it was.'

Those in court had been wrought up to an irrational, but real sense of some monstrosity. They had forgotten the figure in the dock and thought only of the figure in the passage. And the figure in the passage, described by three capable and respectable men who had all seen it, was a shifting nightmare: one called it a woman, and the other a beast, and the other a devil. . . .

The judge was looking at Father Brown with level and piercing eyes. 'You are a most extraordinary witness,' he said; 'but there is something about you that makes me think you are trying to tell the truth. Well, who was the man you saw in the passage?'

'He was myself,' said Father Brown.

Butler, K.C., sprang to his feet in an extraordinary stillness, and said quite calmly: 'Your lordship will allow me to cross-examine?' And then, without stopping, he shot at Brown the apparently disconnected question: 'You have heard about the dagger; you know the experts say the crime was committed with a short blade?'

'A short blade,' assented Brown, nodding solemnly like an owl, 'but a very long hilt.'

Before the audience could quite dismiss the idea that the priest had really seen himself doing murder with a short dagger with a long hilt (which seemed somehow to make it more horrible), he had himself hurried on to explain.

'I mean daggers aren't the only things with short blades. Spears have short blades. And spears catch at the end of the steel just like daggers, if they're that sort of fancy spear they had in theatres; like the spear poor old Parkinson killed his wife with, just when she'd sent for me to settle their family troubles—and I came just too late, God forgive me! But he died penitent—he just died of being penitent. He couldn't bear what he'd done.'

The general impression in court was that the little priest, who was gabbling away, had literally gone mad in the box. But the judge still looked at him with bright and steady eyes of interest; and the counsel for the defence went on with his questions unperturbed.

'If Parkinson did it with that pantomime spear,' said Butler, 'he must have thrust from four yards away. How do you account for signs of struggle, like the dress dragged off the shoulder?' He had slipped into treating this mere witness as an expert; but no one noticed it now.

'The poor lady's dress was torn,' said the witness, 'because it was caught in a panel that slid to just behind her. She struggled to free herself, as she did so Parkinson came out of the prisoner's room and lunged with the spear.'

'A panel?' repeated the barrister in a curious voice.

'It was a looking-glass on the other side,' explained Father Brown. 'When I was in the dressing-room I noticed that some of them could probably be slid out into the passage.'

There was another vast and unnatural silence, and this time it was the judge who spoke. 'So you really mean that when you looked down that passage, the man you saw was yourself—in a mirror?'

'Yes, my lord; that was what I was trying to say,' said Brown, 'but they asked me for the shape; and our hats have corners just like horns, and so I——'

The judge leaned forward, his old eyes yet more brilliant, and said in specially distinct tones: 'Do you really mean to say that when Sir Wilson Seymour saw that wild what-you-call-him with curves and a woman's hair and a man's trousers, what he saw was Sir Wilson Seymour?'

'Yes, my lord,' said Father Brown.

'And you mean to say that when Captain Cutler saw that chimpanzee with humped shoulders and hog's bristles, he simply saw himself?'

'Yes, my lord.'

The judge leaned back in his chair with a luxuriance in which it was hard to separate the cynicism and the admiration. 'And can you tell us why,' he asked, 'you should know your own figure in a looking-glass, when two such distinguished men don't?'

Father Brown blinked even more painfully than before; then he stammered: 'Really, my lord, I don't know . . . unless it's because I don't look at it so often.'

THE MISTAKE OF THE MACHINE

Flambeau and his friend the priest were sitting in the Temple Gardens about sunset; and their neighbourhood or some such accidental influence had turned their talk to matters of legal process. From the problem of the licence in cross-examination, their talk strayed to Roman and mediæval torture, to the examining magistrate in France and the Third Degree in America.

'I've been reading,' said Flambeau, 'of this new psychometric method they talk about so much, especially in America. You know what I mean; they put a pulsometer on a man's wrist and judge by how his heart goes at the pronunciation of certain words. What do you think of it?'

'I think it very interesting,' replied Father Brown; 'it reminds me of that interesting idea in the Dark Ages that blood would flow from a corpse if the murderer touched it.'

'Do you really mean,' demanded his friend, 'that you think the two methods equally valuable?'

'I think them equally valueless,' replied Brown. 'Blood flows, fast or slow, in dead folk or living, for so many more million reasons than we can ever know. Blood will have to flow very funnily; blood will have to flow up the Matterhorn, before I will take it as a sign that I am to shed it.'

'The method,' remarked the other, 'has been guaranteed by some of the greatest American men of science.'

'What sentimentalists men of science are!' exclaimed Father Brown, 'and how such more sentimental must American men of science be! Who but a Yankee would think of proving anything from heart-throbs? Why, they must be as sentimental as a man who thinks a woman is in love with him if she blushes. That's a test from the circulation of the blood, discovered by the immortal Harvey; and a jolly rotten test, too.'

'But surely,' insisted Flambeau, 'it might point pretty straight at something or other.'

'There's a disadvantage in a stick pointing straight,' answered the other. 'What is it? Why, the other end of the stick always points the opposite way. It depends whether you get hold of the

125

stick by the right end. I saw the thing done once and I've never believed in it since.' And he proceeded to tell the story of his disillusionment.

It happened nearly twenty years before, when he was chaplain to his co-religionists in a prison in Chicago—where the Irish population displayed a capacity both for crime and penitence which kept him tolerably busy. The official second-in-command under the Governor was an ex-detective named Greywood Usher, a cadaverous, careful-spoken Yankee philosopher, occasionally varying a very rigid visage with an odd apologetic grimace. He liked Father Brown in a slightly patronizing way; and Father Brown liked him, though he heartily disliked his theories. His theories were extremely complicated and were held with extreme simplicity.

One evening he had sent for the priest, who, according to his custom, took a seat in silence at a table piled and littered with papers, and waited. The official selected from the papers a scrap of newspaper cutting, which he handed across to the cleric, who read it gravely. It appeared to be an extract from one of the pinkest of American Society papers, and ran as follows:

'Society's brightest widower is once more on the Freak Dinner stunt. All our exclusive citizens will recall the Perambulator Parade Dinner, in which Last-Trick Todd, at his palatial home at Pilgrim's Pond, caused so many of our prominent *débutantes* to look even younger than their years. Equally elegant and more miscellaneous and large-hearted in social outlook was Last-Trick's show the year previous, the popular Cannibal Crush Lunch, at which the confections handed round were sarcastically moulded in the forms of human arms and legs, and during which more than one of our gayest mental gymnasts was heard offering to eat his partner. The witticism which will inspire this evening is as yet in Mr Todd's pretty reticent intellect, or locked in the jewelled bosoms of our city's gayest leaders; but there is talk of a pretty parody of the simple manners and customs at the other end of Society's scale. This would be all the more telling, as hospitable Todd is entertaining in Lord Falconroy, the famous traveller, a true-blooded aristocrat fresh from England's oak-groves. Lord Falconroy's travels began before his ancient feudal title was resurrected; he was in the Republic in his youth, and fashion murmurs a sly reason for his return. Miss Etta Todd is one of our deep-souled New Yorkers, and comes into an income of nearly twelve hundred million dollars.'

'Well,' asked Usher, 'does that interest you?'

'Why, words rather fail me,' answered Father Brown. 'I cannot think at this moment of anything in this world that would interest me less. And, unless the just anger of the Republic is at last going to electrocute journalists for writing like that, I don't quite see why it should interest you either.'

'Ah!' said Mr Usher dryly, and handing across another scrap of newspaper. 'Well, does *that* interest you?'

The paragraph was headed 'Savage Murder of a Warder. Convict Escapes,' and ran: 'Just before dawn this morning a shout for help was heard in the Convict Settlement at Sequah in this State. The authorities, hurrying in the direction of the cry, found the corpse of the warder who patrols the top of the north wall of the prison, the steepest and most difficult exit, for which one man has always been found sufficient. The unfortunate officer had, however, been hurled from the high wall, his brains beaten out as with a club, and his gun was missing. Further inquiries showed that one of the cells was empty; it had been occupied by a rather sullen ruffian giving his name as Oscar Rian. He was only temporarily detained for some comparatively trivial assault; but he gave everyone the impression of a man with a black past and a dangerous future. Finally, when daylight had fully revealed the scene of murder, it was found that he had written on the wall above the body a fragmentary sentence, apparently with a finger dipped in blood: "This was self-defence and he had the gun. I meant no harm to him or any man but one. I am keeping the bullet for Pilgrim's Pond—O.R." A man must have used most fiendish treachery or most savage and amazing bodily daring to have stormed such a wall in spite of an armed man.'

'Well, the literary style is somewhat improved,' admitted the priest cheerfully, 'but still I don't see what I can do for you. I should cut a poor figure, with my short legs, running about this State after an athletic assassin of that sort. I doubt whether anybody could find him. The convict settlement at Sequah is thirty miles from here; the country between is wild and tangled enough, and the country beyond, where he will surely have the sense to go, is a perfect no-man's land tumbling away to the prairies. He may be in any hole or up any tree.'

'He isn't in any hole,' said the governor; 'he isn't up any tree.'

'Why, how do you know?' asked Father Brown, blinking.

'Would you like to speak to him?' inquired Usher.

Father Brown opened his innocent eyes wide. 'He is here?' he exclaimed. 'Why, how did your men get hold of him?'

'I got hold of him myself,' drawled the American, rising and lazily stretching his lanky legs before the fire. 'I got hold of him with the crooked end of a walking-stick. Don't look so surprised. I really did. You know I sometimes take a turn in the country lanes outside this dismal place; well, I was walking early this evening up a steep lane with dark hedges, and grey-looking ploughed fields on both sides; and a young moon was up and silvering the road. By the light of it I saw a man running across the field towards the road; running with his body bent and at a good mile-race trot. He appeared to be much exhausted; but when he came to the thick black hedge he went through it as if it were made of spiders' webs; or rather (for I heard the strong branches breaking and snapping like bayonets) as if he himself were made of stone. In the instant in which he appeared up against the moon, crossing the road, I slung my hooked cane at his legs, tripping him and bringing him down. Then I blew my whistle long and loud, and our fellows came running up to secure him.'

'It would have been rather awkward,' remarked Brown, 'if you had found he was a popular athlete practising a mile race.'

'He was not,' said Usher grimly. 'We soon found out who he was; but I had guessed it with the first glint of the moon on him.'

'You thought it was the runaway convict,' observed the priest simply, 'because you had read in the newspaper cutting that morning that a convict had run away.'

'I had somewhat better grounds,' replied the governor coolly. 'I pass over the first as too simple to be emphasized—I mean that fashionable athletes do not run across ploughed fields or scratch their eyes out in bramble hedges. Nor do they run all doubled up like a crouching dog. There were more decisive details to a fairly well-trained eye. The man was clad in coarse and ragged clothes, but they were something more than merely coarse and ragged. They were so ill-fitting as to be quite grotesque; even as he appeared in black outline against the moonrise, the coat-collar in which his head was buried made him look like a hunchback, and the long loose sleeves looked as if he had no hands. It at once occurred to me that he had somehow managed to change his convict clothes for some confederate's clothes which did not fit him. Second, there was a pretty stiff wind against which he was running; so that I must have seen the streaky look of blowing hair, if the hair had not been very short. Then I remembered that beyond these ploughed fields he was crossing lay Pilgrim's Pond, for which (you will remember) the convict was keeping his bullet; and I sent my walking-stick flying.'

'A brilliant piece of rapid deduction,' said Father Brown; 'but had he got a gun?'

As Usher stopped abruptly in his walk the priest added apologetically: 'I've been told a bullet is not half so useful without it.'

'He had no gun,' said the other gravely; 'but that was doubtless due to some very natural mischance or change of plans. Probably the same policy that made him change the clothes made him drop the gun; he began to repent the coat he had left behind him in the blood of his victim.'

'Well, that is possible enough,' answered the priest.

'And it's hardly worth speculating on,' said Usher, turning to some other papers, 'for we know it's the man by this time.'

His clerical friend asked faintly: 'But how?' And Greywood Usher threw down the newspapers and took up the two press-cuttings again.

'Well, since you are so obstinate,' he said, 'let's begin at the beginning. You will notice that these two cuttings have only one thing in common, which is the mention of Pilgrim's Pond, the estate, as you know, of the millionaire Ireton Todd. You also know that he is a remarkable character; one of those that rose on stepping-stones——'

'Of our dead selves to higher things,' assented his companion. 'Yes; I know that. Petroleum, I think.'

'Anyhow,' said Usher, 'Last-Trick Todd counts for a great deal in this rum affair.'

He stretched himself once more before the fire and continued talking in his expansive, radiantly explanatory style.

'To begin with, on the face of it, there is no mystery here at all. It is not mysterious, it is not even odd, that a jailbird should take his gun to Pilgrim's Pond. Our people aren't like the English, who will forgive a man for being rich if he throws away money on hospitals or horses. Last-Trick Todd has made himself big by his own considerable abilities; and there's no doubt that many of those on whom he has shown his abilities would like to show theirs on him with a shot-gun. Todd might easily get dropped by some man he'd never even heard of; some labourer he'd locked out, or some clerk in a business he'd busted. Last-Trick is a man of mental endowments and a high public character; but in this country the relations of employers and employed are considerably strained.

'That's how the whole thing looks supposing this Rian made for Pilgrim's Pond to kill Todd. So it looked to me, till another little discovery woke up what I have of the detective in me. When I had my prisoner safe, I picked up my cane again and strolled down the two or three turns of country road that brought me to one of the side entrances of Todd's grounds, the one nearest to the pool or lake after which the place is named. It was some two hours ago, about seven by this time; the moonlight was more luminous, and I could see the long white streaks of it lying on the mysterious mere with its grey, greasy, half-liquid shores in which they say our fathers used to make witches walk until they sank. I'd forgotten the exact tale; but you know the place I mean; it lies north of Todd's house towards the wilderness, and has two queer wrinkled trees, so dismal that they look more like huge fungoids than decent foliage. As I stood peering at this misty pool, I fancied I saw the faint figure of a man moving from the house towards it, but it was all too dim and distant for one to be certain of the fact, and still less of the details. Besides, my attention was very sharply arrested by something much closer. I crouched behind the fence which ran not more than two hundred yards from one wing of the great mansion, and which was fortunately split in places, as if specially for the application of a cautious eye. A door had opened in the dark bulk of the left wing, and a figure appeared black against the illuminated interior—a muffled figure bending forward, evidently peering out into the night. It closed the door behind it, and I saw it was carrying a lantern, which threw a patch of imperfect light on the dress and figure of the wearer. It seemed to be the figure of a woman, wrapped up in a ragged cloak and evidently disguised to avoid notice; there was something very strange both about the rags and the furtiveness in a person coming out of those rooms lined with gold. She took cautiously the curved garden path which brought her within half a hundred yards of me; then she stood up for an instant on the terrace of turf that looks towards the slimy lake, and holding her flaming lantern above her head she deliberately swung it three times to and fro as for a signal. As she swung it the second time a flicker of its light fell for a moment on her own face, a face that I knew. She was unnaturally pale, and her head was bundled in her borrowed plebian shawl; but I am certain it was Etta Todd, the millionaire's daughter.

'She retraced her steps in equal secrecy and the door closed behind her again. I was about to climb the fence and follow, when I realized that the detective fever that had lured me into the adventure was rather undignified; and that in a more authoritative capacity I already held all the cards in my hand. I was just turning away when a new noise broke on the night. A window was thrown up in one of the upper floors, but just round the corner of the house so that I could not see it; and a voice of terrible distinctness was heard shouting across the dark garden to know where Lord Falconroy was, for he was missing from every room in the house. There was no mistaking that voice. I have heard it on many a political platform or meeting of directors; it was Ireton Todd himself. Some of the others seemed to have gone to the lower windows or on to the steps, and were calling up to him that Falconroy had gone for a stroll down to the Pilgrim's Pond an hour before, and could not be traced since. Then Todd cried "Mighty Murder!" and shut down the window violently; and I could hear him plunging down the stairs inside. Repossessing myself of my former and wiser purpose, I whipped out of the way of the general search that must follow; and returned here not later than eight o'clock.

'I now ask you to recall that little Society paragraph which seemed to you so painfully lacking in interest. If the convict was not keeping the shot for Todd, as he evidently wasn't, it is most likely that he was keeping it for Lord Falconroy; and it looks as if he had delivered the goods. No more handy place to shoot a man than in the curious geological surroundings of that pool, where a body thrown down would sink through thick slime to a depth practically unknown. Let us suppose, then, that our friend with the cropped hair came to kill Falconroy and not Todd. But, as I have pointed out, there are many reasons why people in America might want to kill Todd. There is no reason why anybody in America should want to kill an English lord newly landed, except for the one reason mentioned in the pink paper—that the lord is

131

paying his attentions to the millionaire's daughter. Our crop-haired friend, despite his ill-fitting clothes, must be an aspiring lover.

'I know the notion will seem to you jarring and even comic; but that's because you are English. It sounds to you like saying the Archbishop of Canterbury's daughter will be married in St George's, Hanover Square, to a crossing-sweeper on ticket-of-leave. You don't do justice to the climbing and aspiring power of our more remarkable citizens. You see a good-looking grey-haired man in evening-dress with a sort of authority about him, you know he is a pillar of the State, and you fancy he had a father. You are in error. You do not realize that a comparatively few years ago he may have been in a tenement or (quite likely) in a jail. You don't allow for our national buoyancy and uplift. Many of our most influential citizens have not only risen recently, but risen comparatively late in life. Todd's daughter was fully eighteen when her father first made his pile; so there isn't really anything impossible in her having a hanger-on in low life; or even in her hanging on to him, as I think she must be doing, to judge by the lantern business. If so, the hand that held the lantern may not be unconnected with the hand that held the gun. This case, sir, will make a noise.'

'Well,' said the priest patiently, 'and what did you do next?'

'I reckon you'll be shocked,' replied Greywood Usher, 'as I know you don't cotton to the march of science in these matters. I am given a good deal of discretion here, and perhaps take a little more than I'm given; and I thought it was an excellent opportunity to test that Psychometric Machine I told you about. Now, in my opinion, that machine can't lie.'

'No machine can lie,' said Father Brown; 'nor can it tell the truth.'

'It did in this case, as I'll show you,' went on Usher positively. 'I sat the man in the ill-fitting clothes in a comfortable chair, and simply wrote words on a blackboard; and the machine simply recorded the variations of his pulse; and I simply observed his manner. The trick is to introduce some word connected with the supposed crime in a list of words connected with something quite different, yet a list in which it occurs quite naturally. Thus I wrote "heron" and "eagle" and "owl", and when I wrote "falcon" he was tremendously agitated; and when I began to make an "r" at the end of the word, that machine just bounded. Who else in this republic has any reason to jump at the name of a newly-arrived Englishman like Falconroy except the man who's shot him? Isn't that better evidence than a lot of gabble from witnesses—the evidence of a reliable machine?'

'You always forget,' observed his companion, 'that the reliable machine always has to be worked by an unreliable machine.'

'Why, what do you mean?' asked the detective.

'I mean Man,' said Father Brown, 'the most unreliable machine I know of. I don't want to be rude; and I don't think you will consider Man to be an offensive or inaccurate description of yourself. You say you observed his manner; but how do you know you observed it right? You say the words have to come in a natural way; but how do you know that you did it naturally? How do you know, if you come to that, that he did not observe your manner? Who is to prove that you were not tremendously agitated? There was no machine tied on to your pulse.'

'I tell you,' cried the American in the utmost excitement, 'I was a cool as a cucumber.'

'Criminals also can be as cool as cucumbers,' said Brown with a smile. 'And almost as cool as you.'

'Well, this one wasn't,' said Usher, throwing the papers about. 'Oh, you make me tired!'

'I'm sorry,' said the other. 'I only point out what seems a reasonable possibility. If you could tell by his manner when the word that might hang him had come, why shouldn't he tell from your manner that the word that might hang him was coming? I should ask for more than words myself before I hanged anybody.'

Usher smote the table and rose in a sort of angry triumph.

'And that,' he cried, 'is just what I'm going to give you. I tried the machine first just in order to test the thing in other ways afterwards and the machine, sir, is right.'

He paused a moment and resumed with less excitement. 'I rather want to insist, if it comes to that, that so far I had very little to go on except the scientific experiment. There was really nothing against the man at all. His clothes were ill-fitting, as I've said, but they were rather better, if anything, than those of the submerged class to which he evidently belonged. Moreover, under all the stains of his plunging through ploughed fields or bursting through dusty hedges, the man was comparatively clean. This might mean, of course, that he had only just broken prison; but it reminded me more of the desperate decency of the comparatively respectable poor. His demeanour was, I am bound to confess, quite in accordance with theirs. He was silent and dignified as they are; he seemed to have a big, but buried, grievance, as they do. He professed total ignorance of the crime and the whole question; and showed nothing but a sullen impatience for something sensible that might come to take him out of his meaningless scrape. He asked me more than once if he could telephone for a lawyer who had helped him a long time ago in a trade dispute, and in every sense acted as you would expect an innocent man to act. There was nothing against him in the world except that little finger on the dial that pointed to the change of his pulse.

'Then, sir, the machine was on its trial; and the machine was right. By the time I came with him out of the private room into the vestibule where all sorts of other people were awaiting examination, I think he had already more or less made up his mind to clear things up by something like a confession. He turned to me and began to say in a low voice: "Oh, I can't stick this any more. If you must know all about me——"

'At the same instant one of the poor women sitting on the long bench stood up, screaming aloud and pointing at him with her finger. I have never in my life heard anything more demoniacally distinct. Her lean finger seemed to pick him out as if it were a pea-shooter. Though the word was a mere howl, every syllable was as clear as a separate stroke on the clock.

' "Drugger Davis!" she shouted. "They've got Drugger Davis!"

'Among the wretched women, mostly thieves and street-walkers, twenty faces were turned, gaping with glee and hate. If I had never heard the words, I should have known by the very shock upon his features that the so-called Oscar Rian had heard his real name. But I'm not quite so ignorant, you may be surprised to hear. Drugger Davis was one of the most terrible and depraved criminals that ever baffled our police. It is certain he had done murder more than once long before his last exploit with the warder. But he was never entirely fixed for it, curiously enough because he did it in the same manner as those milder—or meaner—crimes for which he was fixed pretty often. He was a handsome, well-bred looking brute, as he still is, to some extent; and he used mostly to go about with barmaids or shop-girls and do them out of their money. Very often, though, he went a good deal farther; and they were found drugged with cigarettes or chocolates and their whole property missing. Then came one case where the girl was found dead; but deliberation could not quite be proved, and, what was more practical still, the criminal could not be found. I heard a rumour of his having reappeared somewhere in the opposite character this time, lending money instead of borrowing it; but still to such poor widows as he might personally fascinate, and still with the same bad result for them. Well, there is your innocent man, and there is his innocent record. Even, since then, four criminals and three warders have identified him and confirmed the story. Now what have you got to say to my poor little machine after that? Hasn't the machine done for him? Or do you prefer to say that the woman and I have done for him?'

'As to what you've done for him,' replied Father Brown, rising and shaking himself in a floppy way, 'you've saved him from the electrical chair. I don't think they can kill Drugger Davis on that old vague story of the poison; and as for the convict who killed the warder, I suppose it's obvious that you haven't got him. Mr Davis is innocent of that crime, at any rate.'

'What do you mean?' demanded the other. 'Why should he be innocent of that crime?'

'Why, bless us all!' cried the small man in one of his rare moments of animation, 'Why, because he's guilty of the other crimes! I don't know what you people are made of. You seem to think that all sins are kept together in a bag. You talk as if a miser on Monday were always a spendthrift on Tuesday. You tell me this man you have here spent weeks and months wheedling needy women out of small sums of money; that he used a drug at the best, and a poison at the worst; that he turned up afterwards as the lowest kind of moneylender, and cheated most poor people in the same patient and pacific style. Let it be granted—let us admit, for the sake of argument, that he did all this. If that is so, I will tell you what he didn't do. He didn't storm a spiked wall against a man with a loaded gun. He didn't write on the wall with his own hand, to say he had done it. He didn't stop to state that his justification was self-defence. He didn't explain that he had no quarrel with the poor warder. He didn't name the house of the rich man to which he was going with the gun. He didn't write his own initials in a man's blood. Saints alive! Can't you see the whole character is different, in good and evil? Why, you don't seem to be like I am a bit. One would think you'd never had any vices of your own.'

The amazed American had already parted his lips in protest when the door of his private and official room was hammered and rattled in an unceremonious way to which he was totally unaccustomed.

The door flew open. The moment before Greywood Usher had been coming to the conclusion that Father Brown might possibly be mad. The moment after he began to think he was mad himself. There burst and fell into his private room a man in the filthiest rags, with a greasy squash hat still askew on his head, and a shabby green shade shoved up from one of his eyes, both of which were glaring like a tiger's. The rest of his face was almost undiscoverable, being masked with a matted beard and whiskers through which the nose could barely thrust itself, and further buried in a squalid red scarf or handkerchief. Mr Usher prided himself on having seen most of the roughest specimens in the State, but he thought he had never seen such a baboon dressed as a scarecrow as this. But, above all, he had never in all his placid scientific existence heard a man like that speak to him first.

'See here, old man Usher,' shouted the being in the red handkerchief, 'I'm getting tired. Don't you try any of your hide-and-seek on me; I don't get fooled any. Leave go of my guest, and I'll let up on the fancy clockwork. Keep him here for a split instant and you'll feel pretty mean. I reckon I'm not a man with no pull.'

The eminent Usher was regarding the bellowing monster with an amazement which had dried up all other sentiments. The mere shock to his eyes had rendered his ears almost useless. At last he rang a bell with a hand of violence. While the bell was still strong and pealing, the voice of Father Brown fell soft but distinct.

'I have a suggestion to make,' he said, 'but it seems a little confusing. I don't know this gentleman—but—but I think I know him. Now, you know him—you know him quite well—but you don't know him—naturally. Sounds paradoxical, I know.'

'I reckon the Cosmos is cracked,' said Usher, and fell asprawl in his round office chair.

'Now, see here,' vociferated the stranger, striking the table, but speaking in a voice that was all the more mysterious because it was comparatively mild and rational though still resounding. 'I won't let you in. I want——'

136

'Who in hell are you?' yelled Usher, suddenly sitting up straight.

'I think the gentleman's name is Todd,' said the priest.

Then he picked up the pink slip of newspaper.

'I fear you don't read the Society papers properly,' he said, and began to read out in a monotonous voice, ' "Or locked in the jewelled bosoms of our city's gayest leaders; but there is talk of a pretty parody of the manners and customs of the other end of Society's scale." There's been a big Slum Dinner up at Pilgrim's Pond tonight; and a man, one of the guests, disappeared. Mr Ireton Todd is a good host, and has tracked him here, without even waiting to take off his fancy-dress.'

'What man do you mean?'

'I mean the man with the comically ill-fitting clothes you saw running across the ploughed field. Hadn't you better go and investigate him? He will be rather impatient to get back to his champagne, from which he ran away in such a hurry, when the convict with the gun hove in sight.'

'Do you seriously mean——' began the official.

'Why, look here, Mr Usher,' said Father Brown quietly, 'you said the machine couldn't make a mistake; and in one sense it didn't. But the other machine did; the machine that worked it. You assumed that the man in rags jumped at the name of Lord Falconroy, because he was Lord Falconroy's murderer. He jumped at the name of Lord Falconroy because he *is* Lord Falconroy.'

'Then why the blazes didn't he say so?' demanded the staring Usher.

'He felt his plight and recent panic were hardly patrician,' replied the priest, 'so he tried to keep the name back at first. But he was just going to tell it you, when'—and Father Brown looked down at his boots—'when a woman found another name for him.'

'But you can't be so mad as to say,' said Greywood Usher, very white, 'that Lord Falconroy was Drugger Davis.'

The priest looked at him very earnestly, but with a baffling and undecipherable face.

'I am not saying anything about it,' he said. 'I leave all the rest to you. Your pink paper says that the title was recently revived for him; but those papers are very unreliable. It says he was in the States in youth; but the whole story seems very strange. Davis and Falconroy are both pretty considerable cowards, but so are lots of other men. I would not hang a dog on my own opinion about this. But I think,' he went on softly and reflectively, 'I think you Americans are too modest. I think you idealize the English aristocracy—even in assuming it to be so aristocratic. You see a good-looking Englishman in evening-dress; you know he's in the House of Lords; and you fancy he has a father. You don't allow for our national buoyancy and uplift. Many of our most influential noblemen have not only risen recently, but——'

'Oh, stop it!' cried Greywood Usher, wringing one lean hand in impatience against a shade of irony in the other's face.

'Don't stay talking to this lunatic!' cried Todd brutally. 'Take me to my friend.'

Next morning Father Brown appeared with the same demure expression, carrying yet another piece of pink newspaper.

'I'm afraid you neglect the fashionable press rather,' he said, 'but this cutting may interest you.'

Usher read the headlines, 'Last-Trick's Strayed Revellers: Mirthful Incident near Pilgrim's Pond.' The paragraph went on: 'A laughable occurrence took place outside Wilkinson's Motor Garage last night. A policeman on duty had his attention drawn by larrikins to a man in prison dress who was stepping with considerable coolness into the steering-seat of a pretty high-toned Panhard; he was accompanied by a girl wrapped in a ragged shawl. On the police interfering, the young woman threw back the shawl, and all recognized Millionaire Todd's daughter, who had just come from the Slum Freak Dinner at the Pond, where all the choicest guests were in a similar *déshabillé*. She and the gentleman who had donned prison uniform were going for the customary joy-ride.'

Under the pink slip Mr Usher found a strip of a later paper, headed, 'Astounding Escape of Millionaire's Daughter with Convict. She had Arranged Freak Dinner. Now Safe in——'

Mr Greenwood Usher lifted his eyes, but Father Brown was gone.

THE PURPLE WIG

Mr Edward Nutt, the industrious editor of the *Daily Reformer*, sat at his desk, opening letters and marking proofs to the merry tune of a typewriter, worked by a vigorous young lady.

He was a stoutish, fair man, in his shirt-sleeves; his movements were resolute, his mouth firm and his tones final; but his round, rather babyish blue eyes had a bewildered and even wistful look that rather contradicted all this. Nor indeed was the expression altogether misleading. It might truly be said of him, as for many journalists in authority, that his most familiar emotion was one of continuous fear; fear of libel actions, fear of lost advertisements, fear of misprints, fear of the sack.

His life was a series of distracted compromises between the proprietor of the paper (and of him), who was a senile soap-boiler with three ineradicable mistakes in his mind, and the very able staff he had collected to run the paper; some of whom were brilliant and experienced men and (what was even worse) sincere enthusiasts for the political policy of the paper.

A letter from one of these lay immediately before him, and rapid and resolute as he was, he seemed almost to hesitate before opening it. He took up a strip of proof instead, ran down it with a blue eye, and a blue pencil, altered the word 'adultery' to the word 'impropriety,' and the word 'Jew' to the word 'Alien,' rang a bell and sent it flying upstairs.

Then, with a more thoughtful eye, he ripped open the letter from his more distinguished contributor, which bore a postmark of Devonshire, and ran as follows:

'DEAR NUTT,—*As I see you're working Spooks and Dooks at the same time, what about an article on that rum business of the Eyres of Exmoor; or as the old women call it down here, the Devil's Ear of Eyre? The head of the family, you know, is the Duke of Exmoor; he is one of the few really stiff old Tory aristocrats left, a sound old crusted tyrant it is quite in our line to make trouble about. And I think I'm on the track of a story that will make trouble.*

'*Of course I don't believe in the old legend about James I; and as for you, you don't believe in anything, not even in journalism. The legend, you'll probably remember, was about the blackest business in English history—the poisoning of Overbury by that witch's cat Frances Howard, and the quite mysterious terror which forced the King to pardon the murderers. There was a lot of alleged witchcraft mixed up with it; and the story goes that a manservant listening at the keyhole heard the truth in a talk between the King and Carr; and the bodily ear with which he heard grew large and monstrous as by magic, so awful was the secret. And though he had to be loaded with lands and gold and made an ancestor of dukes, the elf-shaped ear is still recurrent in the family. Well, you don't believe in black magic; and if you did, you couldn't use it for copy. If a miracle happened in your office, you'd have to hush it up, now so many bishops are agnostics. But that is not the point. The point is that there really is something queer about Exmoor and his family; something quite natural, I dare say, but quite abnormal. And the Ear is in it somehow, I fancy; either a symbol or a delusion or a disease or something. Another tradition says that Cavaliers just after James I began to wear their hair long only to cover the ear of the first Lord Exmoor. This also is no doubt fanciful.*

'The reason I point this out to you is this: It seems to me that we make a mistake in attacking aristocracy entirely for its champagne and diamonds. Most men rather admire the nobs for having a good time, but I think we surrender too much when we admit that aristocracy has made even the aristocrats happy. I suggest a series of articles pointing out how dreary, how inhuman, how downright diabolist, is the very smell and atmosphere of some of these great houses. There are plenty of instances; but you couldn't begin with a better one than the Ear of the Eyres. By the end of the week I think I can get you the truth about it.—Yours ever, FRANCIS FINN.'

Mr Nutt reflected a moment, staring at his left boot; then he called out in a strong, loud and entirely lifeless voice, in which every syllable sounded alike: 'Miss Barlow, take down a letter to Mr Finn, please.

DEAR FINN,—*I think it would do; copy should reach us second post Saturday.—Yours,* E. NUTT.'

This elaborate epistle he articulated as if it were all one word; and Miss Barlow rattled it down as if it were all one word. Then he took up another strip of proof and a blue pencil, and altered the word 'supernatural' to the word 'marvellous,' and the expression 'shoot down' to the expression 'repress.'

In such happy, healthful activities did Mr Nutt disport himself, until the ensuing Saturday found him at the same desk, dictating to the same typist, and using the same blue pencil on the first instalment of Mr Finn's revelations. The opening was a sound piece of slashing invective about the evil secrets of princes, and despair in the high places of the earth. Though written violently, it was in excellent English; but the editor, as usual, had given to somebody else the task of breaking it up into sub-headings, which were of a spicier sort, as 'Peeress and Poisons,' and 'The Eerie Ear,' 'The Eyres in their Eyrie,' and so on through a hundred happy changes. Then followed the legend of the Ear, amplified from Finn's first letter, and then the substance of his later discoveries, as follows:

'I know it is the practice of jounalists to put the end of the story at the beginning and call it a headline. I know that journalism largely consists in saying "Lord Jones Dead" to people who never knew that Lord Jones was alive. Your present correspondent thinks that this, like many other journalistic customs, is bad journalism; and that the *Daily Reformer* has to set a better example in such things. He proposes to tell his story as it occurred, step by step. He will use the real names of the parties, who in most cases are ready to confirm his testimony. As for the headlines, the sensational proclamations—they will come at the end.

'I was walking along a public path that threads through a private Devonshire orchard and seems to point towards Devonshire cider, when I came suddenly upon just such a place as the path suggested. It was a long, low inn, consisting really of a cottage and two barns; thatched all over with the thatch that looks like brown and grey hair grown before history. But outside the door was a sign which called it the Blue Dragon; and under the sign was one of those long rustic tables that used to stand outside most of the free English inns, before teetotallers and brewers between them destroyed freedom. And at this table sat three gentlemen, who might have lived a hundred years ago.

'Now that I know them all better, there is no difficulty about disentangling the impressions; but just then they looked like three very solid ghosts. The dominant figure, both because he was bigger in all three dimensions, and because he sat centrally in the length of the table, facing me, was a tall, fat man dressed completely in black, with a rubicund, even apoplectic visage, but a rather bald and rather bothered brow. Looking at him again, more strictly, I could not exactly say what it was that gave me the sense of antiquity, except the antique cat of his white clerical necktie and the barred wrinkles across his brow.

'It was even less easy to fix the impression in the case of the man at the right end of the table, who, to say truth, was as commonplace a person as could be seen anywhere, with a round, brown-haired head and a round snub nose, but also clad in clerical black, of a stricter cut. It was only when I saw his broad curved hat lying on the table beside him that I realized why I connected him with anything ancient. He was a Roman Catholic priest.

'Perhaps the third man at the other end of the table, had really more to do with it than the rest, though he was both slighter in physical presence and more inconsiderate in his dress. His lank limbs were clad, I might also say clutched, in very tight grey sleeves and pantaloons; he had a long, sallow, aquiline face which seemed somehow all the more saturnine because his lanterns jaws were imprisoned in his collar and neckcloth more in the style of the old stock; and his hair (which ought to have been dark brown) was of an odd dim, russet colour which, in conjunction with his yellow face looked rather purple than red. The unobtrusive yet unusual colour was all the more notable because his hair was almost unnaturally healthy and curling, and he wore it full. But, after all analysis, I incline to think that what gave me my first old-fashioned impression was simply a set of tall, old-fashioned wine glasses, one or two lemons and two churchwarden pipes. And also, perhaps, the old-world errand on which I had come.

'Being a hardened reporter, and it being apparently a public inn, I did not need to summon much of my impudence to sit down at the long table and order some cider. The big man in black seemed very learned, especially about local antiquities; the small man in black, though he talked much less, surprised me with a yet wider culture. So we got on very well together; but the third man, the old gentleman in the tight pantaloons, seemed rather distant and haughty, until I slid into the subject of the Duke of Exmoor and his ancestry.

'I thought the subject seemed to embarrass the other two a little; but it broke the spell of the third man's silence most successfully.

Speaking with restraint and with the accent of a highly educated gentleman, and puffing at intervals at his long churchwarden pipe, he proceeded to tell me some of the most horrible stories I have ever heard in my life: how one of the Eyres in the former ages had hanged his own father; and another had his wife scourged at the cart tail through the village; and another had set fire to a church full of children, and so on.

'Some of the tales, indeed, are not fit for public print; such as the story of the Scarlet Nuns, the abominable story of the Spotted Dog, or the thing that was done in the quarry. And all this red roll of impieties came from his thin, genteel lips rather primly than otherwise, as he sat sipping the wine out of his tall, thin glass.

'I could see that the big man opposite me was trying, if anything, to stop him; but he evidently held the old gentleman in considerable respect, and could not venture to do so at all abruptly. And the little priest at the other end of the table, though free from any such air of embarrassment, looked steadily at the table, and seemed to listen to the recital with great pain—as well as he might.

' "You don't seem," I said to the narrator, "to be very fond of the Exmoor pedigree."

'He looked at me a moment, his lips still prim, but whitening and tightening; then he deliberately broke his long pipe and glass on the table and stood up, the very picture of a perfect gentleman with the flaming temper of a fiend.

' "These gentlemen," he said, "will tell you whether I have cause to like it. The curse of the Eyres of old has lain heavy on this country, and many have suffered from it. They know there are none who have suffered from it as I have." And with that he crushed a piece of the fallen glass under his heel, and strode away among the green twilight of the twinkling apple-trees.

' "That is an extraordinary old gentleman," I said to the other two; "do you happen to know what the Exmoor family has done to him? Who is he?"

'The big man in black was staring at me with the wild air of a baffled bull; he did not at first seem to take it in. Then he said at last, "Don't you know who he is?"

'I reaffirmed my ignorance, and there was another silence; then the little priest said, still looking at the table, "That is the Duke of Exmoor."

'Then, before I could collect my scattered senses, he added equally quietly, but with an air of regularizing things: "My friend here is Doctor Mull, the Duke's librarian. My name is Brown."

' "But," I stammered, "if that is the Duke, why does he damn all the old dukes like that?"

' "He seems really to believe," answered the priest called Brown, "that they have left a curse on him," Then he added, with some irrelevance, "That's why he wears a wig."

'It was a few moments before his meaning dawned on me. "You don't mean that fable about the fantastic ear?" I demanded. "I've heard of it, of course, but surely it must be a superstitious yarn spun out of something much simpler. I've sometimes thought it was a wild version of one of those mutilation stories. They used to crop criminals' ears in the sixteenth century."

' "I hardly think it was that," answered the little man thoughtfully, "but it is not outside ordinary science or natural law for a family to have some deformity frequently reappearing—such as one ear bigger than the other."

'The big librarian had buried his big bald brow in his big red hands, like a man trying to think out his duty. "No," he groaned. "You do the man a wrong after all. Understand, I've no reason to defend him, or even keep faith with him. He has been a tyrant to me as to everybody else. Don't fancy because you see him sitting simply here that he isn't a great lord in the worst sense of the word. He would fetch a man a mile to ring a bell a yard off—if it would summon another man three miles to fetch a matchbox three yards off. He must have a footman to carry his walking-stick; a body servant to hold up his opera-glasses——"

' "But not a valet to brush his clothes," cut in the priest, with a curious dryness, "for the valet would want to brush his wig, too."

'The librarian turned to him and seemed to forget my presence; he was strongly moved and, I think, a little heated with wine. "I don't know how you know it, Father Brown," he said, "but you are right. He lets the whole world do everything for him—except dress him. And that he insists on doing in a literal solitude like a desert. Anybody is kicked out of the house without a character who is so much as found near his dressing-room door."

' "He seems a pleasant old party," I remarked.

' "No," replied Dr Mull quite simply; "and yet that is just what

144

I mean by saying you are unjust to him after all. Gentlemen, the Duke does really feel the bitterness about the curse that he uttered just now. He does, with sincere shame and terror, hide under that purple wig something he thinks it would blast the sons of man to see. I know it is so; and I know it is not a mere natural disfigurement, like a criminal mutilation, or a hereditary disproportion in the features. I know it is worse than that; because a man told me who was present at a scene that no man could invent, where a stronger man than any of us tried to defy the secret, and was scared away from it."

'I opened my mouth to speak, but Mull went on in oblivion of me, speaking out of the cavern of his hands. "I don't mind telling you, Father, because it's really more defending the poor Duke than giving him away. Didn't you ever hear of the time when he very nearly lost all the estates?"

'The priest shook his head; and the librarian proceeded to tell the tale as he had heard it from his predecessor in the same post, who had been his patron and instructor, and whom he seemed to trust implicitly. Up to a certain point it was a common enough tale of the decline of a great family's fortunes—the tale of a family lawyer. This lawyer, however, had the sense to cheat honestly, if the expression explains itself. Instead of using funds he held in trust, he took advantage of the Duke's carelessness to put the family in a financial hole, in which it might be necessary for the Duke to let him hold them in reality.

'The lawyer's name was Isaac Green, but the Duke always called him Elisha; presumably in reference to the fact that he was quite bald, though certainly not more than thirty. He had risen very rapidly, but from very dirty beginnings; being first a "nark" or informer, and then a moneylender: but as solicitor to the Eyres he had the sense, as I say, to keep technically straight until he was ready to deal the final blow. The blow fell at dinner; and the old librarian said he should never forget the very look of the lampshades and the decanters, as the little lawyer, with a steady smile, proposed to the great landlord that they should halve the estates between them. The sequel certainly could not be overlooked; for the Duke, in dead silence, smashed a decanter on the man's bald head as suddenly as I had seen him smash the glass that day in the orchard. It left a red triangular scar on the scalp, and the lawyer's eyes altered, but not his smile.

'He rose tottering to his feet, and struck back as such men do strike. "I am glad of that," he said, "for now I can take the whole estate. The law will give it to me."

'Exmoor, it seems, was white as ashes, but his eyes still blazed. "The law will give it you," he said; "but you will not take it. . . . Why not? Why? Because it would mean the crack of doom for me, and if you take it *I shall take off my wig* . . . . Why, you pitiful plucked fowl, anyone can see your bare head. But no man shall see mine and live."

'Well, you may say what you like and make it mean what you like. But Mull swears it is the solemn fact that the lawyer, after shaking his knotted fists in the air for an instant, simply ran from the room and never reappeared in the countryside; and since then Exmoor has been feared more for a warlock than even for a landlord and a magistrate.

'Now, Dr Mull told his story with rather wild theatrical gestures, and with a passion I think at least partisan. I was quite conscious of the possibility that the whole was the extravagance of an old braggart and gossip. But before I end this half of my discoveries, I think it due to Dr Mull to record that my two first inquiries have confirmed his story. I learned from an old apothecary in the village that there was a bald man in evening-dress, giving the name of Green, who came to him one night to have a three-cornered cut on his forehead plastered. And I learnt from the legal records and old newspapers that there was a lawsuit threatened, and at least begun, by one Green against the Duke of Exmoor.'

Mr Nutt, of the *Daily Reformer*, wrote some highly incongruous words across the top of the copy, made some highly mysterious marks down the side of it, and called to Miss Barlow in the same loud, monotonous voice: 'Take down a letter to Mr Finn.'

'DEAR FINN,—*Your copy will do, but I have had to headline it a bit; and our public would never stand a Romanist priest in the story—you must keep your eye on the suburbs. I've altered him to Mr Brown, a Spiritualist.*

Yours,
E. NUTT.'

A day or two afterwards found the active and judicious editor examining, with blue eyes that seemed to grow rounder and rounder, the second instalment of Mr Finn's tale of mysteries in high life. It began with the words:

'I have made an astounding discovery. I freely confess it is quite different from anything I expected to discover, and will give a much more practical shock to the public. I venture to say, without any vanity, that the words I now write will be read all over Europe, and certainly all over America and the Colonies. And yet I heard all I have to tell before I left this same little wooden table in this same little wood of apple-trees.

'I owe it all to the small priest Brown; he is an extraordinary man. The big librarian had left the table, perhaps ashamed of his long tongue, perhaps anxious about the storm in which his mysterious master had vanished: anyway, he betook himself heavily in the Duke's tracks through the trees. Father Brown had picked up one of the lemons and was eyeing it with an odd pleasure.

' "What a lovely colour a lemon is!" he said. "There's one thing I don't like about the Duke's wig—the colour."

' "I don't think I understand," I answered.

' "I dare say he's got good reason to cover his ears, like King Midas," went on the priest, with a cheerful simplicity which somehow seemed rather flippant under the circumstances, "I can quite understand that it's nicer to cover them with hair than with brass plates or leather flaps. But if he wants to use hair, why doesn't he make it look like hair? There never was hair of that colour in this world. It looks more like a sunset-cloud coming through the wood. Why doesn't he conceal the family curse better, if he's really so ashamed of it? Shall I tell you? It's because he isn't ashamed of it. He's proud of it.

' "It's an ugly wig to be proud of—and an ugly story," I said.

' "Consider," replied this curious little man, "how you yourself really feel about such things. I don't suggest you're either more snobbish or more morbid than the rest of us: but don't you feel in a vague way that a genuine old family curse is rather a fine thing to have? Would you be ashamed, wouldn't you be a little proud, if the heir of the Glamis horror called you his friend? Or if Byron's family had confided, to you only, the evil adventures of their race? Don't be too hard on the aristocrats themselves if their heads are as weak as ours would be, and they are snobs about their own sorrows."

' "By Jove!" I cried; "and that's true enough. My own mother's family had a banshee; and, now I come to think of it, it has comforted me in many a cold hour."

' "And think," he went on, "of that stream of blood and poison that spurted from his thin lips the instant you so much as mentioned his ancestors. Why should he show every stranger over such a Chamber of Horrors unless he is proud of it? He doesn't conceal his wig, he doesn't conceal his blood, he doesn't conceal his family curse, he doesn't conceal the family crimes—*but*——"

'The little man's voice changed so suddenly, he shut his hand so sharply, and his eyes so rapidly grew rounder and brighter like a waking owl's, that it had all the abruptness of a small explosion on the table.

' "But," he ended, "*he does really conceal his toilet.*"

'It somehow completed the thrill of my fanciful nerves that at that instant the Duke appeared again silently among the glimmering trees, with his soft foot and sunset-hued hair, coming round the corner of the house in company with his librarian. Before he came within earshot, Father Brown had added quite composedly, "Why does he really hide the secret of what he does with the purple wig? Because it isn't the sort of secret we suppose."

"The Duke came round the corner and resumed his seat at the head of the table with all his native dignity. The embarrassment of the librarian left him hovering on his hind legs, like a huge bear. The Duke addressed the priest with great seriousness. "Father Brown," he said, "Doctor Mull informs me that you have come here to make a request. I no longer profess an observance of the religion of my fathers; but for their sakes, and for the sake of the days when we met before, I am very willing to hear you. But I presume you would rather be heard in private."

'Whatever I retain of the gentleman made me stand up. Whatever I have attained of the journalist made me stand still. Before this paralysis could pass, the priest had made a momentarily detaining motion. "If," he said, "your Grace will permit me my real petition, or if I retain any right to advise you, I would urge that as many people as possible should be present. All over this country I have found hundreds, even of my own faith and flock, whose imaginations are poisoned by the spell which I implore you to break. I wish we could have all Devonshire here to see you do it."

' "To see me do what?" asked the Duke, arching his eyebrows.

' "To see you take off your wig," said Father Brown.

'The Duke's face did not move; but he looked at his petitioner with a glassy stare which was the most awful expression I have ever seen on a human face. I could see the librarian's great legs wavering under him like the shadows of stems in a pool; and I could not banish from my own brain the fancy that the trees all around us were filling softly in the silence with devils instead of birds.

' "I spare you," said the Duke in a voice of inhuman pity. "I refuse. If I gave you the faintest hint of the load of horror I have to bear alone, you would lie shrieking at these feet of mine and begging to know no more. I will spare you the hint. You shall not spell the first letter of what is written on the altar of the Unknown God."

' "I know the Unknown God," said the little priest, with an unconscious grandeur of certitude that stood up like a granite tower. "I know his name; it is Satan. The true God was made flesh and dwelt among us. And I say to you, wherever you find men ruled merely by mystery, it is the mystery of iniquity. If the devil tells you something is too fearful to look at, look at it. If he says something is too terrible to hear, hear it. If you think some truth unbearable, bear it. I entreat your Grace to end this nightmare now and here at this table."

' "If I did," said the Duke in a low voice, "you and all you believe, and all by which alone you live, would be the first to shrival and perish. You would have an instant to know the great Nothing before you died."

' "The Cross of Christ be between me and harm," said Father Brown. "Take off your wig."

'I was leaning over the table in ungovernable excitement; in listening to this extraordinary duel half a thought had come into my head. "Your Grace," I cried, "I call your bluff. Take off that wig or I will knock it off."

'I suppose I can be prosecuted for assault, but I am very glad I did it. When he said, in the same voice of stone, "I refuse," I simply sprang on him. For three long instants he strained against me as if he had all hell to help him; but I forced back his head until the hairy cap fell off it. I admit that, whilst wrestling, I shut my eyes as it fell.

'I was awakened by a cry from Mull, who was also by this time at the Duke's side. His head and mine were both bending over the bald head of the wigless Duke. Then the silence was snapped by the librarian exclaiming: "What can it mean? Why, the man had nothing to hide. His ears are just like everybody else's."

' "Yes," said Father Brown, "that is what he had to hide."

'The priest walked straight up to him, but strangely enough did not even glance at his ears. He stared with an almost comical seriousness at his bald forehead, and pointed to a three-cornered cicatrice, long healed, but still discernible. 'Mr Green, I think," he said politely, "and he did get the whole estate after all."

'And now let me tell the readers of the *Daily Reformer* what I think the most remarkable thing in the whole affair. This transformation scene, which will seem to you as wild and purple as a Persian fairy-tale, has been (except for my technical assault) strictly legal and constitutional from its first beginnings. This man with the odd scar and the ordinary ears is not an impostor. Though (in one sense) he wears another man's wig and claims another man's ear, he has not stolen another man's coronet. He really is the one and only Duke of Exmoor. What happened was this. The old Duke really had a slight malformation of the ear, which really was more or less hereditary. He really was morbid about it; and it is likely enough that he did invoke it as a kind of curse in the violent scene (which undoubtedly happened) in which he struck Green with the decanter. But the contest ended very differently. Green pressed his claim and got the estates; the dispossessed nobleman shot himself and died without issue. After a decent interval the beautiful English Government revived the 'extinct' peerage of Exmoor, and bestowed it, as is usual, on the most important person, the person who had got the property.

'This man used the old feudal fables—probably, in his snobbish soul, really envied and admired them. So that thousands of poor English people trembled before a mysterious chieftain with an ancient destiny and a diadem of evil stars—when they are really trembling before a guttersnipe who was a pettifogger and a pawn-broker not twelve years ago. I think it very typical of the real case against our aristocracy as it is, and it will be till God sends us braver men.'

Mr Nutt put down the manuscript and called out with unusual sharpness: 'Miss Barlow, please take down a letter to Mr Finn:

"DEAR FINN,—*You must be mad; we can't touch this. I wanted vampires and the bad old days and aristocracy hand-in-hand with superstition. They like that. But you must know the Exmoors would never forgive this. And what would our people say then, I should like to know! Why, Sir Simon is one of Exmoor's greatest pals; and it would ruin that cousin of the Eyres that's standing for us at Bradford. Besides, old Soap-Suds was sick enough at not getting his peerage last year; he'd sack me by wire if I lost him it with such lunacy as this. And what about Duffey? He's doing us some rattling articles on 'The Heel of the Norman.' And how can he write about Normans if the man's only a solicitor? Do be reasonable.—Yours.*

E. NUTT.'

As Miss Barlow rattled away cheerfully, he crumpled up the copy and tossed it into the waste-paper basket; but not before he had, automatically and by mere force of habit, altered the word 'God' to the word 'circumstances.'

The Arrow of Heaven

It is to be feared that about a hundred detective stories have begun with the discovery that an American millionaire has been murdered; an event which is, for some reason, treated as a sort of calamity. This story, I am happy to say, has to begin with a murdered millionaire; in one sense, indeed, it has to begin with three murdered millionaires, which some may regard as an *embarras de richesse*. But it was chiefly this coincidence or continuity of criminal policy that took the whole affair out of the ordinary run of criminal cases and made it the extraordinary problem that it was.

It was very generally said that they had all fallen victims to some vendetta or curse attaching to the possession of a relic of great value both intrinsically and historically: a sort of chalice inlaid with precious stones and commonly called the Coptic Cup. Its origin was obscure, but its use was conjectured to be religious; and some attributed the fate that followed its possessors to the fanaticism of some Oriental Christian horrified at its passing through such materialistic hands. But the mysterious slayer, whether or no he was such a fanatic, was already a figure of lurid and sensational interest in the world of journalism and gossip. The nameless being was provided with a name, or a nickname. But it is only with the story of the third victim that we are now concerned; for it was only in this case that a certain Father Brown, who is the subject of these sketches, had an opportunity of making his presence felt.

When Father Brown first stepped off an Atlantic liner on to American soil, he discovered, as many another Englishman has done, that he was a much more important person than he had ever supposed. His short figure, his short-sighted and undistinguished countenance, his rather rusty-black clerical clothes, could pass through any crowd in his own country without being noticed as anything unusual, except perhaps unusually insignificant. But America has a genius for the encouragement of fame; and his appearance in one or two curious criminal problems, together with his long association with Flambeau, the ex-criminal and detective, had consolidated a reputation in America out of what was little more than a rumour in England. His round face was blank with surprise when he found himself held up on the quay by a group of journalists, as by a gang of brigands, who asked him questions about all the subjects on which he was least likely to regard himself as an authority, such as the details of female dress and the criminal statistics of the country that he had only that moment clapped his eyes on. Perhaps it was the contrast with the black embattled solidarity of this group that made more vivid another figure that stood apart from it, equally black against the burning white daylight of that brilliant place and season, but entirely solitary; a tall, rather yellow-faced man in great goggles, who arrested him with a gesture when the journalists had finished and said: 'Excuse me, but maybe you are looking for Captain Wain.'

Some apology may be made for Father Brown; for he himself would have been sincerely apologetic. It must be remembered that he had never seen America before, and more especially that he had never seen that sort of tortoise-shell spectacles before; for the fashion at this time had not spread to England. His first sensation was that of gazing at some goggling sea-monster with a faint suggestion of a diver's helmet. Otherwise the man was exquisitely dressed; and to Brown, in his innocence, the spectacles seemed the queerest disfigurement for a dandy. It was as if a dandy had adorned himself with a wooden leg as an extra touch of elegance. The question also embarrassed him. An American aviator of the name of Wain, a friend of some friends of his own in France, was indeed one of a long list of people he had some hope of seeing during his American visit; but he had never expected to hear of him so soon.

'I beg your pardon,' he said doubtfully, 'are you Captain Wain? Do you—do you know him?'

'Well, I'm pretty confident I'm not Captain Wain,' said the man in goggles, with a face of wood. 'I was pretty clear about that when I saw him waiting for you over there in the car. But the other question's a bit more problematical. I reckon I know Wain and his uncle, and old man Merton, too. I know old man Merton, but old man Merton don't know me. And he thinks he has the advantage, and I think I have the advantage. See?'

Father Brown did not quite see. He blinked at the glittering seascape and the pinnacles of the city, and then at the man in goggles. It was not only the masking of the man's eyes that produced the impression of something impenetrable. Something in his yellow face was almost Asiatic, even Chinese; and his conversation seemed to consist of stratified layers of irony. He was a type to be found here and there in that hearty and sociable population; he was the inscrutable American.

'My name's Drage,' he said, 'Norman Drage, and I'm an American citizen, which explains everything. At least I imagine your friend Wain would like to explain the rest; so we'll postpone The Fourth of July till another date.'

Father Brown was dragged in a somewhat dazed condition towards a car at some little distance, in which a young man with tufts of untidy yellow hair and a rather harassed and haggard expression, hailed him from afar and presented himself as Peter Wain. Before he knew where he was he was stowed in the car and travelling with considerable speed through and beyond the city. He was unused to the impetuous practicality of such American action, and felt about as bewildered as if a chariot drawn by dragons had carried him away into fairyland. It was under these disconcerting conditions that he heard for the first time, in long monologues from Wain, and short sentences from Drage, the story of the Coptic Cup and the two crimes already connected with it.

It seemed that Wain had an uncle named Crake who had a partner named Merton, who was number three in the series of rich business men to whom the cup had belonged. The first of them, Titus P. Trant, the Copper King, had received threatening letters from somebody signing himself Daniel Doom. The name was presumably a pseudonym, but it had come to stand for a very public if not a very popular character; for somebody as well known as Robin Hood and Jack the Ripper combined. For it soon became clear that the writer of the threatening letter did not confine himself to threatening. Anyhow, the upshot was that old Trant was found one morning with his head in his own lilypond, and there was not the shadow of a clue. The cup was, fortunately, safe in the bank; and it passed with the rest of Trant's property to his cousin, Brian Horder, who was also a man of great wealth and who was also threatened by the nameless enemy. Brian Horder was picked up dead at the foot of a cliff outside his seaside residence, at which there was a burglary, this time on a large scale. For though the cup apparently again escaped, enough bonds and securities were stolen to leave Horder's financial affairs in confusion.

'Brian Horder's widow,' explained Wain, 'had to sell most of his valuables, I believe, and Brandon Merton must have purchased the cup at that time, for he had it when I first knew him. But you can guess for yourself that it's not a very comfortable thing to have.'

'Has Mr Merton ever had any of the threatening letters?' asked Father Brown, after a pause.

'I imagine he has,' said Mr Drage; and something in his voice made the priest look at him curiously, until he realized that the man in goggles was laughing silently, in a fashion that gave the newcomer something of a chill.

'I'm pretty sure he has,' said Peter Wain, frowning. 'I've not seen the letters, only his secretary sees any of his letters, for he is pretty reticent about business matters, as big business men have to be. But I've seen him real upset and annoyed with letters; and letters that he tore up, too, before even his secretary saw them. The secretary himself is getting nervous and says he is sure somebody is laying for the old man; and the long and the short of it is, that we'd be very grateful for a little advice in the matter. Everybody knows your great reputation, Father Brown, and the secretary asked me to see if you'd mind coming straight out to the Merton house at once.'

'Oh, I see,' said Father Brown, on whom the meaning of this apparent kidnapping began to drawn at last. 'But, really, I don't see that I can do any more than you can. You're on the spot, and must have a hundred times more data for a scientific conclusion than a chance visitor.'

'Yes,' said Mr Drage dryly; 'our conclusions are much too scientific to be true. I reckon if anything hit a man like Titus P. Trant, it just came out of the sky without waiting for any scientific explanation. What they call a bolt from the blue.'

'You can't possibly mean,' cried Wain, 'that it was supernatural!'

But it was by no means easy at any time to discover what Mr Drage could possibly mean; except that if he said somebody was a real smart man, he very probably meant he was a fool. Mr Drage maintained an Oriental immobility until the car stopped, a little while after, at what was obviously their destination. It was rather a singular place. They had been driving through a thinly-wooded country that opened into a wide plain, and just in front of them was a building consisting of a single wall or very high fence, round, like a Roman camp and having rather the appearance of an aerodrome. The barrier did not look like wood or stone, and closer inspection proved it to be of metal.

They all alighted from the car, and one small door in the wall was slid open with considerable caution, after manipulations resembling the opening of a safe. But, much to Father Brown's surprise, the man called Norman Drage showed no disposition to enter, but took leave of them with sinister gaiety.

'I won't come in,' he said. 'It 'ud be too much pleasurable excitement for old man Merton, I reckon. He loves the sight of me so much that he'd die of joy.'

And he strode away, while Father Brown, with increasing wonder, was admitted through the steel door which instantly clicked behind him. Inside was a large and elaborate garden of gay and varied colours, but entirely without any trees or tall shrubs or flowers. In the centre of it rose a house of handsome and even striking architecture, but so high and narrow as rather to resemble a tower. The burning sunlight gleamed on glass roofing here and there at the top, but there seemed to be no windows at all in the lower part of it. Over everything was that spotless and sparkling cleanliness that seemed so native to the clear American air. When they came inside the portal, they stood amid resplendent marble and metals and enamels of brilliant colours, but there was no staircase. Nothing but a single shaft for a lift went up the centre between the solid walls, and the approach to it was guarded by heavy, powerful men like plain-clothes policemen.

'Pretty elaborate protection, I know,' said Wain. 'Maybe it makes you smile a little, Father Brown, to find Merton has to live in a fortress like this without even a tree in the garden for anyone to hide behind. But you don't know what sort of proposition we're up against in this country. And perhaps you don't know just what the name of Brander Merton means. He's a quiet-looking man enough, and anybody might pass him in the street; not that they get much chance nowadays, for he can only go out now and then in a closed car. But if anything happened to Brander Merton there'd be earthquakes from Alaska to the Cannibal Islands. I fancy there was never a king or emperor who had such power over the nations as he has. After all, I suppose if you'd been asked to visit the tsar, or the king of England, you'd have had the curiosity to go. You mayn't care much for tsars or millionaires; but it just means that power like that is always interesting. And I hope it's not against your principles to visit a modern sort of emperor like Merton.'

'Not at all,' said Father Brown, quietly. 'It is my duty to visit prisoners and all miserable men in captivity.'

There was a silence, and the young man frowned with a strange and almost shifty look on his lean face. Then he said, abruptly:

'Well, you've got to remember it isn't only common crooks or the Black Hand that's against him. This Daniel Doom is pretty much like the Devil. Look how he dropped Trant in his own gardens and Horder outside his house, and got away with it.'

The top floor of the mansion, inside the enormously thick walls, consisted of two rooms; an outer room which they entered, and an inner room that was the great millionaire's sanctum. They entered the outer room just as two other visitors were coming out of the inner one. One was hailed by Peter Wain as his uncle—a small but very stalwart and active man with a shaven head that looked bald, and a brown face that looked almost too brown to have ever been white. This was old Crake, commonly called Hickory Crake in reminiscence of the more famous Old Hickory, because of his fame in the last Red Indian wars. His companion was a singular contrast—a very dapper gentleman with dark hair like a black varnish and a broad, black ribbon to his monocle: Barnard Blake, who was old Merton's lawyer and had been discussing with the partners the business of the firm. The four men met in the middle of the outer room and paused for a little polite conversation, in the act of respectively going and coming. And through all goings and comings another figure sat at the back of the room near the inner door, massive and motionless in the half-light from the inner window; a man with a negro face and enormous shoulders. This was what the humorous self-criticism of America playfully calls the Bad Man; whom his friends might call a bodyguard and his enemies a bravo.

This man never moved or stirred to greet anybody; but the sight of him in the outer room seemed to move Peter Wain to his first nervous query.

'Is anybody with the chief?' he asked.

'Don't get rattled, Peter,' chuckled his uncle. 'Wilton the secretary is with him, and I hope that's enough for anybody. I don't believe Wilton ever sleeps for watching Merton. He is better than twenty bodyguards. And he's quick and quiet as an Indian.'

'Well, you ought to know,' said his nephew, laughing. 'I remember the Red Indian tricks you used to teach me when I was a boy and liked to read Red Indian stories. But in my Red Indian stories Red Indians seemed always to have the worst of it.'

'They didn't in real life,' said the old frontiersman grimly.

'Indeed?' inquired the bland Mr Blake. 'I should have thought they could do very little against our firearms.'

'I've seen an Indian stand under a hundred guns with nothing but a little scalping-knife and kill a white man standing on the top of a fort,' said Crake.

'Why, what did he do with it?' asked the other.

'Threw it,' replied Crake, 'threw it in a flash before a shot could be fired. I don't know where he learnt the trick.'

'Well, I hope you didn't learn it,' said his nephew, laughing.

'It seems to me,' said Father Brown, thoughtfully, 'that the story might have a moral.'

While they were speaking Mr Wilton, the secretary, had come out of the inner room and stood waiting; a pale, fair-haired man with a square chin and steady eyes with a look like a dog's; it was not difficult to believe that he had the single-eye of a watchdog.

He only said, 'Mr Merton can see you in about ten minutes,' but it served for a signal to break up the gossiping group. Old Crake said he must be off, and his nephew went out with him and his legal companion, leaving Father Brown for the moment alone with his secretary; for the negroid giant at the other end of the room could hardly be felt as if he were human or alive; he sat so motionless with his broad back to them, staring towards the inner room.

'Arrangements rather elaborate here, I'm afraid,' said the secretary. 'You've probably heard all about this Daniel Doom, and why it isn't safe to leave the boss very much alone.'

'But he is alone just now, isn't he?' said Father Brown.

The secretary looked at him with grave, grey eyes.

'For fifteen minutes,' he said. 'For fifteen minutes out of the twenty-four hours. That is all the real solitude he has; and that he insists on, for a pretty remarkable reason.'

'And what is the reason?' inquired the visitor.

Wilton, the secretary, continued his steady gaze, but his mouth, that had been merely grave, became grim.

'The Coptic Cup,' he said. 'Perhaps you've forgotten the Coptic Cup; but he hasn't forgotten that or anything else. He doesn't trust any of us about the Coptic Cup. It's locked up somewhere and somehow in that room so that only he can find it; and he won't take it out till we're all out of the way. So we have to risk that quarter of an hour while he sits and worships it; I reckon it's the only worshipping he does. Not that there's any risk really; for I've turned all this place into a trap I don't believe the devil himself could get into—or at any rate, get out of. If this infernal Daniel Doom pays us a visit, he'll stay to dinner and a good bit later, by God! I sit here on hot bricks for the fifteen minutes, and the instant I heard a shot or a sound of struggle I'd press this button and an electrocuting current would run in a ring round that garden wall, so that it 'ud be death to cross or climb it. Of course, there couldn't be a shot, for this is the only way in; and the only window he sits at is away up on the top of a tower as smooth as a greasy pole. But, anyhow, we're all armed here, of course; and if Doom did get into that room he'd be dead before he got out.'

Father Brown was blinking at the carpet in a brown study. Then he said suddenly, with something like a jerk:

'I hope you won't mind my mentioning it, but a kind of a notion came into my head just this minute. It's about you.'

'Indeed,' remarked Wilton, 'and what about me?'

'I think you are a man of one idea,' said Father Brown, 'and you will forgive me for saying that it seems to be even more the idea of catching Daniel Doom than of defending Brander Merton.'

Wilton started a little and continued to stare at his companion; then very slowly his grim mouth took on a rather curious smile.

'How did you—what makes you think that?' he asked.

'You said that if you heard a shot you could instantly electrocute the escaping enemy,' remarked the priest. 'I suppose it occurred to you that the shot might be fatal to your employer before the shock was fatal to his foe. I don't mean that you wouldn't protect Mr Merton if you could, but it seems to come rather second in your thoughts. The arrangements are very elaborate, as you say, and you seem to have elaborated them. But they seem even more designed to catch a murderer than to save a man.'

'Father Brown,' said the secretary, who had recovered his quiet tone, 'you're very smart, but there's something more to you than smartness. Somehow you're the sort of man to whom one wants to tell the truth; and besides, you'll probably hear it, anyhow, for in one way it's a joke against me already. They all say I'm a monomaniac about running down this big crook, and perhaps I am. But I'll tell you one thing that none of them know. My full name is John Wilton Horder.' Father Brown nodded as if he were completely enlightened, but the other went on.

'This fellow who calls himself Doom killed my father and uncle and ruined my mother. When Merton wanted a secretary I took the job, because I thought that where the cup was the criminal might sooner or later be. But I didn't know who the criminal was and could only wait for him; and I meant to serve Merton faithfully.'

'I understand,' said Father Brown gently; 'and, by the way, isn't it time that we attended on him?'

'Why, yes,' answered Wilton, again starting a little out of his brooding so that the priest concluded that his vindictive mania had again absorbed him for a moment. 'Go in now by all means.'

Father Brown walked straight into the inner room. No sound of greetings followed, but only a dead silence; and a moment after the priest reappeared in the doorway.

At the same moment the silent bodyguard sitting near the door moved suddenly; and it was as if a huge piece of furniture had come to life. It seemed as though something in the very attitude of the priest had been a signal; for his head was against the light from the inner window and his face was in shadow.

'I suppose you will press that button,' he said with a sort of sigh.

Wilton seemed to awake from his savage brooding with a bound and leapt up with a catch in his voice.

'There was no shot,' he cried.

'Well,' said Father Brown, 'it depends what you mean by a shot.'

Wilton rushed forward, and they plunged into the inner room together. It was a comparatively small room and simply though elegantly furnished. Opposite to them one wide window stood open, over-looking the garden and the wooded plain. Close up against the window stood a chair and a small table, as if the captive desired as much air and light as was allowed him during his brief luxury of loneliness.

On the little table under the window stood the Coptic Cup; its owner had evidently been looking at it in the best light. It was well worth looking at, for that white and brilliant daylight turned its precious stones to many-coloured flames so that it might have been a model of the Holy Grail. It was well worth looking at; but Brander Merton was not looking at it. For his head had fallen back over his chair, his mane of white hair hanging towards the floor, and his spike of grizzled beard thrust up towards the ceiling, and out of his throat stood a long, brown-painted arrow with red feathers at the other end.

'A silent shot,' said Father Brown, in a low voice; 'I was just wondering about those new inventions for silencing firearms. But this is a very old invention, and quite as silent.'

Then, after a moment, he added: 'I'm afraid he is dead. What are you going to do?'

The pale secretary roused himself with abrupt resolution. 'I'm going to press that button, of course,' he said, 'and if that doesn't do for Daniel Doom, I'm going to hunt him through the world till I find him.'

'Take care it doesn't do for any of our friends,' observed Father Brown; 'they can hardly be far off; we'd better call them.'

'That lot know all about the wall,' answered Wilton. 'None of them will try to climb it, unless one of them . . . is in a great hurry.'

Father Brown went to the window by which the arrow had evidently entered and looked out. The garden, with its flat flower-beds, lay far below like a delicately coloured map of the world. The whole vista seemed so vast and empty, the tower seemed set so far up in the sky that as he stared out a strange phrase came back to his memory.

'A bolt from the blue,' he said. 'What was that somebody said about a bolt from the blue and death coming out of the sky? Look how far away everything looks; it seems extraordinary that an arrow could come so far, unless it were an arrow from heaven.'

Wilton had returned, but did not reply, and the priest went on as in soliloquy.

'One thinks of aviation. We must ask young Wain . . . about aviation.'

'There's a lot of it round here,' said the secretary.

'Case of very old or very new weapons,' observed Father Brown. 'Some would be quite familiar to his old uncle, I suppose; we must ask him about arrows. This looks rather like a Red Indian arrow. I don't know where the Red Indian shot it from; but you remember the story the old man told. I said it had a moral.'

'If it had a moral,' said Wilton warmly, 'it was only that a real

Red Indian might shoot a thing farther than you'd fancy. It's nonsense your suggesting a parallel.'

'I don't think you've got the moral quite right,' said Father Brown.

Although the little priest appeared to melt into the millions of New York next day, without any apparent attempt to be anything but a number in a numbered street, he was, in fact, unobtrusively busy for the next fortnight with the commission that had been given him, for he was filled with profound fear about a possible miscarriage of justice. Without having any particular air of singling them out from his other new acquaintances, he found it easy to fall into talk with the two or three men recently involved in the mystery; and with old Hickory Crake especially he had a curious and interesting conversation. It took place on a seat in Central Park, where the veteran sat with his bony hands and hatchet face resting on the oddly-shaped head of a walking-stick of dark red wood, possibly modelled on a tomahawk.

'Well, it may be a long shot,' he said, wagging his head, 'but I wouldn't advise you to be too positive about how far an Indian arrow could go. I've known some bow-shots that seemed to go straighter than any bullets, and hit the mark to amazement, considering how long they had been travelling. Of course, you practically never hear now of a Red Indian with a bow and arrows, still less of a Red Indian hanging about here. But if by any chance there were one of the old Indian marksmen, with one of the old Indian bows, hiding in those trees hundred of yards beyond the Merton outer wall—why, then I wouldn't put it past the noble savage to be able to send an arrow over the wall and into the top window of Merton's house; no, nor into Merton, either. I've seen things quite as wonderful as that done in the old days.'

'No doubt,' said the priest, 'you have done things quite as wonderful, as well as seen them.'

Old Crake chuckled, and then said gruffly: 'Oh, that's all ancient history.'

'Some people have a way of studying ancient history,' the priest said. 'I suppose we may take it there is nothing in your old record to make people talk unpleasantly about this affair.'

'What do you mean?' demanded Crake, his eyes shifting sharply for the first time, in his red, wooden face, that was rather like the head of a tomahawk.

'Well, since you were so well acquainted with all the arts and crafts of the Redskin——' began Father Brown slowly.

Crake had had a hunched and almost shrunken appearance as he sat with his chin propped on its queer-shaped crutch. But the next instant he stood erect in the path like a fighting bravo with the crutch clutched like a cudgel.

'What?' he cried—in something like a raucous screech—'What the hell! Are you standing up to me to tell me I might happen to have murdered my own brother-in-law?'

From a dozen seats dotted about the path people looked towards the disputants, as they stood facing each other in the middle of the path, the bald-headed energetic little man brandishing his outlandish stick like a club, and the black dumpy figure of the little cleric looking at him without moving a muscle, save for his blinking eyelids. For a moment it looked as if the black, dumpy figure would be knocked on the head, and laid out with true Red Indian promptitude and dispatch; and the large form of an Irish policeman could be seen heaving up the distance and bearing down on the group. But the priest only said, quite placidly, like one answering an ordinary query:

'I have formed certain conclusions about it, but I do not think I will mention them till I make my report.'

Whether under the influence of the footsteps of the policeman or of the eyes of the priest, old Hickory tucked his stick under his arm and put his hat on again, grunting. The priest bade him a placid good morning, and passed in an unhurried fashion out of the park, making his way to the lounge of the hotel where he knew that young Wain was to be found. The young man sprang up with a greeting; he looked even more haggard and harassed than before, as if some worry were eating him away; and the priest had a suspicion that his young friend had recently been engaged, with only too conspicuous success, in evading the last Amendment to the American Constitution. But at the first word about his hobby or favourite science he was vigilant and concentrated enough. For Father Brown had asked, in an idle and conversational fashion, whether much flying was done in that district, and had told how he had at first mistaken Mr Merton's circular wall for an aerodrome.

'It's a wonder you didn't see any while we were there,' answered Captain Wain. 'Sometimes they're as thick as flies; that open plain is a great place for them, and I shouldn't wonder if it were the chief

163

breeding-ground, so to speak, for my sorts of birds in the future. I've flown a good deal there myself, of course, and I know most of the fellows about here who flew in the war; but there are a whole lot of people taking to it out there now whom I never heard of in my life. I suppose it will be like motoring soon, and every man in the States will have one.'

'Being endowed by his Creator,' said Father Brown with a smile, 'with the right to life, liberty and the pursuit of motoring—not to mention aviation. So I suppose we may take it that one strange aeroplane passing over that house, at certain times, wouldn't be noticed much.'

'No,' replied the young man; 'I don't suppose it would.'

'Or even if the man were known,' went on the other, 'I suppose he might get hold of a machine that wouldn't be recognized as his. If you, for instance, flew in the ordinary way, Mr Merton and his friends might recognize the rig-out, perhaps; but you might pass pretty near that window on a different pattern of plane, or whatever you call it; near enough for practical purposes.'

'Well, yes,' began the young man, almost automatically, and then ceased, and remained staring at the cleric with an open mouth and eyes standing out of his head.

'My God!' he said, in a low voice; 'my God!'

Then he rose from the lounge seat, pale and shaking from head to foot and still staring at the priest.

'Are you mad?' he said; 'are you raving mad?'

There was a silence and then he spoke again in a swift hissing fashion. 'You positively come here to suggest——'

'No; only to collect suggestions,' said Father Brown, rising. 'I may have formed some conclusions provisionally, but I had better reserve them for the present.'

And then saluting the other with the same stiff civility, he passed out of the hotel to continue his curious peregrinations.

By the dusk of that day they had led him down the dingy streets and steps that straggled and tumbled towards the river in the oldest and most irregular part of the city. Immediately under the coloured lantern that marked the entrance to a rather low Chinese restaurant he encountered a figure he had seen before, though by no means presenting itself to the eye as he had seen it.

Mr Norman Drage still confronted the world grimly behind his great goggles, which seemed somehow to cover his face like a dark mask of glass. But except for the goggles, his appearance had undergone a strange transformation in the mouth that had elapsed since the murder. He had then, as Father Brown had noted, been dressed up to the nines—up to that point, indeed, where there begins to be too fine a distinction between the dandy and the dummy outside a tailor's shop. But now all those externals were mysteriously altered for the worse; as if the tailor's dummy had been turned into a scarecrow. His top hat still existed, but it was battered and shabby; his clothes were dilapidated; his watch-chain and minor ornaments were gone. Father Brown, however, addressed him as if they had met yesterday, and made no demur to sitting down with him on a bench in the cheap eating-house whither he was bound. It was not he, however, who began the conversation.

'Well?' growled Drage; 'and have you succeeded in avenging your holy and sainted millionaire? We know all millionaires are holy and sainted; you can find it all in the papers next day, about how they lived by the light of the Family Bible they read at their mother's knee. Gee! If they'd only read out some of the things there are in the Family Bible, the mother might have been startled some. And the millionaire, too, I reckon. The old Book's full of a lot of grand fierce old notions they don't grow nowadays; sort of wisdom of the Stone Age and buried under the Pyramids. Suppose somebody had flung old man Merton from the top of that tower of his, and let him be eaten by dogs at the bottom, it would be no worse than what happened to Jezebel. Wasn't Agag hacked into little pieces, for all he went walking delicately? Merton walked delicately all his life, damn him—until he got too delicate to walk at all. But the shaft of the Lord found him out, as it might have done in the old Book, and struck him dead on the top of his tower to be a spectacle to the people.'

'The shaft was material, at least,' said his companion.

'The Pyramids are mighty material, and they hold down the dead kings all right,' grinned the man in the goggles. 'I think there's a lot to be said for these old material religions. There's old carvings that have lasted for thousands of years, showing their gods and emperors with bended bows; with hands that look as if they could really bend bow of stone. Material, perhaps—but what materials! Don't you sometimes stand staring at those old Eastern patterns and things, till you have a hunch that that old Lord God is still driving like a dark Apollo, and shooting black rays of death?'

'If he is,' replied Father Brown, 'I might call him by another name. But I doubt whether Merton died by a dark ray or even a stone arrow.'

'I guess you think he's St Sebastian,' sneered Drage, 'killed with an arrow. A millionaire must be a martyr. How do you know he didn't deserve it? You don't know much about your millionaire, I fancy. Well, let me tell you he deserved it a hundred times over.'

'Well,' asked Father Brown gently, 'why didn't you murder him?'

'You want to know why I didn't?' said the other, staring. 'Well, you're a nice sort of clergyman.'

'Not at all,' said the other, as if waving away a compliment.

'I suppose it's your way of saying I did,' snarled Drage. 'Well, prove it, that's all. As for him, I reckon he was no loss.'

'Yes, he was,' said Father Brown, sharply. 'He was a loss to you. That's why you didn't kill him.'

And he walked out of the room, leaving the man in goggles gaping after him.

It was nearly a month later that Father Brown revisited the house where the third millionaire had suffered from the vendetta of Daniel Doom. A sort of council was held of the persons most interested. Old Crake sat at the head of the table with his nephew on his right hand the lawyer on his left; the big man with the African features, whose name appeared to be Harris, was ponderously present, if only as a material witness; a red-haired, sharp-nosed individual addressed as Dixon seemed to be the representative of Pinkerton's or some such private agency; and Father Brown slipped unobtrusively into an empty seat beside him.

Every newspaper in the world was full of the catastrophe of the colossus of finance, of the great organizer of the Big Business that bestrides the modern world; but from the tiny group that had been nearest to him at the very instant of his death very little could be learned. The uncle, nephew, and attendant solicitor declared they were well outside the outer wall before the alarm was raised; and inquiries of the official guardians at both barriers brought answers that were rather confused, but on the whole confirmatory. Only one other complication seemed to call for consideration. It seemed that round about the time of the death, before or after, a stranger had been found hanging mysteriously round the entrance and asking to see Mr Merton. The servants had some difficulty in understanding what he meant, for his language was very obscure; but it was afterwards considered to be also very suspicious, since he had said something about a wicked man being destroyed by a word out of the sky.

Peter Wain leaned forward, the eyes bright in his haggard face, and said:

'I'll bet on that, anyhow, Norman Drage.'

'And who in the world is Norman Drage?' asked his uncle.

'That's what I want to know,' replied the young man. 'I practically asked him, but he has got a wonderful trick of twisting every straight question crooked; it's like lunging at a fencer. He hooked on to me with hints about the flying-ship of the future; but I never trusted him much.'

'But what sort of a man is he?' asked Crake.

'He's a mystagogue,' said Father Brown, with innocent promptitude. 'There are quite a lot of them about; the sort of men about town who hint to you in Paris cafés and cabarets that they've lifted the veil of Isis or know the secret of Stonehenge. In a case like this they're sure to have some sort of mystical explanations.'

The smooth, dark head of Mr Barnard Blake, the lawyer, was inclined politely towards the speaker, but his smile was faintly hostile.

'I should hardly have thought, sir,' he said, 'that you had any quarrel with mystical explanations.'

'On the contrary,' replied Father Brown, blinking amiably at him. 'That's just why I can quarrel with 'em. Any sham lawyer could bamboozle me, but he couldn't bamboozle you; because you're a lawyer yourself. Any fool could dress up as a Red Indian and I'd swallow him whole as the only original Hiawatha; but Mr Crake would see through him at once. A swindler could pretend to me that he knew all about aeroplanes, but not to Captain Wain. And it's just the same with the other, don't you see? It's just because I have picked up a little about mystics that I have no use for mystagogues. Real mystics don't hide mysteries, they reveal them. They set a thing up in broad daylight, and when you've seen it it's still a mystery. But the mystagogues hide a thing in darkness and secrecy, and when you find it, it's a platitude. But in the case of Drage, I admit he had also another and more practical notion in talking about fire from heaven or bolts from the blue.'

'And what was his notion?' asked Wain. 'I think it wants watching, whatever it is.'

'Well,' replied the priest, slowly, 'he wanted us to think the murders were miracles because . . . well, because he knew they weren't.'

'Ah,' said Wain, with a sort of hiss, 'I was waiting for that. In plain words, he is the criminal.'

'In plain words, he is the criminal who didn't commit the crime,' answered Father Brown calmly.

'Is that your conception of plain words?' inquired Blake politely.

'You'll be saying I'm the mystagogue now,' said Father Brown, somewhat abashed, but with a broad smile, 'but it was really quite accidental. Drage didn't commit the crime—I mean this crime. His only crime was blackmailing somebody, and he hung about here to do it; but he wasn't likely to want the secret to be public property or the whole business to be cut short by death. We can talk about him afterwards. Just at the moment, I only want him cleared out of the way.'

'Out of the way of what?' asked the other.

'Out of the way of the truth,' replied the priest, looking at him tranquilly, with level eyelids.

'Do you mean,' faltered the other, 'that you know the truth?'

'I rather think so,' said Father Brown modestly.

There was an abrupt silence, after which Crake cried out suddenly and irrelevantly in a rasping voice:

'Why, where is that secretary fellow? Wilton! He ought to be here.'

'I am in communication with Mr Wilton,' said Father Brown gravely; 'in fact, I asked him to ring me up here in a few minutes from now. I may say that we've worked the thing out together, in a manner of speaking.'

'If you're working together, I suppose it's all right,' grumbled Crake. 'I know he was always a sort of bloodhound on the trail of this vanishing crook, so perhaps it was well to hunt in couples with him. But if you know the truth about this, where the devil did you get it from?'

'I got it from you,' answered the priest, quietly, and continued to gaze mildly at the glaring veteran. 'I mean I made the first guess from a hint in a story of yours about an Indian who threw a knife and hit a man on the top of a fortress.'

'You've said that several times,' said Wain with a puzzled air; 'but I can't see any inference, except that his murderer threw an arrow and hit a man on the top of a house very like a fortress. But of course the arrow wasn't thrown but shot, and would go much farther. Certainly it went uncommonly far; but I don't see how it brings us any farther.'

'I'm afraid you missed the point of the story,' said Father Brown. 'It isn't that if one thing can go far another can go farther. It is that the wrong use of a tool can cut both ways. The men on Crake's fort thought of a knife as a thing for a hand-to-hand fight and forgot that it could be a missile like a javelin. Some other people I know thought of a thing as a missile like a javelin and forgot that, after all, it could be used hand-to-hand as a spear. In short, the moral of the story is that since a dagger can be turned into an arrow, so can an arrow be turned into a dagger.'

They were all looking at him now; but he continued in the same casual and unconscious tone:

'Naturally we wondered and worried a good deal about who shot that arrow through the window and whether it came from far away, and so on. But the truth is that nobody shot the arrow at all. It never came in at the window at all.'

'Then how did it come there?' asked the swarthy lawyer, with a rather lowering face.

'Somebody brought it with him, I suppose,' said Father Brown; 'it wouldn't be hard to carry or conceal. Somebody had it in his hand as he stood with Merton in Merton's own room. Somebody thrust it into Merton's throat like a poignard, and then had the highly intelligent idea of placing the whole thing at such a place and angle that we all assumed in a flash that it had flown in at the window like a bird.'

'Somebody,' said old Crake, in a voice as heavy as stone.

The telephone bell rang with a strident and horrible clamour of insistence. It was in the adjoining room, and Father Brown had darted there before anybody else could move.

'What the devil is it all about?' cried Peter Wain, who seemed all shaken and distracted.

'He said he expected to be rung up by Wilton, the secretary,' replied his uncle in the same dead voice.

'I suppose it is Wilton?' observed the lawyer, like one speaking to fill up a silence. But nobody answered the question until Father Brown reappeared suddenly and silently in the room, bringing the answer.

'Gentlemen,' he said, when he had resumed his seat, 'it was you who asked me to look into the truth about this puzzle; and having found the truth, I must tell it, without any pretence of softening the shock. I'm afraid anybody who pokes his nose into things like this can't afford to be a respecter of persons.'

'I suppose,' said Crake, breaking the silence that followed, 'that means that some of us are accused, or suspected.'

'All of us are suspected,' answered Father Brown. 'I may be suspected myself, for I found the body.'

'Of course we're suspected,' snapped Wain. 'Father Brown kindly explained to me how I could have besieged the tower in a flying-machine.'

'No,' replied the priest, with a smile; 'you described to me how you could have done it. That was just the interesting part of it.'

'He seemed to think it likely,' growled Crake, 'that I killed him myself with a Red Indian arrow.'

'I thought it most unlikely,' said Father Brown, making rather a wry face. 'I'm sorry if I did wrong, but I couldn't think of any other way of testing the matter. I can hardly think of anything more improbable than the notion that Captain Wain went careering in a huge machine past the window, at the very moment of the murder, and nobody noticed it; unless, perhaps, it were the notion that a respectable old gentleman should play at Red Indians with a bow and arrow behind the bushes, to kill somebody he could have killed in twenty much simpler ways. But I had to find out if they had had anything to do with it; and so I had to accuse them in order to prove their innocence.'

'And how have you proved their innocence?' asked Blake the lawyer, leaning forward eagerly.

'Only by the agitation they showed when they were accused,' answered the other.

'What do you mean, exactly?'

'If you will permit me to say so,' remarked Father Brown, composedly enough, 'I did undoubtedly think it my duty to suspect them and everybody else. I did suspect Mr Crake and I did suspect Captain Wain, in the sense that I considered the possibility or probability of their guilt. I told them I had formed conclusions about it; and I will now tell them what those conclusions were. I was sure they were innocent, because of the manner and the moment in which they passed from unconsciousness to indignation. So long as they never thought they were accused, they went on giving me materials to support the accusation. They practically explained to me how they might have committed the crime. Then they suddenly realized with a shock and a shout of rage that they were accused; they realized it long after they might well have expected to be accused, but long before I had accused them. Now no guilty person could possibly do that. He might be snappy and suspicious from the first; or he might simulate unconsciousness and innocence up to the end. But he wouldn't begin by making things worse for himself and then give a great jump and begin furiously denying the notion he had himself helped to suggest. That could only come by his having really failed to realize what he was suggesting. The self-consciousness of a murderer would always be at least morbidly vivid enough to prevent him first forgetting his relation with the thing and then remembering to deny it. So I ruled you both out and others for other reasons I needn't discuss now. For instance, there was the secretary——

'But I'm not talking about that just now. Look here, I've just heard from Wilton on the 'phone, and he's given me permission to tell you some rather serious news. Now I suppose you all know by this time who Wilton was, and what he was after.'

'I know he was after Daniel Doom and wouldn't be happy till he got him,' answered Peter Wain; 'and I've heard the story that he's the son of old Horder, and that's why he's the avenger of blood. Anyhow, he's certainly looking for the man called Doom.'

'Well,' said Father Brown, 'he had found him.'

Peter Wain sprang to his feet in excitement.

'The murderer!' he cried. 'Is the murderer in the lock-up already?'

'No,' said Father Brown, gravely; 'I said the news was serious, and it's more serious than that. I'm afraid poor Wilton has taken a terrible responsibility. I'm afraid he's going to put a terrible responsibility on us. He hunted the criminal down, and just when he had him cornered at last—well, he has taken the law into his own hands.'

'You mean that Daniel Doom——' began the lawyer.

'I mean that Daniel Doom is dead,' said the priest. 'There was some sort of wild struggle, and Wilton killed him.'

'Serve him right,' growled Mr Hickory Crake.

'Can't blame Wilton for downing a crook like that, especially considering the feud,' assented Wain; 'it was like stepping on a viper.'

'I don't agree with you,' said Father Brown. 'I suppose we all talk romantic stuff at random in defence of lynching and lawlessness; but I have a suspicion that if we lose our laws and liberties we shall regret it. Besides, it seems to me illogical to say there is something to be said for Wilton committing murder, without even inquiring whether there was anything to be said for Doom committing it. I rather doubt whether Doom was merely a vulgar assassin; he may have been a sort of outlaw with a mania about the cup, demanding it with threats and only killing after a struggle; both victims were thrown down just outside their houses. The objection to Wilton's way of doing it is that we shall never hear Doom's side of the case.'

'Oh, I've no patience with all this sentimental whitewashing of worthless, murderous blackguards,' cried Wain, heatedly. 'If Wilton croaked the criminal he did a jolly good day's work, and there's an end of it.'

'Quite so, quite so,' said his uncle, nodding vigorously.

Father Brown's face had a yet heavier gravity as he looked slowly round the semicircle of faces.

'Is that really what you all think?' he asked. Even as he did so he realized that he was an Englishman and an exile. He realized that he was among foreigners, even if he was among friends. Around that ring of foreigners ran a restless fire that was not native to his own breed; the fiercer spirit of the western nation that can rebel and lynch, and above all, combine. He knew that they had already combined.

'Well,' said Father Brown, with a sigh, 'I am to understand, then, that you do definitely condone this unfortunate man's crime, or act of private justice, or whatever you call it. In that case it will not hurt him if I tell you a little more about it.'

He rose suddenly to his feet; and though they saw no meaning in his movement, it seemed in some way to change or chill the very air in the room.

'Wilton killed Doom in a rather curious way,' he began.

'How did Wilton kill him?' asked Crake, abruptly.

'With an arrow,' said Father Brown.

Twilight was gathering in the long room, and daylight dwindling to a gleam from the great window in the inner room, where the great millionaire had died. Almost automatically the eyes of the group turned slowly towards it, but as yet there was no sound. Then the voice of Crake came cracked and high and senile in a sort of crowing gabble.

'What you mean? What you mean? Brander Merton killed by an arrow. This crook killed by an arrow——'

'By the same arrow,' said the priest, 'and at the same moment.'

Again there was a sort of strangled and yet swollen and bursting silence, and young Wain began: 'You mean——'

'I mean that your friend Merton was Daniel Doom,' said Father Brown firmly; 'and the only Daniel Doom you'll ever find. Your friend Merton was always crazy after that Coptic Cup that he used to worship like an idol every day; and in his wild youth he had really killed two men to get it, though I still think the deaths may have been in a sense accidents of the robbery. Anyhow, he had it; and that man Drage knew the story and was blackmailing him. But Wilton was after him for a very different purpose; I fancy he only discovered the truth when he'd got into this house. But anyhow, it was in this house, and that in that room, that this hunt ended, and he slew the slayer of his father.'

For a long time nobody answered. Then old Crake could be heard drumming with his fingers on the table and muttering: 'Brander must have been mad. He must have been mad.'

'But, good Lord!' burst out Peter Wain; 'what are we to do? What are we to say? Oh, it's all quite different! What about the papers and the big business people? Brander Merton is a thing like the President or the Pope of Rome.'

'I certainly think it is rather different,' began Barnard Blake, the lawyer, in a low voice. 'The difference involves a whole——'

Father Brown struck the table so that the glasses on it rang; and they could almost fancy a ghostly echo from the mysterious chalice that still stood in the room beyond.

'No!' he cried, in a voice like a pistol-shot. 'There shall be no difference. I gave you your chance of pitying the poor devil when you thought he was a common criminal. You wouldn't listen then; you were all for private vengeance then. You were all for letting him be butchered like a wild beast without a hearing or a public trial, and said he had only got his deserts. Very well then, if Daniel Doom has got his deserts, Brander Merton has got his deserts. If that was good enough for Doom, by all that is holy it is good enough for Merton. Take your wild justice or our dull legality; but in the name of Almighty God, let there be an equal lawlessness or an equal law.'

Nobody answered except the lawyer, and he answered with something like a snarl:

'What will the police say if we tell them we mean to condone a crime?'

'What will they say if I tell them you did condone it?' replied Father Brown. 'Your respect for the law comes rather late, Mr Barnard Blake.'

After a pause he resumed in a milder tone: 'I, for one, am ready to tell the truth if the proper authorities ask me; and the rest of you can do as you like. But as a fact, it will make very little difference. Wilton only rang me up to tell me that I was now free to lay his confession before you; for when you heard it, he would be beyond pursuit.'

He walked slowly into the inner room and stood there by the little table beside which the millionaire had died. The Coptic Cup still stood in the same place, and he remained there for a space staring at its cluster of all the colours of the rainbow, and beyond it into a blue abyss of sky.

The Oracle of the Dog

'Yes,' said Father Brown, 'I always like a dog, so long as he isn't spelt backwards.'

Those who are quick in talking are not always quick in listening. Sometimes even their brilliancy produces a sort of stupidity. Father Brown's friend and companion was a young man named Fiennes, with eager blue eyes and blond hair that seemed to be brushed back, not merely with a hairbrush but with the wind of the world as he rushed through it. But he stopped in the torrent of his talk in a momentary bewilderment before he saw the priest's very simple meaning.

'You mean that people make too much of them?' he said. 'Well, I don't know. They're marvellous creatures. Sometimes I think they know a lot more than we do.'

Father Brown said nothing, but continued to stroke the head of the big retriever in a half-abstracted but apparently soothing fashion.

'Why,' said Fiennes, warming again to his monologue, 'there was a dog in the case I've come to see you about: what they call the "Invisible Murder Case," you know. It's a strange story, but from my point of view the dog is about the strangest thing in it. Of course, there's the mystery of the crime itself, and how old Druce can have been killed by somebody else when he was all alone in the summer-house——'

The hand stroking the dog stopped for a moment in its rhythmic movement, and Father Brown said calmly: 'Oh, it was a summer-house, was it?'

'I thought you'd read all about it in the papers,' answered Fiennes. 'Stop a minute; I believe I've got a cutting that will give you all the particulars.' He produced a strip of newspaper from his pocket and handed it to the priest, who began to read it, holding it close to his blinking eyes with one hand while the other continued its half-conscious caresses of the dog. It looked like the parable of a man not letting his right hand know what his left hand did.

'*Many mystery stories, about men murdered behind locked doors and*

175

windows, and murderers escaping without means of entrance and exit, have come true in the course of the extraordinary events at Cranston on the coast of Yorkshire, where Colonel Druce was found stabbed from behind by a dagger that has entirely disappeared from the scene, and apparently even from the neighbourhood.

'*The summer-house in which he died was indeed accessible at one entrance, the ordinary doorway which looked down the central walk of the garden towards the house. But, by a combination of events almost to be called a coincidence, it appears that both the path and the entrance were watched during the crucial time, and there is a chain of witnesses who confirm each other. The summer-house stands at the extreme end of the garden, where there is no exit or entrance of any kind. The central garden path is a lane between two ranks of tall delphiniums, planted so close that any stray step off the path would leave its traces; and both path and plants run right up to the very mouth of the summer-house, so that no straying from that straight path could fail to be observed, and no other mode of entrance can be imagined.*

'*Patrick Floyd, secretary of the murdered man, testified that he had been in a position to overlook the whole garden from the time when Colonel Druce last appeared alive in the doorway to the time when he was found dead; as he, Floyd, had been on the top of a step-ladder clipping the garden hedge. Janet Druce, the dead man's daughter, confirmed this, saying that she had sat on the terrace of the house throughout that time and had seen Floyd at his work. Touching some part of the time, this is again supported by Donald Druce, her brother—who overlooked the garden—standing at his bedroom windows in his dressing-gown, for he had risen late. Lastly, the account is consistent with that given by Dr Valentine, a neighbour, who called for a time to talk with Miss Druce on the terrace, and by the Colonel's solicitor, Mr Aubrey Traill, who was apparently the last to see the murdered man alive—presumably with the exception of the murderer.*

'*All are agreed that the course of events was as follows: About half-past three in the afternoon, Miss Druce went down the path to ask her father when he would like tea; but he said he did not want any and was waiting to see Traill, his lawyer, who was to be sent to him in the summer-house. The girl then came away and met Traill coming down the path; she directed him to her father and he went in as directed. About half an hour afterwards he came out again, the Colonel coming with him to the door and showing himself to all appearance in health and even high spirits. He had been somewhat annoyed earlier in the day by his son's irregular hours, but seemed to recover his temper in a perfectly normal fashion, and had been rather markedly genial in receiving other visitors, including two of his nephews, who came over for the day. But as these were out walking during the whole period of the tragedy, they had no evidence to give. It is said, indeed, that the Colonel was not on very good terms with Dr Valentine, but that gentleman only had a brief interview with the daughter of the house, to whom he is supposed to be paying serious attentions.*

'Traill, the solicitor, says he left the Colonel entirely alone in the summer-house, and this is confirmed by Floyd's bird's-eye view of the garden, which showed nobody else passing the only entrance. Ten minutes later, Miss Druce again went down the garden and had not reached the end of the path when she saw her father, who was conspicuous by his white linen coat, lying in a heap on the floor. She uttered a scream which brought others to the spot, and on entering the place they found the Colonel lying dead beside his basket-chair, which was also upset. Dr Valentine, who was still in the immediate neighbourhood, testified that the wound was made by some sort of stiletto, entering under the shoulder-blade and piercing the heart. The police have searched the neighbourhood for such a weapon, but no trace of it can be found.'

'So Colonel Druce wore a white coat, did he?' said Father Brown as he put down the paper.

'Trick he learnt in the tropics,' replied Fiennes, with some wonder. 'He'd had some queer adventures there, by his own account; and I fancy his dislike of Valentine was connected with the doctor coming from the tropics, too. But it's all an infernal puzzle. The account there is pretty accurate; I didn't see the tragedy, in the sense of the discovery; I was out walking with the young nephews and the dog—the dog I wanted to tell you about. But I saw the stage set for it as described; the straight lane between the blue flowers right up to the dark entrance, and the lawyer going down it in his blacks and his silk hat, and the red head of the secretary showing high above the green hedge as he worked on it with his shears. Nobody could have mistaken that red head at any distance; and if people say they saw it there all the time, you may be sure they did. This red-haired secretary, Floyd, is quite a character; a breathless bounding sort of fellow, always doing everybody's work as he was doing the gardener's. I think he is an American;

he's certainly got the American view of life—what they call the view-point, bless 'em.'

'What about the lawyer?' asked Father Brown.

There was a silence and then Fiennes spoke quite slowly for him. 'Traill struck me as a singular man. In his fine black clothes he was almost foppish, yet you can hardly call him fashionable. For he wore a pair of long, luxuriant black whiskers such as haven't been seen since Victorian times. He had rather a fine grave face and a fine grave manner, but every now and then he seemed to remember to smile. And when he showed his white teeth he seemed to lose a little of his dignity, and there was something faintly fawning about him. It may have been only embarrassment, for he would also fidget with his cravat and his tie-pin, which were at once handsome and unusual, like himself. If I could think of anybody—but what's the good, when the whole thing's impossible? Nobody knows who did it. Nobody knows how it could be done. At least there's only one exception I'd make, and that's why I really mentioned the whole thing. The dog knows.'

Father Brown sighed and then said absently: 'You were there as a friend of young Donald, weren't you? He didn't go on your walk with you?'

'No,' replied Fiennes smiling. 'The young scoundrel had gone to bed that morning and got up that afternoon. I went with his cousins, two young officers from India, and our conversation was trivial enough. I remember the elder, whose name I think is Herbert Druce and who is an authority on horse-breeding, talked about nothing but a mare he had bought and the moral character of the man who sold her; while his brother Harry seemed to be brooding on his bad luck at Monte Carlo. I only mention it to show you, in the light of what happened on our walk, that there was nothing psychic about us. The dog was the only mystic in our company.'

'What sort of a dog was he?' asked the priest.

'Same breed as that one,' answered Fiennes. 'That's what started me off on the story, your saying you didn't believe in believing in a dog. He's a big black retriever, named Nox, and a suggestive name, too; for I think what he did a darker mystery than the murder. You know Druce's house and garden are by the sea; we walked about a mile from it along the sands and then turned back, going the other way. We passed a rather curious rock called the Rock of Fortune, famous in the neighbourhood because it's one of those examples of one stone barely balanced on another, so that a touch would knock it over. It is not really very high but the hanging outline of it makes it look a little wild and sinister; at least it made it look so to me, for I don't imagine my jolly young companions were afflicted with the picturesque. But it may be that I was beginning to feel an atmosphere; for just then the question arose of whether it was time to go back to tea, and even then I think I had a premonition that time counted for a good deal in the business. Neither Herbert Druce nor I had a watch, so we called out to his brother, who was some paces behind, having stopped to light his pipe under the hedge. Hence it happened that he shouted out the hour, which was twenty past four, in his big voice through the growing twilight; and somehow the loudness of it made it sound like the proclamation of something tremendous. His unconsciousness seemed to make it all the more so; but that was always the way with omens; and particular ticks of the clock were really very ominous things that afternoon. According to Dr Valentine's testimony, poor Druce had actually died just about half-past four.

'Well, they said we needn't go home for ten minutes, and we walked a little farther along the sands, doing nothing in particular—throwing stones for the dog and throwing sticks into the sea for him to swim after. But to me the twilight seemed to grow oddly oppressive, and the very shadow of the top-heavy Rock of Fortune lay on me like a load. And then the curious thing happened. Nox had just brought back Herbert's walking-stick out of the sea and his brother had thrown his in also. The dog swam out again, but just about what must have been the stroke of the half-hour, he stopped swimming. He came back again on to the shore and stood in front of us. Then he suddenly threw up his head and sent up a howl of wail of woe—if ever I heard one in the world.

' "What the devil's the matter with the dog?" asked Herbert; but none of us could answer. There was a long silence after the brute's wailing and whining died away on the desolate shore; and then the silence was broken. As I live, it was broken by a faint and far-off shriek, like the shriek of a woman from beyond the hedges inland. We didn't know what it was then; but we knew afterwards. It was the cry the girl gave when she first saw the body of her father.'

'You went back, I suppose,' said Father Brown patiently. 'What happened then?'

'I'll tell you what happened then,' said Fiennes with a grim emphasis. 'When we got back into that garden the first thing we saw was Traill, the lawyer; I can see him now with his black hat and black whiskers relieved against the perspective of the blue flowers stretching down to the summer-house, with the sunset and the strange outline of the Rock of Fortune in the distance. His face and figure were in shadow against the sunset; but I swear the white teeth were showing in his head and he was smiling.

'The moment Nox saw that man the dog dashed forward and stood in the middle of the path barking at him madly, murderously, volleying out curses that were almost verbal in their dreadful distinctness of hatred. And the man doubled up and fled along the path between the flowers.'

Father Brown sprang to his feet with a startling impatience.

'So the dog denounced him, did he?' he cried. 'The oracle of the dog condemned him. Did you see what birds were flying, and are you sure whether they were on the right hand or the left? Did you consult the augurs about the sacrifices? Surely you didn't omit to cut open the dog and examine his entrails. That is the sort of scientific test you heathen humanitarians seem to trust when you are thinking of taking away the life and honour of a man.'

Fiennes sat gaping for an instant before he found breath to say: 'Why, what's the matter with you? What have I done now?'

A sort of anxiety came back into the priest's eyes—the anxiety of a man who has run against a post in the dark and wonders for a moment whether he has hurt it.

'I'm most awfully sorry,' he said with sincere distress. 'I beg your pardon for being so rude; pray forgive me.'

Fiennes looked at him curiously. 'I sometimes think you are more of a mystery than any of the mysteries,' he said. 'But anyhow, if you don't believe in the mystery of the dog, at least you can't get over the mystery of the man. You can't deny that at the very moment when the beast came back from the sea and bellowed, his master's soul was driven out of his body by the blow of some unseen power that no mortal man can trace or even imagine. And as for the lawyer—I don't go only by the dog—there are other curious details, too. He struck me as a smooth, smiling, equivocal sort of person; and one of his tricks seemed like a sort of hint. You know the doctor and the police were on the spot very quickly; Valentine was brought back when walking away from the house, and he telephoned instantly. That, with the secluded house, small numbers, and enclosed space, made it pretty possible to search everybody who could have been near; and everybody was thoroughly searched—for a weapon. The whole house, garden, and shore were combed for a weapon. The disappearance of the dagger is almost as crazy as the disappearance of the man.'

'The disappearance of the dagger,' said Father Brown, nodding. He seemed to have become suddenly attentive.

'Well,' continued Fiennes, 'I told you that man Traill had a trick of fidgeting with his tie and tie-pin—especially his tie-pin. His pin, like himself, was at once showy and old-fashioned. It had one of those stones with concentric coloured rings that look like an eye; and his own concentration on it got on my nerves, as if he had been a Cyclops with one eye in the middle of his body. But the pin was not only large but long; and it occurred to me that his anxiety about its adjustment was because it was even longer than it looked; as long as a stiletto in fact.'

Father Brown nodded thoughtfully. 'Was any other instrument ever suggested?' he asked.

'There was another suggestion,' answered Fiennes, 'from one of the young Druces—the cousins, I mean. Neither Herbert nor Harry Druce would have struck one at first as likely to be of assistance in scientific detection; but while Herbert was really the traditional type of heavy Dragoon, caring for nothing but horses and being an ornament to the Horse Guards, his younger brother Harry had been in the Indian Police and knew something about such things. Indeed, in his own way he was quite clever; and I rather fancy he had been too clever; I mean he had left the police through breaking some red-tape regulations and taking some sort of risk and responsibility of his own. Anyhow, he was in some sense a detective out of work, and threw himself into this business with more than the ardour of an amateur. And it was with him that I had an argument about the weapon—an argument that led to something new. It began by his countering my description of the dog barking at Traill; and he said that a dog at his worst didn't bark, but growled.'

'He was quite right there,' observed the priest.

'This young fellow went on to say that, if it came to that, he'd heard Nox growling at other people before then; and among others at Floyd, the secretary. I retorted that his own argument answered itself; for the crime couldn't be brought home to two or three people, and least of all to Floyd, who was as innocent as a harum-scarum schoolboy, and had been seen by everybody all the time perched above the garden hedge with his fan of red hair as conspicuous as a scarlet cockatoo. "I know there's difficulties anyhow," said my colleague; "but I wish you'd come with me down the garden a minute. I want to show you something I don't think any one else has seen." This was on the very day of the discovery, and the garden was just as it had been. The step-ladder was still standing by the hedge, and just under the hedge my guide stopped and disentangled something from the deep grass. It was the shears used for clipping the hedge, and on the point of one of them was a smear of blood.'

There was a short silence, and then Father Brown said suddenly. 'What was the lawyer there for?'

'He told us the Colonel sent for him to alter his will,' answered Fiennes. 'And, by the way, there was another thing about the business of the will that I ought to mention. You see, the will wasn't actually signed in the summer-house that afternoon.'

'I suppose not,' said Father Brown; 'there would have to be two witnesses.'

'The lawyer actually came down the day before and it was signed then; but he was sent for again next day because the old man had a doubt about one of the witnesses and had to be reassured.'

'Who were the witnesses?' asked Father Brown.

'That's just the point,' replied his informant eagerly, 'the witnesses were Floyd, the secretary, and this Dr Valentine, the foreign sort of surgeon or whatever he is; and the two have a quarrel. Now I'm bound to say that the secretary is something of a busybody. He's one of those hot and headlong people whose warmth of temperament has unfortunately turned mostly to pugnacity and bristling suspicion; to distrusting people instead of to trusting them. That sort of red-haired red-hot fellow is always either universally credulous or universally incredulous; and sometimes both. He was not only a Jack-of-all-trades, but he knew better than all tradesmen. He not only knew everything, but he warned everybody against everybody. All that must be taken into account in his suspicions about Valentine; but in that particular case there seems to have been something behind it. He said the name of Valentine was not really Valentine. He said he had seen him elsewhere known by the name of De Villon. He said it would invalidate the will; of course he was kind enough to explain to the lawyer what the law was on that point. They were both in a frightful wax.'

Father Brown laughed. 'People often are when they are to witness a will,' he said; 'for one thing, it means that they can't have any legacy under it. But what did Dr Valentine say? No doubt the universal secretary knew more about the doctor's name than the doctor did. But even the doctor might have some information about his own name.'

Fiennes paused a moment before he replied.

'Dr Valentine took it in a curious way. Dr Valentine is a curious man. His appearance is rather striking but very foreign. He is young but wears a beard cut square; and his face is very pale, dreadfully pale and dreadfully serious. His eyes have a sort of ache in them, as if he ought to wear glasses, or had given himself a headache with thinking; but he is quite handsome and always very formally dressed, with a top hat and a dark coat and a little red rosette. His manner is rather cold and haughty, and he has a way of staring at you which is very disconcerting. When thus charged with having changed his name, he merely stared like a sphinx and then said with a little laugh that he supposed Americans had no names to change. At that I think the Colonel also got into a fuss and said all sorts of angry things to the doctor; all the more angry because of the doctor's pretensions to a future place in his family. But I shouldn't have thought much of that but for a few words that I happened to hear later, early in the afternoon of the tragedy. I don't want to make a lot of them, for they weren't the sort of words on which one would like, in the ordinary way, to play the eavesdropper. As I was passing out towards the front gate with my two companions and the dog, I heard voices which told me that Dr Valentine and Miss Druce had withdrawn for a moment into the shadow of the house, in an angle behind a row of flowering plants, and were talking to each other in passionate whisperings—sometimes almost like hissings; for it was something of a lovers' quarrel as well as a lovers' tryst. Nobody repeats the sort of things they said for the most part; but in an unfortunate business like this I'm bound to say that there was repeated more than once a phrase about killing somebody. In fact, the girl seemed to be begging him not to kill somebody, or saying that no provocation could justify killing anybody; which seems an unusual sort of talk to address to a gentleman who has dropped in to tea.'

'Do you know,' asked the priest, 'whether Dr Valentine seemed to be very angry after the scene with the secretary and the Colonel—I mean about witnessing the will?'

'By all accounts,' replied the other, 'he wasn't half so angry as the secretary was. It was the secretary who went away raging after witnessing the will.'

'And now,' said Father Brown, 'what about the will itself?'

'The Colonel was a very wealthy man, and his will was important. Traill wouldn't tell us the alteration at that stage, but I have since heard only this morning in fact—that most of the money was transferred from the son to the daughter. I told you that Druce was wild with my friend Donald over his dissipated hours.'

'The question of motive has been rather over-shadowed by the question of method,' observed Father Brown thoughtfully. 'At that moment, apparently, Miss Druce was the immediate gainer by the death.'

'Good God! What a cold-blooded way of talking,' cried Fiennes, staring at him. 'You don't really mean to hint that she——'

'Is she going to marry that Dr Valentine?' asked the other.

'Some people are against it,' answered his friend. 'But he is liked and respected in the place and is a skilled and devoted surgeon.'

'So devoted a surgeon,' said Father Brown, 'that he had surgical instruments with him when he went to call on the young lady at teatime. For he must have used a lancet or something, and he never seems to have gone home.'

Fiennes sprang to his feet and looked at him in a heat of inquiry. 'You suggest he might have used the very same lancet——'

Father Brown shook his head. 'All these suggestions are fancies just now,' he said. 'The problem is not who did it or what did it, but how it was done. We might find many men and even many tools—pins and shears and lancets. But how did a man get into that room? How did even a pin get into it?'

He was staring reflectively at the ceiling as he spoke, but as he said the last words his eye cocked in an alert fashion as if he had suddenly seen a curious fly on the ceiling.

'Well, what would you do about it?' asked the young man. 'You have a lot of experience; what would you advise now?'

'I'm afraid I'm not much use,' said Father Brown with a sigh. 'I can't suggest very much without having ever been near the place or the people. For the moment you can only go on with local inquiries. I gather that your friend from the Indian Police is more or less in charge of your inquiry down there. I should run down and see how he is getting on. See what he's been doing in the way of amateur detection. There may be news already.'

As his guests, the biped and the quadruped, disappeared, Father Brown took up his pen and went back to his interrupted occupation of planning a course of lectures on the Encyclical *Rerum Novarum*. The subject was a large one and he had to re-cast it more than once, so that he was somewhat similarly employed some two days later when the big black dog again came bounding into the room and sprawled all over him with enthusiasm and excitement. The master who followed the dog shared the excitement if not the enthusiasm. He had been excited in a less pleasant fashion, for his blue eyes seemed to start from his head and his eager face was even a little pale.

'You told me,' he said abruptly and without preface, 'to find out what Harry Druce was doing. Do you know what he's done?'

The priest did not reply, and the young man went on in jerky tones:

'I'll tell you what he's done. He's killed himself.'

Father Brown's lips moved only faintly, and there was nothing practical about what he was saying—nothing that has anything to do with this story or this world.

'You give me the creeps sometimes,' said Fiennes. 'Did you—did you expect this?'

'I thought it possible,' said Father Brown; 'that was why I asked you to go and see what he was doing. I hoped you might not be too late.'

'It was I who found him,' said Fiennes rather huskily. 'It was the ugliest and most uncanny thing I ever knew. I went down that old garden again, and I knew there was something new and unnatural about it besides the murder. The flowers still tossed about in blue masses on each side of the black entrance into the old grey summer-house; but to me the blue flowers looked like blue devils dancing before some dark cavern of the underworld. I looked all round, everything seemed to be in its ordinary place. But the queer notion grew on me that there was something wrong with the very shape of the sky. And then I saw what it was. The Rock of Fortune always rose in the background beyond the garden hedge and against the sea. And the Rock of Fortune was gone.'

Father Brown had lifted his head and was listening intently.

'It was as if a mountain had walked away out of a landscape or a moon fallen from the sky; though I knew, of course, that a touch at any time would have tipped the thing over. Something possessed me and I rushed down that garden path like the wind and went crashing through that hedge as if it were a spider's web. It was a thin hedge really, though its undisturbed trimness had made it serve all the purposes of a wall. On the shore I found the loose rock fallen from its pedestal; and poor Harry Druce lay like a wreck underneath it. One arm was thrown round it in a sort of embrace as if he had pulled it down on himself; and on the broad brown sands beside it, in large crazy lettering, he had scrawled the words: "The Rock of Fortune falls on the Fool." '

'It was the Colonel's will that did that,' observed Father Brown. 'The young man had staked everything on profiting himself by Donald's disgrace, especially when his uncle sent for him on the same day as the lawyer, and welcomed him with so much warmth. Otherwise he was done; he'd lost his police job; he was beggared at Monte Carlo. And he killed himself when he found he'd killed his kinsman for nothing.'

'Here, stop a minute!' cried the staring Fiennes. 'You're going too fast for me.'

'Talking about the will, by the way,' continued Father Brown calmly 'before I forget it, or we go on to bigger things, there was a simple explanation, I think, of all that business about the doctor's name. I rather fancy I have heard both names before somewhere. The doctor is really a French nobleman with the title of the Marquis de Villon. But he is also an ardent Republican and has abandoned his title and fallen back on the forgotten family surname. "With your Citizen Riquetti you have puzzled Europe for ten days." '

'What is that?' asked the young man blankly.

'Never mind,' said the priest. 'Nine times out of ten it is a rascally thing to change one's name; but this was a piece of fine fanaticism. That's the point of his sarcasm about Americans having no names—that is, no titles. Now in England the Marquis of

Hartington is never called Mr Hartington; but in France the Marquis de Villon is called M. de Villon. So it might well look like a change of name. As for the talk about killing, I fancy that also was a point of French etiquette. The doctor was talking about challenging Floyd to a duel, and the girl was trying to dissuade him.'

'Oh, I *see*,' cried Fiennes slowly. 'Now I understand what she meant.'

'And what is that about?' asked his companion, smiling.

'Well,' said the young man, 'it was something that happened to me just before I found that poor fellow's body; only the catastrophe drove it out of my head. I suppose it's hard to remember a little romantic idyll when you've just come on top of a tragedy. But as I went down the lanes leading to the Colonel's old place I met his daughter walking with Dr Valentine. She was in mourning, of course, and he always wore black as if he were going to a funeral; but I can't say that their faces were very funereal. Never have I seen two people looking in their own way more respectably radiant and cheerful. They stopped and saluted me, and then she told me they were married and living in a little house on the outskirts of the town, where the doctor was continuing his practice. This rather surprised me, because I knew that her old father's will had left her his property; and I hinted at it delicately by saying I was going along to her father's old place and had half expected to meet her there. But she only laughed and said: "Oh, we've given up all that. My husband doesn't like heiresses." And I discovered with some astonishment they really had insisted on restoring the property to poor Donald; so I hope he's had a healthy shock and will treat it sensibly. There was never much really the matter with him; he was very young and his father was not very wise. But it was in connexion with that that she said something I didn't understand at the time; but now I'm sure it must be as you say. She said with a sort of sudden and splendid arrogance that was entirely altruistic:

"I hope it'll stop that red-haired fool from fussing any more about the will. Does he think my husband, who has given up a crest and a coronet as old as the Crusades for his principles, would kill an old man in a summer-house for a legacy like that?" Then she laughed again and said, "My husband isn't killing anybody except in the way of business. Why, he didn't even ask his friends to call on the secretary." Now, of course, I see what she meant.'

'I see part of what she meant, of course,' said Father Brown.

'What did she mean exactly by the secretary fussing about the will?'

Fiennes smiled as he answered. 'I wish you knew the secretary, Father Brown. It would be a joy to you to watch him make things hum, as he calls it. He made the house of mourning hum. He filled the funeral with all the snap and zip of the brightest sporting event. There was no holding him, after something had really happened. I've told you how he used to oversee the gardener as he did the garden, and how he instructed the lawyer in the law. Needless to say, he also instructed the surgeon in the practice of surgery; and as the surgeon was Dr Valentine, you may be sure it ended in accusing him of something worse than bad surgery. The secretary got it fixed in his red head that the doctor had committed the crime, and when the police arrived he was perfectly sublime. Need I say that he became, on the spot, the greatest of all amateur detectives? Sherlock Holmes never towered over Scotland Yard with more Titanic intellectual pride and scorn than Colonel Druce's private secretary over the police investigating Colonel Druce's death. I tell you it was a joy to see him. He strode about with an abstracted air, tossing his scarlet crest of hair and giving curt impatient replies. Of course it was his demeanour during these days that made Druce's daughter so wild with him. Of course he had a theory. It's just the sort of theory a man would have in a book; and Floyd is the sort of man who ought to be in a book. He'd be better fun and less bother in a book.'

'What was his theory?' asked the other.

'Oh, it was full of pep,' replied Fiennes gloomily. 'It would have been glorious copy if it could have held together for ten minutes longer. He said the Colonel was still alive when they found him in the summer-house, and the doctor killed him with the surgical instrument on pretence of cutting the clothes.'

'I see,' said the priest. 'I suppose he was lying flat on his face on the mud floor as a form of siesta.'

'It's wonderful what hustle will do,' continued his informant. 'I believe Floyd would have got his great theory into the papers at any rate, and perhaps had the doctor arrested, when all these things were blown sky high as if by dynamite by the discovery of that dead body lying under the Rock of Fortune. And that's what we come back to after all. I suppose the suicide is almost a confession. But nobody will ever know the whole story.'

There was a silence, and then the priest said modestly: 'I rather think I know the whole story.'

Fiennes stared. 'But look here,' he cried; 'how do you come to know the whole story, or to be sure it's the true story? You've been sitting here a hundred miles away writing a sermon; do you mean to tell me you really know what happened already? If you've really come to the end, where in the would do you begin? What started you off with your own story?'

Father Brown jumped up with a very unusual excitement and his first exclamation was like an explosion.

'The dog!' he cried. 'The dog, of course! You had the whole story in your hands in the business of the dog on the beach, if you'd only noticed the dog properly.'

Fiennes stared still more. 'But you told me before that my feelings about the dog were all nonsense, and the dog had nothing to do with it.'

'The dog had everything to do with it,' said Father Brown, 'as you'd have found out if you'd only treated the dog as a dog, and not as God Almighty judging the souls of men.'

He paused in an embarrassed way for a moment, and then said, with a rather pathetic air of apology: 'The truth is, I happen to be awfully fond of dogs. And it seemed to me that in all this lurid halo of dog superstitions nobody was really thinking about the poor dog at all. To begin with a small point, about his barking at the lawyer or growling at the secretary. You asked how I could guess things a hundred miles away; but honestly it's mostly to your credit, for you described people so well that I know the types. A man like Traill, who frowns usually and smiles suddenly, a man who fiddles with things, especially at his throat, is a nervous, easily embarrassed man. I shouldn't wonder if Floyd, the efficient secretary, is nervy and jumpy, too; those Yankee hustlers often are. Otherwise he wouldn't have cut his fingers on the shears and dropped them when he heard Janet Druce scream.

'Now dogs hate nervous people. I don't know whether they make the dog nervous, too; or whether, being after all a brute, he is a bit of a bully; or whether his canine vanity (which is colossal) is simply offended at not being liked. But anyhow there was nothing in poor Nox protesting against those people, except that he disliked them for being afraid of him. Now I know you're awfully clever, and nobody of sense sneers at cleverness. But I sometimes fancy, for instance, that you are too clever to understand animals. Sometimes you are too clever to understand men, especially when they act almost as simply as animals. Animals are very literal; they live in a world of truisms. Take this case: a dog barks at a man and a man runs away from a dog. Now you do not seem to be quite simple enough to see the fact: that the dog barked because he disliked the man and the man fled because he was frightened of the dog. They had no other motives and they needed none; but you must read psychological mysteries into it and suppose the dog had supernormal vision, and was a mysterious mouthpiece of doom. You must suppose the man was running away, not from the dog but from the hangman. And yet, if you come to think of it, all this deeper psychology is exceedingly improbable. If the dog really could completely and consciously realize the murderer of his master he wouldn't stand yapping as he might at a curate at a tea-party; he's much more likely to fly at his throat. And on the other hand, do you really think a man who had hardened his heart to murder an old friend and then walk about smiling at the old friend's family, under the eyes of his old friend's daughter and post-mortem doctor—do you think a man like that would be doubled up by mere remorse because a dog barked? He might feel the tragic irony of it; it might shake his soul, like any other tragic trifle. But he wouldn't rush madly the length of a garden to escape from the only witness whom he knew to be unable to talk. People have a panic like that when they are frightened, not of tragic ironies, but of teeth. The whole thing is simpler than you can understand.

'But when we come to that business by the seashore, things are much more interesting. As you stated them, they were much more puzzling. I didn't understand that tale of the dog going in and out of the water; it didn't seem to me a doggy thing to do. If Nox had been very much upset about something else, he might possibly have refused to go after the stick at all. He'd probably go off nosing in whatever direction he suspected the mischief. But when once a dog is actually chasing a thing, a stone or a stick or a rabbit, my experience is that he won't stop for anything but the most peremptory command, and not always for that. That he should turn round because his mood changed seems to me unthinkable.'

'But he did turn round,' insisted Fiennes; 'and came back without the stick.'

'He came back without the stick for the best reason in the world,' replied the priest. 'He came back because he couldn't find it. He whined because he couldn't find it. That's the sort of thing a dog really does whine about. A dog is a devil of a ritualist. He is as particular about the precise routine of a game as a child about the precise repetition of a fairy-tale. In this case something had gone wrong with the game. He came back to complain seriously of the conduct of the stick. Never had such a thing happened before. Never had an eminent and distinguished dog been so treated by a rotten old walking-stick.'

'Why, what had the walking-stick done?' inquired the young man.

'It had sunk,' said Father Brown.

Fiennes said nothing, but continued to stare; and it was the priest who continued:

'It had sunk because it was not really a stick, but a rod of steel with a very thin shell of cane and a sharp point. In other words, it was a swordstick. I suppose a murderer never gets rid of a bloody weapon so oddly and yet so naturally as by throwing it into the sea for a retriever.'

'I begin to see what you mean,' admitted Fiennes; 'but even if a swordstick was used, I have no guess of how it was used.'

'I had a sort of guess,' said Father Brown, 'right at the beginning when you said the word summerhouse. And another when you said that Druce wore a white coat. As long as everybody was looking for a short dagger, nobody thought of it; but if we admit a rather long blade like a rapier, it's not so impossible.'

He was leaning back, looking at the ceiling, and began like one going back to his own first thoughts and fundamentals.

'All that discussion about detective stories like the Yellow Room, about a man found dead in sealed chambers which no one could enter, does not apply to the present case, because it is a summer-house. When we talk of a Yellow Room, or any room, we imply walls that are really homogeneous and impenetrable. But a summer-house is not made like that; it is often made, as it was in this case, of closely interlaced but separate boughs and strips of wood, in which there are chinks here and there. There was one of them just behind Druce's back as he sat in his chair up against the wall. But just as the room was a summer-house, so the chair was a basket-chair. That also was a lattice of loopholes. Lastly, the summer-house was close up under the hedge; and you have just told me that it was really a thin hedge. A man standing outside it could easily see, amid a network of twigs and branches and canes, one white spot of the Colonel's coat as plain as the white of a target.

'Now, you left the geography a little vague; but it was possible to put two and two together. You said the Rock of Fortune was not really high; but you also said it could be seen dominating the garden like a mountain peak. In other words, it was very near the end of the garden, though your walk had taken you a long way round to it. Also, it isn't likely the young lady really howled so as to be heard half a mile. She gave an ordinary involuntary cry, and yet you heard it on the shore. And among other interesting things that you told me, may I remind you that you said Harry Druce had fallen behind to light his pipe under a hedge.'

Fiennes shuddered slightly. 'You mean he drew his blade there and sent it through the hedge at the white spot. But surely it was a very odd chance and a very sudden choice. Besides, he couldn't be certain the old man's money had passed to him, and as a fact it hadn't.'

Father Brown's face became animated.

'You misunderstand the man's character,' he said, as if he himself had known the man all his life. 'A curious but not unknown type of character. If he had really *known* the money would come to him, I seriously believe he wouldn't have done it. He would have seen it as the dirty thing it was.'

'Isn't that rather paradoxical?' asked the other.

'This man was a gambler,' said the priest, 'and a man in disgrace for having taken risks and anticipated orders. It was probably for something pretty unscrupulous, for every imperial police is more like a Russian secret police than we like to think. But he had gone beyond the line and failed. Now, the temptation of that type of man is to do a mad thing precisely because the risk will be wonderful in retrospect. He wants to say, "Nobody but I could have seized that chance or seen that it was then or never. What a wild and wonderful guess it was, when I put all those things together; Donald in disgrace; and the lawyer being sent for; and Herbert and I sent for at the same time—and then nothing more but the way the old man grinned at me and shook hands. Anybody would say I was mad to risk it; but that is how fortunes are made, by the man mad enough to have a little foresight. 'In short, it is the vanity of guessing. It is the megalomania of the gambler. The more incongruous the coincidence, the more instantaneous the decision, the more likely he is to snatch the chance. The accident, the very triviality of the white speck and the hole in the hedge intoxicated him like a vision of the world's desire. Nobody clever enough to see such a combination of accidents could be cowardly enough not to use them! That is how the devil talks to the gambler. But the devil himself would hardly have induced that unhappy man to go down in a dull, deliberate way and kill an old uncle from whom he'd always had expectations. It would be too respectable.'

He paused a moment, and then went on with a certain quiet emphasis.

'And now try to call up the scene, even as you saw it yourself. As he stood there, dizzy with his diabolical opportunity, he looked up and saw that strange outline that might have been the image of his own tottering soul; the one great crag poised perilously on the other like a pyramid on its point, and remembered that it was called the Rock of Fortune. Can you guess how such a man at such a moment would read such a signal? I think it strung him up to action and even to vigilance. He who would be a tower must not fear to be a toppling tower. Anyhow, he acted; his next difficulty was to cover his tracks. To be found with a sword-stick, let alone a blood-stained sword-stick, would be fatal in the search that was certain to follow. If he left it anywhere, it would be found and probably traced. Even if he threw it into the sea the action might be noticed, and thought noticeable—unless indeed he could think of some more natural way of covering the action. As you know, he did think of one, and a very good one. Being the only one of you with a watch, he told you it was not yet time to return, strolled a little farther and started the game of throwing in sticks for the retriever. But how his eyes must have rolled darkly over all that desolate sea-shore before they alighted on the dog!'

Fiennes nodded, gazing thoughtfully into space. His mind seemed to have drifted back to a less practical part of the narrative.

'It's queer,' he said, 'that the dog really was in the story after all.'

'The dog could almost have told you the story, if he could talk,' said the priest. 'All I complain of is that because he couldn't talk, you made up his story for him, and made him talk with the tongues of men and angels. It's part of something I've noticed more and more in the modern world, appearing in all sorts of newspaper rumours and conversational catchwords; something that's arbitrary without being authoritative. People readily swallow the untested claims of this, that, or the other. It's drowning all your old rationalism and scepticism, it's coming in like a sea; and the name of it is superstition.' He stood up abruptly, his face heavy with a sort of frown, and went on talking almost as if he were alone. 'It's the first effect of not believing in God that you lose your common sense and can't see things as they are. Anything that anybody talks about, and says there's a good deal in it, extends itself indefinitely like a vista in a nightmare. And a dog is an omen, and a cat is a mystery, and a pig is a mascot and a beetle is a scarab, calling up all the menagerie of polytheism from Egypt and old India; Dog Anubis and great green-eyed Pasht and all the holy howling Bulls of Bashan; reeling back to the bestial gods of the beginning, escaping into elephants and snakes and crocodiles; and all because you are frightened of four words: "He was made Man".'

The young man got up with a little embarrassment, almost as if he had overheard a soliloquy. He called to the dog and left the room with vague but breezy farewells. But he had to call the dog twice, for the dog had remained behind quite motionless for a moment, looking up steadily at Father Brown as the wolf looked at St Francis.

The Doom of the Darnaways

Two landscape-painters stood looking at one landscape, which was also a seascape, and both were curiously impressed by it, though their impressions were not exactly the same. To one of them, who was a rising artist from London, it was new as well as strange. To the other, who was a local artist but with something more than a local celebrity, it was better known; but perhaps all the more strange for what he knew of it.

In terms of tone and form, as these men saw it, was a stretch of sands against a stretch of sunset, the whole scene lying in strips of sombre colour, dead green and bronze and brown and a drab that was not merely dull but in that gloaming in some way more mysterious than gold. All that broke these level lines was a long building which ran out from the fields into the sands of the sea, so that its fringe of dreary weeds and rushes seemed almost to meet the seaweed. But its most singular feature was that the upper part of it had the ragged outlines of a ruin, pierced by so many wide windows and large rents as to be a mere dark skeleton against the dying light; while the lower bulk of the building had hardly any windows at all, most of them being blind and bricked up and their outlines only faintly traceable in the twilight. But one window at least was still a window; and it seemed strangest of all that it showed a light.

'Who on earth can live in that old shell?' exclaimed the Londoner, who was a big, bohemian-looking man, young but with a shaggy red beard that made him look older; Chelsea knew him familiarly as Harry Payne.

'Ghosts, you might suppose,' replied his friend Martin Wood. 'Well, the people who live there really are rather like ghosts.'

It was perhaps rather a paradox that the London artist seemed almost bucolic in his boisterous freshness and wonder, while the local artist seemed a more shrewd and experienced person, regarding him with mature and amiable amusement; indeed, the latter was altogether a quieter and more conventional figure, wearing darker clothes and with his square and stolid face clean-shaven.

'It is only a sign of the times, of course,' he went on, 'or of the passing of old times and old families with them. The last of the great Darnaways live in that house, and not many of the new poor are as poor as they are. They can't even afford to make their own top-story habitable; but have to live in the lower rooms of a ruin, like bats and owls. Yet they have family portraits that go back to the Wars of the Roses and the first portrait-painting in England, and very fine some of them are; I happen to know, because they asked for my professional advice in overhauling them. There's one of them especially, and one of the earliest, but it's so good that it gives you the creeps.'

'The whole place gives you the creeps, I should think by the look of it,' replied Payne.

'Well,' said his friend, 'to tell you the truth, it does.'

The silence that followed was stirred by a faint rustle among the rushes by the moat; and it gave them, rationally enough, a slight nervous start when a dark figure brushed along the bank, moving rapidly and almost like a startled bird. But it was only a man walking briskly with a black bag in his hand: a man with a long sallow face and sharp eyes that glanced at the London stranger in a slightly darkling and suspicious manner.

'It's only Dr Barnet,' said Wood with a sort of relief. 'Good evening, Doctor. Are you going up to the house? I hope nobody's ill.'

'Everybody's always ill in a place like that,' growled the doctor; 'only sometimes they're too ill to know it. The very air of the place is a blight and a pestilence. I don't envy the young man from Australia.'

'And who,' asked Payne abruptly and rather absently, 'may the young man from Australia be?'

'Ah!' snorted the doctor; 'hasn't your friend told you about him? As a matter of fact I believe he is arriving today. Quite a romance in the old style of melodrama: the heir back from the colonies to his ruined castle, all complete even down to an old family compact for his marrying the lady watching in the ivied tower. Queer old stuff, isn't it? But it really happens sometimes. He's even got a little money, which is the only bright spot there ever was in this business.'

'What does Miss Darnaway herself, in her ivied tower, think of the business?' asked Martin Wood dryly.

'What she thinks of everything else by this time,' replied the doctor. 'They don't think in this weedy old den of superstitions, they only dream and drift. I think she accepts the family contract and the colonial husband as part of the Doom of the Darnaways, don't you know. I really think that if he turned out to be a hump-backed negro with one eye and a homicidal mania, she would only think it added a finishing touch and fitted in with the twilight scenery.'

'You're not giving my friend from London a very lively picture of my friends in the country,' said Wood, laughing. 'I had intended taking him there to call; no artist ought to miss those Darnaway portraits if he gets the chance. But perhaps I'd better postpone it if they're in the middle of the Australian invasion.'

'Oh, do go in and see them, for the Lord's sake,' said Dr Barnet warmly. 'Anything that will brighten their blighted lives will make my task easier. It will need a good many colonial cousins to cheer things up, I should think; and the more the merrier. Come, I'll take you in myself.'

As they drew nearer to the house it was seen to be isolated like an island in a moat of brackish water which they crossed by a bridge. On the other side spread a fairly wide stony floor or embankment with great cracks across it, in which little tufts of weed and thorn sprouted here and there. This rock platform looked large and bare in the grey twilight, and Payne could hardly have believed that such a corner of space could have contained so much of the soul of a wilderness. This platform only jutted out on one side, like a giant doorstep and beyond it was the door; a very low-browed Tudor archway standing open, but dark like a cave.

When the brisk doctor led them inside without ceremony, Payne had, as it were, another shock of depression. He could have expected to find himself mounting to a very ruinous tower, by very narrow winding staircases; but in this case the first steps into the house were actually steps downwards. They went down several short and broken stairways into large twilit rooms which, but for their lines of dark pictures and dusty bookshelves, might have been the traditional dungeons beneath the castle moat. Here and there a candle in an old candlestick lit up some dusty accidental detail of a dead elegance; but the visitor was not so much impressed or depressed by this artificial light as by the one pale gleam of natural light. As he passed down the long room he saw the only window in that wall—a curious low oval window of a late seventeenth-century fashion. But the strange thing about it was that it did not look out directly on any space of sky but only on a reflection of sky; a pale strip of daylight merely mirrored in the moat, under the hanging shadow of the bank. Payne had a memory of the Lady of Shallot who never saw the world outside except in a mirror. The lady of this Shallot not only in some sense saw the world in a mirror, but even saw the world upside-down.

'It's as if the house of Darnaway were falling literally as well as metaphorically,' said Wood in a low voice; 'as if it were sinking slowly into a swamp or a quicksand, until the sea goes over it like a green roof.'

Even the sturdy Dr Barnet started a little at the silent approach of the figure that came to receive them. Indeed, the room was so silent that they were all startled to realize that it was not empty. There were three people in it when they entered: three dim figures motionless in the dim room; all three dressed in black and looking like dark shadows. As the foremost figure drew nearer the grey light from the window, he showed a face that looked almost as grey as its frame of hair. This was old Vine, the steward, long left *in loco parentis* since the death of that eccentric parent, the last Lord Darnaway. He would have been a handsome old man if he had had no teeth. As it was, he had one which showed every now and then and gave him a rather sinister appearance. He received the doctor and his friends with a fine courtesy and escorted them to where the other two figures in black were seated. One of them seemed to Payne to give another appropriate touch of gloomy antiquity to the castle by the mere fact of being a Roman Catholic priest, who might have come out of a priest's hole in the dark old days. Payne could imagine him muttering prayers or telling beads, or tolling bells or doing a number of indistinct and melancholy things in that melancholy place. Just then he might be supposed to have been giving religious consolation to the lady; but it could hardly be supposed that the consolation was very consoling, or at any rate that it was very cheering. For the rest, the priest was personally insignificant enough, with plain and rather expressionless features; but the lady was a very different matter. Her face was very far from being plain or insignificant; it stood out from the darkness of her dress and hair and background with a pallor that was almost awful, but a beauty that was almost awfully alive. Payne looked at it as long as he dared; and he was to look at it a good deal longer before he died.

Wood merely exchanged with his friends such pleasant and polite phrases as would lead up to his purpose of revisiting the portraits. He apologized for calling on the day which he heard was to be one of family welcome; but he was soon convinced that the family was rather mildly relieved to have visitors to distract them or break the shock. He did not hesitate, therefore, to lead Payne through the central reception-room into the library beyond, where hung the portrait, for there was one which he was especially bent on showing, not only as a picture but almost as a puzzle. The little priest trudged along with them; he seemed to know something about old pictures as well as about old prayers.

'I'm rather proud of having spotted this,' said Wood. 'I believe it's a Holbein. If it isn't, there was somebody living in Holbein's time who was as great as Holbein.'

It was a portrait in the hard but sincere and living fashion of the period, representing a man clad in black trimmed with gold and fur, with a heavy, full, rather pale face but watchful eyes.

'What a pity art couldn't have stopped for ever at just that transition stage,' cried Wood, 'and never transitioned any more. Don't you see it's just realistic enough to be real? Don't you see the face speaks all the more because it stands out from a rather stiffer framework of less essential things? And the eyes are even more real than the face. On my soul, I think the eyes are too real for the face! It's just as if those sly, quick eyeballs were protruding out of a great pale mask.'

'The stiffness extends to the figure a little, I think,' said Payne. 'They hadn't quite mastered anatomy when mediævalism ended, at least in the north. That left leg looks to me a good deal out of drawing.'

'I'm not so sure,' replied Wood quietly. 'Those fellows who painted just when realism began to be done, and before it began to be overdone, were often more realistic than we think. They put real details of portraiture into things that are thought merely conventional. You might say this fellow's eyebrows or eye-sockets are a little lop-sided; but I bet if you knew him you'd find that one of his eyebrows did really stick up more than the other. And I shouldn't wonder if he was lame or something, and that black leg was meant to be crooked.'

'What an old devil he looks!' burst out Payne suddenly. 'I trust his reverence will excuse my language.'

'I believe in the devil, thank you,' said the priest with an inscrutable face. 'Curiously enough there was a legend that the devil was lame.'

'I say,' protested Payne, 'you can't really mean that he was the devil; but who the devil was he?'

'He was the Lord Darnaway under Henry VII and Henry VIII,' replied his companion. 'But there are curious legends about him, too; one of them is referred to in that inscription round the frame, and further developed in some notes left by somebody in a book I found here. They are both rather curious reading.'

Payne leaned forward, craning his head so as to follow the archaic inscription round the frame. Leaving out the antiquated lettering and spelling, it seemed to be a sort of rhyme running somewhat thus:

> In the seventh heir I shall return:
> In the seventh hour I shall depart:
> None in that hour shall hold my hand:
> And woe to her that holds my heart.

'It sounds creepy somehow,' said Payne, 'but that may be partly because I don't understand a word of it.'

'It's pretty creepy even when you do,' said Wood in a low voice. 'The record made at a later date, in the old book I found, is all about how this beauty deliberately killed himself in such a way that his wife was executed for his murder. Another note commemorates a later tragedy, seven successions later—under the Georges—in which another Darnaway committed suicide, having first thoughtfully left poison in his wife's wine. It's said that both suicides took place at seven in the evening. I suppose the inference is that he does really return with every seventh inheritor and makes things pleasant, as the rhyme suggests, for any lady unwise enough to marry him.'

'On that argument,' replied Payne, 'it would be a trifle uncomfortable for the next seventh gentleman.'

Wood's voice was lower still as he said:

'The new heir will be the seventh.'

Harry Payne suddenly heaved up his great chest and shoulders like a man flinging off a burden.

'What crazy stuff are we all talking?' he cried. 'We're all educated men in an enlightened age, I suppose. Before I came into this damned dank atmosphere I'd never have believed I should be talking of such things, except to laugh at them.'

'You are right,' said Wood. 'If you lived long enough in this underground palace you'd begin to feel differently about things. I've begun to feel very curiously about that picture, having had so much to do with handling and hanging it. It sometimes seems to me that the painted face is more alive than the dead faces of the people living here; that it is a sort of talisman or magnet: that it commands the elements and draws out the destinies of men and things. I suppose you would call it very fanciful.'

'What is that noise?' cried Payne suddenly.

They all listened, and there seemed to be no noise except the dull boom of the distant sea; then they began to have the sense of something mingling with it; something like a voice calling through the sound of the surf, dulled by it at first, but coming nearer and nearer. The next moment they were certain: someone was shouting outside in the dusk.

Payne turned to the low window behind him and bent to look out. It was the window from which nothing could be seen except the moat with its reflection of bank and sky. But that inverted vision was not the same that he had seen before. From the hanging shadow of the bank in the water depended two dark shadows reflected from the feet and legs of a figure standing above upon the bank. Through that limited aperture they could see nothing but the two legs black against the reflection of a pale and livid sunset. But somehow that very fact of the head being invisible, as if in the clouds, gave something dreadful to the sound that followed; the voice of a man crying aloud what they could not properly hear or understand. Payne especially was peering out of the little window with an altered face, and he spoke with an altered voice:

'How queerly he's standing!'

'No, no,' said Wood, in a sort of soothing whisper. 'Things often look like that in reflection. It's the wavering of the water that makes you think that.'

'Think what?' asked the priest shortly.

'That his left leg is crooked,' said Wood.

Payne had thought of the oval window as a sort of mystical mirror; and it seemed to him that there were in it other inscrutable images of doom. There was something else beside the figure that he did not understand; three thinner legs showing in dark lines against the light, as if some monstrous three-legged spider or bird were standing beside the stranger. Then he had the less crazy thought of a tripod like that of the heathen oracles; and the next moment the thing had vanished and the legs of the human figure passed out of the picture.

He turned to meet the pale face of old Vine, the steward, with his mouth open, eager to speak, and his single tooth showing.

'He has come,' he said. 'The boat arrived from Australia this morning.'

Even as they went back out of the library into the central salon they heard the footsteps of the newcomer clattering down the entrance steps, with various items of light luggage trailed behind him. When Payne saw one of them, he laughed with a reaction of relief. His tripod was nothing but the telescopic legs of a portable camera, easily packed and unpacked; and the man who was carrying it seemed so far to take on equally solid and normal qualities. He was dressed in dark clothes, but of a careless and holiday sort; his shirt was of grey flannel, and his boots echoed uncompromisingly enough in those still chambers. As he strode forward to greet his new circle his stride had scarcely more than the suggestion of a limp. But Payne and his companions were looking at his face, and could scarcely take their eyes from it.

He evidently felt there was something curious and uncomfortable about his reception; but they could have sworn that he did not himself know the cause of it. The lady, supposed to be in some sense already betrothed to him, was certainly beautiful enough to attract him; but she evidently also frightened him. The old steward brought him a sort of feudal homage, yet treated him as if he were the family ghost. The priest still looked at him with a face which was quite indecipherable, and therefore perhaps all the more unnerving. A new sort of irony, more like the Greek irony, began to pass over Payne's mind. He had dreamed of the stranger as a devil, but it seemed almost worse that he was an unconscious destiny. He seemed to march towards crime with the monstrous innocence of Œdipus. He had approached the family mansion in so blindly buoyant a spirit as to have set up his camera to photograph his first sight of it; and even the camera had taken on the semblance of the tripod of a tragic pythoness.

Payne was surprised, when taking his leave a little while after, at something which showed that the Australian was already less unconscious of his surroundings. He said in a low voice:

'Don't go . . . or come again soon. You look like a human being. This place fairly gives me the jumps.'

When Payne emerged out of those almost subterranean halls and came into the night air and the smell of the sea, he felt as if he had come out of that underworld of dreams in which events tumble on top of each other in a way at once unrestful and unreal. The arrival of the strange relative had been somehow unsatisfying and, as it were, unconvincing. The doubling of the same face in the old portrait and the new arrival troubled him like a two-headed monster. And yet it was not altogether a nightmare; nor was it that face, perhaps, that he saw most vividly.

'Did you say?' he asked of the doctor, as they strode together across the striped dark sands by the darkening sea; 'did you say that young man was betrothed to Miss Darnaway by a family compact or something? Sounds rather like a novel.'

'But an historical novel,' answered Dr Barnet. 'The Darnaways all went to sleep a few centuries ago, when things were really done that we only read of in romances. Yes; I believe there's some family tradition by which second or third cousins always marry when they stand in a certain relation of age, in order to unite the property. A damned silly tradition, I should say; and if they often married in and in, in that fashion, it may account on principles of heredity for their having gone so rotten.'

'I should hardly say,' answered Payne a little stiffly, 'that they had all gone rotten.'

'Well,' replied the doctor, 'the young man doesn't *look* rotten, of course, though he's certainly lame.'

'The young man!' cried Payne, who was suddenly and unreasonably angry. 'Well, if you think the young lady looks rotten, I think it's you who have rotten taste.'

The doctor's face grew dark and bitter. 'I fancy I know more about it than you do,' he snapped.

They completed the walk in silence, each feeling that he had been irrationally rude and had suffered equally irrational rudeness; and Payne was left to brood alone on the matter, for his friend Wood had remained behind to attend to some of his business in connexion with the pictures.

Payne took very full advantage of the invitation extended by the colonial cousin, who wanted somebody to cheer him up. During the next few weeks he saw a good deal of the dark interior of the Darnaway home; though it might be said that he did not confine himself entirely to cheering up the colonial cousin. The lady's melancholy was of longer standing and perhaps needed more lifting; anyhow, he showed a laborious readiness to lift it. He was not without a conscience, however, and the situation made him doubtful and uncomfortable. Weeks went by and nobody could discover from the demeanour of the new Darnaway whether he considered himself engaged according to the old compact or no. He went mooning about the dark galleries and stood staring vacantly at the dark and sinister picture. The shades of that prison-house were certainly beginning to close on him, and there was little of his Australian assurance left. But Payne could discover nothing upon the point that concerned him most. Once he attempted to confide in his friend Martin Wood, as he was pottering about in his capacity of picture-hanger; but even out of him he got very little satisfaction.

'It seems to me you can't butt in,' said Wood shortly, 'because of the engagement.'

'Of course I shan't butt in if there is an engagement,' retorted his friend; 'but is there? I haven't said a word to her of course; but I've seen enough of her to be pretty certain she doesn't think there is, even if she thinks there may be. He doesn't say there is, or even hint that there ought to be. It seems to me this shilly-shallying is rather unfair on everybody.'

'Especially on you, I suppose,' said Wood a little harshly. 'But if you ask me, I'll tell you what I think—I think he's afraid.'

'Afraid of being refused?' asked Payne.

'No; afraid of being accepted,' answered the other. 'Don't bite my head off—I don't mean afraid of the lady. I mean afraid of the picture.'

'Afraid of the picture!' repeated Payne.

'I mean afraid of the curse,' said Wood. 'Don't you remember the rhyme about the Darnaway doom falling on him and her?'

'Yes, but look here,' cried Payne; 'even the Darnaway doom can't have it both ways. You tell me first that I mustn't have my own way because of the compact, and then that the compact mustn't have its own way because of the curse. But if the curse can destroy the compact, why should she be tied to the compact? If they're frightened of marrying each other, they're free to marry anybody else, and there's an end of it. Why should I suffer for the observance of something they don't propose to observe? It seems to me your position is very unreasonable.'

'Of course it's all the tangle,' said Wood rather crossly, and went on hammering at the frame of a canvas.

Suddenly, one morning, the new heir broke his long and baffling silence. He did it in a curious fashion, a little crude, as was his way, but with an obvious anxiety to do the right thing. He asked frankly for advice, not of this or that individual as Payne had done, but collectively as of a crowd. When he did speak he threw himself on the whole company like a statesman going to the country. He called it 'a show-down.' Fortunately the lady was not included in this large gesture; and Payne shuddered when he thought of her feelings. But the Australian was quite honest; he thought the natural thing was to ask for help and for information, calling a sort of family council at which he put his cards on the table. It might be said that he flung down his cards on the table, for he did it with a rather desperate air, like one who had been harassed for days and nights by the increasing pressure of a problem. In that short time the shadows of that place of low windows and sinking pavements had curiously changed him, and increased a certain resemblance that crept through all their memories.

The five men, including the doctor, were sitting round a table; and Payne was idly reflecting that his own light tweeds and red hair must be the only colours in the room, for the priest and the steward were in black, and Wood and Darnaway habitually wore dark grey suits that looked almost like black. Perhaps this incongruity had been what the young man had meant by calling him a human being. At that moment the young man himself turned abruptly in his chair and began to talk. A moment after the dazed artist knew that he was talking about the most tremendous thing in the world.

'Is there anything in it?' he was saying. 'That is what I've come to asking myself till I'm nearly crazy. I'd never have believed I should come to thinking of such things; but I think of the portrait and the rhyme and the coincidences or whatever you call them, and I go cold. Is there anything in it? Is there any Doom of the Darnaways or only a damned queer accident? Have I got a right to marry, or shall I bring something big and black out of the sky, that I know nothing about, on myself and somebody else?'

His rolling eye had roamed round the table and rested on the plain face of the priest, to whom he now seemed to be speaking. Payne's submerged practicality rose in protest against the problem of superstition being brought before that supremely superstitious tribunal. He was sitting next to Darnaway and struck in before the priest could answer.

'Well, the coincidences are curious, I admit,' he said, rather forcing a note of cheerfulness; 'but surely we——' and then he stopped as if he had been struck by lightning. For Darnaway had turned his head sharply over his shoulder at the interruption, and with the movement, his left eyebrow jerked up far above its fellow and for an instant the face of the portrait glared at him with a ghastly exaggeration of exactitude. The rest saw it; and all had the air of having been dazzled by an instant of light. The old steward gave a hollow groan.

'It is no good,' he said hoarsely; 'we are dealing with something too terrible.'

'Yes,' assented the priest in a low voice, 'we are dealing with something terrible; with the most terrible thing I know, and the name of it is nonsense.'

'What did you say?' said Darnaway, still looking towards him.

'I said nonsense,' repeated the priest. 'I have not said anything in particular up to now, for it was none of my business; I was only taking temporary duty in the neighbourhood and Miss Darnaway wanted to see me. But since you're asking me personally and point-blank, why, it's easy enough to answer. Of course there's no Doom of the Darnaways to prevent your marrying anybody you have any decent reason for marrying. A man isn't fated to fall into the smallest venial sin, let alone into crimes like suicide and murder. You can't be made to do wicked things against your will because your name is Darnaway, any more than I can because my name is Brown. The Doom of the Browns,' he added with relish—'the Weird of the Browns would sound even better.'

'And you of all people,' repeated the Australian, staring, 'tell me to think like that about it.'

'I tell you to think about something else,' replied the priest cheerfully. 'What has become of the rising art of photography? How is the camera getting on? I know it's rather dark downstairs, but those hollow arches on the floor above could easily be turned into a first-rate photographic studio. A few workmen could fit it out with a glass roof in no time.'

'Really,' protested Martin Wood, 'I do think you should be the last man in the world to tinker about with those beautiful Gothic arches, which are about the best work your own religion has ever done in the world. I should have thought you'd have had some feeling for that sort of art; but I can't see why you should be so uncommonly keen on photography.'

'I'm uncommonly keen on daylight,' answered Father Brown, 'especially in this dingy business; and photography has the virtue of depending on daylight. And if you don't know that I would grind all the Gothic arches in the world to powder to save the sanity of a single human soul, you don't know so much about my religion as you think you do.'

The young Australian had sprung to his feet like a man rejuvenated. 'By George! that's the talk,' he cried; 'though I never thought to hear it from that quarter. I'll tell you what, reverend sir, I'll do something that will show I haven't lost my courage after all.'

The old steward was still looking at him with quaking watchfulness, as if he felt something fey about the young man's defiance. 'Oh,' he cried, 'what are you going to do now?'

'I am going to photograph the portrait,' replied Darnaway.

Yet it was barely a week afterwards that the storm of the catastrophe seemed to stoop out of the sky, darkening the sun of sanity to which the priest had appealed in vain, and plunging the mansion once more in the darkness of the Darnaway doom. It had been easy enough to fit up the new studio; and seen from inside it looked very like any other such studio, empty except for the fullness of the white light. A man coming from the gloomy rooms below had more than normally the sense of stepping into a more than modern brilliancy, as blank as the future. At the suggestion of Wood, who knew the castle well and had got over his first aesthetic grumblings, a small room remaining intact in the upper ruins was easily turned into a dark room, into which Darnaway went out of the white daylight to grope by the crimson gleams of a red lamp. Wood said, laughing, that the red lamp had reconciled him to the vandalism; as that bloodshot darkness was as romantic as an alchemist's cave.

Darnaway had risen at daybreak on the day that he meant to photograph the mysterious portrait, and had it carried up from the library by the single corkscrew staircase that connected the two floors. There he had set it up in the wide white daylight on a sort of easel and planted his photographic tripod in front of it. He said he was anxious to send a reproduction of it to a great antiquary who had written on the antiquities of the house; but the others knew that this was an excuse covering much deeper things. It was, if not exactly a spiritual duel between Darnaway and the demoniac picture, at least a duel between Darnaway and his own doubts. He wanted to bring the daylight of photography face to face with that dark masterpiece of painting; and to see whether the sunshine of the new art would not drive out the shadows of the old.

Perhaps this was why he preferred to do it by himself, even if some of the details seemed to take longer and involve more than normal delay. Anyhow, he rather discouraged the few who visited his studio during the day of the experiment, and who found him focussing and fussing about in a very isolated and impenetrable fashion. The steward had left a meal for him, as he refused to come down; the old gentleman also returned some hours afterwards and found the meal more or less normally disposed of; but when he brought it he got no more gratitude than a grunt. Payne went up once to see how he was getting on, but finding the photographer disinclined for conversation came down again. Father Brown had wandered that way in an unobtrusive style to take Darnaway a letter from the expert to whom the photograph was to be sent. But he left the letter on a tray, and whatever he thought of that great glasshouse full of daylight and devotion to a hobby, a world he had himself in some sense created, he kept it to himself and came down. He had reason to remember very soon that he was the last to come down the solitary staircase connecting the floors, leaving a lonely man and an empty room behind him. The others were standing in the salon that led into the library, just under the great black ebony clock that looked like a titantic coffin.

'How was Darnaway getting on,' asked Payne, a little later, 'when you last went up?'

The priest passed a hand over his forehead. 'Don't tell me I'm getting psychic,' he said with a sad smile. 'I believe I'm quite dazzled with daylight up in that room and couldn't see things straight. Honestly, I felt for a flash as if there were something uncanny about Darnaway's figure standing before that portrait.'

'Oh, that's the lame leg,' said Barnet promptly. 'We know all about that.'

'Do you know,' said Payne abruptly, but lowering his voice, 'I don't think we do know all about it or anything about it. What's the matter with his leg? What was the matter with his ancestor's leg?'

'Oh, there's something about that in the book I was reading in there, in the family archives,' said Wood; 'I'll fetch it for you.' And he stepped into the library just beyond.

'I think,' said Father Brown quietly, 'Mr Payne must have some particular reason for asking that.'

'I may as well blurt it out once and for all,' said Payne, but in a yet lower voice. 'After all, there is a rational explanation. A man from anywhere might have made up to look like the portrait: What do we know about Darnaway? He is behaving rather oddly——'

The others were staring at him in a rather started fashion; but the priest seemed to take it very calmly.

'I don't think the old portrait's ever been photographed,' he said. 'That's why he wants to do it. I don't think there's anything odd about that.'

'Quite an ordinary state of things, in fact,' said Wood with a smile; he had just returned with the book in his hand. And even as he spoke there was a stir in the clockwork of the great dark clock behind him and successive strokes thrilled through the room up to the number of seven. With the last stroke there came a crash from the floor above that shook the house like a thunderbolt; and Father Brown was already two steps up the winding staircase before the sound had ceased.

'My God!' cried Payne involuntarily; 'he is alone up there.'

'Yes,' said Father Brown without turning, as he vanished up the stairway. 'We shall find him alone.'

When the rest recovered from their first paralysis and ran helter-skelter up the stone steps and found their way to the new studio, it was true in that sense that they found him alone. They found him lying in a wreck of his tall camera, with its long splintered legs standing out grotesquely at three different angles; and Darnaway had fallen on top of it with one black crooked leg lying at a fourth angle along the floor. For the moment the dark heap looked as if he were entangled with some huge and horrible spider. Little more than a glance and a touch were needed to tell them that he was dead. Only the portrait stood untouched upon the easel, and one could fancy the smiling eyes shone.

An hour afterwards Father Brown, in helping to calm the confusion of the stricken household, came upon the old steward muttering almost as mechanically as the clock had ticked and struck the terrible hour. Almost without hearing them, he knew what the muttered words must be.

> *In the seventh heir I shall return*
> *In the seventh hour I shall depart.*

As he was about to say something soothing, the old man seemed suddenly to start awake and stiffen into anger; his mutterings changed to a fierce cry.

'You!' he cried; 'you and your daylight! Even you won't say now there is no Doom for the Darnaways.'

'My opinion about this is unchanged,' said Father Brown mildly.

Then after a pause he added: 'I hope you will observe poor Darnaway's last wish, and see the photograph is sent off.'

'The photograph!' cried the doctor sharply. 'What's the good of that? As a matter of fact, it's rather curious; but there isn't any photograph. It seems he never took it after all, after pottering about all day.'

Father Brown swung round sharply. 'Then take it yourselves,' he said. 'Poor Darnaway was perfectly right. It's most important that the photograph should be taken.'

As all the visitors, the doctor, the priest and the two artists trailed away in a black and dismal procession across the brown and yellow sands, they were at first more or less silent, rather as if they had been stunned. And certainly there had been something like a crack of thunder in a clear sky about the fulfilment of that forgotten superstition at the very time when they had most forgotten it; when the doctor and the priest had both filled their minds with rationalism as the photographer had filled his rooms with daylight. They might be as rationalistic as they liked; but in broad daylight the seventh heir had returned, and in broad daylight at the seventh hour he had perished.

'I'm afraid everybody will always believe in the Darnaway superstition now,' said Martin Wood.

'I know one who won't,' said the doctor sharply. 'Why should I indulge in superstition because somebody else indulges in suicide?'

'You think poor Mr Darnaway committed suicide?' asked the priest.

'I'm sure he committed suicide,' replied the doctor.

'It is possible,' agreed the other.

'He was quite alone up there, and he had a whole drug-store of poisons in the dark room. Besides, it's just the sort of thing that Darnaways do.'

'You don't think there's anything in the fulfilment of the family curse?'

'Yes,' said the doctor; 'I believe in one family curse, and that is the family constitution. I told you it was heredity, and they are all half mad. If you stagnate and breed in and brood in your own swamp like that, you're bound to degenerate whether you like it or not. The laws of heredity can't be dodged; the truths of science can't be denied. The minds of the Darnaways are falling to pieces, as their blighted old sticks and stones are falling to pieces, eaten away by the sea and the salt air. Suicide—of course he commited suicide; I dare say all the rest will commit suicide. Perhaps the best thing they could do.'

As the man of science spoke there sprang suddenly and with startling clearness into Payne's memory the face of the daughter of the Darnaways, a tragic mask pale against an unfathomable blackness, but itself of a blinding and more than mortal beauty. He opened his mouth to speak and found himself speechless.

'I see,' said Father Brown to the doctor; 'so you do believe in the superstition after all?'

'What do you mean—believe in the superstition? I believe in the suicide as a matter of scientific necessity.'

'Well,' replied the priest, 'I don't see a pin to choose between your scientific superstition and the other magical superstition. They both seem to end in turning people into paralytics, who can't move their own legs or arms or save their own lives or souls. The rhyme said it was the Doom of the Darnaways to be killed, and the scientific textbook says it is the Doom of the Darnaways to kill themselves. Both ways they seem to be slaves.'

'But I thought you said you believed in rational views of these things.' said Dr Barnet. 'Don't you believe in heredity?'

'I said I believed in daylight,' replied the priest in a loud and clear voice, 'and I won't choose between two tunnels of subterranean superstition that both end in the dark. And the proof of it is this; that you are all entirely in the dark about what really happened in that house.'

'Do you mean about the suicide?' asked Payne.

'I mean about the murder,' said Father Brown; and his voice, though only slightly lifted to a louder note, seemed somehow to resound over the whole shore. 'It was murder: but murder is of the will, which God made free.'

What the others said at the moment in answer to it Payne never knew. For the word had a rather curious effect on him; stirring him like the blast of a trumpet and yet bringing him to a halt. He stood still in the middle of the sandy waste and let the others go on in front of him; he felt the blood crawling through all his veins and the sensation that is called the hair standing on end; and yet he felt a new and unnatural happiness. A psychological process too quick and too complicated for himself to follow had already reached a conclusion that he could not analyse; but the conclusion was one of relief. After standing still for a moment he turned and went back slowly across the sands to the house of the Darnaways.

He crossed the moat with a stride that shook the bridge, descended the stairs and traversed the long rooms with a resounding tread, till he came to the place where Adelaide Darnaway sat haloed with the low light of the oval window, almost like some forgotten saint left behind in the land of death. She looked up, and an expression of wonder made her face yet more wonderful.

'What is it?' she said. 'Why have you come back?'

'I have come for the Sleeping Beauty,' he said in a tone that had the resonance of a laugh. 'This old house went to sleep long ago, as the doctor said; but it is silly for you to pretend to be old. Come up into the daylight and hear the truth. I have brought you a word; it is a terrible word, but it breaks the spell of your captivity.'

She did not understand a word he said, but something made her rise and let him lead her down the long hall and up the stairs and out under the evening sky. The ruins of a dead garden stretched towards the sea, and an old fountain with the figure of a triton, green with rust, remained poised there, pouring nothing out of a dried horn into an empty basin. He had often seen that desolate outline against the evening sky as he passed, and it had seemed to him a type of fallen fortunes in more ways than one. Before long, doubtless, those hollow fonts would be filled, but it would be with the pale green bitter waters of the sea and the flowers would be drowned and strangled in seaweed. So, he had told himself, the daughter of the Darnaways might indeed be wedded; but she would be wedded to death and a doom as deaf and ruthless as the sea. But now he laid a hand on the bronze triton that was like the hand of a giant, and shook it as if he meant to hurl it over like an idol or an evil god of the garden.

'What do you mean?' she asked steadily. 'What is the word that will set us free?'

'The word is murder,' he said, 'and the freedom it brings is as fresh as the flowers of spring. No; I do not mean I have murdered anybody. But the fact that anybody can be murdered is itself good news, after the evil dreams you have been living in. Don't you understand? In that dream of yours everything that happened to you came from inside you; the Doom of the Darnaways was stored up in the Darnaways; it unfolded itself like a horrible flower. There was no escape even by happy accident; it was all inevitable; whether it was Vine and his old-wives' tales, or Barnet and his new-fangled heredity. But this man who died was not the victim of a magic curse or an inherited madness. He was murdered; and for us that murder is simply; yes, *requiescat in pace*: but a happy accident. It is a ray of daylight, because it comes from outside.'

She suddenly smiled. 'Yes, I believe I understand. I suppose you are talking like a lunatic, but I understand. But who murdered him?'

'I do not know,' he answered calmly, 'but Father Brown knows. And as Father Brown says, murder is at least done by the will, free as that wind from the sea.'

'Father Brown is a wonderful person,' she said after a pause; 'he was the only person who ever brightened my existence in any way at all until——'

'Until what?' asked Payne, and made a movement almost impetuous, leaning towards her and thrusting away the bronze monster so that it seemed to rock on its pedestal.

'Well, until you did,' she said and smiled again.

So was the sleeping palace awakened, and it is no part of this story to describe the stages of its awakening, though much of it had come to pass before the dark of that evening had fallen upon the shore. As Harry Payne strode homewards once more, across those dark sands that he had crossed in so many moods, he was at the highest turn of happiness that is given in this mortal life, and the whole red sea within him was at the top of its tide. He would have had no difficulty in picturing all that place again in flower, and the bronze triton bright as a golden god and the fountain flowing with water or with wine. But all this brightness and blossoming had been unfolded for him by the one word 'murder,' and it was still a word that he did not understand. He had taken it on trust, and he was not unwise; for he was one of those who have a sense of the sound of truth.

It was more than a month later that Payne returned to his London house to keep an appointment with Father Brown, taking the required photograph with him. His personal romance had prospered as well as was fitting under the shadow of such a tragedy, and the shadow itself therefore lay rather more lightly on him; but it was hard to view it as anything but the shadow of a family fatality. In many ways he had been much occupied; and it was not until the Darnaway household had resumed its somewhat stern routine, and the portrait had long been restored to its place in the library, that he had managed to photograph it with a magnesium flare. Before sending it to the antiquary, as originally arranged, he brought it to the priest who had so pressingly demanded it.

'I can't understand your attitude about all this, Father Brown,' he said. 'You act as if you had already solved the problem in some way of your own.'

The priest shook his head mournfully. 'Not a bit of it,' he answered. 'I must be very stupid, but I'm quite stuck; stuck about the most practical point of all. It's a queer business; so simple up to a point and then——Let me have a look at that photograph, will you?'

He held it close to his screwed, short-sighted eyes for a moment, and then said: 'Have you got a magnifying glass?'

Payne produced one, and the priest looked through it intently for some time and then said: 'Look at the title of that book at the edge of the bookshelf beside the frame: it's "The History of Pope Joan." Now, I wonder . . . yes, by George; and the one above is something or other of Iceland. Lord! What a queer way to find it out! What a dolt and donkey I was not to notice it when I was there!'

'But what have you found out?' asked Payne impatiently.

'The last link,' said Father Brown, 'and I'm not stuck any longer. Yes; I think I know how that unhappy story went from first to last now.'

'But why?' insisted the other.

'Why, because,' said the priest with a smile, 'the Darnaway library contained books about Pope Joan and Iceland, not to mention another I see with the title beginning "The Religion of Frederick," which is not so very hard to fill up.' Then, seeing the other's annoyance, his smile faded and he said more earnestly:

'As a matter of fact, this last point, though it is the last link, is not the main business. There were much more curious things in the case than that. One of them is rather a curiosity of evidence. Let me begin by saying something that may surprise you. Darnaway did not die at seven o'clock that evening. He had been already dead for a whole day.'

'Surprise is rather a mild word,' said Payne grimly, 'since you and I both saw him walking about afterwards.'

'No, we did not,' replied Father Brown quietly. 'I think we both saw him, or thought we saw him, fussing about with the focussing of his camera. Wasn't his head under that black cloak when you passed through the room? It was when I did. And that's why I felt there was something queer about the room and the figure. It wasn't that the leg was crooked, but rather than it wasn't crooked. It was dressed in the same sort of dark clothes; but if you see what you believe to be one man standing in the way that another man stands, you will think he's in a strange and strained attitude.'

'Do you really mean,' cried Payne with something like a shudder, 'that it was some unknown man?'

'It was the murderer, said Father Brown. 'He had already killed Darnaway at daybreak and hid the corpse and himself in the dark room—an excellent hiding-place, because nobody normally goes into it or can see much if he does. But he let it fall out on the floor at seven o'clock, of course, that the whole thing might be explained by the curse.'

'But I don't understand,' observed Payne. 'Why didn't he kill him at seven o'clock then, instead of loading himself with a corpse for fourteen hours?'

'Let me ask you another question,' said the priest. 'Why was there no photograph taken? Because the murderer made sure of killing him when he first got up, and before he could take it. It was essential to the murderer to prevent that photograph reaching the expert on the Darnaway antiquities.'

There was a sudden silence for a moment, and then the priest went on in a lower tone:

'Don't you see how simple it is? Why, you yourself saw one side of the possibility; but it's simpler even than you thought. You said a man might be faked to resemble an old picture. Surely it's simpler that a picture should be faked to resemble a man. In plain words, it's true in a rather special way that there was no Doom of the Darnaways. There was no old picture; there was no old rhyme; there was no legend of a man who cause his wife's death. But there was a very wicked and a very clever man who was willing to cause another man's death in order to rob him of his promised wife.'

The priest suddenly gave Payne a sad smile, as if in reassurance. 'For the moment I believe you thought I meant you,' he said, 'But you were not the only person who haunted that house for sentimental reasons. You know the man, or rather you think you do. But there were depths in the man called Martin Wood, artist and antiquary, which none of his mere artistic acquaintances were likely to guess. Remember that he was called in to criticize and catalogue the pictures; in an aristocratic dustbin of that sort that practically means simply to tell the Darnaways what art treasures they had got. They would not be surprised at things turning up they had never noticed before. It had to be done well, and it was; perhaps he was right when he said that if it wasn't Holbein it was somebody of the same genius.'

'I feel rather stunned,' said Payne; 'and there are twenty things I don't see yet. How did he know what Darnaway looked like? How did he actually kill him? The doctors seem rather puzzled at present.'

'I saw a photograph the lady had which the Australian sent on before him,' said the priest, 'and there are several ways in which he could have learned things when the new heir was once recognized. We may not know these details; but they are not difficulties. You remember he used to help in the dark room; it seems to me an ideal place, say, to prick a man with a poisoned pin, with the poisons all handy. No; I say these were not difficulties. The difficulty that stumped me was how Wood could be in two places at once. How could he take the corpse from the dark-room and prop it against the camera so that it would fall in a few seconds, without coming downstairs, when he was in the library looking out a book? And I was such a fool that I never looked at the books in the library; and it was only in this photograph, by very undeserved good luck, that I saw the simple fact of a book about Pope Joan.'

'You've kept your best riddle for the end,' said Payne grimly. 'What on earth can Pope Joan have to do with it?'

'Don't forget the book about the Something of Iceland,' advised the priest, 'or the religion of somebody called Frederick. It only remains to ask what sort of man was the late Lord Darnaway.'

'Oh does it?' observed Payne heavily.

'He was a cultivated, humorous sort of eccentric, I believe,' went on Father Brown. 'Being cultivated, he knew there was no such person as Pope Joan. Being humorous, he was very likely to have thought of the title of "The Snakes of Iceland" or something else that didn't exist. I venture to reconstruct the third title as "The Religion of Frederick the Great"—which also doesn't exist. Now, doesn't it strike you that those would be just the titles to put on the backs of books that didn't exist; or in other words on a bookcase that wasn't a bookcase?'

'Ah!' cried Payne; 'I see what you mean now. There was some hidden staircase——'

'Up to the room Wood himself selected as a dark room,' said the priest nodding. 'I'm sorry. It couldn't be helped. It's dreadfully banal and stupid, as stupid as I have been on this pretty banal case. But we were mixed up in a real musty old romance of decayed gentility and a fallen family mansion; and it was too much to hope that we could escape having a secret passage. It was a priest's hole; and I deserve to be put in it.'

THE MIRROR OF THE MAGISTRATE

James Bagshaw and Wilfred Underhill were old friends, and were fond of rambling through the streets at night, talking interminably as they turned corner after corner in the silent and seemingly lifeless labyrinth of the large suburb in which they lived. The former, a big, dark, good-humoured man with a strip of black moustache, was a professional police detective; the latter, a sharp-faced, sensitive-looking gentleman with light hair, was an amateur interested in detection. It will come as a shock to the readers of the best scientific romance to learn that it was the policeman who was talking and the amateur who was listening, even with a certain respect.

'Ours is the only trade,' said Bagshaw, 'in which the professional is always supposed to be wrong. After all, people don't write stories in which hairdressers can't cut hair and have to be helped by a customer; or in which a cabman can't drive a cab until his fare explains to him the philosophy of cab-driving. For all that, I'd never deny that we often tend to get into a rut: or, in other words, have the disadvantages of going by a rule. Where the romancers are wrong is, that they don't allow us even the advantages of going by a rule.'

'Surely,' said Underhill, 'Sherlock Holmes would say that he went by a logical rule.'

'He may be right,' answered the other; 'but I mean a collective rule. It's like the staff work of an army. We pool our information.'

'And you don't think detective stories allow for that?' asked his friend.

'Well, let's take any imaginary case of Sherlock Holmes, and Lestrade, the official detective. Sherlock Holmes, let us say, can guess that a total stranger crossing the street is a foreigner, merely because he seems to look for the traffic to go to the right instead of the left. I'm quite ready to admit Holmes might guess that. I'm quite sure Lestrade wouldn't guess anything of the kind. But what they leave out is the fact that the policeman, who couldn't guess, might very probably know. Lestrade might know the man was a foreigner merely because his department has to keep an eye on all foreigners; some would say on all natives, too. As a policeman I'm glad the police know so much; for every man wants to do his own job well. But as a citizen, I sometimes wonder whether they don't know too much.'

'You don't seriously mean to say,' cried Underhill incredulously, 'that you know anything about strange people in a strange street. That if a man walked out of that house over there, you would know anything about him?'

'I should if he was the householder,' answered Bagshaw. 'That house is rented by a literary man of Anglo-Roumanian extraction, who generally lives in Paris, but is over here in connection with some poetical play of his. His name's Osric Orm, one of the new poets, and pretty steep to read, I believe.'

'But I mean all the people down the road,' said his companion. 'I was thinking how strange and new and nameless everything looks, with these high blank walls and these houses lost in large gardens. You can't know all of them.'

'I know a few,' answered Bagshaw. 'This garden we're walking under is at the end of the grounds of Sir Humphrey Gwynne, better known as Mr Justice Gwynne, the old judge who made such a row about spying during the war. The house next door to it belongs to a wealthy cigar merchant. He comes from Spanish-America and looks very swarthy and Spanish himself; but he bears the very English name of Buller. The house beyond that—did you hear that noise?'

'I heard something,' said Underhill, 'but I really don't know what it was.'

'I know what it was,' replied the detective, 'it was a rather heavy revolver, fired twice, followed by a cry for help. And it came straight out of the back garden of Mr Justice Gwynne, that paradise of peace and legality.'

He looked up and down the street sharply and then added:

'And the only gate of the back garden is half a mile round on the other side. I wish this wall were a little lower, or I were a little lighter; but it's got to be tried.'

'It is lower a little farther on,' said Underhill, 'and there seems to be a tree that looks helpful.'

They moved hastily along and found a place where the wall seemed to stoop abruptly, almost as if it had half-sunk into the earth; and a garden tree, flamboyant with the gayest garden blossom, straggled out of the dark enclosure and was gilded by the gleam of a solitary street-lamp. Bagshaw caught the crooked branch and threw one leg over the low wall; and the next moment they stood knee-deep amid the snapping plants of a garden border.

The garden of Mr Justice Gwynne by night was rather a singular spectacle. It was large and lay on the empty edge of the suburb, in the shadow of a tall, dark house that was the last in its line of houses. The house was literally dark, being shuttered and unlighted, at least on the side overlooking the garden. But the garden itself, which lay in its shadow and should have been a tract of absolute darkness, showed a random glitter, like that of fading fireworks; as if a giant rocket had fallen in fire among the trees. As they advanced they were able to locate it as the light of several coloured lamps, entangled in the trees like the jewel fruits of Aladdin, and especially as the light from a small, round lake or pond, which gleamed with pale colours as if a lamp were kindled under it.

'Is he having a party?' asked Underhill. 'The garden seems to be illuminated.'

'No,' answered Bagshaw. 'It's a hobby of his, and I believe he prefers to do it when he's alone. He likes playing with a little plant of electricity that he works from that bungalow or hut over there, where he does his work and keeps his papers. Buller, who knows him very well, says the coloured lamps are rather more often a sign he's not to be disturbed.'

'Sort of red danger signals,' suggested the other.

'Good Lord! I'm afraid they are danger signals!' and he began suddenly to run.

A moment after Underhill saw what he had seen. The opalescent ring of light, like the halo of the moon, round the sloping sides of the pond, was broken by two black stripes or streaks which soon proved themselves to be the long, black legs of a figure fallen head downwards into the hollow, with the head in the pond.

'Come on,' cried the detective sharply, 'that looks to me like——'

His voice was lost, as he ran on across the wide lawn, faintly luminous in the artificial light, making a bee-line across the big garden for the pool and the fallen figure. Underhill was trotting steadily in that straight track, when something happened that startled him for the moment. Bagshaw, who was travelling as steadily as a bullet towards the black figure by the luminous pool, suddenly turned at a sharp angle and began to run even more rapidly towards the shadow of the house. Underhill could not imagine what he meant by the altered direction. The next moment, when the detective had vanished into the shadow of the house, there came out of that obscurity the sound of a scuffle and a curse; and Bagshaw returned lugging with him a little struggling man with red hair. The captive had evidently been escaping under the shelter of the building, when the quicker ears of the detective had heard him rustling like a bird among the bushes.

'Underhill,' said the detective, 'I wish you'd run on and see what's up by the pool. And now, who are you?' he asked, coming to a halt. 'What's your name?'

'Michael Flood,' said the stranger in a snappy fashion. He was an unnaturally lean little man, with a hooked nose too large for his face, which was colourless, like parchment, in contrast with the ginger colour of his hair. 'I've got nothing to do with this. I found him lying dead and I was scared; but I only came to interview him for a paper.'

'When you interview celebrities for the Press,' said Bagshaw, 'do you generally climb over the garden wall?'

And he pointed grimly to a trail of footprints coming and going along the path towards the flower bed.

The man calling himself Flood wore an expression equally grim.

'An interviewer might very well get over the wall,' he said, 'for I couldn't make anybody hear at the front door. The servant had gone out.'

'How do you know he'd gone out?' asked the detective suspiciously.

'Because,' said Flood, with an almost unnatural calm, 'I'm not the only person who gets over garden walls. It seems just possible that you did it yourself. But, anyhow, the servant did; for I've just this moment seen him drop over the wall, away on the other side of the garden, just by the garden door.'

'Then why didn't he use the garden door?' demanded the cross-examiner.

'How should I know?' retorted Flood. 'Because it was shut, I suppose. But you'd better ask him, not me; he's coming towards the house at this minute.'

There was, indeed, another shadowy figure beginning to be visible through the fire-shot gloaming, a squat, square-headed figure, wearing a red waistcoat as the most conspicuous part of a rather shabby livery. He appeared to be making with unobtrusive haste towards a side-door in the house, until Bagshaw hallooed to him to halt. He drew nearer to them very reluctantly, revealing a heavy, yellow face, with a touch of something Asiastic which was consonant with his flat, blue-black hair.

Bagshaw turned abruptly to the man called Flood. 'Is there anybody in this place,' he said, 'who can testify to your identity?'

'Not many, even in this country,' growled Flood. 'I've only just come from Ireland; the only man I know round here is the priest at St Dominic's Church—Father Brown.'

'Neither of you must leave this place,' said Bagshaw, and then added to the servant: 'But you can go into the house and ring up St Dominic's Presbytery and ask Father Brown if he would mind coming round here at once. No tricks, mind.'

While the energetic detective was securing the potential fugitives, his companion, at his direction, had hastened on to the actual sense of the tragedy. It was a strange enough scene; and, indeed, if the tragedy had not been tragic it would have been highly fantastic. The dead man (for the briefest examination proved him to be dead) lay with his head in the pond, where the glow of the artificial illumination encircled the head with something of the appearance of an unholy halo. The face was gaunt and rather sinister, the brow bald, and the scanty curls dark grey, like iron rings; and, despite the damage done by the bullet wound in the temple, Underhill had no difficulty in recognizing the features he had seen in the many portraits of Sir Humphrey Gwynne. The dead man was in evening-dress, and his long, black legs, so thin as to be almost spidery, were sprawling at different angles up the steep bank from which he had fallen. As by some weird whim of diabolical arabesque, blood was eddying out, very slowly, into the luminous water in snaky rings, like the transparent crimson of sunset clouds.

Underhill did not know how long he stood staring down at this macabre figure, when he looked up and saw a group of four figures standing above him on the bank. He was prepared for Bagshaw and his Irish captive, and he had no difficulty in guessing the status of the servant in the red waistcoat. But the fourth figure had a sort of grotesque solemnity that seemed strangely congruous to that incongruity. It was a stumpy figure with a round face and a hat like a black halo. He realized that it was, in fact, a priest; but there was something about it that reminded him of some quaint old black woodcut at the end of a Dance of Death.

Then he heard Bagshaw saying to the priest:

'I'm glad you can identify this man; but you must realize that he's to some extent under suspicion. Of course, he may be innocent; but he did enter the garden in an irregular fashion.'

'Well, I think he's innocent myself,' said the little priest in a colourless voice. 'But, of course, I may be wrong.'

'Why do you think he is innocent?'

'Because he entered the garden in an irregular fashion,' answered the cleric. 'You see, I entered it in a regular fashion myself. But I seem to be almost the only person who did. All the best people seem to get over garden walls nowadays.'

'What do you mean by a regular fashion?' asked the detective.

'Well,' said Father Brown, looking at him with limpid gravity, 'I came in by the front door. I often come into houses that way.'

'Excuse me,' said Bagshaw, 'but does it matter very much how you came in, unless you propose to confess to the murder?'

'Yes, I think it does,' said the priest mildly. 'The truth is, that when I came in at the front door I saw something I don't think any of the rest of you have seen. It seems to me it might have something to do with it.'

'What did you see?'

'I saw a sort of general smash-up,' said Father Brown in his mild voice. 'A big looking-glass broken, and a small palm tree knocked over, and the pot smashed all over the floor. Somehow, it looked to me as if something had happened.'

'You are right,' said Bagshaw after a pause. 'If you saw that, it certainly looks as if it had something to do with it.'

'And if it had anything to do with it,' said the priest very gently, 'it looks as if there was one person who had nothing to do with it; and that is Mr Michael Flood, who entered the garden over the wall in an irregular fashion, and then tried to leave it in the same irregular fashion. It is his irregularity that makes me believe in his innocence.'

'Let us go into the house,' said Bagshaw abruptly.

As they passed in at the side-door, the servant leading the way, Bagshaw fell back a pace or two and spoke to his friend.

'Something odd about that servant,' he said. 'Says his name is Green, though he doesn't look it; but there seems no doubt he's really Gwynne's servant, apparently the only regular servant he had. But the queer thing is, that he flatly denied that his master was in the garden at all, dead or alive. Said the old judge had gone out to a grand legal dinner and couldn't be home for hours, and gave that as his excuse for slipping out.'

'Did he,' asked Underhill, 'give any excuse for his curious way of slipping in?'

'No, none that I can make sense of,' answered the detective. 'I can't make him out. He seems to be scared of something.'

Entering by the side-door, they found themselves at the inner end of the entrance hall, which ran along the side of the house and ended with the front door, surmounted by a dreary fanlight of the old-fashioned pattern. A faint, grey light was beginning to outline its radiation upon the darkness, like some dismal and discoloured sunrise; but what light there was in the hall came from a single, shaded lamp, also of an antiquated sort, that stood on a bracket in a corner. By the light of this Bagshaw could distinguish the debris of which Brown had spoken. A tall palm, with long sweeping leaves, had fallen full length, and its dark red pot was shattered into shards. They lay littered on the carpet, along with pale and gleaming fragments of a broken mirror, of which the almost empty frame hung behind them on the wall at the end of the vestibule. At right angles to this entrance, and directly opposite the side-door as they entered, was another and similar passage leading into the rest of the house. At the other end of it could be seen the telephone which the servant had used to summon the priest; and a half-open door, showing, even through the crack, the serried ranks of great leather-bound books, marked the entrance to the judge's study.

Bagshaw stood looking down at the fallen pot and the mingled fragments at his feet.

'You're quite right,' he said to the priest; 'there's been a struggle here. And it must have been a struggle between Gwynne and his murderer.'

'It seemed to me,' said Father Brown modestly, 'that something had happened here.'

'Yes; it's pretty clear what happened,' assented the detective. 'The murderer entered by the front door and found Gwynne; probably Gwynne let him in. There was a death grapple, possibly a chance shot, that hit the glass, though they might have broken it with a stray kick or anything. Gwynne managed to free himself and fled into the garden, where he was pursued and shot finally by the pond. I fancy that's the whole story of the crime itself; but, of course, I must look round the other rooms.'

The other rooms, however, revealed very little, though Bagshaw pointed significantly to the loaded automatic pistol that he found in a drawer of the library desk.

'Looks as if he was expecting this,' he said; 'yet it seems queer he didn't take it with him when he went out into the hall.'

Eventually they returned to the hall, making their way towards the front door, Father Brown letting his eye rove around in a rather absent-minded fashion. The two corridors, monotonously papered in the same grey and faded pattern, seemed to emphasize the dust and dingy floridity of the few early Victorian ornaments, the green rust that devoured the bronze of the lamp, the dull gold that glimmered in the frame of the broken mirror.

'They say it's bad luck to break a looking-glass,' he said. 'This looks like the very house of ill-luck. There's something about the very furniture——'

'That's rather odd,' said Bagshaw sharply. 'I thought the front door would be shut, but it's left on the latch.'

There was no reply; and they passed out of the front door into the front garden, a narrower and more formal plot of flowers, having at one end a curiously clipped hedge with a hole in it, like a green cave, under the shadow of which some broken steps peeped out.

Father Brown strolled up to the hole and ducked his head under it. A few moments after he had disappeared they were astonished to hear his quiet voice in conversation above their heads, as if he were talking to somebody at the top of a tree. The detective followed, and found that the curious covered stairway led to what looked like a broken bridge, over-hanging the darker and emptier spaces of the garden. It just curled round the corner of the house, bringing in sight the field of coloured lights beyond and beneath. Probably it was the relic of some abandoned architectural fancy of building a sort of terrace on arches across the lawn. Bagshaw thought it a curious cul-de-sac in which to find anybody in the small hours between night and morning; but he was not looking at the details of it just then. He was looking at the man who was found.

As the man stood with his back turned—a small man in light grey clothes—the one outstanding feature about him was a wonderful head of hair, as yellow and radiant as the head of a huge dandelion. It was literally outstanding like a halo, and something in that association made the face, when it was slowly and sulkily turned on them, rather a shock of contrast. That halo should have enclosed an oval face of the mildly angelic sort; but the face was crabbed and elderly with a powerful jowl and a short nose that somehow suggested the broken nose of a pugilist.

'This is Mr Orm, the celebrated poet, I understand,' said Father Brown, as calmly as if he were introducing two people in a drawing-room.

'Whoever he is,' said Bagshaw, 'I must trouble him to come with me and answer a few questions.'

Mr Osric Orm, the poet, was not a model of self-expression when it came to the answering of questions. There, in that corner of the old garden, as the grey twilight before dawn began to creep over the heavy hedges and the broken bridge, and afterwards in a succession of circumstances and stages of legal inquiry that grew more and more ominous, he refused to say anything except that he had intended to call on Sir Humphrey Gwynne, but had not done so because he could not get anyone to answer the bell. When it was pointed out that the door was practically open, he snorted. When it was hinted that the hour was somewhat late, he snarled. The little that he said was obscure, either because he really knew hardly any English, or because he knew better than to know any. His opinions seemed to be of a nihilistic and destructive sort, as was indeed the tendency of his poetry for those who could follow it; and it seemed possible that his business with the judge, and perhaps his quarrel with the judge, had been something in the anarchist line. Gwynne was known to have had something of a mania about Bolshevist spies, as he had about German spies. Anyhow, one coincidence, only a few moments after his capture, confirmed Bagshaw in the impression that the case must be taken seriously. As they went out of the front gate into the street, they so happened to encounter yet another neighbour, Buller, the cigar merchant from next door, conspicuous by his brown, shrewd face and the unique orchid in his buttonhole; for he had a name in that branch of horticulture. Rather to the surprise of the rest, he hailed his neighbour, the poet, in a matter-of-fact manner, almost as if he had expected to see him.

'Hallo, here we are again,' he said. 'Had a long talk with old Gwynne, I suppose?'

'Sir Humphrey Gwynne is dead,' said Bagshaw. 'I am investigating the case and I must ask you to explain.'

Buller stood as still as the lamp-post beside him, possibly stiffened with surprise. The red end of his cigar brightened and darkened rhythmically, but his brown face was in shadow; when he spoke it was with quite a new voice.

'I only mean,' he said, 'that when I passed two hours ago Mr Orm was going in at this gate to see Sir Humphrey.'

'He says he hasn't seen him yet,' observed Bagshaw, 'or even been into the house.'

'It's a long time to stand on the doorstep,' observed Buller.

'Yes,' said Father Brown; 'it's rather a long time to stand in the street.'

'I've been home since then,' said the cigar merchant. 'Been writing letters and came out again to post them.'

'You'll have to tell all that later,' said Bagshaw. 'Good night—or good morning.'

The trial of Osric Orm for the murder of Sir Humphrey Gwynne, which filled the newspapers for so many weeks, really turned entirely on the same crux as that little talk under the lamp-post, when the grey-green dawn was breaking about the dark streets and gardens. Everything came back to the enigma of those two empty hours between the time when Buller saw Orm going in at the garden gate, and the time when Father Brown found him apparently still lingering in the garden. He had certainly had the time to commit six murders, and might almost have committed them for want of something to do; for he could give no coherent account of what he was doing. It was argued by the prosecution that he had also the opportunity, as the front door was unlatched, and the side-door into the larger garden left standing open. The court followed, with considerable interest, Bagshaw's clear reconstruction of the struggle in the passage, of which the traces were so evident; indeed, the police had since found the shot that had shattered the glass. Finally, the hole in the hedge to which he had been tracked, had very much the appearance of a hiding-place. On the other hand, Sir Matthew Blake, the very able counsel for the defence, turned this last argument the other way: asking why any man should entrap himself in a place without possible exit, when it would obviously be much more sensible to slip out into the street. Sir Matthew Blake also made effective use of the mystery that still rested upon the motive for the murder. Indeed, upon this point, the passages between Sir Matthew Blake and Sir Arthur Travers, the equally brilliant advocate for the prosecution, turned rather to the advantage of the prisoner. Sir Arthur could only throw out suggestions about a Bolshevist conspiracy which sounded a little thin. But when it came to investigating the facts of Orm's mysterious behaviour that night he was considerably more effective.

The prisoner went into the witness-box, chiefly because his astute counsel calculated that it would create a bad impression if he did not. But he was almost an uncommunicative to his own counsel as to the prosecuting counsel. Sir Arthur Travers made all possible capital out of his stubborn silence, but did not succeed in breaking it. Sir Arthur was a long, gaunt man, with a long, cadaverous face, in striking contrast to the sturdy figure and bright, bird-like eye of Sir Matthew Blake. But if Sir Matthew suggested a very cocksure sort of cock-sparrow, Sir Arthur might more truly have been compared to a crane or stork; as he leaned forward, prodding the poet with questions, his long nose might have been a long beak.

'Do you mean to tell the jury,' he asked, in tones of grating incredulity, 'that you never went in to see the deceased gentleman at all?'

'No!' replied Orm shortly.

'You wanted to see him, I suppose. You must have been very anxious to see him. Didn't you wait two whole hours in front of his front door?'

'Yes,' replied the other.

'And yet you never even noticed the door was open?'

'No,' said Orm.

'What in the world were you doing for two hours in somebody's else's front garden?' insisted the barrister. 'You were doing something I suppose?'

'Yes.'

'Is it a secret?' asked Sir Arthur, with adamantine jocularity.

'It's a secret from you,' answered the poet.

It was upon this suggestion of a secret that Sir Arthur seized in developing his line of accusation. With a boldness which some thought unscrupulous, he turned the very mystery of the motive, which was the strongest part of his opponent's case, into an argument for his own. He gave it as the first fragmentary hint of some far-flung and elaborate conspiracy, in which a patriot had perished like one caught in the coils of an octopus.

'Yes,' he cried in a vibrating voice, 'my learned friend is perfectly right! We do not know the exact reason why this honourable public servant was murdered. We shall not know the reason why the next public servant is murdered. If my learned friend himself falls a victim to his eminence, and the hatred which the hellish powers of destruction feel for the guardians of law, he will be murdered, and he will not know the reason. Half the decent people in this court will be butchered in their beds, and we shall not know the reason. And we shall never know the reason and never arrest the massacre, until it has depopulated our country, so long as the defence is permitted to stop all proceedings with this stale tag about "motive," when every other fact in the case, every glaring incongruity, every gaping silence, tells us that we stand in the presence of Cain.'

'I never knew Sir Arthur so excited,' said Bagshaw to his group of companions afterwards. 'Some people are saying he went beyond the usual limit and that the prosecutor in a murder case oughtn't to be so vindictive. But I must say there was something downright creepy about that little goblin with the yellow hair, that seemed to play up to the impression. I was vaguely recalling, all the time, something that De Quincey says about Mr Williams, that ghastly criminal who slaughtered two whole families almost in silence. I think he says that Williams had hair of a vivid unnatural yellow; and that he thought it had been dyed by a trick learned in India, where they dye horses green or blue. Then there was his queer, stony silence, like a troglodyte's; I'll never deny that it all worked me up until I felt there was a sort of monster in the dock. If that was only Sir Arthur's eloquence, then he certainly took a heavy responsibility in putting so much passion into it.'

'He was a friend of poor Gwynne's, as a matter of fact,' said Underhill, more gently; 'a man I know saw them hobnobbing together after a great legal dinner lately. I dare say that's why he feels so strongly in this case. I suppose it's doubtful whether a man ought to act in such a case on mere personal feeling.'

'He wouldn't,' said Bagshaw. 'I bet Sir Arthur Travers wouldn't act only on feeling, however strongly he felt. He's got a very stiff sense of his own professional position. He's one of those men who are ambitious even when they've satisfied their ambition. I know nobody who'd take more trouble to keep his position in the world.

No; you've got hold of the wrong moral to his rather thundering sermon. If he lets himself go like that, it's because he thinks he can get a conviction, anyhow, and wants to put himself at the head of some political movement against the conspiracy he talks about. He must have some very good reason for wanting to convict Orm and some very good reason for thinking he can do it. That means that the facts will support him. His confidence doesn't look well for the prisoner.' He became conscious of an insignificant figure in the group.

'Well, Father Brown,' he said with a smile; 'what do you think of our judicial procedure?'

'Well,' replied the priest rather absently, 'I think the thing that struck me most was how different men look in their wigs. You talk about the prosecuting barrister being so tremendous. But I happened to see him take his wig off for a minute, and he really looks quite a different man. He's quite bald, for one thing.'

'I'm afraid that won't prevent his being tremendous,' answered Bagshaw. 'You don't propose to found the defence on the fact that the prosecuting counsel is bald, do you?'

'Not exactly,' said Father Brown good-humouredly. 'To tell the truth, I was thinking how little some kinds of people know about other kinds of people. Suppose I went among some remote people who had never even heard of England. Suppose I told them that there is a man in my country who won't ask a question of life and death, until he has put an erection made of horse-hair on the top of his head, with little tails behind, and grey corkscrew curls at the side, like an Early Victorian old woman. They would think he must be rather eccentric; but he isn't at all eccentric, he's only conventional. They would think so, because they don't know anything about English barristers; because they don't know what a barrister is. Well, that barrister doesn't know what a poet is. He doesn't understand that a poet's eccentricities wouldn't seem eccentric to other poets. He thinks it odd that Orm should walk about in a beautiful garden for two hours, with nothing to do. God bless my soul! A poet would think nothing of walking about in the same backyard for ten hours if he had a poem to do. Orm's own counsel was quite as stupid. It never occurred to him to ask Orm the obvious question.'

'What question do you mean?' asked the other.

'Why, what poem he was making up, of course,' said Father

Brown rather impatiently. 'What line he was stuck at, what epithet he was looking for, what climax he was trying to work up to. If there were any educated people in court, who know what literature is, they would have known well enough whether he had had anything genuine to do. You'd have asked a manufacturer about the conditions of his factory; but nobody seems to consider the conditions under which poetry is manufactured. It's done by doing nothing.'

'That's all very well,' replied the detective; 'but why did he hide? Why did he climb up that crooked little stairway and stop there; it led nowhere.'

'Why, because it led nowhere, of course,' cried Father Brown explosively. 'Anybody who clapped eyes on that blind alley ending in mid-air might have known an artist would want to go there, just as a child would.'

He stood blinking for a moment, and then said apologetically: 'I beg your pardon; but it seems odd that none of them understand these things. And then there was another thing. Don't you know that everything has, for an artist, one aspect or angle that is exactly *right*? A tree, a cow, and a cloud, in a certain relation only, mean something; as three letters, in one order only, mean a word. Well, the view of that illuminated garden from that unfinished bridge was the right view of it. It was as unique as the fourth dimension. It was a sort of fairy foreshortening; it was like looking *down* at heaven and seeing all the stars growing on trees and that luminous pond like a moon fallen flat on the fields in some happy nursery tale. He could have looked at it for ever. If you told him the path led nowhere, he would tell you it had led him to the country at the end of the world. But do you expect him to tell you that in the witnessbox? What would you say to him if he did? You talk about a man having a jury of his peers. Why don't you have a jury of poets?'

'You talk as if you were a poet yourself,' said Bagshaw..

'Thank your stars I'm not,' said Father Brown. 'Thank your lucky stars a priest has to be more charitable than a poet. Lord have mercy on us, if you knew what a crushing, what a cruel contempt he feels for the lot of you, you'd feel as if you were under Niagara.'

'You may know more about the artistic temperament than I do,' said Bagshaw after a pause; 'but, after all, the answer is simple. You can only show that he might have done what he did, without committing the crime. But it's equally true that he might have committed the crime. And who else could have commited it?'

'Have you thought about the servant, Green?' asked Father Brown, reflectively. 'He told a rather queer story.'

'Ah,' cried Bagshaw quickly, 'you think Green did, after all.'

'I'm quite sure he didn't,' replied the other. 'I only asked if you'd thought about his queer story. He only went out for some trifle, a drink or an assignation or what not. But he went out by the garden door and came back over the garden wall. In other words, he left the door open, but he came back to find it shut. Why? Because Somebody Else had already passed out that way.'

'The murderer,' muttered the detective doubtfully. 'Do you know who he was?'

'I know what he looked like,' answered Father Brown quietly. 'That's the only thing I do know. I can almost see him as he came in at the front door, in the gleam of the hall lamp; his figure, his clothes, even his face!'

'What's all this?'

'He looked like Sir Humphrey Gwynne,' said the priest.

'What the devil do you mean?' demanded Bagshaw. 'Gwynne was lying dead with his head in the pond.'

'Oh, yes,' said Father Brown.

After a moment he went on: 'Let's go back to that theory of yours, which was a very good one, though I don't quite agree with it. You suppose the murderer came in at the front door, met the judge in the front hall, struggling with him and breaking the mirror; that the judge then retreated into the garden, where he was finally shot. Somehow, it doesn't sound natural to me. Granted he retreated down the hall, there are two exits at the end, one into the garden and one into the house. Surely, he would be more likely to retreat into the house? His gun was there; his telephone was there; his servant, so far as he knew, was there. Even the nearest neighbours were in that direction. Why should he stop to open the garden door and go out alone on the deserted side of the house?'

'But we know he did go out of the house,' replied his companion, puzzled. 'We know he went out of the house, because he was found in the garden.'

'He never went out of the house, because he never was in the house,' said Father Brown. 'Not that evening, I mean. He was sitting in that bungalow. I read *that* lesson in the dark, at the beginning, in red and golden stars across the garden. They were worked from the hut; they wouldn't have been burning at all if he hadn't been in the hut. He was trying to run across to the house and the telephone, when the murderer shot him beside the pond.'

'But what about the pot and the palm and the broken mirror?' cried Bagshaw. 'Why, it was you who found them! It was you yourself who said there must have been a struggle in the hall.'

The priest blinked rather painfully. 'Did I?' he muttered. 'Surely, I didn't say that. I never thought that. What I think I said, was that something had happened in the hall. And something did happen; but it wasn't a struggle.'

'Then what broke the mirror?' asked Bagshaw shortly.

'A bullet broke the mirror,' answered Father Brown gravely; 'a bullet fired by the criminal. The big fragments of falling glass were quite enough to knock over the pot and the palm.'

'Well, what else could he have been firing at except Gwynne?' asked the detective.

'It's rather a fine metaphysical point,' answered his clerical companion almost dreamily. 'In one sense, of course, he was firing at Gwynne. But Gwynne wasn't there to be fired at. The criminal was alone in the hall.'

He was silent for a moment, and then went on quietly. 'Imagine the looking-glass at the end of the passage, before it was broken, and the tall palm arching over it. In the half-light, reflecting these monochrome walls, it would look like the end of the passage. A man reflected in it would look like a man coming from inside the house. It would look like the master of the house—if only the reflection were a little like him.'

'Stop a minute,' cried Bagshaw. 'I believe I begin——'

'You begin to see,' said Father Brown. 'You begin to see why all the suspects in this case must be innocent. Not one of them could possibly have mistaken his own reflection for old Gwynne. Orm would have known at once that his bush of yellow hair was not a bald head. Flood would have seen his own red head, and Green his own red waistcoat. Besides, they're all short and shabby; none of them could have thought his own image was a tall, thin, old gentleman in evening dress. We want another, equally tall and thin, to match him. That's what I meant by saying that I knew what the murderer looked like.'

'And what do you argue from that?' asked Bagshaw, looking at him steadily.

The priest uttered a sort of sharp, crisp laugh, oddly different from his ordinary mild manner of speech.

'I am going to argue,' he said, 'the very thing that you said was so ludicrous and impossible.'

'What do you mean?'

'I'm going to base the defence,' said Father Brown, 'on the fact that the prosecuting counsel has a bald head.'

'Oh, my God!' said the detective quietly, and got to his feet, staring.

Father Brown had resumed his monologue in an unruffled manner.

'You've been following the movements of a good many people in this business; you policemen were prodigiously interested in the movements of the poet, and the servant, and the Irishman. The man whose movements seem to have been rather forgotten is the dead man himself. His servant was quite honestly astonished at finding his master had returned. His master had gone to a great dinner of all the leaders of the legal profession, but had left it abruptly and come home. He was not ill, for he summoned no assistance; he had almost certainly quarrelled with some leader of the legal profession. It's among the leaders of that profession that we should have looked first for his enemy. He returned, and shut himself up in the bungalow, where he kept all his private documents about treasonable practices. But the leader of the legal profession, who knew there was something against him in those documents, was thoughtful enough to follow his accuser home; he also being in evening-dress, but with a pistol in his pocket. That is all; nobody could ever have guessed it except for the mirror.'

He seemed to be gazing into vacancy for a moment, and then added:

'A queer thing is a mirror; a picture frame that holds hundreds of different pictures, all vivid and all vanished for ever. Yet, there was something specially strange about the glass that hung at the end of that grey corridor under that green palm. It is as if it was a magic glass and had a different fate from others, as if its picture could somehow survive it, hanging in the air of that twilight house like a spectre; or at least like an abstract diagram, the skeleton of an argument. We could, at least, conjure out of the void the thing that

Sir Arthur Travers saw. By the way, there was one very true thing that you said about him.'

'I'm glad to hear it,' said Bagshaw with grim good-nature. 'And what was it?'

'You said,' observed the priest, 'that Sir Arthur must have some good reason for wanting to get Orm hanged.'

A week later the priest met the police detective once more, and learned that the authorities had already been moving on the new lines of inquiry when they were interrupted by a sensational event.

'Sir Arthur Travers,' began Father Brown.

'Sir Arthur Travers is dead,' said Bagshaw, briefly.

'Ah!' said the other, with a little catch in his voice; 'you mean that he——'

'Yes,' said Bagshaw, 'he shot at the same man again, but not in a mirror.'

The Song of the Flying Fish

The soul of Mr Peregrine Smart hovered like a fly round one possession and one joke. It might be considered a mild joke, for it consisted merely of asking people if they had seen his goldfish. It might also be considered an expensive joke; but it is doubtful whether he was not secretly more attached to the joke than to the evidence of expenditure. In talking to his neighbours in the little group of new houses that had grown up round the old village green, he lost no time in turning the conversation in the direction of his hobby. To Dr Burdock, a rising biologist with a resolute chin and hair brushed back like a German's, Mr Smart made the easy transition. 'You are interested in natural history; have you seen my goldfish?' To so orthodox an evolutionist as Dr Burdock doubtless all nature was one; but at first sight the link was not close, as he was a specialist who had concentrated entirely upon the primitive ancestry of the giraffe. To Father Brown, from a church in the neighbouring provincial town, he traced a rapid train of thought which touched on the topics of 'Rome—St Peter—fisherman—fish—goldfish.' In talking to Mr Imlack Smith, the bank manager, a slim and sallow gentleman of dressy appearance but quiet demeanour, he violently wrenched the conversation to the subject of the gold standard, from which it was merely a step to goldfish. In talking to that brilliant Oriental traveller and scholar, Count Yvon de Lara (whose title was French and his face rather Russian, not to say Tartar), the versatile conversationalist showed an intense and intelligent interest in the Ganges and the Indian Ocean, leading naturally to the possible presence of goldfish in those waters. From Mr Harry Hartopp, the very rich but very shy and silent young gentleman who had recently come down from London, he had at last extorted the information that the embarrassed youth in question was *not* interested in fishing, and had then added: 'Talking about fishing, have you seen my goldfish?'

The peculiar thing about the goldfish was that they were made of gold. They were part of an eccentric but expensive toy, said to have been made by the freak of some rich Eastern prince, and Mr Smart had picked it up at some sale or in some curiosity shop, such as he frequented for the purpose of lumbering up his house with unique and useless things. From the other end of the room it looked like a rather unusually large bowl containing rather unusually large living fish; a closer inspection showed it to be a huge bubble of beautifully blown Venetian glass, very thin and delicately clouded with faintly iridescent colour, in the tinted twilight of which hung grotesque golden fishes with great rubies for eyes. The whole thing was undoubtedly worth a great deal in solid material; how much more would depend upon the waves of lunacy passing over the world of collectors. Mr Smart's new secretary, a young man named Francis Boyle, though an Irishman and not credited with caution, was mildly surprised at his talking so freely of the gems of his collection to the group of comparative strangers who happened to have alighted in a rather nomadic fashion in the neighbourhood; for collectors are commonly vigilant and sometimes secretive. In the course of settling down to his new duties, Mr Boyle found he was not alone in this sentiment, and that in others, it passed from a mild wonder to a grave disapproval.

'It's a wonder his throat isn't cut,' said Mr Smart's valet, Harris, not without a hypothetical relish, almost as if he had said, in a purely artistic sense: 'It's a pity.'

'It's extraordinary how he leaves things about,' said Mr Smart's head clerk, Jameson, who had come up from the office to assist the new secretary, 'and he won't even put up those ramshackle old bars across his ramshackle old door.'

'It's all very well with Father Brown and the doctor,' said Mr Smart's housekeeper, with a certain vigorous vagueness that marked her opinions, 'but when it comes to foreigners, I call it tempting providence. It isn't only the Count, either; that man at the bank looks to me much too yellow to be English.'

'Well, that young Hartopp is English enough,' said Boyle good-humouredly, 'to the extent of not having a word to say for himself.'

'He thinks the more,' said the housekeeper. 'He may not be exactly a foreigner, but he is not such a fool as he looks. Foreign is as foreign does, I say,' she added darkly.

Her disapproval would probably have deepened if she had heard the conversation, in her master's drawing-room that afternoon, a conversation of which the goldfish were the text, though the offensive foreigner tended more and more to be the central figure.

It was not that he spoke so very much; but even his silences had something positive about them. He looked the more massive for sitting in a sort of heap on a heap of cushions, and in the deepening twilight his wide Mongolian face seemed faintly luminous, like a moon. Perhaps his background brought out something atmospherically Asiatic about his face and figure, for the room was a chaos of more or less costly curiosities, amid which could be seen the crooked curves and burning colours of countless Eastern weapons, Eastern pipes and vessels, Eastern musical instruments and illuminated manuscripts. Anyhow, as the conversation proceeded, Boyle felt more and more that the figure seated on the cushions and dark against the twilight had the exact outline of a huge image of Buddha.

The conversation was general enough, for all the little local group were present. They were, indeed, often in the habit of dropping in at each other's houses, and by this time constituted a sort of club, of people coming from the four or five houses standing round the green. Of these houses Peregrine Smart's was the oldest, largest, and most picturesque; it straggled down almost the whole of one side of the square, leaving only room for a small villa, inhibited by a retired colonel named Varney, who was reported to be an invalid, and certainly was never seen to go abroad. At right angles to these stood two or three shops that served the simpler needs of the hamlet, and at the corner the inn of the Blue Dragon, at which Mr Hartopp, the stranger from London, was staying. On the opposite side were three houses, one rented by the Count de Lara, one by Dr Burdock, and the third still standing empty. On the fourth side was the bank, with an adjoining house for the bank manager, and a line of fence enclosing some land that was let for building. It was thus a very self-contained group, and the comparative emptiness of the open ground for miles round it threw the members more and more on each other's society. That afternoon, one stranger had indeed broken into the magic circle: a hatchet-faced fellow with fierce tufts of eyebrows and moustache, and so shabbily dressed that he must have been a millionaire or a duke if he had really (as was alleged) come down to do business with the old collector. But he was known, at the Blue Dragon at least, as Mr Harmer.

To him had been recounted anew the glories of the gilded fish and the criticisms regarding their custody.

'People are always telling me I ought to lock them up more carefully,' observed Mr Smart, cocking an eyebrow over his shoulder at the dependant who stood there holding some papers from the office. Smart was a round-faced, round-bodied little old man rather like a bald parrot. 'Jameson and Harris and the rest are always at me to bar the doors as if it were a mediæval fortress, though really these rotten old rusty bars are too mediæval to keep anybody out, I should think. I prefer to trust to luck and the local police.'

'It is not always the best bars that keep people out,' said the Count. 'It all depends on who's trying to get in. There was an ancient Hindu hermit who lived naked in a cave and passed through the three armies that encircled the Mogul and took the great ruby out of the tyrant's turban, and went back unscathed like a shadow. For he wished to teach the great how small are the laws of space and time.'

'When we really study the small laws of space and time,' said Dr Burdock dryly, 'we generally find out how those tricks are done. Western science had let in daylight on a good deal of Eastern magic. Doubtless a great deal can be done with hypnotism and suggestion, to say nothing of sleight-of-hand.'

'The ruby was not in the royal tent,' observed the Count in his dreamy fashion; 'but he found it among a hundred tents.'

'Can't all that be explained by telepathy?' asked the doctor sharply.

The question sounded the sharper because it was followed by a heavy silence, almost as if the distinguished Oriental traveller had, with imperfect politeness, gone to sleep.

'I beg your pardon,' he said rousing himself with a sudden smile. 'I had forgotten we were talking with words. In the east we talk with thoughts, and so we never misunderstand each other. It is strange how you people worship words and are satisfied with words. What difference does it make to a thing that you now call it telepathy, as you once called it tomfoolery? If a man climbs into the sky on a mango-tree, how is it altered by saying it is only levitation, instead of saying it is only lies. If a mediæval witch waved a wand and turned me into a blue baboon, you would say it was only atavism.'

The doctor looked for a moment as if he might say that it would not be so great a change after all. But before his irritation could find that or any other vent, the man called Harmer interrupted gruffly:

'It's true enough those Indian conjurors can do queer things, but I notice they generally do them in India. Confederates, perhaps, or merely mass psychology. I don't think those tricks have ever been played in an English village, and I should say our friend's goldfish were quite safe.'

'I will tell you a story,' said de Lara, in his motionless way, 'which happened not in India, but outside an English barrack in the most modernized part of Cairo. A sentinel was standing inside the grating of an iron gateway looking out between the bars on to the street. There appeared outside the gate a beggar, barefoot and in native rags, who asked him, in English that was startlingly distinct and refined, for a certain official document kept in the building for safety. The soldier told the man, of course, that he could not come inside; and the man answered, smiling: "What is inside and what is outside?" The soldier was still staring scornfully through the iron grating when he gradually realized that, though neither he nor the gate had moved, he was actually standing in the street and looking in at the barrack yard, where the beggar stood still and smiling and equally motionless. Then, when the beggar turned towards the building, the sentry awoke to such a sense as he had left, and shouted a warning to all the soldiers within the gate enclosure to hold the prisoner fast. "You won't get out of there anyhow," he said vindictively. Then the beggar said in his silvery voice: "What is outside and what is inside?" And the soldier, still glaring through the same bars, saw that they were once more between him and the street, where the beggar stood free and smiling with a paper in his hand.'

Mr Imlack Smith, the bank manager, was looking at the carpet with his dark sleek head bowed, and he spoke for the first time.

'Did anything happen about the paper?' he asked.

'Your professional instincts are correct, sir,' said the Count with grim affability. 'It was a paper of considerable financial importance. Its consequences were international.'

'I hope they don't occur often,' said young Hartopp gloomily.

'I do not touch the political side,' said the Count serenely, 'but only the philosophical. It illustrates how the wise man can get behind time and space and turn the levers of them, so to speak, so that the whole world turns round before our eyes. But is it so hard for you people to believe that spiritual powers are really more powerful than material ones.'

'Well,' said old Smart cheerfully, 'I don't profess to be an authority on spiritual powers. What do you say, Father Brown?'

'The only thing that strikes me,' answered the little priest, 'is that all the supernatural acts we have yet heard of seem to be thefts. And stealing by spiritual methods seem to me much the same as stealing by material ones.'

'Father Brown is a Philistine,' said the smiling Smith.

'I have a sympathy with the tribe,' said Father Brown. 'A Philistine is only a man who is right without knowing why.'

'All this is too clever for me,' said Hartopp heartily.

'Perhaps,' said Father Brown with a smile, 'you would like to speak without words, as the Count suggests. He would begin by saying nothing in a pointed fashion, and you would retort with a burst of taciturnity.'

'Something might be done with music,' murmured the Count dreamily. 'It would be better than all these words.'

'Yes, I might understand that better,' said the young man in a low voice.

Boyle had followed the conversation with curious attention, for there was something in the demeanour of more than one of the talkers that seemed to him significant or even odd. As the talk drifted to music, with an appeal to the dapper bank manager (who was an amateur musician of some merit), the young secretary awoke with a start to his secretarial duties, and reminded his employer that the head clerk was still standing patiently with the papers in his hand.

'Oh, never mind about those just now, Jameson,' said Smart rather hurriedly. 'Only something about my account; I'll see Mr Smith about it later. You were saying that the 'cello, Mr Smith——

But the cold breath of business had sufficed to disperse the fumes of transcendental talk, and the guests began one after another to say farewell. Only Mr Imlack Smith, bank manager and musician, remained to the last; and when the rest were gone he and his host went into the inner room, where the goldfish were kept, and closed the door.

The house was long and narrow, with a covered balcony running along the first floor, which consisted mostly of a sort of suite of rooms used by the householder himself, his bedroom and dressing-room, and an inner room in which his very valuable treasures were sometimes stored for the night instead of being left in the rooms below. This balcony, like the insufficiently barred door below it, was a matter of concern to the housekeeper, and the head clerk and the others who lamented the carelessness of the collector; but, in truth, that cunning old gentleman was more careful than he seemed. He professed no great belief in the antiquated fastenings of the old house, which the housekeeper lamented to see rusting in idleness, but he had an eye to the more important point of strategy. He always put his favourite goldfish in the room at the back of his bedroom for the night, and slept in front of it, as it were, with a pistol under his pillow. And when Boyle and Jameson, awaiting his return from the *tête-à-tête*, at length saw the door open and their employer reappear, he was carrying the great glass bowl as reverently as it if had been the relic of a saint.

Outside, the last edges of the sunset still clung to the corners of the green square; but inside, a lamp had already been kindled; and in the mingling of the two lights the coloured globe glowed like some monstrous jewel, and the fantastic outlines of the fiery fishes seemed to give it, indeed, something of the mystery of a talisman, like strange shapes seen by a seer in the crystal of doom. Over the old man's shoulder the olive face of Imlack Smith stared like a sphinx.

'I am going up to London tonight, Mr Boyle,' said Old Smart, with more gravity than he commonly showed. 'Mr Smith and I are catching the six-forty-five. I should prefer you, Jameson, to sleep upstairs in my room tonight; if you put the bowl in the back room as usual, it will be quite safe then. Not that I suppose anything could possibly happen.'

'Anything may happen anywhere,' said the smiling Mr Smith. 'I think you generally take a gun to bed with you. Perhaps you had better leave it behind in this case.'

Peregrine Smart did not reply, and they passed out of the house on to the road round the village green.

The secretary and the head clerk slept that night as directed in their employer's bedroom. To speak more strictly, Jameson, the head clerk, slept in a bed in the dressing-room, but the door stood open between, and the two rooms running along the front were practically one. Only the bedroom had a long french window giving on the balcony, and an entrance at the back into the inner apartment where the goldfish bowl had been placed for safety. Boyle dragged his bed right across so as to bar this entrance, put the revolver under his pillow, and then undressed and went to bed, feeling that he had taken all possible precautions against an impossible or improbable event. He did not see why there should be any particular danger of normal burglary; and as for the spiritual burglary that figured in the traveller's tales of the Count de Lara, if his thoughts ran on them so near to sleep it was because they were such stuff as dreams are made of. They soon turned into dreams with intervals of dreamless slumber. The old clerk was a little more restless as usual; but after fussing about a little longer and repeating some of his favourite regrets and warnings, he also retired to his bed in the same manner and slept. The moon brightened and grew dim again above the green square and the grey blocks of houses in a solitude and silence that seemed to have no human witness; and it was when the white cracks of daybreak had already appeared in the corners of the grey sky that the thing happened.

Boyle, being young, was naturally both the healthier and the heavier sleeper of the two. Though active enough when he was once awake, he always had a load to lift in waking. Moreover, he had dreams of the sort that cling to the emerging minds like the dim tentacles of an octopus. They were a medley of many things, including his last look from the balcony across the four grey roads and the green square. But the pattern of them changed and shifted and turned dizzily, to the accompaniment of a low grinding noise, which sounded somehow like a subterranean river, and may have been no more than old Mr Jameson snoring in the dressing-room. But in the dreamer's mind all that murmur and motion was vaguely connected with the words of the Count de Lara, about a wisdom that could hold the levers of time and space and turn the world. In the dream it seemed as if a vast murmuring machinery under the world were really moving whole landscapes hither and thither, so that the ends of the earth might appear in a man's front garden, or his own front garden be exiled beyond the sea.

The first complete impressions he had were the words of a song, with a rather thin metallic accompaniment; they were sung in a foreign accent and a voice that was still strange and yet faintly familiar. And yet he could hardly feel sure that he was not making up poetry in his sleep.

> *Over the land and over the sea*
> *My flying fishes will come to me,*

For the note is not of the world that wakes them,
But in——

He struggled to his feet and saw that his fellow-guardian was already out of bed; Jameson was peering out of the long window on to the balcony and calling out sharply to someone in the street below.

'Who's that?' he called out sharply. 'What do you want?'

He turned to Boyle in agitation, saying: 'There's somebody prowling about just outside. I knew it wasn't safe. I'm going down to bar that front door, whatever they say.'

He ran downstairs in a flutter and Boyle could hear the clattering of the bars upon the front door; but Boyle himself stepped out upon the balcony and looked out on the long grey road that led up to the house, and he thought he was still dreaming.

Upon that grey road leading across that empty moor and through that little English hamlet, there had appeared a figure that might have stepped straight out of the jungle or the bazaar—a figure out of one of the Count's fantastic stories; a figure out of the 'Arabian Nights.' The rather ghostly grey twilight which begins to define and yet to discolour everything when the light in the east has ceased to be localized, lifted slowly like a veil of grey gauze and showed him a figure wrapped in outlandish raiment. A scarf of a strange sea-blue, vast and voluminous, went round the head like a turban, and then again round the chin, giving rather the general character of a hood; so far as the face was concerned it had the effects of a mask. For the raiment round the head was drawn close as a veil; and the head itself was bowed over a queer-looking musical instrument made of silver or steel, and shaped like a deformed or crooked violin. It was played with something like a silver comb, and the notes were curiously thin and keen. Before Boyle could open his mouth, the same haunting alien accent came from under the shadow of the burnous, singing words of the same sort:

> *As the golden birds go back to the tree*
> *My golden fishes return to me.*
> *Return——*

'You've no right here,' called out Boyle in exasperation, hardly knowing what he said.

'I have a right to the goldfish,' said the stranger, speaking more like King Solomon than an unsandalled Bedouin in a ragged blue cloak. 'And they will come to me. Come!'

He struck his strange fiddle as his voice rose sharply on the word. There was a pang of sound that seemed to pierce the mind, and then there came a fainter sound, like an answer: a vibrant whisper. It came from the dark room behind where the bowl of goldfish was standing.

Boyle turned towards it; and even as he turned the echo in the inner room changed to a long tingling sound like an electric bell, and then to a faint crash. It was still a matter of seconds since he had challenged the man from the balcony; but the old clerk had already regained the top of the stairs, panting a little, for he was an elderly gentleman.

'I've locked up the door, anyhow,' he said.

'The stable door,' said Boyle out of the darkness of the inner room.

Jameson followed him into that apartment and found him staring down at the floor, which was covered with a litter of coloured glass like the curved bits of a broken rainbow.

'What do you mean by the stable door?' began Jameson.

'I mean that the steed is stolen,' answered Boyle. 'The flying steeds. The flying fishes our Arab friend outside has just whistled to like so many performing puppies.'

'But how could he?' exploded the old clerk, as if such events were hardly respectable.

'Well, they're gone,' said Boyle shortly. 'The broken bowl is here, which would have taken a long time to open properly, but only a second to smash. But the fish are gone, God knows how, though I think our friend ought to be asked.'

'We are wasting time,' and the distracted Jameson. 'We ought to be after him at once.'

'Much better be telephoning the police at once,' answered Boyle. 'They ought to outstrip him in a flash with motors and telephones that go a good deal farther than we should ever get, running through the village in our nightgowns. But it may be there are things even the police cars and wires won't outstrip.'

While Jameson was talking to the police station through the telephone in an agitated voice, Boyle went out again on to the balcony and hastily scanned that grey landscape of daybreak. There was no trace of the man in the turban, and no other sign of life, except some faint stirrings an expert might have recognized in the hotel of the Blue Dragon. Only Boyle, for the first time, noted consciously something that he had all along been noting unconsciously. It was like a fact struggling in the submerged mind and demanding its own meaning. It was simply the fact that the grey landscape had never been entirely grey; there was one gold spot amid its stripes of colourless colour, a lamp lighted in one of the houses on the other side of the green. Something, perhaps irrational, told him that it had been burning through all the hours of the darkness and was only fading with the dawn. He counted the houses, and his calculation brought out a result which seemed to fit in with something, he knew not what. Anyhow, it was apparently the house of the Count Yvon de Lara.

Inspector Pinner had arrived with several policemen, and done several things of a rapid and resolute sort, being conscious that the very absurdity of the costly trinkets might give the case considerable prominence in the newspapers. He had examined everything, measured everything, taken down everybody's deposition, taken everybody's fingerprints, put everybody's back up, and found himself at the end facing a fact which he could not believe. An Arab from the desert had walked up the public road and stopped in front of the house of Mr Peregrine Smart, where a bowl of artificial goldfish was kept in an inner room; he had then sung or recited a little poem, and the bowl had exploded like a bomb and the fishes vanished into thin air. Nor did it soothe the inspector to be told by a foreign Count—in a soft, purring voice—that the bounds of experience were being enlarged.

Indeed, the attitude of each member of the little group was characteristic enough. Peregrine Smart himself had come back from London the next morning to hear the news of his loss. Naturally he admitted a shock; but it was typical of something sporting and spirited in the little old gentleman, something that always made his small strutting figure look like a cock-sparrow's, that he showed more vivacity in the search than depression at the loss. The man named Harmer, who had come to the village on purpose to buy the goldfish, might be excused for being a little testy of learning they were not there to be bought. But, in truth, his rather aggressive moustache and eyebrows seemed to bristle with something more definite than disappointment, and the eyes that darted over the company were bright with a vigilance that might well be suspicion. The sallow face of the bank manager, who had also returned from London though by a later train, seemed again and again to attract those shining and shifting eyes like a magnet. Of the two remaining figures of the original circle, Father Brown was generally silent when he was not spoken to, and the dazed Hartopp was often silent even when he was.

But the Count was not a man to let anything pass that gave an apparent advantage to his views. He smiled at his rationalistic rival, the doctor, in the manner of one who knows how it is possible to be irritating by being ingratiating.

'You will admit, doctor,' he said, 'that at least some of the stories you thought so improbable look a little more realistic today than they did yesterday. When a man as ragged as those I described is able, by speaking a word, to dissolve a solid vessel inside the four walls of the house he stands outside, it might perhaps be called an example of what I said about spiritual powers and material barriers.'

'And it might be called an example of what I said,' said the doctor sharply, 'about a little scientific knowledge being enough to show how the tricks are done.'

'Do you really mean, doctor,' asked Smart in some excitement, 'that you can throw any scientific light on this mystery?'

'I can throw light on what the Count calls a mystery,' said the doctor, 'beccause it is not a mystery at all. That part of it is plain enough. A sound is only a wave of vibration, and certain vibrations can break glass, if the sound is of a certain kind and the glass of a certain kind. The man did not stand in the road and think, which the Count tells us is the ideal method when Orientals want a little chat. He sang out what he wanted, quite loud, and struck a shrill note on an instrument. It is similar to many experiments by which glass of special composition has been cracked.'

'Such as the experiment,' said the Count lightly, 'by which several lumps of solid gold have suddenly ceased to exist.'

'Here comes Inspector Pinner,' said Boyle. 'Between ourselves, I think he would regard the doctor's natural explanation as quite as much of a fairy tale as the Count's preternatural one. A very sceptical intellect, Mr Pinner's, especially about me. I rather think I am under suspicion.'

'I think we are all under suspicion,' said the Count.

It was the presence of this suspicion in his own case that led

Boyle to seek the personal advice of Father Brown. They were walking round the village green together, some hours later in the day, when the priest, who was frowning thoughtfully at the ground as he listened, suddenly stopped.

'Do you see that?' he asked. 'Somebody's been washing the pavement here—just this little strip of pavement outside Colonel Varney's house. I wonder whether that was done yesterday.'

Father Brown looked rather earnestly at the house, which was high and narrow, and carried rows of striped sun-blinds of gay but already faded colours. The chinks or crannies that gave glimpses of the interior looked all the darker; indeed, they looked almost black in contrast with the façade thus golden in the morning light.

'That is Colonel Varney's house, isn't it?' he asked. 'He comes from the East, too, I fancy. What sort of man is he?'

'I've never even seen him,' answered Boyle. 'I don't think anybody's seen him, except Dr Burdock, and I rather fancy the doctor doesn't see him more than he need.'

'Well, I'm going to see him for a minute,' said Father Brown.

The big front door opened and swallowed the small priest, and his friend stood staring at it in a dazed and irrational manner, as if wondering whether it would ever open again. It opened in a few minutes, and Father Brown emerged, still smiling, and continued his slow and pottering progress round the square of roads. Sometimes he seemed to have forgotten the matter in hand altogether, for he would make passing remarks on historical and social questions, or on the prospects of development in the district. He remarked on the soil used for the beginning of a new road by the bank; he looked across the old village green with a vague expression.

'Common land. I suppose people ought to feed their pigs and geese on it, if they had any pigs or geese; as it is, it seems to feed nothing but nettles and thistles. What a pity that what was supposed to be a sort of large meadow has been turned into a small and petty wilderness. That's Dr Burdock's house opposite, isn't it?'

'Yes,' answered Boyle, almost jumping at this abrupt postscript.

'Very well,' answered Father Brown, 'then I think we'll go indoors again.'

As they opened the front door of Smart's house and mounted the stairs, Boyle repeated to his companion many details of the drama enacted there at daybreak.

'I suppose you didn't doze off again?' asked Father Brown, 'giving time for somebody to scale the balcony while Jameson ran down to secure the door.'

'No,' answered Boyle; 'I am sure of that. I woke up to hear Jameson challenging the stranger from the balcony; then I heard him running downstairs and putting up the bars, and then in two strides I was on the balcony myself.'

'Or could he have slipped in between you from another angle? Are there any other entrances besides the front entrance?'

'Apparently there are not,' said Boyle gravely.

'I had better make sure, don't you think?' asked Father Brown apologetically, and scuttled softly downstairs again. Boyle remained in the front bedroom gazing rather doubtfully after him. After a comparatively brief interval the round and rather rustic visage appeared again at the head of the stairs, looking rather like a turnip ghost with a broad grin.

'No; I think that settles the matter of entrances,' said the turnip ghost, cheerfully. 'And now, I think, having got everything in a tight box, so to speak, we can take stock of what we've got. It's rather a curious business.'

'Do you think,' asked Boyle, 'that the Count or the colonel, or any of these Eastern travellers have anything to do with it? Do you think it is—preternatural?'

'I will grant you this,' said the priest gravely, 'if the Count or the colonel, or any of your neighbours did dress up in Arab masquerade and creep up to this house in the dark—then it *was* preternatural.'

'What do you mean? Why?'

'Because the Arab left no footprints,' answered Father Brown. 'The colonel on the one side and the banker on the other are the nearest of your neighbours. That loose red soil is between you and the bank, it would print off bare feet like a plaster cast and probably leave red marks everywhere. I braved the colonel's curry-seasoned temper to verify the fact that the front pavement was washed yesterday and not today; it was wet enough to make wet footprints all along the road. Now, if the visitor were the Count or the doctor in the houses opposite, he might possibly, of course, have come across the common. But he must have found it exceedingly uncomfortable with bare feet, for it is, as I remarked, one mass of thorns and thistles and stinging nettles. He would surely have pricked himself and probably left traces of it. Unless, as you say, he was a preternatural being.'

Boyle looked steadily at the grave and indecipherable face of his clerical friend.

'Do you mean that he was? he asked, at length.

'There is one general truth to remember,' said Father Brown, after a pause. 'A thing can sometimes be too close to be seen, as, for instance, a man cannot see himself. There was a man who had a fly in his eye when he looked through the telescope, and he discovered that there was a most incredible dragon in the moon. And I am told that if a man hears the exact reproduction of his own voice it sounds like the voice of a stranger. In the same way, if anything is right in the foreground of our life we hardly see it, and if we did we might think it quite odd. If the thing in the foreground got into the middle distance, we should probably think it had come from the remote distance. Just come outside the house again for a moment. I want to show you how it looks from another standpoint.'

He had already risen, and as they descended the stairs he continued his remarks in a rather groping fashion as if he were thinking aloud.

'The Count and the Asiatic atmosphere all come in, because, in a case like this, everything depends on the preparation of the mind. A man can reach a condition in which a brick, falling on his head, will seem to be a Babylonian brick carved with cuneiform, and dropped from the Hanging Gardens of Babylon, so that he will never even look at the brick and see it is of one pattern with the bricks of his own house. So in your case——'

'What does this mean?' interrupted Boyle, staring and pointing at the entrance. 'What in the name of wonder does it mean? The door is barred again.'

He was staring at the front door by which they had entered but a little while before, and across which stood, once more, the great dark bands of rusty iron which had once, as he had said, locked the stable door too late.

There was something darkly and dumbly ironic in those fastenings closing behind them and imprisoning them as if of their own motion.

'Oh those!' said Father Brown casually. 'I put up those bars myself, just now. Didn't you hear me?'

'No,' answered Boyle, staring. 'I heard nothing.'

'Well, I rather thought you wouldn't,' said the other equably. 'There's really no reason why anybody upstairs should hear those bars being put up. A sort of hook fits easily into a sort of hole. When you're quite close you hear a dull click; but that's all. The only thing that makes any noise a man could hear upstairs, is this.'

And he lifted the bar out of its socket and let it fall with a clang at the side of the door.

'It does make a noise if you *unbar* the door,' said Father Brown gravely, 'even if you do it pretty carefully.'

'You mean——'

'I mean,' said Father Brown, 'that what you heard upstairs was Jameson opening the door and not shutting it. And now let's open the door ourselves and go outside.'

When they stood outside in the street, under the balcony, the little priest resumed his previous explanation as coolly as if it had been a chemical lecture.

'I was saying that a man may be in the mood to look for something very distant, and not realize that it is something very close, something very close to himself, perhaps something very like himself. It was a strange and outlandish thing that you saw when you looked down at this road. I suppose it never occurred to you to consider what he saw when he looked up at that balcony?'

Boyle was staring at the balcony and did not answer, and the other added:

'You thought it very wild and wonderful that an Arab should come through civilized England with bare feet. You didn't not remember that at the same moment you had bare feet yourself.'

Boyle at last found words, and it was to repeat words already spoken.

'Jameson opened the door,' he said mechanically.

'Yes,' assented his friend. 'Jameson opened the door and came out into the road in his nightclothes, just as you came out on the balcony. He caught up two things that you had seen a hundred times: the length of old blue curtain that he wrapped round his head, and the Oriental musical instrument you must have often seen in that heap of Oriental curiosities. The rest was atmosphere and acting, very fine acting, for he is a very fine artist in crime.'

'Jameson!' exclaimed Boyle incredulously. 'He was such a dull old stick that I never even noticed him.'

'Precisely,' said the priest, 'he was an artist. If he could act a wizard or a troubadour for six minutes, do you think he could not act a clerk for six weeks?'

'I am still not quite sure of his object,' said Boyle.

'His object has been achieved,' replied Father Brown, 'or very nearly achieved. He had taken the goldfish already, of course, as he had twenty chances of doing. But if he had simply taken them, everybody would have realized that he had twenty chances of doing it. By creating a mysterious magician from the end of the earth, he set everybody's thoughts wandering far afield to Arabia and India, so that you yourself can hardly believe that the whole thing was so near home. It was too close to you to be seen.'

'If this is true,' said Boyle, 'it was an extraordinary risk to run, and he had to cut it very fine. It's true I never heard the man in the street say anything while Jameson was talking from the balcony, so I suppose that was all a fake. And I suppose it's true that there was time for him to get outside before I had fully woken up and got out on to the balcony.'

'Every crime depends on somebody not waking up too soon,' replied Father Brown; 'and in every sense most of us wake up too late. I, for one, have woken up much too late. For I imagine he's bolted long ago, just before or just after they took his finger-prints.'

'You woke up before anybody else, anyhow,' said Boyle, 'and I should never have woken up in that sense. Jameson was so correct and colourless that I forgot all about him.'

'Beware of the man you forget,' replied his friend; 'he is the one man who has you entirely at a disadvantage. But I did not suspect him, either, until you told me how you had heard him barring the door.'

'Anyhow, we owe it all to you,' said Boyle warmly.

'You owe it all to Mrs Robinson,' said Father Brown with a smile.

'Mrs Robinson?' questioned the wondering secretary. 'You don't mean the housekeeper?'

'Beware of the woman you forget, and even more,' answered the other. 'This man was a very high-class criminal; he had been an excellent actor, and therefore he was a good psychologist. A man like the Count never hears any voice but his own; but this man could listen, when you had all forgotten he was there, and gather exactly the right materials for his romance and know exactly the

252

right note to strike to lead you all astray. But he made one bad mistake in the psychology of Mrs Robinson, the housekeeper.'

'I don't understand,' answered Boyle, 'what she can have to do with it.'

'Jameson did not expect the doors to be barred,' said Father Brown. 'He knew that a lot of men, especially careless men like you and your employer, could go on saying for days that something ought to be done, or might as well be done. But if you convey to a woman that something ought to be done, there is always a dreadful danger that she will suddenly do it.'

The Vampire of the Village

At the twist of a path in the hills, where two poplars stood up like pyramids dwarfing the tiny village of Potter's Pond, a mere huddle of houses, there once walked a man in a costume of a very conspicuous cut and colour, wearing a vivid magenta coat and a white hat tilted upon black ambrosial curls, which ended with a sort of Byronic flourish of whisker.

The riddle of why he was wearing clothes of such fantastic antiquity, yet wearing them with an air of fashion and even swagger, was but one of the many riddles that were eventually solved in solving the mystery of his fate. The point here is that when he had passed the poplars he seemed to have vanished; as if he had faded into the wan and widening dawn or been blown away upon the wind of morning.

It was only about a week afterwards that his body was found a quarter of a mile away, broken upon the steep rockeries of a terraced garden leading up to a gaunt and shuttered house called The Grange. Just before he had vanished, he had been accidentally overheard apparently quarrelling with some bystanders, and especially abusing their village as 'a wretched little hamlet'; and it was supposed that he had aroused some extreme passions of local patriotism and eventually been their victim. At least the local doctor testified that the skull had suffered a crushing blow that might have caused death, though probably only inflicted with some sort of club or cudgel. This fitted in well enough with the notion of an attack by rather savage yokels. But nobody ever found any means of tracing any particular yokel; and the inquest returned a verdict of murder by some persons unknown.

A year or two afterwards the question was re-opened in a curious way; a series of events which led a certain Dr Mulborough, called by his intimates Mulberry in apt allusion to something rich and fruity about his dark rotundity and rather empurpled visage, travelling by train down to Potter's Pond, with a friend whom he had often consulted upon problems of the kind. In spite of the somewhat port-winy and ponderous exterior of the doctor, he had a shrewd eye and was really a man of very remarkable sense; which he considered that he showed in consulting a little priest named Brown, whose acquaintance he had made over a poisoning case long ago. The little priest was sitting opposite to him, with the air of a patient baby absorbing instruction; and the doctor was explaining at length the real reasons for the journey.

'I cannot agree with the gentleman in the magenta coat that Potter's Pond is only a wretched little hamlet. But it is certainly a very remote and secluded village; so that it seems quite outlandish, like a village of a hundred years ago. The spinsters are really spinsters—damn it, you could almost imagine you saw them spin. The ladies are not just ladies. They are gentlewomen; and their chemist is not a chemist, but an apothecary; pronounced potecary. They do just admit the existence of an ordinary doctor like myself to assist the apothecary. But I am considered rather a juvenile innovation, because I am only fifty-seven years old and have only been in the county for twenty-eight years. The solicitor looks as if he had known it for twenty-eight thousand years. Then there is the old Admiral, who is just like a Dickens illustration; with a house full of cutlasses and cuttle-fish and equipped with a telescope.'

'I suppose,' said Father Brown, 'there are always a certain number of Admirals washed up on the shore. But I never understood why they get stranded so far inland.'

'Certainly no dead-alive place in the depths of the country is complete without one of these little creatures,' said the doctor. 'And then, of course, there is the proper sort of clergyman; Tory and High Church in a dusty fashion dating from Archbishop Laud; more of an old woman than any of the old women. He's a white-haired studious old bird, more easily shocked than the spinsters. Indeed, the gentlewomen, though Puritan in their principles, are sometimes pretty plain in their speech; as the real Puritans were. Once or twice I have known old Miss Carstairs-Carew use expressions as lively as anything in the Bible. The dear old clergyman is assiduous in reading the Bible; but I almost fancy he shuts his eyes when he comes to those words. Well, you know I'm not particularly modern. I don't enjoy this jazzing and joy-riding of the Bright Young Things——'

'The Bright Young Things don't enjoy it,' said Father Brown. 'That is the real tragedy.'

'But I am naturally rather more in touch with the world than the people in this prehistoric village,' pursued the doctor. 'And I had reached a point when I almost welcomed the Great Scandal.'

'Don't say the Bright Young Things have found Potter's Pond after all,' observed the priest, smiling.

'Oh, even our scandal is on old-established melodramatic lines. Need I say that the clergyman's son promises to be our problem? It would be almost irregular, if the clergyman's son were quite regular. So far as I can see, he is very mildly and almost feebly irregular. He was first seen drinking ale outside the Blue Lion. Only it seems he is a poet, which in those parts is next door to being a poacher.'

'Surely,' said Father Brown, 'even in Potter's Pond that cannot be the Great Scandal.'

'No,' replied the doctor gravely. 'The Great Scandal began thus. In the house called The Grange, situated at the extreme end of The Grove, there lives a lady. A Lonely Lady. She calls herself Mrs Maltravers (that is how we put it); but she only came a year or two ago and nobody knows anything about her. "I can't think why she wants to live here," said Miss Carstairs-Carew; "we do not visit her."'

'Perhaps that's why she wants to live there,' said Father Brown.

'Well, her seclusion is considered suspicious. She annoys them by being good-looking and even what is called good style. And all the young men are warned against her as a vamp.'

'People who lose all their charity generally lose all their logic,' remarked Father Brown. 'It's rather ridiculous to complain that she keeps herself to herself; and then accuse her of vamping the whole male population.'

'That is true,' said the doctor. 'And yet she is really rather a puzzling person. I saw her and found her intriguing; one of those brown women, long and elegant and beautifully ugly, if you know what I mean. She is rather witty, and though young enough certainly gives me an impression of what they call—well, experience. What the old ladies call a Past.'

'All the old ladies having been born this very minute,' observed Father Brown. 'I think I can assume she is supposed to have vamped the parson's son.'

'Yes, and it seems to be a very awful problem to the poor old parson. She is supposed to be a widow.'

Father Brown's face had a flash and spasm of his rare irritation. 'She is supposed to be a widow, as the parson's son is supposed to be the parson's son, and the solicitor is supposed to be a solicitor and you are supposed to be a doctor. Why in thunder shouldn't she be a widow? Have they one speck of *prima facie* evidence for doubting that she is what she says she is?'

Dr Mulborough abruptly squared his broad shoulders and sat up.

'Of course you're right again,' he said. 'But we haven't come to the scandal yet. Well, the scandal is that she is a widow.'

'Oh,' said Father Brown; and his face altered and he said something soft and faint, that might almost have been 'My God!'

'First of all,' said the doctor, 'they have made one discovery about Mrs Maltravers. She is an actress.'

'I fancied so,' said Father Brown. 'Never mind why. I had another fancy about her, that would seem even more irrelevant.'

'Well, at that instant it was scandal enough that she was an actress. The dear old clergyman of course is heartbroken, to think that his white hairs should be brought in sorrow to the grave by an actress and adventuress. The spinsters shriek in chorus. The Admiral admits he has sometimes been to a theatre in town; but objects to such things in what he calls "our midst". Well, of course I've no particular objections of that kind. This actress is certainly a lady, if a bit of a Dark Lady, in the manner of the Sonnets; the young man is very much in love with her; and I am no doubt a sentimental old fool in having a sneaking sympathy with the misguided youth who is sneaking round the Moated Grange; and I was getting into quite a pastoral frame of mind about this idyll, when suddenly the thunderbolt fell. And I, who am the only person who ever had any sympathy with these people, am sent down to be the messenger of doom.'

'Yes,' said Father Brown, 'and why *were* you sent down?'

The doctor answered with a sort of groan:

'Mrs Maltravers is not only a widow, but she is the widow of Mr Maltravers.'

'It sounds a shocking revelation, as you state it,' acknowledged the priest seriously.

'And Mr Maltravers,' continued his medical friend, 'was the man who was apparently murdered in this very village a year or two ago; supposed to have been bashed on the head by one of the simple villagers.'

'I remember you told me,' said Father Brown. 'The doctor, or some doctor, said he had probably died of being clubbed on the head with a cudgel.'

Dr Mulborough was silent for a moment in frowning embarrassment, and then said curtly:

'Dog doesn't eat dog, and doctors don't bite doctors, not even when they are mad doctors. I shouldn't care to cast any reflection on my eminent predecessor in Potter's Pond, if I could avoid it; but I know you are really safe for secrets. And, speaking in confidence, my eminent predecessor at Potter's Pond was a blasted fool; a drunken old humbug and absolutely incompetent. I was asked, originally by the Chief Constable of the County (for I've lived a long time in the county, though only recently in the village), to look into the whole business; the depositions and reports of the inquest and so on. And there simply isn't any question about it. Maltravers may have been hit on the head; he was a strolling actor passing through the place; and Potter's Pond probably thinks it is all in the natural order that such people should be hit on the head. But whoever hit him on the head did not kill him; it is simply impossible for the injury, as described, to do more than knock him out for a few hours. But lately I have managed to turn up some other facts bearing on the matter; and the result of it is pretty grim.'

He sat louring at the landscape as it slid past the window, and then said more curtly:

'I am coming down here, and asking your help, because there's going to be an exhumation. There is very strong suspicion of poison.'

'And here we are at the station,' said Father Brown cheerfully. 'I suppose your idea is that poisoning the poor man would naturally fall among the household duties of his wife.'

'Well, there never seems to have been anyone else here who had any particular connection with him,' replied Mulborough, as they alighted from the train. 'At least there is one queer old crony of his, a broken-down actor, hanging around; but the police and the local solicitor seem convinced he is an unbalanced busybody; with some *idée fixe* about a quarrel with an actor who was his enemy; but who certainly wasn't Maltravers. A wandering accident, I should say, and certainly nothing to do with the problem of the poison.'

Father Brown had heard the story. But he knew that he never knew a story until he knew the characters in the story. He spent the next two or three days in going the rounds, on one police excuse or another, to visit the chief actors of the drama. His first interview with the mysterious widow was brief but bright. He brought away from it at least two facts; one that Mrs Maltravers sometimes talked in a way which the Victorian village would call cynical; and, second, that like not a few actresses, she happened to belong to his own religious communion.

He was not so illogical (nor so unorthodox) as to infer from this alone that she was innocent of the alleged crime. He was well aware that his old religious communion could boast of several distinguished poisoners. But he had no difficulty in understanding its connection, in this sort of case, with a certain intellectual liberty which these Puritans would call laxity; and which would certainly seem to this parochial patch of an older England to be almost cosmopolitan. Anyhow, he was sure she could count for a great deal, whether for good or evil. Her brown eyes were brave to the point of battle, and her enigmatic mouth, humorous and rather large, suggested that her purposes touching the parson's poetical son, whatever they might be, were planted pretty deep.

The parson's poetical son himself, interviewed amid vast village scandal on a bench outside the Blue Lion, gave an impression of pure sulks. Hurrel Horner, son of the Rev Samuel Horner, was a square-built young man in a pale grey suit with a touch of something arty in a pale green tie, otherwise mainly notable for a mane of auburn hair and a permanent scowl. But Father Brown had a way with him in getting people to explain at considerable length why they refused to say a single word. About the general scandalmongering in the village, the young man began to curse freely. He even added a little scandalmongering of his own. He referred bitterly to alleged past flirtations between the Puritan Miss Carstairs-Carew and Mr Carver the solicitor. He even accused that legal character of having attempted to force himself upon the acquaintance of Mrs Maltravers. But when he came to speak of his own father, whether out of an acid decency or piety, or because his anger was too deep for speech, he snapped out only a few words.

'Well, there it is. He denounces her day and night as a painted adventuress; a sort of barmaid with gilt hair. I tell him she's not; you've met her yourself, and you know she's not. But he won't even meet her. He won't even see her in the street or look at her out of a window. An actress would pollute his house and even his holy presence. If he is called a Puritan he says he's proud to be a Puritan.'

'Your father,' said Father Brown, 'is entitled to have his views respected, whatever they are; they are not views I understand very well myself. But I agree he is not entitled to lay down the law about a lady he has never seen and then refuse even to look at her, to see if he is right. That is illogical.'

'That's his very stiffest point,' replied the youth. 'Not even one momentary meeting. Of course, he thunders against my other theatrical tastes as well.'

Father Brown swiftly followed up the new opening, and learnt much that he wanted to know. The alleged poetry, which was such a blot on the young man's character, was almost entirely dramatic poetry. He had written tragedies in verse which had been admired by good judges. He was no mere stage-struck fool; indeed he was no fool of any kind. He had some really original ideas about acting Shakespeare; it was easy to understand his having been dazzled and delighted by finding the brilliant lady at the Grange. And even the priest's intellectual sympathy so far mellowed the rebel of Potter's Pond that at their parting he actually smiled.

It was that smile which suddenly revealed to Father Brown that the young man was really miserable. So long as he frowned, it might well have been only sulks; but when he smiled it was somehow a more real revelation of sorrow.

Something continued to haunt the priest about that interview with the poet. As inner instinct certified that the sturdy young man was eaten from within, by some grief greater even than the conventional story of conventional parents being obstacles to the course of true love. It was all the more so, because there were not any obvious alternative causes. The boy was already rather a literary and dramatic success; his books might be said to be booming. Nor did he drink or dissipate his well-earned wealth. His notorious revels at the Blue Lion reduced themselves to one glass of light ale; and he seemed to be rather careful with his money. Father Brown thought of another possible complication in connection with Hurrel's large resources and small expenditure; and his brow darkened.

The conversation of Miss Carstairs-Carew, on whom he called next, was certainly calculated to paint the parson's son in the darkest colours. But as it was devoted to blasting him with all the special vices which Father Brown was quite certain the young man did not exhibit, he put it down to a common combination of Puritanism and gossip. The lady, though lofty, was quite gracious, however, and offered the visitor a small glass of port-wine and a slice of seed-cake, in the manner of everybody's most ancient great-aunts, before he managed to escape from a sermon on the general decay of morals and manners.

His next port of call was very much of a contrast; for he disappeared down a dark and dirty alley, where Miss Carstairs-Carew would have refused to follow him even in thought; and then into a narrow tenement made noisier by a high and declamatory voice in an attic. . . . From this he re-emerged, with a rather dazed expression, pursued on to the pavement by a very excited man with a blue chin and a black frock-coat faded to bottle-green, who was shouting argumentatively:

'He did not disappear! Maltravers never disappeared! He appeared: he appeared dead and I've appeared alive. But where's all the rest of the company? Where's that man, that monster, who deliberately stole my lines, crabbed my best scenes and ruined my career? I was the finest Tubal that ever trod the boards. He acted Shylock—he didn't need to act much for that! And so with the greatest opportunity of my whole career. I could show you press-cuttings on my renderings of Fortinbras——'

'I'm quite sure they were splendid and very well-deserved,' gasped the little priest. 'I understood the company had left the village before Maltravers died. But it's all right. It's quite all right.' And he began to hurry down the street again.

'He was to act Polonius,' continued the unquenchable orator behind him. Father Brown suddenly stopped dead.

'Oh,' he said very slowly, 'he was to act Polonius.'

'That villain Hankin!' shrieked the actor. 'Follow his trail. Follow him to the ends of the earth! Of course he'd left the village; trust him for that. Follow him—find him; and may the curses——' But the priest was against hurrying away down the street.

Two much more prosaic and perhaps more practical interviews followed this melodramatic scene. First the priest went into the bank, where he was closeted for ten minutes with the manager; and then paid a very proper call on the aged and amiable clergyman. Here again all seemed very much as described, unaltered and seemingly unalterable; a touch or two of devotion from more austered traditions, in the narrow crucifix on the wall, the big Bible on the bookstand and the old gentleman's opening lament over the increasing disregard of Sunday; but all with a flavour of gentility that was not without its little refinements and faded luxuries.

The clergyman also gave his guest a glass of port; but accompanied by an ancient British biscuit instead of seed-cake. The priest had again the weird feeling that everything was almost too perfect, and that he was living a century before his time. Only on one point the amiable old parson refused to melt into any further amiability; he meekly but firmly maintained that his conscience would not allow him to meet a stage player. However, Father Brown put down his glass of port with expressions of appreciation and thanks; and went off to meet his friend the doctor by appointment at the corner of the street; whence they were to go together to the offices of Mr Carver, the solicitor.

'I suppose you've gone the dreary round,' began the doctor, 'and found it a very dull village.'

Father Brown's reply was sharp and almost shrill.

'Don't call your village dull. I assure you it's a very extraordinary village indeed.'

'I've been dealing with the only extraordinary thing that ever happened there, I should think,' observed Dr Mulborough. 'And even that happened to somebody from outside. I may tell you they managed the exhumation quietly last night; and I did the autopsy this morning. In plain words we've been digging up a corpse that's simply stuffed with poison.'

'A corpse stuffed with poison,' repeated Father Brown rather absently. 'Believe me, your village contains something much more extraordinary than that.'

There was abrupt silence, followed by the equally abrupt pulling of the antiquated bell-pull in the porch of the solicitor's house; and they were soon brought into the presence of that legal gentleman, who presented them in turn to a white-haired, yellow-faced gentleman with a scar, who appeared to be the Admiral.

By this time the atmosphere of the village had sunk almost into the subconsciousness of the little priest; but he was conscious that the lawyer was indeed the sort of lawyer to be the adviser of people like Miss Carstairs-Carew. But though he was an archaic old bird, he seemed something more than a fossil. Perhaps it was the uniformity of the background; but the priest had again the curious feeling that he himself was transplanted back into the early nineteenth century, rather than that the solicitor had survived into the early twentieth. His collar and cravat contrived to look almost like a stock as he settled his long chin into them; but they were clean as well as clean-cut; and there was even something about him of a very dry old dandy. In short, he was what is called well preserved, even if partly by being petrified.

The lawyer and the Admiral, and even the doctor, showed some surprise on finding that Father Brown was rather disposed to defend the parson's son against the local lamentations on behalf of the parson.

'I thought our young friend rather attractive, myself,' he said. 'He's a good talker and I should guess a good poet; and Mrs Maltravers, who is serious about that at least, says he's quite a good actor.'

'Indeed,' said the lawyer. 'Potter's Pond, outside Mrs Maltravers, is rather more inclined to ask if he is a good son.'

'He is a good son,' said Father Brown. 'That's the extraordinary thing.'

'Damn it all,' said the Admiral. 'Do you mean he's really fond of his father?'

The priest hesitated. Then he said, 'I'm not quite so sure about that. That's the other extraordinary thing.'

'What the devil do you mean?' demanded the sailor with nautical profanity.

'I mean,' said Father Brown, 'that the son still speaks of his father in a hard unforgiving way; but he seems after all to have done more than his duty by him. I had a talk with the bank manager, and as we were inquiring in confidence into a serious crime, under authority from the police, he told me the facts. The old clergyman has retired from parish work; indeed, this was never actually his parish. Such of the populace, which is pretty pagan, as goes to church at all, goes to Dutton-Abbot, not a mile away. The old man has no private means, but the son is earning good money; and the old man is well looked after. He gave me some port of absolutely first-class vintage; I saw rows of dusty old bottles of it; and I left him sitting down to a little lunch quite *recherché* in an old-fashioned style. It must be done on the young man's money.'

'Quite a model son,' said Carver with a slight sneer.

Father Brown nodded, frowning, as if revolving a riddle of his own; and then said:

'A model son. But rather a mechanical model.'

At this moment a clerk brought in an unstamped letter for the lawyer; a letter which the lawyer tore impatiently across after a single glance. As it fell apart, the priest saw a spidery, crazy crowded sort of handwriting and the signature of 'Phoenix Fitzgerald'; and made a guess which the other curtly confirmed.

'It's that melodramatic actor that's always pestering us,' he said. 'He's got some fixed feud with some dead and gone fellow mummer of his, which can't have anything to do with the case. We all refuse to see him, except the doctor, who did see him; and the doctor says he's mad.'

'Yes,' said Father Brown, pursing his lips thoughtfully. 'I should say he's mad. But of course there can't be any doubt that he's right.'

'Right?' cried Carver sharply. 'Right about what?'

'About this being connected with the old theatrical company,' said Father Brown. 'Do you know the first thing that stumped me about this story? It was that notion that Maltravers was killed by villagers because he insulted their village. It's extraordinary what coroners can get jurymen to believe; and journalists, of course, are quite incredibly credulous. They can't know much about English rustics. I'm an English rustic myself; at least I was grown, with other turnips, in Essex. Can you imagine an English agricultural labourer idealising and personifying his village, like the citizen of an old Greek city state; drawing the sword for its sacred banner, like a man in the tiny mediaeval republic of an Italian town? Can you hear a jolly old gaffer saying, "Blood alone can wipe out one spot on the escutcheon of Potter's Pond"? By St George and the Dragon, I only wish they would! But, as a matter of fact, I have a more practical argument for the other notion.'

He paused for a moment, as if collecting his thoughts, and then went on:

'They misunderstood the meaning of those few last words poor Maltravers was heard to say. He wasn't telling the villagers that the village was only a hamlet. He was talking to an actor; they were going to put on a performance in which Fitzgerald was to be Fortinbras, the unknown Hankin to be Polonius, and Maltravers, no doubt, the Prince of Denmark. Perhaps somebody else wanted the part or had views on the part; and Maltravers said angrily,

"You'd be a miserable little Hamlet"; that's all.'

Dr Mulborough was staring; he seemed to be digesting the suggestion slowly but without difficulty. At last he said, before the others could speak:

'And what do you suggest that we should do now?'

Father Brown arose rather abruptly; but he spoke civilly enough. 'If these gentlemen will excuse us for a moment, I propose that you and I, doctor, should go round at once to the Horners. I know the parson and his son will both be there just now. And what I want to do, doctor, is this. Nobody in the village knows yet, I think, about your autopsy and its result. I want you simply to tell both the clergyman and his son, while they are there altogether, the exact fact of the case; that Maltravers died by poison and not by a blow.'

Dr Mulborough had reason to reconsider his incredulity when told that it was an extraordinary village. The scene which ensued, when he actually carried out the priest's programme, was certainly of the sort in which a man, as the saying is, can hardly believe his eyes.

The Rev Samuel Horner was standing in his black cassock, which threw up the silver of his venerable head; his hand rested at the moment on the lectern at which he often stood to study the Scriptures, now possibly by accident only; but it gave him a greater look of authority. And opposite to him his mutinous son was sitting asprawl in a chair, smoking a cheap cigarette with an exceptionally heavy scowl; a lively picture of youthful impiety.

The old man courteously waved Father Brown to a seat, which he took and sat there silent, staring blandly at the ceiling. But something made Mulborough feel that he could deliver his important news more impressively standing up.

'I feel,' he said, 'that you ought to be informed, as in some sense the spiritual father of this community, that one terrible tragedy in its record has taken on a new significance; possibly even more terrible. You will recall the sad business of the death of Maltravers; who was adjudged to have been killed with the blow of a stick, probably wielded by some rustic enemy.'

The clergyman made a gesture with a wavering hand. 'God forbid,' he said, 'that I should say anything that might seem to palliate murderous violence in any case. But when an actor brings his wickedness into this innocent village, he is challenging the judgment of God.'

'Perhaps,' said the doctor gravely. 'But anyhow it was not so that the judgment fell. I have just been commissioned to conduct a post-mortem on the body; and I can assure you, first, that the blow on the head could not conceivably have caused the death; and, second, that the body was full of poison, which undoubtedly caused death.'

Young Hurrel Horner sent his cigarette flying and was on his feet with the lightness and swiftness of a cat. His leap landed him within a yard or so of the reading-desk.

'Are you certain of this?' he gasped. 'Are you absolutely certain that that blow could not cause death?'

'Absolutely certain,' said the doctor.

'Well,' said Hurrel, 'I almost wish this one could.'

In a flash, before anyone could move a finger, he had struck the parson a stunning crack on the mouth, dashing him backwards like a disjointed black doll against the door.

'What are you doing?' cried Mulborough, shaken from head to foot with the shock and mere sound of the blow. 'Father Brown, what is this madman doing?'

But Father Brown had not stirred; he was still staring serenely at the ceiling.

'I was waiting for him to do that,' said the priest placidly. 'I rather wonder he hasn't done it before.'

'Good God,' cried the doctor. 'I know we thought he was wronged in some ways; but to strike his father; to strike a clergy-man and a non-combatant——'

'He has not struck his father; and he has not struck a clergyman,' said Father Brown. 'He has struck a blackmailing blackguard of an actor dressed up as a clergyman, who has lived on him like a leech for years. Now he knows he is free of the blackmail, he lets fly; and I can't say I blame him much. More especially as I have very strong suspicions that the blackmailer is a poisoner as well. I think, Mulborough, you had better ring up the police.'

They passed out of the room uninterrupted by the two others, the one dazed and staggered, the other still blind and snorting and panting with passions of relief and rage. But as they passed, Father Brown once turned his face to the young man; and the young man was one of the very few human beings who have seen that face implacable.

266

'He was right there,' said Father Brown. 'When an actor brings his wickedness into this innocent village, he challenges the judgment of God.'

'Well,' said Father Brown, as he and the doctor again settled themselves in a railway carriage standing in the station of Potter's Pond. 'As you say, it's a strange story; but I don't think it's any longer a mystery story. Anyhow, the story seems to me to have been roughly this. Maltravers came here, with part of his touring company; some of them went straight to Dutton-Abbot, where they were all presenting some melodrama about the early nineteenth century; he himself happened to be hanging about in his stage dress, the very distinctive dress of a dandy of that time. Another character was an old-fashioned parson, whose dark dress was less distinctive and might pass as being merely old-fashioned. This part was taken by a man who mostly acted old men; had acted Shylock and was afterwards going to act Polonius.

'A third figure in the drama was our dramatic poet, who was also a dramatic performer, and quarrelled with Maltravers about how to present *Hamlet*, but more about personal things, too. I think it likely that he was in love with Mrs Maltravers even then; I don't believe there was anything wrong with them; and I hope it may now be all right with them. But he may very well have resented Maltravers in his conjugal capacity; for Maltravers was a bully and likely to raise rows. In some such row they fought with sticks, and the poet hit Maltravers very hard on the head, and, in the light of the inquest, had every reason to suppose he had killed him.

'A third person was present or privy to the incident, the man acting the old parson; and he proceeded to blackmail the alleged murderer, forcing from him the cost of his upkeep in some luxury as a retired clergyman. It was the obvious masquerade for such a man in such a place, simply to go on wearing his stage clothes as a retired clergyman. But he had his own reason for being a very retired clergyman. For the true story of Maltravers' death was that he rolled into a deep undergrowth of bracken, gradually recovered, tried to walk towards a house, and was eventually overcome, not by the blow, but by the fact that the benevolent clergyman had given him poison an hour before, probably in a glass of port. I was beginning to think so, when I drank a glass of the parson's port. It made me a little nervous. The police are working on that theory

267

now; but whether they will be able to prove that part of the story, I don't know. They will have to find the exact motive; but it's obvious that this bunch of actors was buzzing with quarrels and Maltravers was very much hated.'

'The police may prove something now they have got the suspicion,' said Dr Mulborough. 'What I don't understand is why you ever began to suspect. Why in the world should you suspect that very blameless black-coated gentleman?'

Father Brown smiled family. 'I suppose in one sense,' he said, 'it was a matter of special knowledge; almost a professional matter, but in a peculiar sense. You know our controversialists often complain that there is a great deal of ignorance about what our religion is really like. But it is really more curious than that. It is true, and it is not at all unnatural, that England does not know much about the Church of Rome. But England does not know much about the Church of England. Not even as much as I do. You would be astonished at how little the average public grasps about the Anglican controversies; lots of them don't really know what is meant by a High Churchman or a Low Churchman, even on the particular points of practice, let alone the two theories of history and philosophy behind them. You can see this ignorance in any newspaper; in any merely popular novel or play.

'Now the first thing that struck me was that this venerable cleric had got the whole thing incredibly mixed up. No Anglican parson could be wrong about every Anglican problem. He was supposed to be an old Tory High Churchman; and then he boasted of being a Puritan. A man like that might personally be rather Puritanical; but he would never call it being a Puritan. He professed a horror of the stage; he didn't know that High Churchmen generally don't have that special horror, though Low Churchmen do. He talked like a Puritan about the Sabbath; and then he had a crucifix in his room. He evidently had no notion of what a very pious parson ought to be, except that he ought to be very solemn and venerable and frown upon the pleasures of the world.

'All this time there was a subconscious notion running in my head; something I couldn't fix in my memory; and then it came to me suddenly. This is a Stage Parson. That is exactly the vague venerable old fool who would be the nearest notion a popular playwright or playactor of the old school had of anything so odd as a religious man.'

'To say nothing of a physician of the old school,' said Mulborough good-humouredly, 'who does not set up to know much about being a religious man.'

'As a matter of fact,' went on Father Brown, 'there was a plainer and more glaring cause for suspicion. It concerned the Dark Lady of the Grange, who was supposed to be the Vampire of the Village. I very early formed the impression that this black blot was rather the bright spot of the village. She was treated as a mystery; but there was really nothing mysterious about her. She had come down here quite recently, quite openly, under her own name, to help the new inquiries to be made about her own husband. He hadn't treated her too well; but she had principles, suggesting that something was due to her married name and to common justice. For the same reason, she went to live in the house outside which her husband had been found dead. The other innocent and straightforward case, besides the Vampire of the Village, was the Scandal of the Village, the parson's profligate son. He also made no disguise of his profession or past connection with the acting world. That's why I didn't suspect him as I did the parson. But you'll already have guessed a real and relevant reason for suspecting the parson.'

'Yes, I think I see,' said the doctor, 'that's why you bring in the name of the actress.'

'Yes, I mean his fanatical fixity about not seeing the actress,' remarked the priest. 'But he didn't really object to seeing her. He objected to her seeing him.'

'Yes, I see that,' assented the other.

'If she had seen the Rev Samuel Horner, she would instantly have recognized the very unreverend actor Hankin, disguised as a sham parson with a pretty bad character behind the disguise. Well, that is the whole of this simple village idyll, I think. But you will admit I kept my promise; I have shown you something in the village considerably more creepy than a corpse; even a corpse stuffed with poison. The black coat of a parson stuffed with a blackmailer is at least worth noticing and my live man is much deadlier than your dead one.'

'Yes,' said the doctor, settling himself back comfortably in the cushions. 'If it comes to a little cosy company on a railway journey, I should prefer the corpse.'